ONCE
MORE
FROM
THE
TOP

ALSO BY EMILY LAYDEN

All Girls

ONCE MORE FROM THE TOP

A Novel

EMILY LAYDEN

MARINER BOOKS

New York   Boston

ONCE MORE FROM THE TOP. Copyright © 2024 by Emily Layden. All rights reserved. Printed in the United States of America. No part of this book may be used or reproduced in any manner whatsoever without written permission except in the case of brief quotations embodied in critical articles and reviews. For information, address HarperCollins Publishers, 195 Broadway, New York, NY 10007.

HarperCollins books may be purchased for educational, business, or sales promotional use. For information, please email the Special Markets Department at SPsales@harpercollins.com.

FIRST EDITION

Designed by Jennifer Chung
Title page art © kolonko/stock.adobe.com

Library of Congress Cataloging-in-Publication Data
has been applied for.

ISBN 978-0-06-331509-9

24 25 26 27 28 LBC 5 4 3 2 1

For Kristen

Fame is a bee.
    It has a song—
It has a sting—
    Ah, too, it has a wing.

                  —Emily Dickinson

ONCE MORE FROM THE TOP

Lake Tahawus is shaped like a long, jagged scratch. When I see her on a map I think of a bear claw slashing at a tent, tearing a curved tatter in the canvas. Thirty-five miles point to point and four hundred feet at her deepest, the lake was born millions of years ago when the glaciers crept from north to south over the land, carving great gashes in the earth. In time the angry, uneven slice that cuts a crooked y-axis through upstate New York filled with water and sediment and algae and fish and, eventually, the endless debris of human life: private camps, built by the railroad tycoons in the Gilded Age; KOAs and hiking trails; bait shops and gas stations; marinas and members-only clubs.

In Thompson Landing, where I grew up, we think of Tahawus as ours. We learn to swim in her shallows and work summer jobs as lifeguards and camp counselors and fishing guides. We keep her secrets—the trails to the best jumping rocks, which islands have the sandiest beaches, where the loons nest on the western shores—like our own.

She does not always repay the favor. This is how it was with Kelsey Copestenke's body.

It was Canadian tourists who found her, on a portaging trip across the islands. The article in the *Post-Ledger* doesn't say *which* of Kelsey's remains they discovered on the beach that afternoon—only that they were "partial"—but I learn from a quick google that when a body decays underwater the first pieces to break off are, typically, the extremities, and so it was most likely the delicate bones of a finger or a metatarsal that washed ashore. Although the details of the initial discovery are slim, the newspaper is meticulous in chronicling how the rest of Kelsey was found, later: the father-and-son duo called in from Seattle; the special sonar technology they use to trawl deep basins of water. There's even a diagram of a tiny action-figure person on a pixelated lake floor, arms spread wide like a crucifixion. Because of something called an "instinctive drowning response," a corpse usually descends chest-up, the father is quoted as saying, hits the bottom feetfirst, then falls backward, coming to rest in a winged position. "That's the image we look for on the sonar," he said, and held his arms out to a T. The writer explains how deep a lake must be to hold a body down, and how because the water in Tahawus is very cold and slightly alkaline, the remains were, in general, remarkably well-preserved for their age.

The victim went missing fifteen years ago, and the case of her disappearance had long gone cold. Kelsey Copestenke was a seventeen-year-old junior at George Thompson High School when she vanished, and a classmate—the article literally says this, and I don't blame the writer, not really, because including my name will invariably boost this floundering local paper's SEO performance, even if it makes it sound like this is my story and not the story of my dead best friend—*and a classmate*, he writes, *of Diamond-selling and Grammy Award–winning singer-songwriter Dylan Read.*

I t's Sloane who sends me the article about Kelsey Copestenke's body. Every day, her two assistants comb the internet's chatter about me, sifting through forums and Google Alerts and social media for anything that might require our attention. Most days they flag a few posts on Twitter and Instagram that I could engage with if I wanted, because it long ago stopped feeling safe for me to riffle through my own notifications; very rarely is there legitimate news we don't already know about, and most mornings it's nonsense—"Hear Dylan Read's ex's un-filtered opinion on singer's new beau"; "Dylan Read's $900 Gucci Sweat-shirt: Get the Look"; "Dylan Read records at Highway 61—fans think new music coming this year!" (In the last case—I'm caught exiting the studio downtown, we hadn't expected the paparazzi storm, thought I'd snuck in unnoticed—Sloane might scan the resulting photos, just to be sure there's none that someone could unfairly distort. I keep my eyes trained on the ground three feet in front of me, walk very carefully—you never know what they might say if I roll my ankle on a crack in the sidewalk. "Dylan Read Drunk at the Studio: Famed Good Girl Finally Gone Bad?")

The subject line of Sloane's email is *news alert* and the body of the message is simply *Did you know this girl?* I don't blame her for being so direct: First of all, Sloane's style is to cut straight to the chase, which is why I hired her; second of all, I understand that her default position is skepticism. The press will do anything to morph even the most tan-gential connections into something material; why would she think this story—sad as it may be—is any different from the usual grasping at straws?

I'm reading the article for the fourth time when Nick texts. Good morning, babe, he writes, followed by a selfie, shot unflatteringly from below, his green eyes wide and eyebrows raised.

We've been together for almost six years and I am still shy about sending him unflattering photos of my own. I reply with a heart-eyed emoji instead. How's set?

Behind schedule already . . .

It's 11 a.m. on the East Coast, where they're shooting Nick's adaptation in the Long Island purgatory that is neither Queens nor the Hamptons, an American stand-in for the exurbs he called home in Ireland. The series is based on his debut novel, a multigenerational family narrative about addiction. Its initial sales were average, but there's been a renewed interest in his back projects since *Leesider* sold two million copies, or maybe since we started dating.

When's your meeting? he asks.

Two hours.
Of course. Nothing in LA starts before 10.

This fucking city. Our shared refrain: LA is perfect; LA is impossible. We call the place in New York "Home," capital *H*, because it's the place I bought because of us and the place that feels most like ours, but the truth is we live nomadically. A career in entertainment means you go where the work is. I think I mind it—the travel, the distance, the lack of feeling settled—less than Nick does.

Good luck, Nick says. And just remember: if you can't make whatever the fuck you want, the rest of us don't stand a chance.

He's right that another artist in my position—with six number-one albums, eight Grammys, and a catalog valued at nearly half a billion dollars—might not feel the need for *luck* before a label listening session. Another artist might feel, by now, that the label's opinion is no longer relevant. They need me more than I need them.

But Nick knows that I don't see any professional obligation that way. He knows that I always feel like I have something to prove. I don't want to *ignore* the executive notes; I want to make something so good they don't have any. I love you, I type, and then click my phone to black.

When I lift my eyes from the screen my heart throttles into my throat. Kelsey Copestenke is tucked into the chair across the room, feet on the seat, knees to chest. She looks exactly as she did fifteen years ago: dark hair; pale, pore-less skin; that ovalish jaw, a little asymmetrical on the left side.

He seems sweet, she says, her amber eyes blazing. *Why didn't you tell him about me?*

WE TAKE TWO SUVS TO THE LABEL OFFICES IN SANTA MONICA, me and Sloane and my security in one, lawyers and assistants in the other. (I do not have the traditional management structure; where most people in my position have a manager, agents, a publicist, and a bevy of assistants, I have Sloane: she is my consigliere, my chief of staff, my Huma Abedin. I engineered it this way because I dole out my trust in teaspoonfuls.)

The car is silent and a little tense. Sloane's fingers dart over her phone. I didn't reply to her email about Kelsey—it was one of a dozen she sent this morning, about the new demos and a fall merch drop and an ask to do a private gig in Silicon Valley; I could see how, for her, the girl from my hometown was just one entry in a checklist—but still some part of me wants to know: *What are people saying about us?*

But if Sloane's job is to assess and triage, mine is to compartmentalize. I rub my thumb over the top of my middle finger, flicking the indented edge of a callus, feeling for where the dead skin will give way, and listen as the radio clicks over: "all the houses look the same," by Vanessa Taylor.

They say that Vanessa is like me. I know this because it has become such a part of her story that it is impossible to avoid. She's been profiled in *Manhattan* and *Vanity Fair*, done song diaries for *Rhapsody* and the *Times*. She's only seventeen and looks it, if you're paying attention to the way she holds herself: she's lanky like a model but moves in the jittery way of a teenager—fiddles with her long, dark hair, laughs constantly, eyes darting. She is incredibly likable, endlessly charming.

This is not what people mean when they say she is like me. Vanessa is young enough for her goodness to be endearing; at thirty-one, my own goodness is suspect. No: when people say that Vanessa is like me, what they really mean is that her music is like mine, autobiographical and lyrics-forward; like me, Vanessa *emotes*—her delivery manages to capture a full range of nuanced feelings. You can *hear* the smiles, the eye rolls, the shrugs. On the radio her voice strains over the bridge, gasping and wobbly, a sonic reflection of her heartbreak. The writing is smart, an ironic takedown of American suburbia, and I admire how she's fit "McMansion" into a melody without fully lapsing into talk-singing: *makeouts in your bonus room and beer games in your basement / shoulda known this thing was doomed, mcmansion love's just entertainment.*

"Did we send her anything?" I ask Sloane.

"Vanessa?"

"Yeah. For her new album. It's out Friday, I think?"

"I'll have Allison send flowers."

I nod. "I think that would be meaningful," I say. Last week she posted a video screaming along to the bridge of "Tell Me How to Be" in her car with the caption *Dylan Read raised me.*

"Unless—" I ask, reconsidering: "It won't look like I'm co-opting her moment, will it?" We're constantly calibrating for the portion of the internet that believes I am like Ursula in the third act of *The Little Mermaid*, feigning sweetness to steal a kingdom. To them, I've overcorrected for my few public stumbles; they feel my worst mistakes are my truest self, and all the rest is cover.

"'Dylan Read sends flowers just to *look nice*,'" Sloane says in her mock-headline voice.

I laugh, but the truth is: I *don't* always know whether I do something because I feel I'm supposed to or because I want to. The only difference between my point of view and the strangers online is that I can trace the doubt much further back.

A THING THAT HAPPENED WITHOUT MY REALIZING IS THAT I started to be *whisked* places. This is how journalists describe it in profiles: *I have one hour with Dylan Read before her venerable publicist* whisks *her off to her next meeting; in the five-hour afternoon I spend with her, Dylan is* whisked *from one press event to the next . . . ; the star is* whisked *from wardrobe to hair and makeup to set . . .* I think it implies some sort of passive movement, as if I am merely a passenger in the progress of my days, but what it really feels like is this: When we arrive at Prismatic Records, I do not touch a door or an elevator button. I do not say a word at the security gate or at the reception desk. I follow a half step behind Sloane, one member of my security team in front of me and one behind, so they make a kind of strategic formation around my body. I am planted in a floor-wide conference room in one of the music industry's biggest labels without so much as having to say hello to anyone who works there. *This* is whisking.

The room is noisy and a little bit warm, packed with only a handful of people who genuinely belong and a whole lot of others—assistants, junior execs, marketing managers—who just want to be able to say they heard the record first. Sloane makes a beeline for the label head, Ben, leaving me to mingle with the executives: Shane and Jeff are all ice-white veneers and wrists roped with leather bracelets, their tanned and ludicrously fit bodies vibrating with manic intensity.

"Dylan!" Shane says, shaking my hand and patting me on the shoulder in kind of a half bro-hug. "Thanks so much for coming in!"

"We're so stoked about this," Jeff adds.

"Oh, please—*I'm* so excited," I tell Shane and Jeff, before gesturing toward the table. "Shall we?"

When I moved from my first label, Melody, to Prismatic, I probably could have done away with the listening session—it's a kind of old-school Nashville thing; the music scene is different here, less traditional, and I have more power now. I could have skipped the charade of presenting the new record in person and simply shared the files via text: *Thoughts?* But I've always felt that I'm my music's best advocate. I can pitch a concept, warm a room, charm the executives. So I kept the listening session through *Shipwrecked* and *The Book of Us*, and I think at least *pretending* to solicit feedback in real time was key in getting the more experimental aspects of those records off the ground. I have to make the same case today, because *Split the Lark* doesn't sound like anything I've made before.

"When I was coming up, everybody told me to act like I belonged. I was supposed to walk into these rooms and onto those stages and behave as if I was totally unfazed by the stakes," I begin. "Somewhere along the way, we decided—as a culture—that there is nothing *worse* than trying. Trying makes us uncomfortable. It pokes at our insecurities. It makes us wonder if maybe—if we weren't so lazy, or if we could just get by with a little less sleep, or if we were better at staying off TikTok—*maybe* all our dreams could come true too. And so rather than applaud the workhorse, we diminish her behavior. The only kind of success that is permissible is the kind that happens almost accidentally."

As I talk, the room around me evaporates. My perception is winnowed to my body's most essential functions: a metronome of breath and blood in and out, in and out, keeping time to my speech. I'm used to this cleaving of myself from the moment, the way my body dissociates when it's busy delivering. Except: this time, the thrum of adrenaline is noisier than usual, like a crunchy, blown-out guitar, clouding the mix with static. I breathe and focus on laying the words down like planks, one after another.

"In quarantine I hired a PhD student from Harvard to tutor me," I continue, grateful for how the hours spent practicing stitched this script into my brain, allowing me to speak almost without thinking, "and together we read as many of the classics as we could—all the plays and books and poetry I might have studied if I'd gone to college instead of to Nashville. And maybe it was because no one knew we were doing it, maybe because I was holed up in Wicklow on Zoom, but for the first time in a long time I didn't feel like I had to hide how much I loved learning. How much I genuinely *love* language, and writing, and how much I treasure the process of creating."

Some performers get off on the ego trip. An audience of eighty thousand makes you feel like a god. For me, the impulse is simpler: I want to *please*. It's that instinct that propels me through the rest of this speech, monster truck tires thundering over my anxiety, more afraid of quitting than I am finishing. "I wrote this album because I *want* to be known as a try-hard. I want the world to see that my work isn't easy for me. I titled the record after a Dickinson poem not just because of her influence on my writing or because I want to position myself among the great poets but also because *Split the Lark* is like Dickinson herself: ambitious, weird, surprising, effortful—and, if I do say so myself, brilliant."

We recorded a lot of the album remotely; I did vocals in a pantry off the kitchen, with thick quilts anchored to the top shelves to muffle as much reverb as possible. It was imperfect: listening now, you can still hear the sound of my clothes, the wires, the random creaks of the house. But there's something kind of gracefully DIY about it, and a metaphorical weight to it too—this is a record about creation. It makes sense to leave a little bit of the process buried in the mix.

"It's bold," Ben says when we finish. "Quiet, but bold."

Fuck. "Bold" is Ben's way of saying he has notes.

"It's definitely a new sound for you. Almost—bedroom pop, but not," Shane says.

"The vocals are clear in a way that bedroom pop isn't, obviously," Jeff adds. "But there is an experimentation to the arrangement that's interesting."

"Mhmm, absolutely." Shane nods. "I'm just wondering, lyrically, whether some of it feels a little . . . academic?"

"Yeah, I had the same note," Jeff says. "Like, even with the title—are people going to *get* that?"

You think rejection will get easier, but the truth is some wounds always hurt. "It's from a poem," I explain, "about—you know, slaughtering the bird to find where the music comes from." It's conceivable that Emily Dickinson was writing about the impossibility of locating the muse, but "Split the Lark" always seemed to me like a broader, distinctly modern rebuke: Stop asking for more, it says. Listen to the song (or read the poem), and leave the rest alone.

Ben looks at me over the top of his thick-rimmed glasses, his arms crossed in front of his chest. "That's a lot of abstraction for a record that's professing to be vulnerable."

With her hip pressed into a filing cabinet against the wall, Kelsey raises an eyebrow at me. *Wonder why that might be?*

WE TAKE THE FREEWAY HOME. THE 10 CRAWLS IN BOTH DIREC-tions. Meanwhile I've moved swiftly from embarrassment to the much easier emotional meter of outrage. "I mean, are we really not past the notes-giving portion of my career?" I say to Sloane.

My publicist's thumbs dart over her phone. "One of your goals with this record was to try to confront this dialogue about your authenticity, and I think that's a goal you share with the label," she says. "The way *you've* come at it is by trying to explain that, for you, *trying* happens naturally."

"Exactly." My ambition—or my success—has gotten me into a little bit of trouble, publicly. The same people who are suspicious of my Good Girl affect also doubt the emotional nature of my songwriting: that my feelings might be a capitalist ploy; that I'm only pretending to share my secrets with the world because I know a rabid, parasocial fan base will help me sell records.

"I think the label might prefer we combat that dialogue more straight-forwardly, in a less craft-oriented way," she says. "They don't actually want *Fetch the Bolt Cutters*, you know?"

I like Sloane because she doesn't give an easy yes. She isn't afraid of me, and it means I get the truth from her, or at least she challenges my thinking. I am skeptical of people who tell me I'm wonderful. (Ironically, since it is the only thing I want to hear. I just don't trust it when it comes too frequently or unequivocally.)

"I've made a record that isn't very commercial," I say. "There's not much more I can do to prove I'm not some kind of emotional scammer than intentionally ignoring the bottom line."

"I know it's not fair that we're in this position," Sloane says. "Men never get called *calculating*."

I sigh, a frustrated, noisy exhale. And then my phone rings: *Mom.* I frown. "I thought she had clients all day," I say to Sloane. I tap the button to add a message to my decline: call you later.

"How is she doing?"

"Busy, allegedly."

Sloane laughs. "It's amazing that she's still practicing."

"It would be different if she worked at a hospital or something, but with a private practice she can control her client roster pretty well. She doesn't take on anyone without a referral. And when one of my stalkers slips through the cracks, she just reframes it as an opportunity to get them the help they need."

Sloane laughs grimly. "And we quietly file for another restraining order."

My phone rings again. Nick this time.

"You can take that," Sloane says.

I shake my head. "It's fine." Debriefing with Sloane, I type.

"He's out on Long Island?"

I nod.

"Is he working on anything new?"

"A new novel?"

Sloane nods.

"Hmm. I think he'd want me to say yes, but I think all the development work—since *Leesider*—is keeping him busy. And the money is better." Not that he needs it.

Your mom is trying to use me as a back channel, Nick types.

And then Sloane's phone pings. She looks at the alert, then begins tap-tapping into her screen, hurried. "What did you say your relationship was to that girl?" she asks. "The one from your hometown."

I feel something heavy slide from my throat to my belly button. "I—I didn't."

"But you knew her?"

"Yeah."

Sloane is still typing. "How well?"

"Why?"

Sloane makes three quick taps on her phone and then turns the screen to show me a grainy, pixelated image—a photo of a photo, as if someone has taken a picture of a newspaper clipping. In the shot, a dozen high schoolers stand on a stage in warm amber light. Their costuming is a chaotic mash-up: some are dressed in ballet leotards, others in basketball shorts; one like a magician, in a caped suit like Dracula. At the far end of the group are two girls, both dressed in jeans, one with dark hair, the other a honeyed brown. The production quality is low enough that they might be anyone—regular teenagers in a regular suburban auditorium. If one of those two girls didn't grow into one of the most recognizable faces on the planet, you wouldn't look twice.

Until this morning, only a few very weird corners of the internet had stumbled across my hometown's fifteen-year-old cold case. I know because I googled Kelsey from time to time and always ended up on a true-crime message board where her story never quite made the cut when the citizen detectives mined for new obsessions. There were no interesting aberrations—no phone calls that pinged the wrong cell tower; no friendship bracelets found fifty feet from the crime scene; no crime scene at all, actually. The cops believed she ran away. I liked to imagine her boarding a Greyhound to Nashville, chasing the one dream she wanted more than all the rest.

I haven't talked about Kelsey in fifteen years. No interviewer ever asked me if I had a friend who went missing. No fans combed my lyrics for references to the girl who disappeared. Why would they? A teenage girl from the wrong side of the tracks goes missing every day. Certainly no one ever dug up this photo, a nothing piece of feel-good journalism covering the local high school's talent show.

Sloane speaks first. "*I* think it's impossible to tell who this is," she says. "But you know my rule."

Outside, the car next to us thumps its bass in a rhythmic vibration. A traffic helicopter chops through the sky above. In my lap, I press my thumbnail into the crack at the top of my middle finger, where the bubbled callus made by my guitar strings pitches into healthy skin. I allow the nail to funnel into the contour like a tidal pull, back and forth, back and forth. On the sixth or tenth trace it catches, and I use my thumb to flick, gently, at the shedding skin.

We never lie to the press. Evade, sure. Lean into *technical* truths, absolutely. But Sloane's one absolute, unyielding principle is this: we do not, under any circumstances, lie.

The Debut

J oni Mitchell never liked that people called her writing *confessional*. There was something distinctly gendered about it—did anybody call Bob Dylan "confessional"?—but most of all apologetic, like she had something to feel guilty about. The descriptor itself implies a wrongdoing; confessing is what you do when you've sinned.

I agree with Joni in principle, obviously. I didn't like when people started calling my work "confessional" either—in addition to her argument, I felt it undermined the process, as if borrowing from my life was inherently juvenile. It was easier to see me as a seventeen-year-old with a diary than a savant, and so that's what they called me.

But it's also true that it might be right to characterize my work in that way. I do have things to be sorry for, and I've been writing about them from the very beginning.

I WAITED A MONTH AFTER KELSEY WENT MISSING BEFORE DELETING our MySpace. The fact of it had a habit of sucker punching me at random times: in line at the grocery store with my mom, charting a parabola in math class, walking the dog after school. All of a sudden, unloading bell peppers onto the checkout counter, I'd remember that all those songs I'd written for Kelsey—*with* Kelsey—still existed on the internet, like a digital graveyard of the person I'd been with her.

The day I finally logged in, I scanned through our profile while one of the singles we'd uploaded ("Made Just For You") played on low, listening to Kelsey's velveteen voice drawn up from the digital ether. I was right about this place, I thought, listening to this disembodied, digitized version of my friend: It wasn't a memorial. It was haunted land.

I turned the music off and clicked into our inbox, performing one last obligatory sweep before shutting the whole thing down. Most of the messages were from men, only some of them truly creepy, with subject lines like *hey* and *hi pretty* above uninspired missives—*just wanted to say ur the most beautiful girl ive ever seen*. Adam's caught my eye because it adhered to the rules of grammar and punctuation: *Hi, my name is Adam McIver*, he wrote.

I'm an A&R scout for Melody here in Nashville. I'd love to talk about your music and how Melody might support your career. Give me a call, he wrote, and then a phone number.

I closed my eyes and pictured Kelsey setting up our profile, her left leg crossed on top of her right in the desk chair, rolling her bottom teeth over her top lip with the effort of concentrating. "It's not only established bands," she explained. "All the guys who play at Junior's have one." Junior's: the local shorthand for the Jolly Roger, the dive bar in town where Kelsey had managed to persuade the owner to let her perform. ("Only on Mondays!" he'd barked, worn down by her nagging. "And at four p.m. See how you like that crowd.")

It didn't matter that Adam's message was exactly the kind of thing Kelsey was hoping for when she made the page—she wasn't here to play for him. I wrote his number down in ballpoint pen on a sheet of printer paper, scrawled diagonally in the corner, then deleted our page in two clicks.

AND THAT MIGHT HAVE BEEN THE END OF IT. I MIGHT HAVE PUT Adam's number in the sleeve pocket of my notebook and allowed enough time to pass until I couldn't be sure whether he worked at Melody anymore, whether his number was still the same, until—probably—he had moved on, forgotten us, found something better. It could have happened that way—it might have—if it weren't for Ms. Twyman and her lesson on sonnets.

I'd been having a hard time writing since Kelsey disappeared. Songs were off-limits, obviously—I didn't even want to try, didn't think it was even worth it without Kelsey showing me the way—but I thought poetry would come back to me, that I could slip back into the artist I was before we met. But my brain felt broken, like there was a glitch in the mechanism I needed to toggle between songwriter and poet, so I could hear words only for their melodic potential. Where "goldfinch" and "crustacean" and "eucalyptus" might have given me poems before, now I heard them only as unsingable, devoid of critical long vowel sounds, no potential for slant rhymes. Ms. Twyman's lesson seemed safe to me because it gave me no choice: we would select, at random, a single word from a hat, and build out from there. Ready-made inspiration, I thought. When she got to my desk I reached my fingertips into the paper nest—a little damp after so much fondling—and pulled out a single folded slip. *Barnacle*, it read, in Ms. Twyman's looped, elegant cursive.

I said it quietly to myself, feeling for the way my lips rolled in on each other with the *b*, the press of my tongue against the roof of my mouth at the *-na*, the clucking *cull* at the end. Nothing came to me. No images of thimble-shaped shells forested onto a ship's hull, no acne-like stippling on a whale's chin, no visions of coralish reefs on the docks in Maine. All I could see was Kelsey, tucked into her desk chair in her bedroom, haloed in twinkle lights, laughing, uproarious. *Rein it in, Keats*, she'd say. *I'll sound like shit trying to sing "barnacle."*

They say anger is a stage of grief. This is because anger is armor: you wrap yourself in it to avoid the hurt. Sadness will paralyze you, but *anger* allows you to keep moving.

What I mean is: For the first time since she disappeared, I wasn't sad about losing Kelsey. I was furious with her.

I raised my hand. Ms. Twyman lifted her head at me, eyebrows cocked, teacher-speak for *Yes?*

"Can I go to the bathroom?"

"You don't need to ask, Dylan," Ms. Twyman said, waving her hand at the door.

It was one of those occasions—there were many, I'm sure—where my reputation as Thompson High's Model Citizen worked as a shield: I passed three hall monitors as I made my way to the building's sole pay phone in a mostly deserted wing off the art classrooms, each of whom smiled at me without asking to see a pass; Mrs. Tarlton, the ceramics teacher, and Mr. Hotaling, who taught Drawing & Painting, both saw me walk through the studio wing and let me proceed without question. I'm sure they all thought: *Dylan Read's a good girl.*

I hadn't meant to commit Adam's number to memory. It's a gift of mine, this capacity to remember minutiae without really trying. In high school I developed a habit of pretending to forget things just so that I wouldn't seem like a freak, overly attentive, devoid of any interior world, without a life of her own. While I waited for the phone to ring I read the graffiti tattooed on the particleboard cubicle: *steph swallows*; a penis with cartoonishly hairy balls; *big titty goth* above two melon-shaped boobs with perfect-circle areolas.

"Melody Music, this is Adam McIver speaking."

"Hi," I began, and then the next part came without even thinking, without any sense of how I'd see it through later: "My name is Cameron Cope," I said, "and you messaged me on MySpace?"

CAMERON WAS KELSEY'S IDEA. "NO ONE WANTS TO BE A *KELSEY Copestenke* fan," she said, sitting at my computer, one hand on the mouse while the other fiddled with one of her necklaces at her chest. Kelsey was restless, always in motion—tapping her foot, bouncing her knee up and down, drumming her fingernails across the flat face of her guitar body.

I lay outstretched on my bed, chin propped on my fists. We were at my house that afternoon because Kelsey didn't have her own computer—her family had an old, clunky Dell on the desk in the living room and dial-up internet only. "But it's your name," I said to her.

"What's in a name?" she said, her voice pitched into a Shakespearean actor's lilt. "That which we call a rose by any other name would smell as sweet." She grinned. "Isn't that how it goes? You're the expert."

I rolled over, grabbed a throw pillow, and launched it across the room at her. In sixth grade I won a school-wide monologue competition—I'd chosen Rosalind from *As You Like It*, "at which time would I, being but a moonish youth, grieve, be effeminate, changeable, longing and liking," et cetera—and for the next three months my classmates spoke to me only in affect: *Taketh one and pass it back; Dylan, wouldst thou hand me the pinnies?* Even Kelsey, a year older—a lifetime in middle school; there was hardly any cross-pollination between the sixth and seventh graders—had heard the way people talked to me, and she loved to tease me about it once we became friends, to use it as a reminder of all the ways my try-hard-ness got me into trouble. "I think the point of that speech is that the name is irrelevant; it's Romeo and Juliet's *love* that matters," I said to her. "So, in this case, it's the music that matters."

"Oh, Dylan. You sweet, naive, good little girl. It's the whole package! You're giving them an *experience*. The name is part of the fantasy."

"I would never write under another name," I said.

"Because you're a *poet*. Obviously you don't care about fame." She paused. "Also, you already have the perfect country-music name. Androgynous but not too edgy, sweet in a down-home kinda way."

I shook my head, conceding the point. "So what's your stage name?"

"Well, I'd like to do something that's, you know, derived from my actual name."

I turned "Copestenke" over in my head, tumbling the letters at the front of my brain. "What about just 'Cope'? C-o-p-e?"

"Kelsey Cope," she said. "Kelsey Cope." She looked at me, the amber core of her hazel eyes glowing. "It's sort of adorable. Is it too adorable? Hmm." She tugged on her necklace again, pulling the charm back and forth across its gold thread—a pendant pressed with tiny diamond stars in the shape of her zodiac sign. It looked expensive, not like the rest of her Claire's jewelry: silver chains greening, gold bracelets molding to brass. I'd asked about it once, and she'd told me it was a gift from some rich old lady she knew at the summer camp she worked at on Lake Tahawus. "What about my middle name?"

"Cameron?"

"Yeah. 'Cameron Cope.' Everybody loves an alliteration."

"Kelsey Cope is also alliterative."

"Shut up. You know what I mean. It's like . . . polished. Intentional. 'Cameron Cope,'" she said again.

I watched as she tucked a section of her dark hair behind her ear. She had a way of doing it so that some pieces stayed pinned at her temple, tumbling along her jaw. It looked purposefully casual. "I think it's perfect," I said, and Kelsey grinned at me.

"Good," she said, "because it's your nom de plume as well."

MY MOM IS A FAMILY THERAPIST. WHEN I WAS EIGHT SHE opened a private practice and turned our pool house into a home office. That summer I floated in the shallow end with two noodles hooked beneath my armpits and watched as contractors in paint-splotched pants bumped their calves against the corners of the diving board. After that, I watched her clients come and go from my bedroom window overlooking the backyard. Often they were very young, like me, with jackets flapping open and dirtied nylon backpacks slipping from their shoulders. Their parents steered them across the crushed gravel laid by the landscaping crew in a neat path from the driveway through the gate and around the pool. In the fall the hydrangeas lost their petals, scattering them across the pearled stones like dusty pink confetti.

At the time my understanding of my mother's work was basic in the general sense but sophisticated for a second grader. When my dad, a cardiologist, bought me a plastic model heart—the kind that comes apart at the seams, ventricle split from ventricle, aorta unhooked from vena cava—my mom gave me a brain. "Dad fixes people's hearts," she explained, pointing to the temporal lobe, "and I help them with their feelings."

I knew that my mom was itching to talk to me about Kelsey's disappearance. For weeks, I'd listened to her clock every spat—every flare of my temper—through her therapist's lens, to the point where I knew that when I told her about Cameron and Adam, she wouldn't ask questions about this stray piece of digital evidence. She wouldn't wonder whether we needed to share this information with the police, who were calling Kelsey a runaway. She'd see only a patient who'd finally decided to walk through the door. Here I was, ready to process.

"I know I shouldn't have lied to Adam," I said to my mom that afternoon, sitting across from her at the kitchen island while she cleaned and diced rhubarb, quarts of bleeding strawberries already heaped on the cutting board.

"It wasn't really a lie," she said. "Like you said, Cameron is something you and Kelsey made up. A persona spun from your music and her voice."

"It was Kelsey's stage name."

My mom shrugged, the way she does when she thinks her clients are oversimplifying, flattening something that is morally ambiguous. "I understand why it would be hard to let her go, is all I'm saying."

I picked a halved strawberry from the cutting board and popped it into my mouth, chewing it slowly. It was room temperature and candied, perfect. "I want to go."

"To Nashville?"

I nodded. "To audition for Adam."

My mom lifted the cutting board from the counter and used the edge of her knife to slide the fruit into the saucepan on the stove. As she did so she nodded, not like she was saying yes but like she was thinking it over.

"Did you read the article I gave you on ambiguous loss?"

This had been my mom's technique for most of my life: she left reading material in conspicuous places. A new picture book about a lost balloon when my grandmother died. *Our Bodies, Ourselves* on my pillow in middle school. Most recently: essays by C. S. Lewis and Elisabeth Kübler-Ross. More than once in my adolescence I told her this was passive-aggressive, like leaving notes about the dishes for your roommates. "Is it possible you're projecting onto my intentions?" she'd asked.

There in the kitchen I shook my head. "Not yet."

My mom nodded again. "You should."

I *had* skimmed the article. It told me that in instances of ambiguous loss—which included missing-person cases and presumed deaths in which there are no remains (e.g., many families of the victims of 9/11 experienced ambiguous loss)—*closure* is a myth. I'd stopped reading because nothing about Kelsey's vanishing seemed uncertain to me.

"Let me talk to your father about it," my mom said then. "But I do think it could be useful."

She thought taking me to Tennessee for a few days would help me process my grief. She had no way of knowing it would change my entire life.

AS A KID I HAD A NORTHEASTERNER'S SENSE OF THE COUNTRY. I'd been to California and Florida and, once, we took a national parks trip through a swath of the American west, but those were exceptions to my geographic rule; everything else south of Pennsylvania and west of Buffalo was uncharted. My trees were maples and sandy pines; my herons blue; my deer white-tailed.

In Nashville, magnolias tipped their wax leaf–choked branches out over 16th Avenue. Black walnuts with arrowhead leaves umbrellaed across the sidewalk. The Tennessee flag caught my eye in my periphery over and over again, a stomach-flipping double take: its three stars centered in navy on a red background like a ghost image of the Confederacy.

On Music Row craftsman cottages with porch swings and small, black-trimmed Tudors inconspicuously housed their artistry: music notes detailed onto a balcony railing; a placard marking a driveway *for Mixtape Records only*; in a few places, a campaign-style yard sign planted in the grass, celebrating a writer or artist—*Congratulations Georgia Riley on your Billboard #1 "Not Over You"!* As we drove closer to the highrises of downtown and the Gulch, the buildings grew more corporate, houses swapped for multistoried brick rectangles. Melody was in a large tan office space with teal-glossed windows and a semiopaque atrium. While the label offices on the southern ends of 16th and 17th might have been, in another city, fraternities or yoga studios or undergrad apartments, Melody could just as easily have been a Kaiser or a Salesforce, one of a million routine corporations in a mass-produced commercial space. My mother hung back while I gave my name at the front desk— "Cameron Cope here to see Adam McIver"—and then we both circled the lobby in opposite directions, appraising the trophies on the walls: platinum records, tour posters, a collection of Grammy Awards arranged in a bouquet in a glass case.

Adam was in his thirties, with crystalline blue eyes and a permanent scruff. When he said our name it echoed across the waiting area, pinging off the high ceilings. I turned to him and felt the cold of the air-conditioning breeze up my skirt—I'd chosen a yellow dress, dotted with small purple flowers, something Kelsey would have made fun of me for wearing: *It concerns me that you only have church dresses*, I could hear her saying, *especially since you don't even go to mass.*

I shifted my guitar case into my left hand and extended my right. "Actually," I said, "it's Dylan."

Adam didn't flinch. "A stage name. Sure. Smart, although I like 'Dylan' too." He turned and gestured beyond him, down a brightly lit hallway. "You'll have to tell me all about the choice. And this must be your—?"

My mom reached toward him. "Marion Breiner. Dylan's mother."

"Very cool." Adam's delivery was flat. Then he added: "A lot of girls just come with their managers."

He led us down a narrow hall to an airy conference room, a white-walled rectangle with large tinted windows over the avenue and a table surrounded by Eames swivel chairs. Adam gestured for me to have the open space in the front of the room, while he and my mother took their seats. They chatted about hot chicken as I opened my guitar case, triple-checked the tuning.

"You know," he said as I stood up, guitar slung over my shoulders now, "the picture you have online—"

On our MySpace, Kelsey's face was half covered with a curtain of hair, turning over her shoulder, shot into the setting sun.

"That's not me either." Kelsey and I didn't look anything alike. In high school she was tall and thin while my proportions were average—five four and athletic more than skinny. Her hair was a glossy almost-black; mine was a dusty brown. In fact everything about me was sort of muted—medium-beige skin that pinked with rosacea; pale gray eyes, matte rather than kaleidoscopic—while Kelsey was carved of contrasts. I was pretty, I think, in my own way, but Kelsey was *interesting*.

Before Adam had time to process it—before I allowed any silence between us to bloat with suspicion and doubt—I delivered an explanation I'd practiced on the flight: "That's my friend Kelsey. We made the MySpace page together. We were a team. I was the writer and she was the singer. But she's gone now, and when you messaged, I thought, this is all Kelsey wanted—a chance like this."

"She's gone? As in . . . ?"

My mom spoke: "Kelsey went missing earlier this spring. The police believe that she ran away. I think we're here because Dylan wanted to . . . honor their project, to see it through to the end."

Adam nodded his head very slowly, his eyebrows slightly narrowed. "I'm sorry to hear that."

"Thank you," I said.

"So . . ." Adam ventured carefully. It was clear he didn't want to seem cold or unsympathetic—but also that he wasn't sure we weren't just wasting his time for the sake of a therapy exercise. "You don't sing?" he asked.

"I do. I can."

"But it was this Kelsey girl's voice I heard online?"

I nodded.

"She had a gorgeous sound. Like a thirty-five-year-old."

I caught my mother's face then, a quick pinched expression—a tightening at the jaw, the outside corners of the eyes, the temple.

"But they were your lyrics?"

"Kelsey and I wrote together," I explained.

Adam inhaled deeply and leaned back in his chair, his hands together at his chest. "Do you have anything original to play?"

"Something I wrote without Kelsey?"

"Yes."

My mom reached a hand across the table. "I don't think that's—"

"Yes," I said. I didn't look at my mother.

"Okay." Adam nodded. "Let's hear that then, please."

THREE WEEKS AFTER KELSEY DISAPPEARED, I WENT TO A PARTY at Megan O'Neill's. I don't think Megan would have invited me, ordinarily; I think I happened to be in the vicinity when she was talking about it in studio art, and I think she probably felt sorry for me, because some people did then. I could tell from the way they spoke more softly in my presence and how they smiled at me in a closed-mouth way that they imagined I must have really been going through it. And I don't think I would have gone to Megan's if it weren't for the way the weekends had become perilous vacuums of nothingness, giant black holes that devoured me with their lack of structure, and anyway Megan lived in the same subdivision as me, so I could walk there and walk home without having to ask my parents—because I had only my permit then—for a ride.

I heard the music as soon as I turned onto Megan's street. They'd thrown open the garage doors, and Nate Morello and Julian Burke and Sean Torres had set up inside in the port not occupied by Megan's brother's air hockey table. I joined a handful of girls leaning against the table's edge, their Old Navy flip-flops dangling over the concrete floor in primary colors: varsity blue and paper white and banana yellow. They sipped their beers while the boys "jammed," mostly not talking to one another, their faces entirely, determinedly placid.

After "Free Bird," Megan leaned over to me and said, "Dylan, you play the guitar, right?"

I nodded.

Nate Morello extended his instrument in my direction, the neck curled in his fist. "Wanna have a go?"

I looked from Megan to Nate and back again. I couldn't tell if they were serious or pitying, if this was an authentic invitation to share the stage or if this was one of those times when a boy asks a girl to do something so he can watch her fumble. Just the day before, in math class, Amelia Clark had fallen into the very same trap, been given a turn trying to throw a paper ball into the trash can at a distance, and failed so miserably—her aim was three feet short and another three to the left—that the boys then shifted to trying to see who could take a *worse* shot than Amelia.

But this wasn't trash can basketball or lunch table Texas Hold'em or powder-puff football. This was something I knew I was good at. "Okay," I said. Nate pressed his guitar pick into my palm and it felt hot in an unpleasant kind of way, like when you sat in a desk at school and the seat was still warm.

I looked to Julian and Sean on the bass and drums.

"Do you know any Queen?" Julian asked.

I could hear Kelsey's open-mouthed cackle. *Idiots. They only know how to play songs from Guitar Hero.*

I shook my head.

"You and Kelsey wrote your own stuff, yeah?" Megan asked.

I clocked her use of the past tense. "Yeah."

"Play one of those."

I paused. I looked back to Julian and Sean. "You guys just want to . . . jump in?" I asked.

"Yeah, that's chill." Julian nodded, and with the back of his hand he pushed his long hair from where it had fallen across his forehead, his drumstick curled in his fist.

I began to play a song called "Never Have I Ever," one Kelsey and I stumbled into in her bedroom one night, secret-sharing transformed into lyrics. "Is this anything?" I remembered her saying, squinting in the semi-serious way she did. *It's a real simple question you asked in the neon light / and I've got all your attention but it just doesn't feel right / cause I've kissed lots and lots of boys but never have I ever kissed a boy like you.*

The melody unfurled slowly over the opening line, tumbled quickly over *never have I ever*, slowed down again to a talky *kissed a boy like you*.

At some point Julian kicked in on the drums, a very basic four-on-the-floor kind of rhythm that actually worked just fine, even though I was sure it was a decision borne from a shallow toolbox rather than any kind of creative discernment. When I finished there was silence for three seconds too long, and in the gap between the last note and when Megan said, "That was really good," and Nate said, "Nice," I caught Jack Rowley's raised eyebrow and a stifled smirk on Becca Mahoney's lips, which she hid quickly behind a long pull on her beer.

I knew my mistake immediately. I should have known that this wasn't the place to do something earnest, a smart, blurry torch song about slut-shaming. If Kelsey had been there, she would have done something funny, like "Too Old For Young Life," a jokey bit she did about the one time she tried going to youth group, or maybe "Summer Camp Crush," another playful-ironic tune she wrote about how she fell in love every July at Camp Tahawus. These were less songs than they were quasi-parodies, meant to charm with their warmth and wit. Kelsey laughed when she sang them, winked, inserted long pauses between the verse and the hook, teasing the audience.

She would have known that even if Megan O'Neill and her friends wanted to use me and our music as some sort of proxy for the gone girl, they didn't actually want to think about the weight of it, the heaviness of Kelsey's absence. They didn't want a little ballad to help them *feel*; they wanted to be entertained. That night I decided, *never again will I forget this lesson*. Never again will I be unclear on the terms of the bargain, the power in the room, how to take it when it's not mine.

I PLAYED ADAM THREE SONGS THAT DAY, WRITTEN IN A BLIND fury after we'd committed to the trip. The pressure of the audition unlocked something in me—my need to be the A-plus student greater than any anxiety or grief or guilt that otherwise clogged my creative pathways—and I showed up at Melody with a trio of tracks that spun my feelings about my failed friendship into lyrics: first, an elegiac scene-setter on a lake sparkling with stars; second, a withering takedown of the narrator's insecurities, framed as a flipped version of the country revenge song; and, finally, having warmed the room, walked Adam by the hand into my world, an atmospheric study of regret.

That one made it onto *Moonless*: *I rewind the tape, watch again from the top / my brain is on fire, I'm there but I'm not / and all of these stories end the same way / with me saying sorry too little too late.*

When I finished, Adam leaned back, resting his hands on his midsection. "Most girls come in here and do a version of *dun dun dun-na-na nuh nuh*," he hummed, mimicking the opening riff of a ubiquitous crossover hit from the late nineties. "Which is fine. Good, even. Obviously we're all looking for the next version of that. But I knew as soon as I saw you in the lobby that wouldn't work for you." He gestured vaguely at my body, or maybe at my clothes. "There's a kind of . . . wholesomeness here, which is particularly interesting set against all these very intense feelings you're exploring in your writing."

The clinical, detached way Adam spoke—almost as if I wasn't there, almost as if the two of us together were observing some other version of myself—helped steady the thundering I felt in my ribs.

"There's a vulnerability to your work that's bracing without being edgy. The writing is so ferocious, but really elegant too—I loved that line in the second song about the moonless night, how'd that go?"

I sang it in a nervous, lilting way for him: *have you ever looked up in the middle of a fight / and seen how the sky is clearest on a moonless night.*

"Yeah," Adam said, impressed. "Whew. It's so weary and wise, where another writer your age would have drafted a song that just felt . . . angsty. These songs are about your friend, yeah?"

He said it neutrally but I felt an immediate flush of shame, as if I'd been caught cheating on a test. "Yes," I admitted.

Adam nodded, unshaken. "We'll just want to be careful about that. Damage is sexy and interesting for a record or two, but it doesn't have legs. Commercially or creatively."

Kelsey had told me, once, that women in country had to sneak their messiest feelings in through the back door. I nodded.

Adam breathed, then slapped the table with both hands. "Okay, here's what I think we should do. We'll get you in here on a publishing deal, set you up with some songwriters, start generating a bunch of material, and see what we come up with."

Kelsey had only ever talked about a *record* deal. This was something else: a lesser prize, maybe, but one that saw me as a *writer*. I recognized the hum inside my stomach, how the vibrating in my core had shifted from nervous tremors to a deep-bellied reverb. It wasn't excitement. It wasn't happiness. I thought in the moment it was something like desperation: this was a chance to start over.

Adam misunderstood my silence for disappointment. "Look, I know it sounds like, well, this isn't a record deal, so it's not a guarantee. But we don't call Nashville a ten-year town for nothing. This is a place for people who are hungry to get better, and we're gonna put you in rooms with Jess Britt and Bill Heathers and, man, I think Sam Jordan would be great at producing you—and it'll be like getting a private master class from some of the most brilliant minds working in music today."

I didn't know any of these people. Instead I asked, "And then what?"

Adam leaned back. "And then in six months or a year, we'll see what we've got, okay?"

"But Dylan has school," my mom said.

Adam laughed. "This is where having brought your manager rather than your mother might have been beneficial," he said to me, still chuckling, and my mom sucked her cheek in, creating a pinched hollow.

"What if I came for summer?" I said. "It's June. I can spend ten weeks here, writing every day."

Adam looked at my mom, who looked at me. I'd violated a family rule: we didn't argue in front of other people. "Your father and I have jobs, Dylan," she said. "Neither one of us can move to Nashville for three months."

I watched Adam's face deaden, annoyed. He didn't have time for this kind of thing, a mother-daughter spat. He was used to being treated like a savior, a hero. "We can figure it out," I said, at the same time Adam sighed and began to stand.

"Why don't you think it over and give me a call tomorrow," he said, and I nodded quickly.

"I appreciate that, Adam," my mom said. "We could use a beat to digest this information."

Adam nodded in a pained kind of way. "Sure thing, Mrs. Read," he said.

"Dr. Breiner."

"Dr. Breiner. My apologies." Adam looked at me and winked. "I'll talk to you tomorrow, Dylan."

I MOVED TO NASHVILLE A WEEK LATER. I SEE NOW THAT I'D PUT my parents in an impossible situation: how I exploited their bewilderment, how there wasn't actually—not even for my exceedingly well-read therapist mother and cardiologist father—a specific playbook for a sixteen-year-old coping with loss. I see how even my parents—grounded, responsible, enduringly thoughtful and wise adults with a copse of advanced degrees between them—might have been seduced. I think that to some extent all parents wonder whether their child is truly exceptional or just exceptional *to them*, but this wasn't the JV soccer team we were talking about, some kind of moderate aspiration like wanting to play Division I athletics. What would you do if your kid stumbled into the kind of opportunity people spend decades chasing? What would you do if you thought it might heal her? Or—just as likely—if you thought it might destroy her?

In the end they let me go because I'm a good girl. That's how I persuaded them: a flawless track record; a childhood defined by being the teacher's helper, Student of the Month, captain of the modified basketball team, Volunteer of the Year in eighth grade, summer jobs oriented around responsibility—lifeguard, soccer camp counselor, a pack of eight- and nine-year-olds in two neat lines behind me. Was this really any different, I argued, from Eleanor, my friend who spent her summers as a swim instructor at a camp in Vermont? Or Lindsay, who was going to Costa Rica with Habitat for Humanity?

My dad had a med school classmate who taught at Vanderbilt. He and his wife were empty nesters now, and happy to host me at their house in Brentwood for the summer. I could bike to the bus stop and from there catch a ride to Music Row, but the first time Mrs. Greenhouse saw me trying to balance on her daughter's unwieldy beach cruiser with my guitar on my back she came running out of the house with her car keys in one hand, the other fluttering nervously: "It's a fifteen-minute drive, just up the highway!" she cried. "I have a haircut this afternoon anyway, I can run a couple errands while I'm out!" It was a twenty-minute drive, actually, which meant Nancy spent close to an hour and a half shuttling me to and from session every day. She played country radio in the car and sang in a glottal twang—she didn't have a southern accent, she was from New Jersey—and asked me every day about my work as if I were her own kid, home from school. I always said "please" and "thank you" and did the dishes after dinner and folded the towels if there was ever a load in the dryer, but I lay in bed every night thinking that there was something unequal about the arrangement, that I was exploiting the kindness of strangers. I'd only come to Nashville because of Kelsey; I only got to stay because of my dad's rich friends. At what point, I wondered, would I begin to feel that this was mine?

I was always anxious before going to write, like an athlete before a major race. I combatted my nerves with preparation: I showed up with notes, melodies, ideas—never ever empty-handed. My cowriters looked over my lyrics and gave me a crash course in music writing: that country songs should tell a story, first and foremost; that they should have a point of view and a sense of place; that we would employ a kind of lyrical manipulation in the chorus and/or final verse, so that the story has a sense of evolution and conclusion. The girl gets the guy; the girl gets a new guy; the narrator reveals she's singing about her parents. This is what gives a song longevity: the desire to learn it, to know it, and then to pass it on.

The trouble was that writers' rooms have a culture of sharing, and all roads led back to Kelsey. She was a boulder I could not move out of the way to tunnel toward some other inspiration. But Adam was right: I didn't want to be known as the sad girl, the one whose every review would begin with a kind of disclaimer. For so many reasons, I couldn't afford to be forever labeled by my trauma.

So I wrote about myself instead. My grief and guilt, my fears and regrets—these could just be feelings, not necessarily tied to any specific loss. I didn't have to tell my cowriters about Kelsey; it was Sam who saw the connective tissue among the lyrics about riding in cars with boys and night skies fuzzed with stars; about missed phone calls and moon slivers tugging on the tides. He noticed that all the songs *worried*; thematically, the music was confident in its lack of confidence. The album we were working toward was a mood, he said, like Joni Mitchell's *Blue*— except instead of love or heartbreak we were writing about anxiety, using the endless, layered expanse of a clear night sky as a metaphor for my own infinite insecurities. Everybody makes mistakes, he said. It's just when you're young they're both bigger *and* smaller than you think.

He thought I was writing from a constellation of failures, not one single black hole. Some part of me was proud: I'd nailed the first rule of songwriting. I'd made the specific universal.

And then we brought the songs to writers' nights around the city, where I sat in the round with two or three other musicians with just our guitars or our keyboards in front of an audience of seventy-five or ninety and workshopped not only the music but also the mythology. At these shows the performers—some who were young like me, others who were older, industry vets, a cluster of hits composed for other artists under their belts—told stories about their writing, fleshing out the world of a song, explaining how they spun a trio of verses from a canceled date or a Bible study group or a dive bar in Chattanooga. I learned how the context for a song could win an audience over as much as the music itself, how you could pull a crowd back onto your side with a good story. In strip-mall music halls and tiny cafés I learned how to narrate my way into authority while Sam sat at the corner of the bar in the back and took notes: *Is this working? Is this something real?*

MOONLESS CAME OUT ON A FRIDAY IN OCTOBER OF WHAT would have been my senior year. For fifteen months I'd pinged between Nashville and upstate New York, taking weeks off from school at a time, begging my teachers to accommodate my schedule. Thompson had a professional-child program—a series of waivers and forms that allowed a student to receive various academic accommodations while also pursuing an extracurricular goal; in our south-of-the-mountains town, Lake Tahawus pointing toward the foothills of the Adirondacks, it was really meant for aspiring Olympians, biathletes and ski jumpers who went to eastern Europe for all of January and February—but by the album's launch I had transitioned fully to an online program through a school in LA. I would never walk at a graduation, never wear a cap and gown, never go to a grad party at someone's lake house.

For the album release we did a press junket in Nashville. It would pale in comparison to the ones I would do for future records, the marathon days in hotel rooms shuffling in one reporter after another for an endless string of three-minute interviews, the green screen set up in the same space for the television appearances, the whole thing bookended by performances on morning shows and late-night shows. But that first launch day felt impossibly busy, impossibly stressful. In the morning on our way to my first radio interview my mom squeezed my hand in the back seat of the label's SUV and said, "Try to be present," and all I could say was "I feel like I'm going to puke," and then "Quiz me." My mom—who was quick to clarify for any interviewer that she was there simply as emotional support, not at all as my "momager"—laughed but obliged, and together we sat in traffic while she asked me a series of very basic questions about my album and my career and I delivered prepared answers, committed to memory down to the inflection points, even the various verbal crutches—"so" and "well" and "I mean"—incorporated into my lines to sound natural, off-the-cuff.

I did a half dozen radio interviews that morning, each one ending in a play of "Moonless," the titular single that had already been on the radio for a month, and one television appearance, on CMT. My publicist at the time—assigned by Melody—said we were lucky to have landed the slot; I could tell that from her point of view, we had a lot of factors working against us: I was a New Yorker in a city notoriously skeptical of carpetbaggers; a seventeen-year-old in a ten-year town; a writer whose anxious lyrics were more reminiscent of Fiona Apple than Loretta Lynn.

In fact all the interviewers that day focused on my self-scrutinizing songwriting. Six times I explained that "Water Bearer" was about the weight of my own insecurities, a riff on my introspective astrological sign. Six times I described the intrusive thoughts that inspired "What If": *my superpower is seeing everything that isn't / till I can't breathe or think or even feel my own heart skipping.* Six times I was asked who I was talking about when I said *I wish I'd never even met you* in "Night Traveler." Was it a boy? They wanted to know. Did somebody break my heart?

"I think a lot of this album is less about the things that happen to us than it is about our reaction to those things. It's internal, not external," I said to the DJs. "What I mean is, I'm the one who broke my own heart." My publicist smiled from outside the booth like she'd never heard such a perfect answer: the kind that gave everything away and nothing at all.

Later, back in my hotel, I stared at my CD on the rumpled duvet while the white noise of the interstate hummed out the window, the black snake of the Cumberland rippling in the distance. Before I could stop myself, I slid my phone from my pocket and dialed.

"Did I do the wrong thing?"

Kelsey's brother's voice was thick with sleep. "Hmm?"

I turned my back to the city and leaned against the glass. "I thought it would help. But now I just feel like I took her dream."

I heard Kelsey's brother moving on his side of the line, the cotton rustle of sheets, the shuffle of slippered feet.

"Sorry. I didn't mean to wake Fiona," I said, soft. I pictured Matt's daughter's toddler bed wedged in the corner of his room, shaped like a Barbie Corvette in pink plastic.

A door slid open and shut, and I knew Matt was standing out on the Copestenkes' back porch, the same deck that had given Fiona a splinter the spring Kelsey vanished, an hour wailing in the bathroom before she agreed to let her aunt retrieve it with a pair of tweezers.

"She's fine. She's been sleeping in Kelsey's bed," Matt said.

We were both quiet for a moment.

"I miss her," I said then.

"Me too."

On the bed, the overhead light caught on the plastic of my CD case and warped the cover art, blotting out my face with the glare. "I miss you," I said, softer.

Matt sighed. I felt the tops of my thighs liquefy, my body puddling with shame. "We can't do this," Matt said.

Anger came next, hot and buzzing at my cheeks, my temples. "Then why did you pick up the phone?"

"I thought maybe you needed to hear it again."

"Hear what?" I snapped. I wanted him to spell it out, to have to suffer through the shame of our behavior right along with me.

Instead I heard him draw a steadying breath. "I don't know if it was the right thing, Dylan. But it's done, and you need to go live your new life. Forget about us. For everyone's sake."

I threw my phone onto the mattress, a pathetic, unsatisfying thump. My CD bounced slightly, and I picked that up instead and hurled it across the room, piercing a scar in the hotel wallpaper.

I hated him for the rejection, for the cliché of his phrasing, but most of all I hated him for being the only person I could talk to about any of it. I hated him for asking me to do something impossible.

My high school is exactly as I left it: two stories and gamma-shaped, with a curved brick facade and a glassy entrance space connecting the academic wings to the gyms, the cafeteria, the music and band rooms and the auditorium. In the late summer the grass that cloaks the football field in front is brown and tan, a speckled, half-hearted green, and the tennis courts are streaked with dust. We park in the visitor lot in front and I'm briefly drowned in the feeling of not-belonging, of having made an error: *over there*, I want to say, pointing to the student parking lot, the back-middle row where Matt would pick us up in his hatchback. *That's where we park*. Here is for interlopers, for parents, for administrators from the district. Over there is where I'm from.

For a moment we sit in the car, my face pressed close to the window, looking out at the crowd funneling inside. I know which attendees are Thompson High grads because they make their way to the side entrance, the little brown door next to the vending machines, while everyone else uses the main entry. I catch a glimpse of the hallway when a man in a navy suit holds the door for a pair of women behind him: brick walls painted an eggy yellow, linoleum flooring speckled brown and white. For a moment I see my younger self, as solid and opaque as the building itself: My arm looped through Kelsey's, walking down the center of the hall in a line-dance step, Kelsey singing "Here You Come Again" at the top of her lungs. I picture her pointing at one of the football players as he exits the athletic trainer's room, pads lazily untied, and she winks: *lookin' better than a body has a right to.*

I shake off the vision, clearing it from my brain like dried leaves from pavement. In the front seat my dad eyes me in the rearview. My mom turns over her shoulder, twisting across the center console. "You okay, sweetie?"

We decided to drive together in one car, my parents' Volvo, because it is inconspicuous and because I'm trying to make as little fuss as possible about my appearance at Kelsey's memorial service. I run the risk of seeming exploitative, insincere; disrespectful of her family's privacy. Sloane and Mike, acting as sole bodyguard for the day, are parked two rows behind us in a black SUV; no matter how hard we might try, the reality is that I am a hurricane—anywhere I go becomes about me.

And yet: There were the posts online. It started with the headlines, every single one of which made Kelsey's story into mine. "HOMETOWN HEARTBREAK: DYLAN READ'S HIGH SCHOOL CLASSMATE DISCOVERED DEAD." "THOMPSON LANDING, HOME TO 'TELL ME' SINGER DYLAN READ, AT CENTER OF TRAGIC 15-YEAR COLD CASE." When the talent show photograph leaked with me standing next to Kelsey—it was Amelia Clark who found it, and posted it on Facebook—what had seemed like a tabloidish tendency to stretch suddenly became a legitimate journalistic concern. Dylan Read actually *knew* this girl.

Sloane's phone started ringing. How well did I know Kelsey? Was I still in touch with the family? How was I coping with the loss? Did I have any plans to make a donation in her honor?

Sloane laid out my options. Say nothing. Say nothing and make a financial contribution—to the family, to the GoFundMe our classmates started for Thompson students looking to pursue a career in music, to some related cause. Make a donation and issue a statement saying I would not be in attendance at the service out of respect for Kelsey's family.

But there was really only one plausible course of action. The world wanted a piece of my grief. I had denied them this part of myself, and it made them question everything they thought they knew about my "diaristic" songwriting. It legitimized the idea that I was only ever pretending to share. Maybe I was cold and calculating after all. What kind of monster doesn't go to their friend's funeral?

"I'm just worried this was a mistake," I say to my mom now from the back seat of their SUV.

"You were a better friend to her than any of these rubberneckers," my dad says, and my mom shoots him a glare.

"You have every right to be here," my mom says. "You are not responsible for the press. That's why you have Sloane." She reaches back and squeezes my wrist resting in my lap, gently prying one hand from the other, as if she'd noticed how I was feeling for the frayed part of the blister on my second finger, and smiles at me. "Ready?"

IN TRUTH, THE PR ANGLE WASN'T MY ONLY REASON FOR COMing home.

It didn't take the police long after finding Kelsey to rule her death an accidental drowning. And if the true-crime sleuths on the internet were disappointed, it was nothing at all compared to the remorse that swept through Thompson Landing like a tidal wave. I knew that Kelsey had been growing distant in the weeks before she disappeared; I knew that she had been talking more and more about making it outside this town. What most of Thompson knew was that Kelsey Copestenke was a little bit of a troublemaker with a complicated home life who had big dreams but almost no resources, and when she disappeared everyone thought that—while it was certainly *sad*—it wasn't exactly a surprise that a girl like her might cut and run.

Now that Kelsey was dead—and now that the police were saying her death was an accident—our hometown felt guilty for whatever role it played in crafting Kelsey's myth. She hadn't run away; she'd been there all along. It wouldn't have changed the outcome if they'd looked harder back then, but they'd spent fifteen years talking about a dead girl as if she just fucked off without saying bye, like she'd been poor and stupid and reckless, like she was a trope in a movie.

I figured this out as I clicked through Thompson Landing's various local news stations online, looking for Matt's dark eyes or her mother Diana's dark curly hair or—would I recognize her?—a teenage Fiona, and found, instead, a chorus of our classmates, Becca Mahoney and Alyssa Alonge and Jeanne Wagner, their faces washed-out in too-close, too-harsh light, saying that *Kelsey was a real firecracker, you know?* And a *class clown* and *I never believed she ran away, because she was a real homebody. You could tell.* With their fake eyelashes and their contoured noses and their bright-colored sweaters—Lilly Pulitzer, really? To be interviewed about a dead girl?—their desperation was obvious. The story had an ending now, but they didn't like how they'd been characterized.

Then came Louie. When I saw his face on News Channel 10, fifteen years older but really not having aged a day—still handsome for a middle-aged man, still radiating a kind of roguishness—I thought, *you coward.* If anyone is supposed to take it on the chin, it's the bartender at the local dive.

"How did you know Miss Copestenke?" the newscaster asked.

Louie cleared his throat. *Business Owner,* his title read on the chyron. "I manage a couple of establishments in the area," he said, "including this little bar." He gestured behind him at the Jolly Roger's paint-chipped sign, its windows covered in bumper stickers and neon signs. *Can't Help Stupid.* "I let folks play live music here some nights, and Kelsey was looking for a gig."

"And what was Kelsey like?"

Louie laughed. His blue eyes crinkled, and the hair he'd slicked back came a little undone. He looked boyish in a menacing kind of way. "Relentless," he said.

It was the first really true thing anyone said about her.

"About what?" the reporter asked.

"Everything, but mainly: she wouldn't take no for an answer. Even if it was perfectly legal, see, I didn't think it was a great idea to let a kid hang out here after school."

"But I take it she wore you down?"

"She had a way of doing that," Louie said, and he smiled like, *what's a guy to do.* "So I let her play her guitar here on Mondays at four p.m. You can imagine what the crowd's like on Monday at four p.m."

"Kelsey played every Monday?"

"Every single Monday. Brought her guitar and her amp and set up right inside the door there, where there's some space next to the jukebox, and sang her little songs for an hour."

"What sort of music?"

Louie frowned. "Country, mostly? I used to rag on her a little because her singing voice had a twang, but that girl had never been south of Pennsylvania."

"Did she ever come here with Dylan Read?"

"Oh yeah," he said, too quickly.

"What was she like back then?" the reporter asked.

Louie feigned a kind of thoughtfulness, as if he hadn't orchestrated this whole interview around exactly this moment. "She was a quiet kid. Shy. Mostly she sat in the corner with a soda while Kelsey did her thing."

I've been writing some new stuff lately, I could hear Kelsey saying as I watched from my booth, a notebook open on the table in front of me. *I thought today would be a good day to test it out. This one's called "Summer Thunder"* . . .

On-screen, Louie was still talking about me. "It surprised me that be-tween the two of them, it was Dylan who ended up the big star. But just goes to show."

"Just goes to show what?"

Louie laughed a little nervously, like someone who wasn't used to clarifying himself. "Here at the bar, we always say that it's the quiet ones you gotta watch out for. You think they're just minding their own busi-ness, but actually they're just waiting for the chance to throw a glass through the window."

"Dylan was a troublemaker?!" the reporter asked, surprised.

"Oh, no, no—nothing like that. But you could tell she always had something on her mind."

"So it sounds like this should be a stop on the Dylan Read Historical Register."

Louie laughed. "Maybe we can get a little plaque out front."

You fucking shark, I thought.

"Just one more question, if you don't mind."

Louie nodded.

"A young girl hanging out at a bar after school. As you said, some might feel that's the sort of behavior that . . . well, isn't the safest."

The bathroom door at Junior's never shut all the way. It had a flimsy hook-and-eye closure that always left the slightest gap, so if somebody wanted, they could stand at the corner of the bar and peer straight through to the toilet. I watched men do it when Kelsey went before her set, angling their bodies away from their beers, feigning a back stretch.

Louie chewed the inside of his cheek. "Kelsey talked a lot about want-ing to leave this place," he said. "It wasn't just kid stuff either. She really meant it. And people loved that about her—that . . . moxie. She'd strike up a conversation with a customer and the next thing I knew they'd be offering to pay for her plane tickets when the time came."

"Did you feel like it was your job to make sure it never went any further than that?"

A memory came to me: Kelsey with her elbows on the counter, waiting for Andy—Louie's weekday bartender—to fill a drink, her ass jutted slightly out, chewing on a cocktail straw. Louie leaned close to her from his usual perch at the bar flap. In the flicker of memory their bodies touched, hip to hip, and they stayed pressed like that, just for a moment, until Andy slid a Coke across the bar to Kelsey, who plunked the straw from between her teeth into the ice and bounced away.

"Well," Louie said, "I did my best. But she didn't always take to fathering."

I studied the tilt of Louie's head and thought again about Kelsey's hip pressed into his. Everyone was trying to avoid being held accountable for Kelsey—reframing their complicity, downplaying how they'd been indifferent or exploitative or judgmental.

I didn't want to be like them. I had to go to Kelsey's funeral because I needed to take responsibility for our friendship. It's the least I could do.

MY MOM AND I WALK IN TOGETHER, DAD TRAILING BEHIND US—A familiar triangulation—and Sloane and Mike last. For the most part the occasion acts as a shield: the white noise of ambient, hushed chatter dims on and off as I move through the room, but no one flocks to us, no one makes a scene. Sometimes I think of fame like an estranged relative: you might say you don't have a relationship with your absent mother, but the reality is that even nonalignment is a response. I've been at this long enough to know when people truly do not know or care who I am, and when people are *choosing* not to care—either to level the playing field (like in LA) or out of respect for the moment (like right now). I exchange a series of small, polite nods, like a member of the royal family on Remembrance Day.

We make our way to a small table near the gym doors, draped in a blue-and-white paper tablecloth (Thompson High's colors) and land-scaped with sympathy bouquets. At the center is a framed photo of Kelsey, frozen at seventeen, and a guest book, spread open in wait. I'm adding my name beneath Jack Rowley's when I hear a man's voice over my shoulder.

"Guess we'll need a security detail for that," he says.

The man's jaw slopes like Kelsey's, the same slight elongation on the left side, and he has her eyes too—that iridescent bronze. He nudges his chin in the direction of the guest book. "Could pay for a year of my kid's college."

My mouth opens, just slightly—a surprised exhale, a small puff of air. Kelsey looks at me from the wall over his shoulder, one leg kicked back against the concrete brick like a cowboy. *Can you believe this asshole?* She laughs and shakes her head, her dark hair curtaining in front of her face. Then she looks at me again. *Talking about his kids as if I wasn't one of them.*

"Luke Sullivan," he says, extending a hand. He has a long, jagged scar through the soft webbing between his thumb and forefinger. "Made the same mistake the fish make," he adds, following my gaze. "Only makes it worse when you pull back on it."

I frown at the image of a hook tunneled in his skin. "I know who you are," I say, still holding the pen aloft. Kelsey's father wasn't in the picture, but the stories about him made their way through the Thompson rumor mill after her disappearance. I've never met Luke, but I know that he's not a good guy.

I smile at him in a deliberately benign way. "You said you want an autograph?" I ask. "Let me sign your arm. See what you could get for that on eBay."

Kelsey's father looks at me in a shell-shocked way that could read as either wounded or amused. Then he laughs, a big, open-mouthed cackle, all his teeth visible. Just like his daughter. The sound echoes in the hushed room.

You don't need to have my publicist's finely calibrated instincts to see there's something volatile here, but it helps. Sloane is at my side immediately, a hand gently tapping at my elbow. "I think it's time?" she says.

"Sloane," I say, "this is Luke Sullivan. Kelsey's biological father."

"Sloane Maxwell," she says, without extending a hand to shake. "My condolences," she adds flatly, before turning to me: "Your parents have already grabbed seats."

I nod and follow Sloane to the gym door, but not without one last, long look at Luke. I don't believe for a second that Kelsey's absent father is ashamed or grieving, like the rest of Thompson Landing. Why, then, is he here? What is he trying to prove?

INSIDE, I TAKE A SEAT BETWEEN MY MOTHER AND SLOANE, ON the bleacher level closest to the gym floor. Mike and my dad sit behind us. I resist the urge to tilt my heels back and feel how the stiletto points skate on the lacquered wood, as if all the sense memories of this place—smells of new paint and rubber and hot plastic; the clamor of so many voices echoing in a high, square, reflective room—have combined to make me feel fifteen again.

Kelsey's photo is propped on an easel at center court, next to a podium on a small temporary stage. Principal Gleason takes the mic first, and this is when I notice Mrs. Copestenke. She looks old, I think; and then I realize that even though everyone I've seen today is older, this is the first time I've had that thought. Kelsey's mother has allowed her hair to go gray, so that her mane of tight curls is shot through with dark streaks rather than the other way around. She's wearing a skirt suit from the nineties, polyester and knee-length with gold pearled buttons, and block kitten heels. In the year Kelsey and I were inseparable I never saw Diana in anything but scrubs, always between hospital shifts, and I think this is kind of adding insult to injury, isn't it, having to perform the pageantry of grief.

Seated next to her is a teenage girl, seventeen or eighteen, tall with curtains of glossy dark hair. I blink once, twice, a cerebral short-circuiting.

My mother leans over to me, whispering: "She looks *so* much like Kelsey, doesn't she?"

Fiona sits with a slight slouch and cool affect, betrayed only slightly by her hands: one resting gently on Diana's thigh, the other wrapped in her father's—the link between them, forever the glue that held their family together.

Kelsey's brother wears his suit uncomfortably, shoulders pressed up to the ears, extra fabric at the elbows, at the ankles. I do the math quickly: Matt is thirty-seven or thirty-eight now, and that number—*almost forty*—knocks the wind out of me. He's an age I remember my own father turning. Time goes liquid while I study his face, his body in its folding chair, that hand that grasps his daughter's. I can see all the rough drafts of him at once: in the driver's seat of his Saab hatchback, pulling the car around front to pick us up from school; teaching Fiona to skate on the lake, tugging her over the bumpy ice with her knees locked; opening a beer in the refrigerator light, home late from work. He still looks like the too-skinny hockey player he wanted to be—something classically American about him with his strong brow and wide nose, and I can see the puckish way he smiles in the gentle curves that parenthesize his lips—but now he has a slight puffiness under his eyes and a pair of lines running across his forehead and he's allowed his hair to grow out. He has incredible hair, I think. He always hid it beneath a buzz cut.

At the podium, Principal Gleason concludes a vague remembrance of

Kelsey, using words like "spirited" and "independent"—plainly teacher-speak for "pain in the ass"—and then the room swells in a round of applause as she extends a hand in Diana's direction, inviting her to the mic.

Kelsey's mother holds a set of index cards. She taps them against the mic stand, filing them together, then rests her wrists against the lectern, the cards gripped between her fingers. "My daughter sang all the time," she begins, but she's too close to the mic and it screams with feedback. She pulls away, adjusts. "Cleaning her room, washing the dishes, making coffee in the morning—" Diana looks at her notes, wanting to land a line. "She was our family's soundtrack.

"I remember, one time, I had a really bad day at the hospital. We lost a kid. Boating accident." She pauses. "It was awful. And I was exhausted, and I walk in the door ready to just—collapse. But the first thing I hear when I get inside is Kelsey, singing 'Coal Miner's Daughter' while she cooked dinner."

The memory seems to fortify her for a moment, exactly as it did two decades ago.

"It's sort of a sad song, I guess, but my daughter's voice just seemed *made* for it. So I stood in our little entryway and I just listened. It didn't fix what happened at work that day but something about Kelsey covering Loretta Lynn made me feel like I would be able to handle it."

I can imagine Kelsey's shimmering delivery precisely. I know exactly how her radiant twang seemed built to carry lyrics that were a little bit melancholy: *We were poor, but we had love / that's the one thing that Daddy made sure of . . .*

"A few weeks before she left, Kelsey got stuck on a loop with 'Never Gonna Give You Up,'" Diana continues. She almost laughs to herself, a little rushed exhale that rasps in the mic. "Her voice wasn't made for that one. Nobody's is, I guess. But she just would. Not. Stop. For days, our lives were nothing but this ridiculous song from the eighties. I remember begging her. Yelling at her. Just please, please stop." Diana shakes her head.

For a little while after Kelsey disappeared, I told myself that at least Diana had hope. She could imagine her daughter busking in Nashville, bartending at the Bluebird, auditioning for open mics all over town. Now I wonder whether her loss has merely doubled: her daughter *and* the fantasy she built for herself as a refuge from grief.

There's a hitch in Diana's voice when she speaks next, as if the moment has finally caught up with her. "Kelsey wanted to be known as the girl who could sing Loretta Lynn like it was written for her. But for me, the one who danced around the kitchen to one-hit wonders was perfect."

Diana turns from the podium to her seat. Gleason touches her on the way, a tender, lingering brush on her upper back. "Thank you, Mrs. Copestenke. We've also invited a friend of Kelsey's—and a fellow musician—to speak on her behalf. I'm sure you all remember her, and I'm certain none of us have been surprised by her success." Gleason finds me in the crowd. "Dylan," she asks, "would you come up?"

The speech was Sloane's idea. She thought it was better to give them—the press, the tabloids, the people online—a Moment, capital *M*, rather than force them to sift through the rubble. If there's a proper photo op and formal quotes, we can avoid any sneaky, covert selling out. "Plus," Sloane pointed out, "this way, the internet can stop guessing why you're there. You can tell them, in your own words, what you want them to know about your relationship with Kelsey."

I bring Gleason into a warm hug, breathing in her scent of Aqua Net and talc and something distinctly female, and then take my place at the mic. I breathe in once, deeply, and allow my smile to expand with my lungs. *Patient. Focused. Calm.* Every time, no matter the stage.

"Hi, everyone," I say, before turning once back to Diana and Fiona and—he keeps his gaze on the floor, a posture of grief or of determined avoidance, I can't be sure—Matt. "And thank you for inviting me to speak today.

"If you remember us from Thompson High, it won't surprise you to hear me say that Kelsey and I weren't very much alike. I was on Science Olympiad; the only club Kelsey went to was ZigZags on a Saturday night. I dressed as the school mascot for Halloween; Kelsey's costume got her sent to the principal's office. My favorite writer was Emily Dickinson. Kelsey's, as we all knew, was Dolly Parton."

The audience laughs at each beat, exactly when and how they're supposed to, in a kind of murmuring, appreciative way. "But these are superficial differences," I continue. "The truth is that—just like Emily Dickinson and Dolly have more in common than we might think, both of them intensely private and ferociously ambitious—Kelsey and I were more alike than we knew too."

I take a deep breath. The internet wants to know if Kelsey and I were actual friends. Were we just classmates? Two acts in one amateur talent show, frozen side by side in a grainy photograph? Or was there something more between us?

Is this personal to me?

"One day that winter, she and I were killing time at the mall during one of those RV shows. Remember them? I never understood how they managed to get those buses inside the mall hallways. Anyway—Kelsey insisted we go inside every single one. She sat in the La-Z-Boy driver seats. She pitched herself backward on the beds, hands behind her head. In a stall that combined a toilet and a shower, she mimed pooping and washing herself at the same time." I flash an apologetic smile at Diana.

"Kelsey and I tucked into the booth seats of a Formica table and leaned against the windows and talked about where we would take our campers. Arches. Zion. Acadia. I wanted to know whether the trees lost their leaves differently in the Midwest, in the Sierras. I wanted to see how the sharp edges of the Rockies and the Tetons compared to our own rolling hills. I imagined watching the sunrise over a mug of coffee beneath my RV's retractable awning.

"Wouldn't it be so nice, Kelsey said, to have everything you needed right in arm's reach? To be able to take it with you everywhere you go?

"The point, I understood, wasn't the sense of adventure, although I know that's what most people associate with Kelsey Copestenke—a certain spontaneity, courage, bravery. A lack of inhibition, maybe. That day in the mall, I understood that what Kelsey loved most—what she *craved* most—was self-sufficiency. Everything she needed right there in one little mobile box.

"I think everybody in high school is a little obsessed with independence, and in some ways these are even older fantasies about American self-reliance: the open road, living off-the-grid. But for Kelsey, this was also about her music. You have to be brave to be an artist. You have to believe that your voice and your perspective are singular. And I think Kelsey was."

I take one careful, patient breath while I smile at the audience. I know not to oversell this, to try as hard as I can to look as though I'm not performing at all. Then I turn again to Kelsey's family, first hugging Diana—she's smaller than I remember, more delicate—then Fiona; "You look so much like her," I whisper into her ear, only to see when we pull apart how her eyes have contracted slightly, the same irritated tell Kelsey had.

And then I'm standing in front of Matt, pulling him in, fitting my chin into the space between his ear and his shoulder and inhaling his Old Spice and disappearing, in an instant, into the black hole of memory: There I am, sitting on his mattress with the navy sheets, staring up at an Islanders poster on the wall. I want him to tell me it's okay, I'm glad to see you, I also had the idea to invite you, so funny, did you know? I want to nudge him in the side and say, it's okay, too. We both made mistakes.

Instead he flicks his gaze away from mine as we separate.

I take my seat with my parents as Principal Gleason is thanking me, her voice bright and thin over the mic, and as she begins to talk about additional ways to contribute to the Kelsey Copestenke Memorial Fund, Sloane whispers "nicely done" in my ear and my dad squeezes me on the shoulder and my mom puts a hand on my thigh, a quick nervous pat. Gleason reminds us that we're all invited for a light lunch at the Copestenkes', and then just like that: it's over. I follow my entourage out into the foyer, George Thompson's brigadier a flat-laid silhouette on the floor, like a piece of Revolutionary-era art.

AS A RULE I TRY TO LEAVE PARTIES OUT THE BACK. OTHERWISE an exit takes too long, everybody trying to get in their last chance to say hello, their courage finally gathered the moment I seem about to slip out of reach. *I just wanted to say.* In following everyone out into the glassy atrium that is the gym's entryway, I've ruined my chance for a quick escape.

Other mothers approach my mom first, eyes flicking to me, and I break the ice. I am grateful for the elephant memory I inherited; like my mother, I'm excellent with names. *Mrs. Strauss, so good to see you; is Rebecca here today? Mr. Jones! How's Kayleigh doing? Ms. Cobley—I heard Paige had a baby! You can't* possibly *be a grandmother!* And on and on. Mr. Pettrucione Ms. McCamy Mr. and Mrs. Smith Mr. and Mrs. McPhillips Mrs. Riley Mrs. Behan—*oh, it's actually Leonig now! Congratulations!* Mike and Sloane keep just enough distance that I do not have to introduce my publicist and my bodyguard, but I watch Ms. McClellan's and Mr. Frazier's and Mrs. Schafer's eyes flit over my shoulder to the large suited man and the birdlike brunette and I know they know that I'm not here the same way they are.

For a while it's only parents who approach, my mother functioning as an intermediary of sorts: they feel comfortable with her. Eventually we're close enough to Kelly Corona's elbow that I can reach out and touch it, gently, and say "Kelly!" and bring her in for a hug, and this creates space for Kelly's friends to draw closer. Everyone is here. I say this: "Everyone's here!" Everyone looks the same, even though I know I look nothing like I did fifteen years ago, and not just because of the money and lasers and Xeomin. Here in Thompson Landing, it's the same faces and bodies but with spouses on their hips (nobody is queer; anyone who might have been queer in 2004 or 2005 or 2006 would not have come back to this place) and, some tell me, one or two children at home. They show me pictures on their phones, scrolling too fast. My cheeks start to ache. I begin to dissociate.

I wish Nick were here. I'm glad he isn't. This is what it means, I think, to be partnered: can't live with 'em, can't live without 'em. I wonder how Nick would feel, meeting all these former friends of mine with their tidy regular lives, their kids and marriages. Our own conversations about the subject are anguished, both of us stuck, certain of our own selfishness but nonetheless intractable. Marriage is an impossibility for me. There is simply too much at stake—a lesson I learned when the recklessness of my first, impossibly brief marriage nearly ruined everything, required a recalibration of my work and my reputation and the way I protected my wealth, even, and I made a promise to myself never to compromise my career with my personal life again. Meanwhile Nick's parents are divorced, estranged, his sister in and out of rehab. His family is fragmented and he longs for us to be made solid, certain. I tell him that while being together is romantic, joining our financial selves in a way that protects my legacy is not. He says that he would never ever force me to choose between him and my art. I ask him to imagine lawyering up against me, because that's what drafting a prenup would require. I promise him, again and again, that I will never leave. *How does the paperwork make it any different?* I ask.

You're a poet, he tells me. *You know the symbolic weight of things.*

Meanwhile Ms. Twyman is telling me about the place she and her husband bought in Edisto, the gardening club, how she always knew I would be a writer. I'm thanking her when Sloane appears over my shoulder, leaning into my ear to tell me that there's a pretty good cluster of paps across the street out in front. They're not allowed on school property but they have long lenses and it's not far; they'll be able to get a good shot.

I know where to go. I pull out my phone to show Sloane a map of campus, telling her where Mike should pull the SUV. I smile at Ms. Twyman once more, then I'm off, back through the gym to the hallway on the opposite side that cuts behind to the languages wing, Spanish and French and Portuguese flags peeling from bulletin boards covered in faded construction paper, all the while thrumming with the same thrilled sensation I used to have at a night basketball game or during Saturday-morning enrichment programs: that this time is stolen, that I am not supposed to be here, that I've found a way to make this school mine.

The small parking lot off the art wing bumps up against the neighborhoods right behind campus and is shielded from view by the tall trees and hedges of the homes belonging to people who would rather pretend they do not share a boundary with teenagers. In photography class we'd sneak out this exit and take pictures in the fields and around the dumpsters, pretending to be the first people to see something beautiful in a rotting apple core, developed in black and white.

Mike's holding the door of my SUV open when I hear a familiar voice: "The Irish exit was always Kelsey's thing," Raff says. He takes a pull on a joint and passes it to the man next to him. "Right until the very end."

I hold up a finger to Sloane and Mike. *Just one minute.*

"Getting high behind the dumpsters?" I say to Raff, who steps away from the trio of soft-shouldered men sharing the joint to move closer to me. I recognize Dan Lawrence, and I assume the other two are also former hockey players. I blink and smell their Axe body spray, the faint wet of their pads, can spot the angry shining zits on the backs of their necks.

"Just trying to recapture the full Thompson High experience," he says. Kelsey's boyfriend's voice is lower than I recall, a slight hoarseness etched into it now, and as he straightens his suit jacket in front of me I think he's softer too: his body absent the hard edging of his chest, his shoulders, his biceps—all that distinct chiseling I remember from watching him down the locker bank.

"What's there to recapture?" I say, my tone light. "Looks like you guys never left."

Raff laughs like someone who is stoned: mouth shut, giggles swallowed. I see the boys turn our way again and check for phones surreptitiously pulled from pockets, recording at waist level—none. "You know," Raff says, catching his breath, "everybody said you'd come, but I said, *no way*. Dylan Read's too good for this place now. She hasn't been seen around here in years."

"I visit my parents," I say, a little defensively. It's true: I take a small plane to a grassy airfield twenty minutes outside of town, then a tinted-window car to my parents', where I hole up before repeating the process in reverse. *Whisking.* "I was her best friend, Raff. I figured I owed it to her, same as her boyfriend."

"Wasn't her boyfriend," Raff says.

This actually makes me laugh, a big spit take of a *bah!* "That seems like a technicality," I say.

Raff's eyes are red-rimmed and watery. His high has crossed from chill to menacing. "You call everyone you fuck your boyfriend?"

Only I'm allowed to call him a piece of shit, I can hear Kelsey saying. *We hate him on* my *terms.* "In high school I think you do, yeah," I say.

"Well, we weren't even fucking then, anyway."

It's not necessarily the lie that knocks the wind out of me—it's that he expects me to buy it. Why does Raff think he can get away with it? I wonder.

Why would he try?

I put Louie and Luke and Raff all on a shelf in my brain and consider the way their revisionist histories seem different, slightly, than my female classmates weeping elegantly for the local news—almost like the stakes are higher for them, somehow. But before I can press, Sloane calls to me from the car door. "Dylan?" she says. "We've got to get to the reception."

"Your carriage awaits," Raff says, and he's still laughing as I slide past Sloane into the SUV, his teammates' huddle opening to reabsorb his round-shouldered frame. For a moment I watch the walled backs of their pack receding through my tinted window and think this, maybe more than anything else so far today, has sent my body hurtling back fifteen years: the feeling that no matter what, no matter how smart I am or how much I think I know, the men are the ones who shape the narrative.

The Breakout

I didn't think of Thompson High as having a stratified hierarchy. I thought of it like a galaxy, with each clique like a spinning planetary system, centralized, symbiotic, with its own gravitational pull: musical theater kids and athletes and artists who smoked cigarettes during their free period just across the street from campus. I drifted among the strivers, forty to sixty kids who'd been funneled off into advanced courses starting in seventh grade so that by sophomore year we were all taking four APs and fretting over our GPAs down to the hundredth decimal place.

Kelsey wasn't a striver. She wasn't a band geek, or on the student newspaper, or one of those girls whose system existed outside of Thompson High—the ballerinas, for example, or the gymnasts. Kelsey was something else entirely: the rare unbound planet—rogue, wandering, interstellar.

Before we met officially, Kelsey existed in my periphery as the sometimes girlfriend of Brendan Raffensburger—"Raff" for short—whose locker, because they were assigned alphabetically, was often in the same bank as mine. Raff played football in the fall and hockey in the winter and was tall and broad with sandy blond hair cut high and tight and a strong, square chin. When he wore his letterman jacket—which was often—I thought he looked almost made-up, as if an anthropologist in a lab somewhere had been tasked with conjuring an American High School Male. Raff's friends dated girls who were pretty, with shining straight hair and delicate features, almond eyes and ski-slope noses, five

foot four in 32B bras. They wore popped-collar polo shirts from Aber-
crombie and silver necklaces from Tiffany and I had the sense, based on
how the boys talked at Raff's locker, that their sex ran in one direction:
the girls gave, the boys received.

Kelsey was different. A year older than us, she was hot in a way that
was not quiet or subtle. She was tall and wore T-shirts that were too
small, so they rode up when she sat down, flashing the skin of her lower
back and the top edge of her lace thong, always highlighter green or hot
pink or neon violet. When she laughed, she did so loudly, her mouth
wide open, the gnarled putty of her chewing gum visible against her
back molars.

When they broke up the first time, Raff went to a party on a Friday
night and slept with Steph Sweeney. I knew this because on Monday
morning I overheard Raff talking to his friends Dan and Vinny about it,
spinning the dial of my combination lock while Raff explained how tight
Steph was compared to Kelsey, how by contrast Kelsey had felt like guiding a hot dog through a hallway. When they got back together a week
after that, nobody said anything about it, and maybe to make up for the
impression that they were having bad sex Raff told the guys about how
Kelsey had let him come on her chest.

The next time they broke up I knew that Raff wasn't telling the whole
story, because Kelsey would slip little notes into his locker when no one
was around, and I'd see Raff slide them into his pocket when his teammates weren't looking.

There's this theory in psychology that refers to the creation of a
"third"—that when two people come together and form a relationship,
that connection is its own separate, distinct space, sort of like a dis-
crete being, a new individual. I don't think that it's possible for someone outside the pair to witness the third, not really—any observation
necessarily inserts a new element, the relationship of the observer to
the original pair. My mom always told me that a good psychologist is

constantly aware of her own projecting: how her own experiences and biases, needs and wants, traumas and family structures might impact her read of another person. What I mean to say is, I understood that I didn't really know anything at all about Kelsey and Raff, and that for all my attention—all my watching from five lockers down—the Kelsey that lived in my head could be only a two-dimensional one, a lithograph version crafted to tell a story that made sense.

I WROTE A LOT OF *SOPHOMORE* FROM A PLACE OF FEAR. I'D moved to Nashville, into a sprawling floor-through penthouse off Music Row, and at night I'd stand in my kitchen and stare across my living room at my home reflected in my ceiling-height windows and think, *this is a house out of a horror movie.* This is the kind of place a serial killer buys. I didn't feel like I belonged, and I feared that at any moment someone might find me out and force me to leave.

I met Aaron Alexander at a holiday party thrown by the owner of the Titans. I wasn't so famous then that people would flock to me upon entering a room, and I wasn't important enough to bring an entourage; as I pulled up to his estate in Forest Hills—a Georgian colonial with a wide porch marked by four two-story columns—my teeth chattered with nerves, a bone-deep freeze on a fifty-five-degree Tennessee night. Inside I made my way to the bar and ordered a cranberry juice with soda, then tried to delay having to navigate the party by slowly picking a cocktail napkin from the stack and adjusting my straw's position among the ice, poking at my wedge of lime like a ship in the red sea.

"I'll have what she's having," Aaron said, and when I turned to look at him my first reaction was "People actually say that?" which was something Kelsey would have said, quick, tongue in cheek; sparkling.

He laughed. "My next question was going to be whether you come here often," he said, and this time I laughed.

"I don't, but I'm guessing you do?"

Aaron adjusted the center button of his suit jacket and puffed out his chest, exaggerating his size, which was considerable. "Was it my shoulders or my all-American looks?"

I pressed my palm to my heart and feigned a gasp. "You think I didn't recognize you from watching you on TV every Sunday?"

"You're a football fan?"

I shook my head, now bringing my hand to his upper arm. "I'm just kidding, I have no idea who you are."

Aaron briefly doubled over, hiding for a moment a broad grin. When he straightened he extended a hand in my direction and I saw that his eyes were the color of the Caribbean, bright turquoise. "Aaron Alexander," he said. "Defensive end."

My hand was small in his, delicate. "Dylan Read," I said. "Singer-songwriter."

"I know. I've heard of you."

"A big country-music listener, are you?"

"Born and raised in Tennessee," he said. "There's no other way."

I nodded, feeling that the conversation had run its course, and felt my stomach start to quake as I fumbled for a clean exit. In a few years, I would never have to do this: there would always be a publicist or assistant over my shoulder.

"This doesn't have any booze?" Aaron held his drink out in front of him, eyeing it like it had duped him in some criminal way.

I smiled, a little embarrassed. "Now you know my secret," I told him. While most people might like a drink to soothe their nerves, I felt I couldn't risk loosening up: I only carried the glass as a prop, camouflage for my control issues.

"I've never met anyone who hides their *lack* of drinking. Isn't it supposed to be the other way around?"

I shrugged. "I don't want people to think I'm uptight."

Aaron frowned, pinching his mouth to one side and raising the opposite eyebrow. "Well, now you're gonna have to prove it to me."

"That I'm not uptight?"

"Yup."

"How?"

"Doesn't sound like something a not-uptight person would say."

I laughed, but Aaron didn't even crack a smile. He just raised the other eyebrow to match the first.

"Hmm," I murmured, thinking. "Did you see that Christmas tree out back?"

"The one on the porch?"

I nodded. The house was decked out in the kind of maximalist-but-tasteful holiday decor that characterizes excess wealth: thick swags of pine boughs around the columns and railings, threaded through with velvet ribbon and gold twinkle lights; steps lined with thriving poinsettias; a twelve-foot blue spruce in the rotunda off the back porch.

"What about it?"

"It seemed . . . under-decorated to me. Don't you think?"

Aaron nodded, slowly at first, playing along. "You know, I think you might be right."

"I think I should help them out, yeah?"

That year, we partnered with Mattel on a line of dolls. They came in six different outfits—Country Dylan (in cowboy boots), Spectacle Dylan (in a sequined dress), Witchy Dylan (after the "Night Traveler" music video outfit), et cetera—and each had her own little acoustic guitar, wood-toned or sparkly gold or deep evergreen, stamped with my autograph. The week of the Christmas party a hundred of these dolls had shown up at Melody's offices, and I'd been driving around with them in the back of my car, unsure what to do with them. They felt like a weird thing to donate to a holiday toy drive, a weirder thing still to have in my house—but not something I could just throw out either.

"I can't decide whether this is the creepiest or most hilarious thing I've ever seen," Aaron said when I opened my trunk. He reached forward and pulled Tennessee Dylan (in a Titans jersey; we had to jump through hoops with the NFL for that one, and it was in part the reason I was at the party) from the stack, then turned the box to face me. Her plastic coffin gleamed in the holiday lights. "Are you a sociopath?" he asked.

"Someone with antisocial personality disorder can't identify their own pathology, duh."

Aaron laughed.

"Come on," I said. "Start unboxing."

The dolls came pinned down in their packaging by little plastic-coated metal ties, each one twisted around a limb and anchored in the back of the box. They took forever to open. We made it a competition, of course, because that's what two competitive young people do, and we teased each other while we worked. He had a sprained middle finger. I had my ugly, gnarled calluses. We joked about who had the strongest hands, the most dexterous fingers. Aaron held each version of the doll up to my face, appraising the likeness even though the only thing that was different, from model to model, was the clothing. "Nah, still doesn't look like you," he'd say, scrunching his nose disapprovingly. He was right: her eyes were too gray, her hair too shiny, her face too perfectly oval.

"Thanks," I said, pretending to be wounded, or pretending to pretend to be wounded, because some part of me, of course, craved doll-like perfection.

"They made an ornament of Crum last year," he told me. "Our quarterback."

"I know who he is!"

"Just making sure. Anyway, it was terrifying. Like they'd taken a Frankenstein ornament and made it a white guy in a Titans jersey." I could picture it: the comically square head, the weirdly thick neck.

"But . . . doesn't he . . . sort of look like Frankenstein?" I asked.

Aaron laughed, and it almost made up for not being doll-like.

When the pile of freed Dylans on the pavement at our feet seemed big enough, I stacked them in Aaron's arms and we crept around the side of the house to the back patio.

"I think they can see us," Aaron hissed, tilting his head quickly toward the open windows. In the kitchen a catering team in white aprons hurried around trays of golden meat, tureens of sauces, platters of silver-dollar quiches.

"They're busy," I said, and then looked over my shoulder. "Are you scared?"

"Of what?"

"Getting caught with a bunch of Barbies," I said. "Might be hard to explain in the locker room."

"Listen, I'm not the one trying to prove something here."

I worked quickly, pulling Dylan dolls from Aaron's arms one by one and nestling them among the ornaments on the spruce. I wrapped her arms around branches, tucked her body in a V shape against a nest of needles, wedged her—legs outstretched—along the flattest, sturdiest limbs of the evergreen. Her little guitars were tethered to her wrist with tiny rubber bands, and every now and then one would snap and fling in the direction of Aaron's face or mine, like tiny bits of toy-making shrapnel.

"Okay," I said to Aaron when there was just one Dylan (Country Dylan) left: "You have to do this one." I pointed the doll in the direction of the treetop.

"How tall do you think I am?"

I made a frustrated grunt. "I can go on your shoulders," I said.

"Is that safe?"

"Can't you lift, like, three times my weight?"

I remember my dress hiked up around my waist, the back of his head against my abdomen, the way his hands wrapped around my calves, thumbs overlapping his forefingers. When he put me down again my skirt rippled over his hair. I stumbled, giggled. He straightened his shirt as we surveyed our handiwork, the tree stippled now with crooked plastic bodies.

"Would an uptight person vandalize a house with her own merch?" I asked.

"No." Aaron laughed. "I don't think she would." He stepped very close to me. "But would she make out with a stranger at a party?"

"Are we strangers?" I nodded in the direction of the tree. "Your hands have been all over my body." When Aaron leaned in to kiss me, I thought, who knew I could talk like that? Where did *that* come from?

IT WAS MY IDEA TO MAKE *SOPHOMORE* A SONG CYCLE, A COHE-sive sonic and lyrical experience built around a single premise—in this case, I wanted to use high school and literal developmental adolescence as a metaphor for my own feelings of adolescence in the music industry, all the fumbling uncertainty I felt despite losing my rookie status, all the ways I was supposed to have a clear, defined sense of my brand when I felt like I was still learning how to be an artist. So much of adolescence is costuming—trying on new experiences and identities and literal clothing to see what fits—and I was doing the same as a musician. Obviously the album title is a little tongue-in-cheek—it's my sophomore record—but even that struck me as kind of useful, artistically. (*Too smart by half*, Kelsey would have said. *Take off the nerd cap for just one second.*) As a freshman, you're granted all this patience, all this time to figure out your way, but as soon as you come back for your sophomore year you're supposed to have it figured out.

That's how I felt the year I met Kelsey: like an indistinct blur of a person. It's strange to think of it that way, as *meeting*—in high school you can orbit a person, be acutely aware of their existence, know their name and birth order and rumored sexual history, but never actually *speak* to them—but we did *meet* that year, as in we spoke for the first time backstage at the Assembly Block performance of the school talent show. My English teacher, Ms. Twyman, encouraged me to perform—"I don't have any talents," I'd argued, and she tapped my poetry portfolio on her desk, the one I'd just submitted, and said, "These are pretty good"—and so I'd written a trio of poems titled "Girlhood" about the men in my life and practiced them in my bedroom every night, timing my breath, manipulating my inflection, saying each part so many ways that when I turned off the light and shut my eyes the lines would keep running in my brain.

Backstage that afternoon, I was the only person without a prop. Tim O'Connor and a couple of guys from the basketball team were performing a Harlem Globetrotters–style routine, and they stood in a wide circle spinning balls on their index fingers, dropping them, sending them pinballing around the chaos; Simone Burgess and Claire Egan had planned a ballet performance, and they sat in a corner reworking their shoes, a small sewing kit on the ground between them; Anthony Campisi was doing a set of magic tricks, and he paced along the wall behind the stage, tugging a string of tied scarves from his sleeve with a flourish, then stuffing them back in, over and over, a rainbow glitch. Meanwhile I stood off to the corner, three sheets of printed paper dampening in my hands.

Onstage, out of view, the head of the art department introduced the show. "Welcome, welcome," we heard Mr. Banks say, and then a high-pitched zip of a whistle pierced the crowd—likely Mrs. Herman, our gym teacher—and everyone fell silent. "Thanks," Banks said. He cleared his throat, gathering himself. "Balanchine. The Beatles. David Blaine," he began, and I heard a small, stifled chuckle from just behind me, farther against the wall. I turned, and a girl in jeans with an acoustic guitar slung from her shoulders pressed the back of her hand to her mouth.

Kelsey caught my eye and mouthed *sorry*, an exaggerated grimace over the second syllable. I smiled at her quickly and then stared at the floor again, at the white A+F logo stenciled to the center-left of my flip-flop strap. Onstage, Simone and Claire began dancing to an orchestral version of "Dreams," and from where Kelsey and I stood, the music projected away from us, we could hear the slip and scuff of their shoes against the vinyl flooring.

Kelsey leaned over to me. "I bet nobody out there even knows this song," she said, raising her eyes in the vague direction of the skating strings.

"That's probably the point," I said, knowing that Claire, at least, was the kind of girl who actively engaged in her own myth-making. Kelsey laughed again, a contained snort.

On the other side of the curtain, applause replaced the music. We heard the fluttered tapping of the girls scampering offstage, and then a single, rhythmic, rubber bouncing—the start of the Globetrotter routine.

"So what's your deal again?" Kelsey asked, flicking her chin at the paper in my hand.

"Oh—um, I write poetry."

Kelsey stared. "Like, spoken word?"

"Not really, just regular poems. I don't do the whole"—I deepened my voice and truncated my rhythm—"you know, the thing, where they talk. Like this." Immediately I wanted to curl into myself, mortified by my own impression, that I'd dared try to be funny or spontaneous.

"Lemme see," Kelsey said.

"Oh no, I'd rather—" I tried to protest, but Kelsey had already pulled the paper from my hand and was unfolding it in her palms, her guitar wedged against the crook of her hip.

"These are all right," Kelsey said after a moment. "But you're just gonna, like, read them?"

"I mean, that's what you do with poetry," I said, a little angry. I reached for my pages but Kelsey held them fast.

"You can't do that."

"Excuse me?"

"It's social suicide."

"What?"

"Look, I mean, *I* don't think it's weird, but this isn't exactly St. Mark's, okay? This is"—she waved her hand vaguely, at the air between us—"upstate New York."

The basketball dribbling—after ascending to a thunderous stampede, a mixture of coordinated beats, some bounced on a four count at shoulder height, others at double time down by the ankles—came to a sudden, sharp stop.

"Shit," Kelsey said. "I'm up." She shoved my poems back in my hand and ran toward the wing, curving the guitar back half-behind her so she could walk casually onstage, one arm waving high. Feeling as though I'd been sideswiped, I stood in the eave between blankets of dusty velvet and watched as Kelsey arranged herself on the edge of a tall stool positioned at center stage. She played simply at first, three repeating notes in a rhythm I could count naturally, and when her voice joined in it was silky with just the slightest drawn syllables of a twang. *When you love somebody*, she began, and despite the tightness in my chest I noticed, too, an involuntary melting in my shoulders and hips. Her delivery—the way she carried the *ooh* at the end of *what do you do-ooh?*; how she turned *sad* into two syllables—was plaintive and desperate, palpably heartbroken, utterly irresistible.

The song was short, and she shifted quickly from the final two notes into a six-note pattern I recognized as distinctly more country. This song sounded more upbeat—even the lyrics seemed triumphant, at the syntactical level: a repeated, confident *here I am*—but there was a melancholy I couldn't quite place, a carried-over longing from the previous, maybe. Kelsey faded the ending, so she almost talk-sang the final *here I am*, adding a little humming as an outro. When she finished she lifted her head and smiled widely at the audience—from where I stood I could see the raised bumps of the apples of her cheeks, the way her eyes squinted at the corners—and the applause was, if not thunderous, at least approving.

Instead of walking offstage, Kelsey stood and dragged her stool slightly back and to the left, at an angle from the center. In the opposite wing Banks hesitated, looking at me across the dais, and I looked at Kelsey, who mouthed *trust me*. I nodded in Banks's direction. As he read my introduction I watched Kelsey fiddle with her guitar, twisting the knobs at the neck, shifting her weight against the foot balanced on the stool's lower rung. And then I strode into the spotlight.

"When I was eight," I began, "my grandfather said you'd never see two hawks in one place." I hated the way my voice sounded back at me, too high and childlike, and I could see, in the lower periphery of my vision, the way the paper shook in my hands. "But I'd seen them circling like vultures, poised like opposing armies in battle."

In the front row, Sean Torres elbowed Nate Morello, their shoulders heaving with silent laughter. A few seats down from them, Megan O'Neill raised a single, devastating eyebrow. I wanted to drop my pages and walk across the stage, into the wings, out the back entrance behind the auditorium, into the staff parking lot, and never return to Thompson High again. But then: a quiet strumming, five notes that echoed the tentative, cautious insistence of the poem.

It was exactly right.

I followed Kelsey's lead, speaking slightly more up-tempo. "At nine he told me that coywolves were an urban legend, but we'd been to California and stood in the Sierras and I'd seen a wild dog, alone, an in-between-sized predator.

"I don't think my grandfather was lying to me, or trying to tell me that I was wrong." I heard Kelsey: one-two-three, one-two. "I just think we lived in different worlds."

From there I moved into a segment about my father, and, finally, a story about a boy I babysat. "I wonder how long we have," I said, and it was somehow timed perfectly, so that Kelsey finished a bar and dropped out for my last line: "Until he, too, will tell me how to be."

We didn't knock it out of the park. But I wasn't humiliated either. Kelsey walked to the front of the stage and placed a hand on the small of my back, the other arm holding her guitar aloft. "Bow," she hissed in my ear, and I did, and then she stood slightly off to one side and extended both arms in my direction, her guitar swung around her back. The crowd followed her lead, swelling to a slightly heightened round of applause.

As we slipped into the wings, the next group—Jay Cohen's band— hustled around us, pressing us into the thick of the drapes. Kelsey stumbled; I grabbed her arm, catching her.

"Thanks," she said, steadying herself. "Assholes."

"How did you do that?" I asked.

"Hmm?"

"Know how to—how to match the music to my lines," I said. "On the fly like that."

Kelsey shrugged. "Guitar's not that hard. Writing is a lot more difficult."

I frowned at her.

"I can show you, if you want," Kelsey said, and then she scanned around us. On a black-and-silver rolling trunk behind us was a stray Sharpie. "C'mere," she said, reaching for my forearm—*518-555-0821*, she wrote into my palm, tracing the numbers twice. She leaned forward and blew softly, her breath cool on the drying ink. "Tell your parents it's a boy," she said.

"Oh, I don't—that'll just get me in trouble."

Kelsey capped the Sharpie and put it back on the storage trunk. "Less trouble than hanging out with me, I think."

FOR *SOPHOMORE*, I WORKED WITH THE SAME WRITING TEAM from my debut. When I showed up to session with Sam with the first verse of "Tell Me How to Be," I was pretty sure it wasn't gonna fly: *Amelia has her nails painted pink / and Tory's hair's in a slicked-back ring / the goth kids in their leather skins / and Rebecca always smells so pretty / The soccer team has its own little clique / and Quiz Bowl knows about Anne Boleyn / all of these girls with their trademark things / but I'm still wondering how to be.* The way I had it in my head, it was a little too folk, and definitely didn't pass the car sing-along test—the idea that a hit song is one that can be sung out loud in a group in a car, windows down, cruise on sixty. Those are never too technical, because precision makes people shy. Radio hits are shameless.

But for however worried I was, I think everyone around me knew we had something big. Number ones are made, not born, and I noticed an uptick in the resources around my album. They gave Sam Jordan the budget to record in a private studio in Berry Hill, when it would have cost far less to do it in Melody's offices. At Mockingjay the studio spaces flexed and expanded like Transformers: ceilings raised and lowered, wall panels opened and shut, velvet drapes pulled tight over stone tiling—everything infinitely adjustable to cushion or reflect sound as needed. Sam hired a new engineer, a tall man named Dave with broad shoulders and chin-length salt-and-pepper hair, who went into the microphone closet and came out with a dozen different options. I sang for a whole afternoon into a series of coded numbers, C12 and 251 and M49 and one that was, Dave told me, worth almost two hundred thousand dollars. They put me in a vocal booth with curved seams and walls made of church plaster and in another blanketed with a silk fabric that flexed to the touch, an absorbent material meant only as an aesthetic cover for the insulation that angled inside the drywall. I asked Sam what Dave was looking for—I could only tell which spaces offered more reverb, where I sounded dry and where I had more warmth—and Sam explained that it was that Sondheim maxim: "content dictates form."

Sam and Dave believed my singing—although far from technically flawless—could be a selling point, and what they were trying to do was capture the particular earnestness of my developing vocal cords. I sounded like a teenager (because I was one), and the way my voice broke or thinned out beyond my range mirrored the emotional turmoil of my lyrics, all that angst and heartache and fear, the vibrating anxiety. They wanted to keep my sound bright and sharp; I often asked to redo mistakes in the booth but noticed, later, when they sent me a demo mix, that they'd used the take where my voice cracked, rasped, where I clearly lost my breath a half beat too soon. If my first reaction when I listened to these was embarrassment—why couldn't I be better, *why wasn't I as good as Kelsey*—my second was always: *that sounds exactly right*. In this case, what I lacked was actually a strength. It made my writing more believable.

WHEN I TOLD AARON ABOUT THE RECORD OVER DINNER AT HIS house, he reached across the patio table and picked a bone from the edge of my plate—he'd made a rack of ribs; when I said I was impressed, he'd insisted that cooking large hunks of meat was his birthright, as a Tennessean—and, after gnawing at the meat I'd left behind until the bone shined gray, he said, "I met Sam at a party once."

"Mm?" I murmured noncommittally. I could tell from his tone there was something more to the story.

Aaron's focus shifted between the gentle parenthesis of the rib and my face. "He sorta hit on my date."

Sam was seeing an artist named Charlie who drove a pickup and baked crispy chocolate chip cookies and dropped them off at the studio on long afternoons. She rode horses on a farm outside the city and her nose was always a little sunburned in an adorable way. I felt like I was constantly meeting people like this in Nashville: women who were such perfectly pieced-together puzzles they seemed made-up.

"Well," I said, "he has a girlfriend now, so you don't have to worry about that."

"The muralist, yeah? They were dating then. I remember because it was the sort of party where you noticed a girl with a pierced nose and a handful of tattoos."

"So you're telling me you hit on her too," I said. I knew I was walking right into his trap: the petulant teenager to his knowing adult.

Aaron set the bone down on his plate and reached for my hand. I yanked it away. "Just be careful with him," he said.

"I know how to handle myself," I snapped.

Aaron's face collapsed the way it could, as if an emotional layer had peeled away to reveal softer tissue. "I know you do," he said. "I didn't mean it like that. You just hear stories—"

I threw my napkin down on my plate and stomped across the slick stone out into the slope of the yard, where the side lawn curved down toward the road. Aaron lived on the river in Lakewood, north of Nashville, on a dead-end street not far from where he grew up, with a private dock tucked into a shady inlet. It was summer and the bugs buzzed and chirped and trilled around me, a shimmering chorus, and I thought about how this, too, was different from what I knew: in New York, the insects vibrated like a hammering heartbeat; in Nashville, the sound was percussive, like a million skittering high hats. I listened as I made my way to the dock, the noise a rain-like baffle for my anger.

Aaron and I started dating after the Christmas party, and not particularly slowly—it was the offseason for him, and so he was home in Nashville; I was writing and recording furiously, trying to finish my album, so I was rooted in the city too. The first time I drove to his house—five thousand rambling, multistoried square feet, cut into the hillside with certain levels visible only from certain angles—I thought that it looked like a home built for a 1970s bachelor. But Aaron's house was tastefully decorated—he'd hired someone, I later learned—in a contemporary take on midcentury modern, lots of curved edges, Eames chairs, everything in black and ivory and warm, reddish mahogany, and I let myself be impressed by the adultness of it, the way it seemed so sure of itself. In the master bath the shower was a walk-in the size of a small bedroom, with two separate rainfall heads and a bench at one end. When Aaron led me to it the first time I thought of asking him how many girls he'd sat on that marble slab, how many times he'd kneeled on the tiles and hooked their thigh over his shoulder, how many other heads had tipped back against the ceramic where my skull pressed against the wet cold—but I knew better than that, better than to be so openly insecure and jealous. Standing out on the dock the night he warned me about Sam, I understood that I'd conceded plenty of power and authority to Aaron in other ways, made countless small errors that had tipped the scales—already weighted in his favor because of his age and gender—even further in his direction.

Because I'd let Aaron show me the way. We ate fried chicken at Zaxby's and drove the winding roads that flexed toward and away from the lake, windows down and heat on high, because I liked the midweight feel of the Tennessee air. In the thin woods north of us where we walked sometimes on the weekends my voice carried endlessly, a seconds-long sonic tail. I think he mistook my marveling at this place as marveling at him—maybe they were the same, a little bit, in the end—and on a Thursday midnight he brought me to his high school and led me through the gate onto his old football field, where the grass was cut thick and short, as carpet-like as a golf course, and in the darkness he lay me at center field and pointed at the stars but I felt my body shaking, bones made of ice. I couldn't tell Aaron that I was hurtling through space toward a memory of another sky just like it, so I pretended to be cold instead— "look how soft you've gotten already," he said, "a New Yorker shivering in fifty degrees"—and let him wrap his body over me, then into me, there on the vertical leg of a twenty-foot block-lettered *M*.

I went home that night, back to my glacial penthouse, and showered until the hot water ran out. The raw spot at the base of my spine where the grass had rubbed a soccer player's injury into my skin stung and I leaned into it, hopeful that the sharp pain of a fresh wound would dull the ache of a much older one. A chorus of lettermanned football players rose around me, and when I shut my eyes against the water I saw Raff's face, his friends laughing at his locker, at Kelsey, at all of us.

KELSEY LIVED ON A LOOPED STREET ON THE NORTHERN EDGE of town, in a neighborhood of single-story homes and raised ranches in crayon-box colors: bright red, mustard yellow, navy blue. The Copestenke house had three bedrooms but they were small and lined with wall-to-wall beige carpeting, and all four of them—Kelsey, Matt, Diana, and Fiona—shared a single bathroom with a butter-colored tub and matching tiled countertop. The first time I went over I felt like I was snooping, like I wasn't supposed to be able to see the grime on their toothbrushes, or the netting of hair that webbed over Diana's hairbrush, or her nail file with its clawed streaks. The house was oriented around a single, windowless hallway, with Kelsey's room at the end, and when I walked by her brother's bedroom Kelsey said over her shoulder, "We can afford a bed; Matt just likes to keep his mattress on the floor like that."

I paused at the threshold of Matt's room, surveying his landscape. On the carpet to the left of the door was a full mattress, unmade, navy flannel sheets tangled at the middle; across from the foot of the bed, against the opposite wall, a dresser spilled its contents from half-shut drawers. Except for a single New York Islanders poster tacked to the wall above the mattress, there was nothing special or distinct about Matt's space at all—except for the fact that he shared it with his daughter.

Because there was Fiona's toddler bed, tucked into the corner, crafted in hot-pink plastic, and Fiona's drawings taped to the closet doors—crayon scribbles and handprint turkeys and finger-painted streaks—and Fiona's stuffed animals, a lamb and a unicorn and a Labrador retriever dotting the path of carpet between her bed and her father's. On the edge of Matt's dresser, a haphazard pile of board books marked the place where their worlds bled together.

Kelsey twisted a piece of hair between her fingertips, watching me. "I wouldn't have anywhere to put all my dirty clothes when my mom tells me to clean," I said, referring to Matt's lack of an under-bed space.

Kelsey laughed. "Well, clearly"—she waved her hand vaguely—"our mom is not the 'clean your room' type. Anyway I think he doesn't want a real bed because it would make too much noise when he brings girls over."

I looked at Fiona's bed. "What about—" I began.

"She sleeps with me half the time. It's like sharing a bed with a fucking furnace, but—" Kelsey shrugged, trailing off. "Anyway, it's better this way. My mom used to date a bit when we were younger, and, I swear to God, we used to be able to hear her headboard." Kelsey pounded her fist rhythmically against the wall. "It was traumatic." She paused again, remembering. "Now that I think about it though, I'm like, way to go, Mom."

"Is she dating anyone now?" I asked, still eyeing Matt's rumpled sheets. There was so much closeness in Kelsey's house, all their lives jammed into one another.

"Nah," Kelsey said. "She says the ship's sailed on that."

"Hey—" A male voice cut through the hall, funneled to our ears by the tightness of the walls.

"Matt," Kelsey said. "This is Dylan. Dylan, my brother, Matt."

Kelsey's brother was tall like her, with the same dark hair, shorn short, but where Kelsey was made of angles, everything long and sharp like a knife, Matt was softer—round eyes where hers were almond-shaped; a wide nose where hers was narrow and ski-sloped.

"Hi," he said, and it was this more than anything else, more than his three-day beard or his daughter or Kelsey's allusions to his sex life or the lab coat hanging from his closet doorknob, the uniform he wore to his full-time job as a pharm tech at the hospital—more than all that, it was Matt's *voice* that reminded me how much older he was. He sounded nothing at all like the boys that high-fived and fist-bumped their way down the Thompson High hallways. He sounded like a man.

"Hi," I said.

"Where's Fiona?" Kelsey asked.

"Mom's off this afternoon. She took her to get ice skates."

"I was gonna help—"

Matt waved her off. "It's fine, I've got it covered." He looked over my shoulder, into his room. "If you two are done poking around here, I need to get changed for work."

"Sorry—" I stammered. "We weren't—"

"We totally were." Kelsey grinned. She grabbed my arm and pulled me out of Matt's doorframe.

"Nice to meet you," I said as Kelsey tugged me down the hall.

"Well, here's where the magic happens," she said as she crossed the threshold, spinning once with her arms wide. "At least, that's what Brendan would tell you."

Kelsey's room was the kind of lived-in that seemed sophisticated, like every detail had been curated. There were twinkle lights wrapped around the ceiling edges and pictures tacked to the walls and all her surfaces were cluttered with little bowls and dishes of memories: faded concert tickets and worn MetroCards and shining guitar picks and little folded matchbooks stamped with the names of bars and restaurants. I moved around her space slowly, allowing my hands to skate over all its little textures, fingering a knotted cluster of plastic beads on her closet door and a tangle of scarves at her bedpost and the wire rounds of a stack of notebooks on her desk, the front covers scrawled with thick, primitive doodles. Her guitar leaned against the side of her dresser and I touched it lightly, just the tips of my index and middle fingers over the curved edge of the head.

"What happened with you and Brendan?" I asked.

With a small hop, Kelsey sat at the edge of her bed. "He's a dickhead."

I laughed. "That's a new one."

"You've never heard the phrase 'dickhead' before?"

"Nope." On the bottom of a Farm Aid poster, band names were stacked in descending font size.

"I think Matt taught it to me."

"Is it like, you *are* the tip of a penis, or you have a dick for a head?"

"*Ooooh!*" Kelsey cried. She lay back on her bed, staring at the ceiling. "I'm an idiot. I only thought of it the first way. The other way makes much more sense."

To the right of Kelsey's bed was a small, single-drawered nightstand. She'd thrown a violet scarf over the lampshade—which, I could see underneath, was a child's light, pale green with stippling on it shaped like caterpillars and butterflies and a fat bumblebee. It was this sort of flourish—a draped piece of silk—that made Kelsey's room seem cared-for in a way mine never did, and, in turn, made her seem engaged in a way I wasn't, an active player in her own existence.

"Shit, toss me that?" On the table next to the lamp was another ceramic dish, this one a nest of hair ties and tiny, shining butterfly clips and a round compact—Kelsey's birth control. I picked up the pastel disc and threw it underhand to where Kelsey lay on the bed. "That you have to take it at the *exact* same time every day has got to be some sort of conspiracy, right? Everything engineered to turn us into little robots."

"I think that was the point of Valium, originally, so. You're not wrong."

"I'm never wrong."

I leaned close to a photo in what was obviously a handmade frame: a collage project of some kind, cut pieces of magazine pictures warped by tacky glue. "Thank God for condoms, I guess," I said absently. Inside the frame, a family of three—a teenage boy and an elementary-aged girl and a middle-aged woman—stood together with their backs turned to a large crowd and an outdoor stage, radiating a foggy halo of orange light.

"Oh no—boys hate them," Kelsey said.

I stared at her, embarrassed—I'd tried to talk about something I didn't yet understand. But also: Wasn't that a line? Wasn't that just a thing they said? In the beat it took me to gather myself, Kelsey's attention shifted to the picture. "My first concert," she said.

"Where?"

"Newport."

"How old were you?"

"Hmm. Like seven or eight? Second grade." Kelsey paused. "I don't know if that makes my mom cool or wildly irresponsible."

I leaned toward the frame slightly, staring at Kelsey's little face. I could see teenage Kelsey in her easily—the glowing eyes, the dark hair, the long face, shrouded beneath a purple bucket hat.

"I know—the hat is way out of character," Kelsey said, and I laughed a little nervously, worried that I'd been staring too long. I shifted my attention to a magazine page tacked on the wall above the nightstand, half obscured by the lampshade.

"You really like her, huh?" I asked.

"Dolly is an icon," Kelsey said, turning over on her stomach and propping herself on her elbows, chin on her fist.

I scrunched my nose and peered closer to the picture. It was old, with the Vaseline-lensed look of the 1970s or '80s—everything soft-focused. Dolly was round-faced and dimpled, and her blond hair, while still big, looked soft, almost natural. "She was really pretty."

"*Really* pretty," Kelsey agreed.

"I feel like I only know her as like, I don't know—" I flailed for the right phrasing, something more polite and less obviously classist than what hovered at the tip of my tongue. "A Vegas act?"

"I know, that's how people think about her now. But you know she writes all her own songs, right?"

I didn't.

"Yeah. She's written hundreds. People forget that about her because they think a songwriter has to look like, I dunno—Joni Mitchell."

I knew what she meant. "It's like how poets have to be very sad," I said.

"Yeah, like, I'm sorry, but wanting to put my head in the oven is not a job requirement," Kelsey said.

This surprised me. "You've read Sylvia Plath?"

Kelsey rolled her eyes. "Twyman assigns the fucking *Bell Jar* every year."

"Have you read any of her poetry?"

Kelsey shook her head. "No thanks. I like being happy."

I laughed. "It's really good, though. It's like . . . it makes me feel kind of—" I wriggled my fingers in the air, as if I were a live wire. "Frayed," I said.

"That sounds terrible?" Kelsey said, and I laughed again. "Miserable is not the only valid artistic expression. Have you listened to any of Dolly's music?"

"I know '9 to 5' and 'Jolene,' and since the talent show I know the ones you sang . . ." I trailed off.

Kelsey popped up from her bed. On her desk she had a small CD player, bullet-shaped with teal accents. "Well, it's time for a little lesson," she said. I perched myself at the edge of her mattress and riffled through a back issue of *Cosmo* while Kelsey swapped the discs in her stereo. "This," she said, "is my personal best-of."

For an hour that afternoon, we listened to Kelsey's CD. She narrated each selection, lending context and backstory to a mix that was softer and more melancholy than I'd expected—more folk too, although I didn't have the musical knowledge to explain it that way at the time. Kelsey knew all the words to every single song, and when she sang along she tucked a lock of brown-almost-black hair behind her ear and tapped the beat with her foot or with her palm against her denimed thigh, and I was the one who felt embarrassed: to witness something so intimate, so pure, so certain.

WE WERE IN THE MIDDLE OF MIXING WHEN THE TEAM AT MEL-ody arranged for a writer from the *Times* magazine to do a long-form profile of me. The reporter would interview me on several occasions in the run-up to my album launch, with the article's publication timed to the record release in October, four months before I turned twenty. It was a big deal: a sign that I was being taken seriously. There was going to be a photo shoot, my first mainstream cover at a magazine billed for a non-teen audience.

I liked Lana Campagna immediately. She had dusty tanned skin like she'd spent an afternoon on an Italian beach and dark, curly hair that tendrilled from her temples. I invited her to my apartment and cooked dinner for her while she sat casually at my kitchen island, her ankle boots wedged against the lower rung of the stool next to her, her red-almost-coral lipstick stained on the edge of her wineglass. Like Kelsey, Lana was the kind of person who could slide into a space and make it hers, and the physical reminder of my friend tugged at my body like a trawler against the sand.

"You like to cook?" she asked, reaching across the counter and plucking a tube of rigatoni from the colander in my sink.

"It's meditative for me, I think," I said, sliding diced onion into a pan of crackling oil. "My mother would say it's the kind of thing that lends itself well to dissociative thinking, like driving, or showering, both of which are great things to do when you need a song idea." I didn't tell her that cooking also allowed me to retain the utmost control over my food. Strange superstitions had begun to pile in my brain: a fear that tortilla chips might scratch my vocal cords; an anxiety around artificial sweeteners, that the temporary thickening of my saliva would remain permanent, my access to pitch altered forever. All the foods on our plates that night were ones I'd deemed safe.

"Your mother is a therapist, right?"

I nodded, tilting the tomatoes into the pan after the onions. "People always find that interesting."

"Well, songwriting is very connected to your feelings."

"I don't think people would like it very much if I started writing songs about *dialectics*," I said, and this made Lana laugh.

"Do you disagree, then? You don't feel your mother's work helped give you a level of comfort processing your emotions in public?"

I cocked my head a little, thinking about this while I julienned strips of basil. People mistook the emotional honesty in *Moonless* for a broader willingness to discuss my personal life; if I could talk so openly about my *feelings*, surely I could talk about their inspiration. The tightrope of these interviews was to make the boundary clear without undermining the intimacy of the art. "If anything," I told Lana, "I think my mother's job taught me that it's really important to have a sense of who you are outside of your work."

"I think that's more complicated in some fields than in others."

In the pot, the tomatoes began to burst, their flesh ripping the grape skin, exposing their muscular insides. I pressed the back of a metal spoon into them, feeling the fruit collapse beneath the silver. "Well, are we talking about writing or are we talking about performing? Because I think those are two different roles."

"Say more about that."

"Now who's the therapist?" I asked, winking.

Lana laughed but let the question hang.

"I do think there's something unique about our expectations on the singer-songwriter when we compare her to another kind of performer. Even my boyfriend, for example," I said, and then thought: *fuck*. But it was too late. I dumped the rigatoni into the tomatoes and stirred once, twice, carefully folding the ridged tubes into the sauce. "We could eat at the table, but this is cozier, right?" I asked, setting the pan in front of Lana.

She nodded and said, "Go on about Aaron."

I sighed, collecting two forks and two spoons from the cutlery drawer. "He's a football player, as you know. But nobody ever asks him if he tackled extra-hard because he's working through something."

Lana looked at me like I was oversimplifying things, and I was. But I didn't want her to look any further under the hood of the ambition that made *Sophomore* and see that it was a product of guilt. Better for her to paint a portrait of the artist as driven solely by her craft.

"Music can be personal to a listener in a way a movie or football game isn't," Lana said.

I laughed. "Aaron would take offense to that, I think."

Lana laughed too, and for the rest of dinner she slid into a series of more benign and expected questions. She asked about the upcoming album (a natural progression from *Moonless*, I said, and when she asked me to elaborate I said that I would still call it pop-country, sonically and lyrically, but it was more cohesive than my debut, because I had a better understanding of the sensibilities of the genre and was able to manipulate them more effectively); about my songwriting process ("Again, sort of the same," I said, "in that the ideas come to me when they come, and I try to write them down in my notebook or sing a little melody into my phone, and sort of noodle on them until we get back into the studio or until I meet up with Jess or Bill or Sam to write"); and about the Grammys, whether I think this could be my year, and I said exactly what I'd practiced a hundred times before, a response that shielded me from the way "Grammys" caused all other thoughts and phrases to slip from my brain into a black hole of nerves and want. "Of course it would be a dream to be recognized by the Recording Academy. But that's exactly what it is—a dream. You've gotta keep your feet firmly on the ground in this place if you want to survive."

I didn't say that the reason I needed a Grammy so badly was because I needed to know this new life wasn't a fluke. I didn't tell Lana that all of this was my best friend's dream, and it should be her here instead of me, and the only way I could see it differently was through the lens of external validation. I didn't admit that I lay awake at night repeating a single, desperate prayer: *This has to have been worth it.*

Instead I stood and walked around the island to the sink, extended a towel in Lana's direction, and said, "I'll wash, you dry?"

SOPHOMORE WAS A SUPERNOVA. WE WOULD SELL OVER THREE million copies in the first year, release five singles, hit number one on the Billboard charts twice (three times on country), and—eventually—become the most-awarded country music album to date. For eighteen months all anyone said to me was a version of *you must be so excited.* I didn't know how to explain that what I felt was the opposite of presence, the opposite of enjoyment: I felt as though I'd vacated my body entirely, that I was sitting in a darkened room watching a film reel of someone else's dream. I thought the prizes would fix my feelings of imposter syndrome but all each one did was remind me how Kelsey wanted it more. I began to fixate instead on the things we *didn't* get: when "Night Games" retreated from two to three on the country chart, a fourth and record-breaking number one suddenly out of reach; when I was nominated for Best *Female* Video but not Video of the Year; when *Pitchfork* refused to review the album. When my team presented me with a list of tour dates—fifty-four cities in thirty-nine states—and I saw *Casper, Moline, Enterprise*, I thought: nowhere towns for a nowhere artist. I asked about the size of the arenas and stadiums and when I heard eight thousand, nine, twelve, I said: "Just for reference, how many in Gillette? How many in Nissan?" Sixty-five and seventy thousand, they told me. Kelsey would have thought it was really something to play for ten thousand fans in a sold-out arena in Indiana. I had to aim higher.

The trouble with that was that—unlike Kelsey—I wasn't a natural performer. Everybody saw me learn how to entertain in real time. I recorded every show and watched the tape on the bus or on my laptop on the plane, like an athlete reviewing game footage. I studied my facial expressions, the verbal crutches I leaned on too heavily in filler commentary, the bodily tics I overused. I thought of how Kelsey's body used to melt into the music, how if she wasn't playing guitar she'd tap a hand on the side of her thigh with the beat or sway in small half circles with the rhythm, leaning into one shoulder then the other, or that smile she kept to herself, like it was just her and the song. Sometimes her movements made their way into my performance and I thought of Matt and Diana watching at home: Did they see Kelsey in me? I wondered. Would I ever be up on that stage alone?

Maybe it doesn't make any sense, that a person could feel so uncertain about her belonging and so desperate for excellence at the same time. But I'd started to suspect that the only way to abandon my origin story was to climb so high I eventually lost sight of where I began.

BECAUSE OF HOW THE GRAMMYS CYCLE WORKS, I WAS NOMI-nated a full calendar year after the album's release. By then Aaron and I were no longer together. When Lana's article came out—"Queen of the Prom," the headline read, alongside a golden-filtered photo spread shot on a high school campus south of Nashville, me in miniskirts and argyle sweater-vests, a borrowed varsity jacket draped over my shoulders, a shimmering, beaded gown and a cheap plastic tiara, waving regally—both Aaron and I had the confused feeling of seeing our reflection in a curved bowl: a version of the truth, but fundamentally distorted. She called Aaron "the jock" to my "American princess"; she wrote that I combined "a poet's nerves and sensitivity" with "the charm and bubble of a regular suburban teen, sentences punctured with 'likes' and 'sort ofs' and lots of excitable hand movement." I felt responsible for the way I'd failed to see this coming, with an album called *Sophomore*; I felt responsible for how I'd allowed Lana to depict me as sixteen rather than what I was—closer to twenty. I'd meant the record as a reflection, but Lana framed it as stalled development: that cliché of the celebrity frozen at the age she became famous.

The first time Aaron came over after the piece I thought it would be best to make light of it, and when he teased me for the amount of soap I used when washing the dishes I said something like *Do I deserve a detention?* "Stop it with that," he said sharply. "The guys are all calling me a fucking cradle robber now. That's not what this is!"

"I know it's not," I said. "That's why—I was joking."

"Yeah, well—it's not fucking funny. It's like people think I'm with you because I have a kiddie fetish or I'm with you because you're, like, ascendant music royalty and it's good for my image. It can't be that I love you."

We hadn't said it to each other yet, and I was critically—fatally—too slow to react. "It doesn't matter what people think," I said.

"That's your response?" Aaron exhaled exaggeratedly. "For a *poet*, you can be a real fucking robot. Maybe that's what I like, huh? They have it all wrong. I don't like teenagers. I like sex dolls."

I told him to get the fuck out.

When I sang "Night Games" ten months later at the Grammys I didn't think about Aaron, even though he lives in those lines—*I don't mind sharing your uniformed smile / 'cause they don't know you like me / for them it's yard counts and touchdowns and / rules I don't care to learn / the only night games I'm playin' are the games that I'm playing with you.* In the dressing room before my performance—this is how these things honor you, by asking you to do *more work*; by coupling one high-stakes moment with another—a singer with brown curly hair and a model's cheekbones sat in the chair next to me, a makeup artist dusting highlighter along the high points of his collarbone and blending foundation into the valleys of his sternum and abdomen (he would perform with an open tuxedo jacket, shirtless underneath the lapels). I recognized Miles from my television: a former Disney Channel star, he went on to join a wildly successful if shortly lived boy band; he and his bandmates were here at the Grammys for a one-off reunion in honor of their producer, who was receiving a Lifetime Achievement Award.

I did my own hair and makeup then—for a long time I worried a full glam squad was too high-maintenance, and that was a label I couldn't afford—and as I dusted finishing powder across my T-zone I caught Miles watching in the mirror. He smiled and flicked his gaze to where the artist Ms. stood waiting for her cue, dressed like Mary Magdalene in eight-inch platform heels, her extensions falling all the way to the floor, so much extra hair that an assistant had to carry it behind her like the train of a wedding gown. When she was out of earshot Miles leaned sideways toward my chair and whispered, "Bet you couldn't do *that* look yourself," and I said, "I don't know, I was a skeleton for Halloween once, and the bones I drew on my hands were *pretty much* the same as a medical textbook."

Miles laughed a kind of shoulder-slumping, full-body cackle that caused his makeup artist to step back, her contouring sponge held aloft. He winced apologetically. "Sorry," he whispered, and then made an *oops* face in my direction.

When I returned to fix my lipstick after my performance, his number was etched on the waxed canvas of my makeup bag, ten digits in shaky liquid liner.

"Miles thought you'd know it was him," the makeup artist said. "But men can be stupid sometimes." She shook her head and rolled her eyes, commiserating.

An hour later I walked onstage to accept my award for Album of the Year. I scanned the audience for Miles, already shaping the memory as it was happening, knowing that one day I'd have to work to uncouple the man from the moment, just like I cleaved my songs from their origins, understanding that no matter how I'd tried to spin it for Lana, the truth was that I did feel a constant splintering, little pieces of me divided again and again and again and scattered on the wind like autumn leaves, appendages I would have to learn to do without.

nside, Kelsey's house is exactly as I remember it: same floral couch, tossed with faded quilts; same desk in the living room (the old Dell traded for a laptop now); same stained linoleum in the kitchen. It's easy enough to slip in here, one more bee in a hive busily tending to grief, and as I do I feel the universe accordion in front of me: There is my sixteen-year-old self, sliding into her best friend's house like it's her own. No need to ring the doorbell; come on in.

But I am not sixteen, and that version of my life is light-years away. In this one, the little dining table where Kelsey and I served Fiona plates of microwaved nachos and smiley-face chocolate chip pancakes groans with aluminum pans of takeout, and the table next to the coat-rack where the Copestenkes dropped their mail and keys and mittens is stacked with condolence cards, and every other available surface—end tables, kitchen counters, the small, low bookcase behind the couch—is cluttered with sympathy bouquets. White roses press against the shimmer of their cellophane wrapping as if gasping for air.

There were no flowers when Kelsey went missing. There was no tip line. There was a police report, and a routine lake drag, and my dad volunteered in a single grid search of the woods near where Kelsey was last seen (at a house party with some friends from Camp Tahawus), but the truth was Kelsey was the kind of kid people expected to pull a stunt like running away. There wasn't a lot to go on except her reputation and a handful of journal entries that weighed the opportunities in New York against those available in LA and Nashville; Diana herself said that

Kelsey had been increasingly withdrawn, even for a girl who'd always seemed convinced her future lay elsewhere and that she had better get there, fast.

Not to mention that this was before the media made a celebrity of every missing young white woman. There was no Twitter, no Instagram, no TikTok. Facebook was for college kids to post embarrassing pictures of their parties. The TLPD checked its boxes and there were no citizen detectives to fill in the gaps, no town that mobilized around the girl who didn't want to be here anyway. Diana couldn't afford to take any shifts off from work, and a week into Kelsey's disappearance she fucked up a patient's EKG, applying the grounding pads incorrectly. The man left with burn marks on his chest, blisters that would take months to heal, a stranger's grief scarred on him forever. My dad called the family, made it go away. My mother delivered enchiladas and frozen soups and Kelsey's eighteenth birthday came and went. She had a history of promising to leave, and it wasn't hard for people to believe that adulthood inspired her to finally go through with it.

Now my classmates prop their thighs on Kelsey's couch and press their noses close to her framed photograph. They move a basket of white dahlias and snapdragons from her coffee table to make room for their cocktail plates of Ritz crackers and cheddar slices. As I make my way through Kelsey's house—the hutch in the living room lined with photos of Fiona, dressed as a cat for Halloween at five or six, arms draped over the shoulders of her basketball teammates at twelve or thirteen, pinning a corsage on her homecoming date at fourteen or fifteen—I begin to feel a claustrophobia I never experience in even the most chaotic rope lines or stadium walks, thousands of people reaching for my arms, my back, my hair, my clothes. I watch Claire Egan deliver beers to Jack Rowley and Sean Torres, two long-necked bottles pinched in one hand, swinging through the living room like a hostess. I slip into the bathroom, pressing my back against the shut door and finding my breath.

From the window over the toilet I can see out into Kelsey's backyard. The ladder on Fiona's old playset is broken, and two men in their thirties drag their feet lazily across the dirt beneath the swings, rocking back and forth.

Kelsey pops up onto the counter next to the sink, hands clutching the tiled edge, kicking a distracted rhythm against the cabinet with her dangling ankles. She sighs and pitches her skull against the mirror, pressing the backs of her two heads into one another. *Weird being here, huh?*

I wash my hands even though I didn't pee.

She still uses the same soap.

Two-dollar grocery-store Dial. I know.

Don't be such a snob.

I'm not. I'm just saying, I could recognize that smell anywhere.

When I leave the bathroom I do a quick double take down the hall. Instead of heading back into the party I turn left, toward the bedrooms. I hear Kelsey peeking out the bathroom behind me: *You never could resist snooping*, she calls.

Walking into the bedroom at the end of the hallway, I'm reminded of those stories about layered paintings: a Van Gogh of potted flowers inked over a sketch of two women; a winged angel buried beneath a portrait of the Virgin Mary. Vines of fake ivy trail in the places where Kelsey strung ropes of twinkle lights; Polaroids are lined in neat rows above the desk where Kelsey once tacked a bulletin board with ticket stubs and concert flyers. Unburned candles in pastel colors accent Kelsey's old wire-frame bookshelf like a small wax sculpture gallery: a seashell, a rose, a woman's torso. I recognize the aesthetic from a million TikToks, the ones my Gen Z fans post.

I allow my hand to trail along Fiona's surfaces, the torn edges of my blistered fingertips catching on the faux-fur plush of one of her blankets; around the crystal knobs of her dresser drawers; along the spines of her record collection, packed tightly in a lavender-colored milk crate. On her desk I swirl my index finger in a plastic tray of brightly colored beads, the kind Kelsey used to keep in mason jars, camp-style friendship bracelets at the ready. In the pictures on the wall I see Kelsey's dark hair on Fiona's face; I hear Kelsey's deep, diaphragmatic laugh from Fiona's open mouth.

I stoop to examine her bookshelf, spines crooked and tumbling into one another, paperbacks piled on top of neat hardcovers. Like Kelsey, even Fiona's haphazardness seems purposeful, somehow: *Harry Potter* next to Joan Didion next to *The Hunger Games* beneath a jumbled cluster of slim poetry collections. She has a thing for nineteenth-century romance—*Pride and Prejudice* and *Middlemarch* and *Jane Eyre*—and her fondness for the marriage plot strikes me as exactly the sort of surprising personality quirk that defined Kelsey.

On the middle shelf, between copies of *Sula* and *Veronica*, is a dusty edition of Sylvia Plath's *Ariel*, the white on its spine gone the color of buttermilk. Using one finger I ease it from the ledge, gently tipping the collection on its axis and then slipping it so the Morrison and Gaitskill fall into one another like knocked knees. The cover is rendered in the slightly anarchic style of 1960s modern design: the letters of the title are arranged in an uneven row; it might be a madcap screwball comedy rather than a posthumous arrangement of abandoned work.

Once again a hatch opens in my memory, and I'm back in this room for the very first time, watching Kelsey wrinkle her nose as I tried to explain what it was I liked about Sylvia Plath's poetry. I wanted Kelsey to understand that I wished I could write like that, in a way that made the reader feel like their nervous system had been ripped out and stitched back on the outside of their skin. I open the book tenderly, and make a small, involuntary gasp: it's a first edition.

I move even more carefully now, paging through the collection with extreme caution, peeling each poem gently at its corner until my hand feels the cleave of a bookmark—no: a note.

My body goes electric with intrigue, all my senses tunneled on the card in my hand. Thick and creamy, ivory yellowed with time, it has the weight of an expensive piece of cardstock—but there's no monogram or detailing, so that besides its obvious age the card is nondescript. I flip it over to find a brief, hasty message in a tight scrawl: *Kelsey—The best songwriters know their poets!* Then simply a short dash and a single initial, *L.*

I feel my pulse throb at the hollow of my neck. This book isn't Fiona's, or it wasn't originally—it belonged to Kelsey. I flip the notecard over and back again in my hand. *L*, I think. *Who is L?* And why on earth would they have given my friend a first-edition Plath?

"Find anything good?"

I stand up quickly, feeling caught, and slip the notecard back into the book. Kelsey's brother waves me off from the doorway, evading eye contact as he begins to trace his own small circle around his daughter's room. "Don't mind me," he says.

I watch Matt for a moment, his back to me, and try to steady myself. I've imagined this moment—alone with Kelsey's brother, with a chance for us to really talk after everything that happened—so many times it almost feels like déjà vu. My throat is choked with all the dialogue I've practiced, all the fantasies I played of driving over here on a visit home and asking Matt if enough time had passed yet, if we could process it together, if maybe he'd changed his mind about the promise we'd made all those years ago.

Instead I hold up the Plath. "I think this was Kelsey's."

This surprises Matt—maybe not the Plath, but that I didn't have a better opening gambit. "So?"

I look at it again, turning the cover over in my hands. "She hated Sylvia Plath."

"You never bought a book you didn't like?" There's a sudden sharpness to Matt's voice, and I feel the quick tremors of an adrenal response, a vibrating in my core. I try to remind myself that the scales are rebalanced between us: When I was fifteen and sixteen, Matt's seven years felt like a canyon. Now—both of us in our thirties—we're more squarely peers. And I have a power I didn't have then.

"She didn't buy it," I say, slipping the note from *L* from within the text. "Looks like it was a gift." An expensive one, I think.

I want Matt to step closer to me, to run his hands over the old ink and tell me he recognizes the handwriting, he knows someone Kelsey called *L*. Instead he stays ten feet away, his body rigid with determination. He doesn't want to engage. "Does it matter? It won't change what happened."

"I guess not," I say to Matt.

"Why are you here, Dylan?"

A tangled knot of reasons unfurls in my mind: because no one is taking responsibility for her; because my job requires some public performance of my feelings; because I never had a chance for closure before; because there is simply too much at stake, and I felt I could control the situation only if I was close to it. But I can see in Matt's body language that he doesn't want to hear any of this. The question is rhetorical; he only wants me to leave.

"Matt," I try, my voice softer, "we never even *talked* about her." I look around the empty room. "It's just us here now—"

"I asked you to leave us alone," he snaps. "I didn't mean for fifteen years, or until you felt like it had been long enough. I meant forever."

In an instant my body hardens against him, fury snapping tight over guilt and grief. "You didn't have any problem hearing from me when it had to do with my money," I snap.

Matt's face twitches. I feel immediately dirty.

"That was for Fiona," he says, each word like a dart. "I would do anything for her."

"I know you would," I say, pointed. We each understand the other's weak spots.

Matt nods, slowly. "Keep the book. Consider it a thank-you for Fiona's college fund."

Later, in the back of my armored SUV, Sloane asks me about the copy of *Ariel*. It was Kelsey's, I tell her. I think of my fans finding Easter eggs in my work, counting the number of diamonds in the wallpaper in the background of an Instagram post—thirty-two—and guessing that it means my next album will come in thirty-two days, or seeing that I used an image of a bird in flight in a lyric and guessing the song must be about Aaron because he had an eagle tattoo. But the truth is it was just the wall I happened to be standing in front of when I took the picture and I just like bird metaphors.

Maybe I am doing the same with Kelsey and *L* now: exercising an old, familiar desire to slip into her mind, to learn absolutely everything about her, to believe that I know her best—no, that we are *the same*. And if there's one thing I should have learned from my fans, it's that all our efforts to *feel* close only ultimately underline the galaxies between us.

MY PARENTS STILL LIVE IN THE HOUSE I GREW UP IN, AT THE start of a cul-de-sac in a subdivision that's grown, over the course of my lifetime, from seventy-five homes to nearly four hundred. A drive through our neighborhood is a lesson in McMansion trends: over there, the years of Too Many Roof Cuts; down Rolling Brook Drive, the Bonus Garage—the weird tacked-on third port to your standard two-car; along Beacon Hill, the season of the oversized craftsman; finally, most recently, the modern farmhouse, every single one rendered in black and white.

Ours is a brick colonial revival with evergreen shutters and a small columned front over the door we never use (we always go in through the garage). Off the eastern side of the house is a single-story sunroom, lined with built-in bookshelves, and over the garage is the bonus room I used for birthday party sleepovers that now houses my parents' security team (an expense I cover, obviously). They resisted it, for a while—my mom wasn't particularly bothered by strangers driving slowly past the house, occasionally jumping out of the car for a selfie—but after their third break-in it started to feel like ADT wasn't enough.

Nick loves this house. He's fascinated by the American commitment to sameness and newness. I love the history in Ireland, the light chaos of the cramped and cluttered streets. Nick thrills at the newness here, the SimCity feel of American suburbia: *Look! I made it overnight!* I'm not saying his Range Rover is in my parents' driveway right now because he's here as some sort of anthropologist, but I bet he'll want to go wander around a Target while he's in town.

Nick and I agree that it's not ideal for him to accompany me to every work-related appearance. That was the reason I gave him when I said he shouldn't come with me this weekend. But the truth is also that I have kept all of this from him, and I need to process my own feelings about what happened between me and Kelsey before I can talk to Nick about it. I'm annoyed to see his car even though I know it's not his fault: he made the choice to come here armed with only the information I'd given him.

"A friend from home died," I told him. It was so far from the complete truth as to be laughable, but Nick's patience and empathy are boundless. Where another partner might have asked, *Who?* or *Did I know her?* Nick didn't look for himself in the story.

"I'm so sorry," he said. "What do you need?"

"I have to speak at her service," I told him.

"You'll be terrific," he said.

"I started writing songs because of her," I admitted then. "I was just a poet before. She taught me about music."

"Well," he said on the phone, "you owe her a hell of a eulogy, then."

Inside, I hear my boyfriend before I see him—a silvery, bright tenor from the kitchen—and then it's the back of his head, thick, brown, wavy hair, and the broadness of his shoulders in his threadbare sweatshirt, and for a moment I wish I could stay just like this, invisible, watching my family without me. What do they say when I'm not here? I wonder. Is it more peaceful, quieter, simpler?

"There she is!"

Nick turns from the counter, following my dad's gaze.

"Hey you," I say.

"Hey you." Nick smiles, strides down the hallway, and wraps me in his arms. He smells like a road trip—stale, metallic.

"You didn't have to come up," I whisper.

"You flew across the country. I could drive a few hours from the city." He kisses my forehead. "You wanted me to just hang out in that big, empty apartment when we could steal an extra weekend together?"

"Quit being such a narcissist!" my dad says, pushing a set of napkins into my chest and shoving a fistful of cutlery at Nick. "Who says he's not here to see me?!"

AT DINNER, EVERYONE DOES THEIR BEST TO FORGET— OR TO pretend to forget—why we're all here, in my parents' house on a random August weekend. Nick slides into my family easily, teasing my dad about his craft beer obsession and sparring with my mother about his creative influences. A writer and a therapist are a natural coupling, each of them endlessly curious and unafraid to ask invasive questions.

"How is it writing about your family?" my mom asks.

Nick is used to people misunderstanding a writer's source material. "As soon as they became characters on the page they stopped being my family."

"You don't think your subconscious is doing any work?"

"I thought I read that the Freudian approach is falling out of style in your field," Nick observes, sly.

My mom loves a client who can make her laugh. *Of course we have favorites*, she said to me once. "It's true," she says. "We got tired of our kids blaming us for everything, so as an industry we decided to pivot to psychedelics."

Nick laughs. "In all seriousness, I'm a long way from that novel now. We've made so many changes to the source material that I barely recognize it."

"Did that feel freeing? Or dishonest?" my mom asks.

"It just feels like the job," Nick says.

"It must be lonely, though. To be so hyper-compartmentalized about your work."

"Okay, Mom—" I begin, but Nick places a hand on top of mine on the table, squeezing lightly.

"I'm not lonely at all," he says, smiling at me.

My heart, so carefully held together today, shatters like dropped glass. Of all the things I don't deserve, there's nothing I feel less worthy of than Nick's love.

LIKE ME, NICK BELIEVES THAT A WRITER EXISTS ON A KNIFE'S edge. It's one of the ways he made himself a safe space for me: here, finally, was someone who understood me; someone who believed me when I said that the songs I wrote were both based on real life and entirely made-up; someone who shared my guilt and self-righteousness—the certainty that the stories we told were ours to write, and yet still, sometimes, at 3 a.m., we lie awake counting the betrayals.

Nick's first novel, *The Soundings*, is the one he calls his contribution to the family splintering. He says this like a joke, dry, dark. He means it and he doesn't. Surely, if he hadn't written his novel, another breaking point would have come along for the Devlins. The dissolution was fated, foretold in the fabric.

Nick was born in Dublin, where his father, John—an English economist—was consulting on a resource management issue. His mother, Kathleen, is Irish—she was born and raised in Cork, the daughter of two teachers—and a journalist, a job she could keep while the family of three bounced around the world for John's career: first Ireland, then Italy, then a stint in London, where Nick's younger sister, Caitríona, was born, five years after her brother.

Cait didn't take to the family's nomadic lifestyle as well as Nick did. She was hypersensitive as a child. When Cait was two and Nick was seven, he read her a story about a little girl who had a pet seashell, and Cait started crying when he got to the part where the little girl was building her shell a sandcastle. "Oh no, oh no!" Cait wailed. Nick couldn't figure out what was wrong.

In the illustration, a bucket of sand was tipped over. Cait couldn't handle the disruption.

It continued in this vein. For years there was no television for Cait except *Sesame Street*. Every picture book had to be carefully proofread by both parents, and sometimes they removed pages, skipping over the part where the hippo broke the chair or the dinosaur's tail knocked over a rock cairn. Even at seven, eight, nine, Nick recognized his sister's behavior as extreme, but this was the nineties and early aughts, and his family was half-Irish: there was no real cultural dialogue around emotional regulation, and the Devlin family didn't talk about feelings.

My mom would say that Nick was "parentified"—the clinical term for when a child finds themselves acting as a caretaker—but he just thought of it as trying to be a good older brother. He held Cait's hand in airports across Europe. He kept track of her earplugs and her blanket. He pushed the furniture to the edges of the room and played soccer with her in their rented homes in Milan and Hong Kong. He wanted to go to boarding school for high school because it would allow him to stay put in one place, with one set of friends, but he worried about how his sister would fare with one less steady thing in her life. So he stayed.

But there was no avoiding it when he went to Trinity. Cait was thirteen, fourteen. Nick noticed she snuck liquor when it was around on vacation or at family gatherings, but he'd done the same thing as a teenager. Later, Cait would tell Nick that when she had her first whiskey, everything went quiet for the first time in her whole life. A car alarm blared outside and it didn't make her feel like her brain was pulsing against the fence of her skull. It was manageable. Fine, even.

Then it was Cait's turn to want to go to boarding school. She got into St. Paul's, in New Hampshire, and off she went. Good, Nick thought. She'll make her own home.

She got caught with Xanax in October of her freshman year. Nick still wonders whether the excess of prescription drugs in America was, in this case, a blessing or a curse. Maybe it might never have happened if she'd stayed in Ireland. Maybe it would have been heroin.

Cait came home and the family moved to Dublin. More than John and Kathleen thought Cait needed stability, they thought she needed attention. Nick came home every weekend for a family meal and noticed things about his sister: a slowness to her speech, the way her eyelids seemed to hang a little low. She picked at her food and excused herself to take impossibly long showers in the evenings. Their parents didn't mention it; Nick wondered if he was imagining things.

The dominoes fell quickly. Cait got arrested for peeing in an alley, then showed up drunk to school, then skipped out on a debate competition. For ten hours nobody could find her. She came home at two in the morning. Kathleen had Cait dump her backpack there in the living room. The Ativan tumbled across the floor like tiny breath mints.

This was when Nick developed a fear of his phone: bad news could come at any time, without warning. His dad called to say that the Garda had picked Cait up, shoplifting from a pharmacy; that she'd landed in the hospital again, tripped and fell and smashed her head on a lamppost; that she told a teacher to fuck themselves at school.

Each of those anecdotes eventually made their way into *The Soundings*.

Cait spent thirty days in a private residential facility an hour north of the city. They would learn, later, that it was rehab-lite: unlimited phone and internet usage after one week, unlimited family visits. The serious places don't just take away the drugs; they leave you alone with yourself. But the Devlins didn't know. So she went and came back a month later and seemed clear-eyed and sharp-tongued. They put her in a Catholic school where she wore a uniform with a blue sweater-vest.

School was part of the problem, though. Cait was reactive and sensitive and there's no place more likely to make a person feel overwhelmed—by people, by smells, by sounds; by the pressure of constant assessment—than a secondary school. By then she had learned to get angry rather than to melt down when something upset her. She failed a math test and Saoirse Doyle whispered to Clare Quinn, "Hard to do maths when you're a zombie," to which Clare replied, "She's even starting to dress like one," and the next thing anybody knew Cait had grabbed the back of Clare's braid and yanked it so hard that Clare's head smacked into Cait's desk.

Nick wrote that into *The Soundings*, nearly exactly as it happened. It came out funny and dark and quintessentially Irish, the whole book's mood in a single scene.

Cait started breaking things at home. She put her fist through walls, smashed a window, kicked her mom's car door, twice threw a plate across the kitchen. Nick would come home and see the cabinet ripped off its rails or the patch of all-weather tape on the windowpane or the dent in the third step on the staircase and worry about what would happen if Cait decided to hit a person rather than a thing. Sometimes he stayed home for the night rather than go back to his apartment at school, just in case. His mom is small and his dad was getting old and he worried they wouldn't be able to handle Cait if it got bad. One night she threw a vase through the TV and that's when they called the Garda, who put her in the hospital on a psych hold, where they realized just how much Klonopin she'd been taking, and that the outbursts were due, in part, to withdrawal. So: back to rehab, this time with a week in a proper detox facility first.

Nick noticed the fraying at the seams in his relationship with his parents before he noticed the unraveling in theirs. If he offered his opinion about Cait's treatment they fought, said he was judging them, that he couldn't possibly understand how hard it was to feel this powerless. All the energy he had once channeled into caring for his little sister he now directed into being as little trouble as possible for his parents. He never asked for money. He didn't tell them about his grades. He didn't tell them he'd applied to Trinity for his MA until he'd been accepted. He got a job coaching soccer for a kids' club and stopped coming home for Sunday dinners.

And he started writing his debut novel. Everything about his reality seemed precarious but inside the world of his fiction he could feel steady, on solid ground. *These* people he had control over; *these* events he could see coming.

While Nick was getting his MA and writing *The Soundings*, Cait managed her leaving cert. Her parents got her a little apartment and a job at a café. She told a customer to fuck off, tossed a cup of coffee in their face, got fired, trashed the flat, disappeared for three days. They sent her to a catastrophically expensive rehab in Malibu, then to a sober-living facility in Santa Monica. She stayed there for a year. Nick began to think of her like a distant cousin.

The Soundings came out, its title borrowed from a line in a Seamus Heaney poem. The novel's sales were middling but it was longlisted for the Booker. Neither of his parents finished it. It wasn't his story, they said. It was Cait's.

"Then let her be mad at me," he said, but of course the point was his parents also viewed it as *their* story, same as Nick.

Six months later they told him they were getting divorced, and it only felt like the completion of something. There: the destruction of their unit seen through to the end.

AFTER DINNER, I TAKE A LONG, HOT SHOWER WHILE NICK HELPS my parents do the dishes. When I get out, I find him stretched out on my childhood bed, legs crossed at the ankles, his laptop open but tossed to the side, his body curved over a book. I stand where the bathroom tile slips into the hardwood of the bedroom and watch him for a beat, twisting my wet hair into a tight spiral, wringing it onto the floor, thinking about how all that unpredictability made him the opposite: reliable, patient; here whenever I need him.

"Whatchya reading?" I ask.

He holds the book up. My stomach turns to eels. "Where'd you get a first edition of *Ariel*?" he asks.

I step across the room, towel held tight around my chest with one hand, and reach for the book. "Kelsey's brother gave it to me," I say. "It was hers."

Immediately Nick's face collapses. "I'm sorry, I didn't mean—"

"No, no—" I say, realizing what I've done. "It's fine. I just—" What? I think. I'm being insane. The police believe her death was an accident. Matt said that knowing who gave the book to Kelsey wouldn't change what happened. But I'm holding on to this collection of poetry the same way I've tucked away Luke's and Louie's and Raff's behavior, as one more out-of-place thing in a story that wants to be told differently.

"Hey," he says, soft. "It's okay. You don't need to say anything."

I close the book carefully and put it on my nightstand, then look toward the computer, trying to reset. "Last-minute rewrites?"

Nick shakes his head. "Just reviewing some emails about protocol for Monday. We've got a closed set."

For a sex scene. "Hmm," I say, tiptoeing closer to the bed. "Do you know the choreography?"

Nick pushes forward from the headboard, sliding across the mattress toward me. "That's the intimacy coordinator's job," he says, reaching for the edge of my towel. His fingers dance along the bottom of the terry, so the fabric moves across my thighs as if by a light breeze: barely, almost imperceptibly. "I know how I imagined it when I wrote it, though," he says.

"Yeah?" I breathe. "You think you could show me?"

Nick grins. He slips one hand under my towel, his palm moving up my inner thigh, a thumb just tracing the edge of me. It's the kind of touch I like most—teasing, anticipatory—but also cannot bear, the devastating vulnerability of wanting something. I take his face in my hands, allowing the towel to drop from my chest, and my mouth is on his for only a moment before he moves to my neck, my chest, each of my nipples, tiny and hard.

Fooling around in my childhood bedroom I feel like a teenager again, small and nervous, hyperalert. I kiss with my eyes open. I'm worried about wet noises, the smack of skin, and I rush, moving to my knees and taking him in my mouth quickly. It's usually just an opening gambit for us, never the main event, but when he pulls at my shoulders and I hear him whisper, husky—"I want you"—I press my palm against his stomach (*no*) and keep going. I'm aware of him reaching for something on the floor, and then I hear him rasp that he's coming, and then he pushes me off him—hard; I rock back onto my tailbone from my knees, surprised—and watch as he finishes into the T-shirt in his hands.

"Sorry," he says, wiping himself off. "I—we don't usually—it seemed safer to assume you didn't want—" He means he's never come in my mouth. It's a cautiousness I should have expected from Nick—our sex is communicative, full of questions and check-ins—but it has the effect of only making me more embarrassed, of having been caught slipping into performance mode: this time, the teenage girl. Kelsey giggles over the top of a beer bottle, face washed in moonlight. *Spit or swallow?*

The Collaboration

None of us needed the Wildflowers, not from a professional standpoint.

Annie Carey was a reigning queen of country, and not the cliché of the fading artist grasping for relevancy either. She rode into Nashville on the heels of Faith and Shania, slipping onto the charts right before the door shut entirely on that brief era of women ruling the genre. Now she had a line of cookware and wrote a guest column every month for *Better Homes & Gardens* and was in conversation with HGTV about a talk show. She sat comfortably atop an empire.

Meanwhile Rachel Pratt was one of Nashville's most in-demand songwriters, with more than a dozen number one cuts under her belt, an Oscar for Best Original Song, and an MFA in poetry. She would never be stupid, fuck-you rich like Annie, but she didn't have to worry about a personal brand or interfacing with the public. When Rachel released a solo record—she'd put out a couple of EPs—it was because she had a handful of songs no one else wanted to cut that she believed in and wanted to exist in the world. It had nothing to do with money or fame or a desire to cross into her own superstardom. She was intensely private, almost manically anxious, and had carved a lane in the industry that allowed her to be successful without exposing herself.

And then there was me. Melody was skeptical about Annie Carey's supergroup. They worried the project would distract me from my next solo record, which they wanted out as soon as possible; they feared that such an openly feminist endeavor would make me enemies at country radio, where sometimes a whole hour would pass before you would hear a song by a woman. They liked the image of Annie anointing the genre's next sovereign, us photographed together like a line of succession—but they weren't sure I *needed* it, not when *Sophomore* was as big as anything Annie had ever done. The coronation was there in the data.

But just because we didn't *need* the Wildflowers didn't mean we weren't getting something out of it. Annie wanted a place to experiment. Rachel wanted more of her songs going to women.

And I wanted to know whether collaboration was ruined for me. I wanted to know if every partnership I entered was inevitably doomed. Would it work out differently this time?

Could the Wildflowers be my do-over?

AFTER I WENT TO KELSEY'S HOUSE THE FIRST TIME, I TRIED avoiding her. If I went online and saw copeofmanycolors7 in my buddy list, I signed off. At school, I loaded all of my books into my backpack so I wouldn't have to go to my locker between classes and risk running into her with Raff. I understood that the next logical step in our relationship was for me to invite Kelsey over to *my* house, and I couldn't bear the thought of her judging the white sleigh bed I'd begged for from Pottery Barn Teen, or the American Girl dolls I still kept in their glossy white boxes, or—worst of all—the small collection of CDs I kept next to my stereo: boy bands, divas, a handful of movie soundtracks. I imagined her walking through my door and seeing my pinboard tacked with spelling bee ribbons and Broadway tickets and thinking, *I've clearly made a mistake.* I was a child. Kelsey was something else.

She found me in the library during study hall. I sat in the back, my two-inch binders and assignment journal and accordion folder spread out in front of me, carefully composing an essay on Lady Macbeth's sleepwalking scene, when Kelsey jumped up onto the table next to me, her denimed thighs knocking my notebook out from under my hand.

I looked over my shoulder, trying to see where she'd come from, and saw Raff with a few of his teammates by the lounge chairs in front. Two of them sat with girls draped in their laps. "'The use of prose in Lady Macbeth's final scene indicates her psychosis and foreshadows her eventual suicide,'" Kelsey said, leaning over to read my notes. "'Psychosis'? Can't you just say that she loses her mind?"

I frowned and pulled my notebook back in front of me, stacking my copy of *Macbeth* on top of my rough draft, hoping she couldn't tell I'd been thinking about how kids hooked up in the stacks sometimes, wondering whether Raff had pressed Kelsey against the shelves and slipped his hand inside her jeans. "It's not *lost*. It's just . . . you know, she's having a hard time."

"I guess that's how you talk when your mom's a therapist," Kelsey said, laughing.

"Lady Macbeth *is* having a hard time," I said, which just made Kelsey laugh harder. It didn't feel like she was mocking me—it felt like an approval. I tried not to smile too hard. "What are you doing here?" I asked.

Kelsey looked across the library at Raff. "Idiot is failing *history*, of all subjects. Like, it's just memorization." She shrugged. "I let him copy one of my old essays." She picked up my assignment pad and flipped through my homework. "Do you use a ruler to make these cross-outs? These are, like, really fucking straight lines."

I rolled my eyes and grabbed it back from her. Kelsey gave it up willingly but then reached for the notebook that had been hidden underneath.

"Oh, no—" I stammered. "That one's not—"

But she was already reading my poems. I thought about how stupid I was for carrying that book around, how inevitable it seemed that this would happen, the million and one times I'd panic-checked my back-pack or my locker to make sure it was still exactly where I left it because what if I'd forgotten it in chemistry? What if I left it in the basket under-neath my desk chair? I never wrote whole poems during the day but I used that notebook to jot down little ideas, tiny snippets of thought that I might want to hold on to for later. It was the fragmented collection of an insane person.

"I like this one," Kelsey said, and then held the notebook at an angle for me to read. *I'm like the trees when your storm came sweeping through / leaves shimmer in the breeze but my roots hold on true.* She talk-sang it out loud, mumble-tracking a light melody, the slightest rushed cadence in the middle, a slowing down at the end. I looked around us, reflexively embar-rassed by her singing. No one was paying any attention. "What's it about?"

I shrugged, resigned to the sharing. "I just liked how the leaves turned silver in the wind. I only added the relationship to give it story. Sometimes it's not so much that I'm looking for a metaphor to explain a feeling or an experience, but instead I'm looking for a situation to fit the metaphor. Does that make sense?"

Kelsey squinted at me, smiling. "That's such a boring answer it's actu-ally interesting." Kelsey shut my notebook and put it down on the stack of papers in front of me, then slipped a tiny, flip-top pad from her back pocket. "I need help with this one," she said, folding it open and tossing it onto the table between us.

I squinted at a line that had a series of scratch-outs beneath it. *They nurse their lonely hearts / with dive bar whiskey and daydreams / and they cure their morning hangovers . . .*

I could see the beginnings of the rejections that followed: *with super-ficial apologies . . . with visits to the priest . . .*

"What are you going for?" I asked.

"I'm just trying to write about those sad motherfuckers who sit at Junior's all day. But everything I tried was too—I dunno, pretentious."

She pulled her lip to one side, thinking. ". . . and they cure their morning hangovers . . . with Gatorade and cheap Chinese?"

"That's gross. Who eats Chinese in the morning?"

Kelsey laughed, her head tipped back. "You do when it's still night," she said.

"Well, that line makes me picture eating lo mein with coffee, which is disgusting." Kelsey was still laughing, but I leaned over her notebook, an idea sparking. "What about 'with diner coffee and some grease'?"

Kelsey looked at her lyrics, mumbling the lines. "Yeah," she said, soft at first, and then more confidently: "That's perfect." She scribbled my words in the margin.

It wasn't a particularly impressive line. But still my stomach rippled. "Cool," I said, trying to speak normally.

Kelsey folded her notebook and smacked it lightly against my upper arm. "Come on," she said. "I wanna show you something."

ANNIE LIVED FORTY-FIVE MINUTES OUTSIDE THE CITY, ON A HUN-dred pristine acres with a barn she converted into a studio, two rescue horses, a dozen heritage-breed chickens, four dogs, and so many barn cats that I sometimes mistook them for racoons or possums. Her husband, Andrew, was a producer who could play any instrument you handed him; her daughters, Joan and Loretta, were five and seven and often popped into our writing sessions bearing small gifts—a ripe Sungold tomato, fresh-picked from the garden; a single rumpled marigold, clipped from the pollinator strips Annie planted in neat borders around the property; a hunk of dripping honeycomb, peeled from the hives Andrew tended like pets. Annie would take their tiny, sticky fingers in her mouth and lick the honey from their knuckles one by one while the girls dissolved into fits of giggles in her lap.

It was Rachel who kept us on task. Rachel was trained in songwriting camps and on publishing teams; she brought icebreakers and books of freewriting prompts and therapy exercises, all kinds of strategies for drumming up material on the spot. I had experience writing on command before—our first sessions as the Wildflowers reminded me of those early days at Melody with Bill and Jess and Sam—and experience crafting for a vision that wasn't exactly my own, but I'd always felt that there was something lesser about those forms of creativity, like I was at best a student and at worst an imposter. Watching Rachel slip in and out of voices like an actor might try on dialects helped me to see that wasn't the case at all. Rachel was brilliant.

"What if we did something character-based?" she asked one day, fingering the fretboard of a guitar once owned by Hank Williams. Her hands were long and delicate as they noodled Andrew's collectors' item. "Like *The Ghost of Tom Joad* or an Americana *Ziggy Stardust*?"

"Or what about a sessions-style record?" Annie said, carefully untangling a knot in Loretta's hair. "We hole up somewhere really iconic, like Bristol or Macon," she explained, naming lesser-known entries in country music's history, "and reclaim a creative experience that has typically excluded women? No one questions a man prioritizing his art, but a woman is never allowed to just fuck off like that, especially if she has kids and a family."

"Maybe it's a response record," Rachel pitched, "like a country *Exile in Guyville*?"

Annie laughed. "'Daddies, Don't Let Your Babies Grow Up to Be Cowgirls'?"

We were having some trouble coalescing around a concept, initially; "country music by three women" wasn't a unifying enough frame. But while Annie and Rachel suggested Americana riffs on indie rock or "contemporary bluegrass," the ideas I worked up after hours—a live album from the Bluebird, or a travelogue that told the stories of women around the world—felt reductive and overdone next to theirs. Any effort I made to match their sophistication was sidelined by distraction: the way Annie fiddled with the trio of thin diamond bands she wore on her ring finger; the tattoo Rachel had on the soft, smooth skin on the inside of her left forearm, a line by Mary Oliver ("look, and look again"); how, when they were in the same room, Annie's and Andrew's bodies angled toward each other like magnets; the perfect midsize weight and shape of Rachel's gold hoop earrings, not so small you would describe them as delicate nor so large you would call them chunky. I was there to write but I kept losing myself in the lessons of their adult womanhood, desperate for scraps of their self-actualization.

These long days of preoccupied, languishing creativity often spilled into dinner, eaten under a cloak of wisteria while the blooms lost their petals in our bourbon, and then again into nights where we let loose as the sky turned to black and more and more cars filled Annie's drive, some invisible Bat-Signal calling friends and cowriters and bandmates to the farm for bonfires and s'mores, for chasing Loretta and Joan around the yard with sparklers past their bedtime, for trading stories about the business while sampling a bottle of something someone was calling "luxury moonshine" as the fire turned to embers. I began to think of myself like a 1920s expat, an artist who fled her hometown for a new creative community abroad.

It was on one of those long musical evenings that I ran into Miles Hart. I hadn't seen him since the Grammys—I never called that number scratched on my makeup bag, paralyzed by the middle school version of myself that would always see Miles as older and more famous—but I knew he'd moved to Nashville as part of his prolonged attempt to break out as a serious singer-songwriter. He came to Annie's with the owner of a guitar shop, and sat next to me by the fire with one of the store's custom instruments perched against his hip. He fiddled with the tuning while I watched his cheekbones sharpen in the firelight.

"Shit," he said.

"Something wrong with it?" I asked, leaning closer to the guitar. The owner Frankensteined them together from the scraps of old instruments, and the result was an intentionally kind of deadened sound. The notes were meant to hang in the air only fleetingly.

Miles shook his head. "I fell into a cliché."

"What cliché?"

"The guy playing his guitar at the girl, hoping to impress her."

I laughed a little too loudly, flexing against the twitch in my stomach. "No you haven't," I told him. "In the cliché, it's not actually about the girl at all. It's about your own ego. You're clearly *much* more self-aware than that."

Miles laughed and began to play "Ring of Fire," and I thought for a moment—I realized, later, he must have thought it too—that he and I would be the next Johnny and June.

I KNEW ABOUT THE OLD ATHLETIC TRAINING ROOM UNDER THE Thompson High rink. It was abandoned in the nineties when an alum who graduated in the eighties and went pro donated money to put in a whole new suite for the hockey team. I'd never seen it—it was where kids went to smoke during their free periods or to hook up after school—but as soon as Kelsey led me to the ice, I knew that's where we were headed.

It turned out, though, that "abandoned" didn't do the old training room justice; it was apocalyptic. Moss crept down from leaky casement windows. Mildew blackened the drop ceiling. Gray light slashed through dust motes into the drained belly of an old hot tub.

"Cool, huh?" Kelsey said, tracing a loop around the room's perimeter.

"Do you come down here a lot?" I asked. A cluster of smashed beer cans huddled in the corner of the whirlpool; cigarette butts peppered the ground. A padded training table spilled yellow foam from a slash in its center like a mushroomy pus.

"Nah," Kelsey said. "It's a little hard-core for me."

I didn't know what she meant by that.

"But there is one thing I like," she said, walking down into the center of the old hot tub and sitting cross-legged on the cement floor. I tried to imagine five or six hockey players in here, elbows cocked against the edge, bodies reclining in the churning water.

"I'm not sure you should sit on that," I said, but Kelsey took her little notepad from her pocket, rested it open against her thigh, and started singing.

I didn't recognize the song at first; she had to get to the line about *dive bar whiskey and daydreams* before I realized this was the one we'd just revised in the library. When she said my line—*and they cure their morning hangovers / with diner coffee and some grease*—I caught an echo in *dive bar* and *diner* that I hadn't even noticed before. I still love that about music, and about writing: the decisions your subconscious makes for you, the choices that reveal themselves later.

"You sing in the shower, right?" Kelsey said when she finished.

"What?"

"Everybody does."

"Um—yeah, sure. I guess."

"The acoustics aren't *good* in a bathroom, technically, but there's a lot of reverb, so your voice sounds more full, which makes it sound better to you. This room does the same thing, especially right here." She patted the floor next to her. "Sit."

Admiring the room was one thing; touching its filth was another. I debated, then finally put my backpack on the ground and perched on the edge of it, like a cushion. Kelsey laughed.

"Okay, I played you all my favorite songs. What's one of yours?"

"Oh, no," I said, sensing where this was headed. "I don't sing."

"You just said you do. In the shower. So come on. What's one song you know all the lyrics to?"

I still hate questions like this. I came up with stock answers, later in my career, safe responses to "who are your biggest influences, creatively?" that felt entirely neutral: interesting but not so niche that I sounded snobby or try-hard; a little boring but believably so. *Carole King. Peter Gabriel.* That day with Kelsey the question seemed only like a trap.

I sighed. "'Homeward Bound'?"

Kelsey leaned back and cocked her head to one side, surprised. Impressed, even. "Okay," she said, and then—without so much as clearing her throat, without gathering herself at all, she just started singing: *I'm sittin' in the railway station / got a ticket for my destination . . .*

She did the little *mm-mmm* between couplets and wriggled her eyebrows at me as if to say, *come on.* Seeing no way out of it, I sighed and jumped in somewhere between *one-night stands* and *guitar in hand.* Kelsey smacked my thigh triumphantly and nudged her shoulder into mine, never breaking stride in the melody.

She was right about the room. The round pool acted like a kind of amphitheater, layering our voices on top of each other and fattening them so that I couldn't exactly separate hers from mine in what funneled up and around us. Together we wove a whole new texture, one that blanketed my nerves. I sang a little louder, marveling at what I'd already identified as Kelsey's vast depth and breadth of music knowledge: She knew every word of the Simon & Garfunkel hit, every inflection, and when we finished she added one extra *silently for me* so I could hear her alone, all luster. Then she put her hands on her crossed knees and turned to face me. Her hair fell from her temple in a sheet. "See? That wasn't so bad."

I smiled, unsure about her point.

"You've gotta be comfy with your own voice if you're gonna make music."

"Am I going to be making music?"

"We are," she said. "Together."

I was beginning to see that this wasn't an entirely spontaneous trip. "I don't know anything about songwriting," I admitted.

She shrugged and shook her head, like it was beside the point. "Yes you do. Songs are poems."

"Okay, well—I'm not a performer."

"That's my job. You just be the wordsmith."

"Like Cyrano," I said, and Kelsey wrinkled her nose, confused. "It's a play," I explained. "From like the 1800s."

"You're such a nerd," she told me. "Never change."

WE WERE CALLED THE WILDFLOWERS AFTER THE DOLLY PARTON song, not the Tom Petty one, and that was kind of the point. Annie wanted to make a very explicit statement about women as integral to the history of country music. Not only was "Wildflowers" a Dolly song, but also it was a cut on *Trio*, the first album by the supergroup consisting of Dolly, Linda Ronstadt, and Emmylou Harris. Rachel liked that it didn't pander: she never would have abided a name like Rodeo Queens or Neon Cowgirls. Privately, I thought of it as a tribute to Kelsey, who loved Dolly more than either Annie or Rachel.

And it worked because the record itself was a hat-tip of sorts. In the end we landed on a concept inspired by the mythology we'd grown up on: Country music is filled with subgenre—there's the "other woman" song, like "Jolene"; the kiss-off ("These Boots Are Made for Walkin'"); the revenge track ("Goodbye Earl"); the name-drop ("If You Don't Like Hank Williams")—and is shameless about its fondness for formula. All we had to do, in the end, was use that to our advantage.

It started when Annie brought in "Loretta," with three verses that traced the origin of her daughter's name. The next day, Rachel shared

"Bone Dry," a drinking song that flipped the script—this was about *not* drinking—to tell the story of her wife's pregnancy, and the anxiety she felt about her role in their parenting. *At night I hear the skeletons / rap their knuckles on my closet door / and whisper false comparisons / till I go reaching for another pour.* It was 2012 but it was Nashville; Rachel was out but quietly, and her willingness to write a queer-coded song about motherhood and miscarriage set a new standard for our songwriting. We weren't merely parodying country tropes; we were expanding them. The genre was a big tent, if only we would let it be.

It took me a while to think of something worth saying. Annie and Rachel had real, full lives, and I was consumed by whether Miles Hart wanted to be my boyfriend. I spent most nights at his place in East Nashville, "where the real artists lived," hanging out in the back while he played gigs at the dives up north off Gallatin, airless brick buildings wedged between chain pharmacies and grocery stores. "Only the locals know these places," he told me the first time. "The tourists are blown away by just the *concept* of a writers' round. You've won them over by existing. *These* are the tough crowds." I was too busy noticing the way his kite tattoo peeked out from under the V of his white T-shirt to realize it all might have been posturing for the fact that he couldn't get into a round somewhere better.

I spent that summer seesawing between Miles and my bandmates, constantly recalibrating for the other perspectives in the room. I wanted to be grown-up enough for Rachel and Annie but cool enough for Miles. I wanted to be talented enough for the Wildflowers but not so big that Miles would be intimidated by me. One night I picked up Miles's rubber-bridge guitar and fiddled with it in bed as he trailed a finger along the inside of my thigh. "Rachel wants to use these on our record," I told him, squeezing my legs together. "She's been tinkering with all these old-school instruments. The other day she was wandering around the studio with a fiddle from the Depression." I told him this neutrally, waiting to see whether it was something he thought was interesting or pretentious.

"Checks out," Miles said, inching his hand closer to my groin. "People think Rachel's cool because she's gay and her solo stuff has a different vibe. But she's really pretty Nashville." He emphasized the city like an adjective.

I frowned. Later I would be able to see Miles's characterization for the sexist bullshit that it was, but in that moment I only felt my own bruised ego. What did Miles think of *my* music, then, if I felt Rachel was infinitely more gifted than me?

I began to noodle the chorus of "Like Her," the first song I was nearly confident enough to bring into a Wildflowers writing session. *I know that she's tall and I'm five foot three / and I know that she's hot and I'm just plain pretty . . .*

"Babe," Miles said, "I could never date a tall girl." He put one hand on my chin and pulled me in for a kiss while his other hand pushed the guitar out of the way.

When I played the song for Annie and Rachel the next day they knew it wasn't an ordinary "other woman" track, and not only because that was the whole point of the record we were making—to flip the lens on the usual tropes. They understood it wasn't about jealousy or desperation. They heard the yearning in it, and knew the song had nothing to do with men at all.

WE STARTED HANGING OUT ALMOST DAILY. KELSEY SHOWED me how she recorded everything on a handheld tape recorder, the kind journalists use, her lips trained close to the speaker. The device caught all her breath, so that sometimes listening to the playback felt more intimate than listening to her tinkering with melodies in real time. Kelsey would press the recorder's edge to her ear, craning her neck to get the sound as close as possible, while I'd tuck my chin into my chest in her egg chair in the corner of her room, making hash marks in my notebook, transcribing syllable counts, avoiding eye contact. Sometimes she would lift her chin in my direction and say, "It sounds like I'm saying 'honestly' there, right?" and hold the recorder out toward my face, or "'Vanished,' that's a great word, did you write that down?"

If Kelsey landed on a phrase, I might try to build out from there—to take "vanished," the idea of something disappearing, the suddenness of it, the trauma, and craft a narrative from the experience. I had an inclination toward scene-setting, world-building: a retreating tide, sand fleas burrowing invisibly into the ground in a carbonated flurry; my grandmother's ashes scattered on the wind. Kelsey would say, *Mm, I can see it,* but that's the location of the song, not its story. We need an arc, a sense of conflict. Why are the lovers on the beach? Who brought them there? Will they leave together?

Sometimes Kelsey would fiddle with chords on her guitar—she was always saying it was out of tune, but at the time I couldn't tell the difference—and come up with a harmony she liked, then layer a melody over it made of things she saw in the room: *bedsheet, scarf, homemade picture frame* (me: "there's a nice internal rhyme there"). After that we'd strip the words and work from a hummed track, and I'd ask Kelsey questions while doodling in the margins: Was it sad or just melancholy? Was it happy or just up-tempo? Was it curious or fumbling, flailing?

"You have such a big emotional vocabulary," she said to me once, and in response I told her about the color wheel my mom gave me that broke down feelings into increasingly minute gradations: sad branched into vulnerable or guilty or lonely; lonely to isolated or abandoned.

Kelsey laughed and immediately lapsed into a goofy, jokey melody, the kind you might hear on a TV commercial: "I got my *wheeeelin' feelins* . . . is this anything?"

I laughed then too, and said probably not, but I remember thinking: how ridiculous that Kelsey's voice sounded like that just messing around—silky, golden, warm. How much older she seemed than me, how much more complex, how much more vast and mysterious her inner world.

At my house, Kelsey liked to stay for dinner, where the four of us ate together—me, my mom and dad, and Kelsey—lingering over meals Kelsey called "fucking elaborate": pasta tossed with leeks; risotto topped with pan-seared shrimp; steak, marinated and grilled and served over mixed greens, sourdough on the side, thick pads of the good butter. When she told my mother that she found it surprising that a woman like her cooked dinner every night—"It's confusing to me," she said, "because it's, like, a very typical gender role, but you're this self-possessed career woman"—they had a long conversation about second- and third-wave feminism, arguing in a friendly way over the constraints of the movements, how in some ways, if you think about it, feminism just created a new set of handcuffs: it was merely a reframe of the same old questions about what it meant to be a good girl, or a good woman, or a good wife. I picked at cubes of crumbling hard cheese at the kitchen counter, half listening to the substance of the conversation but really watching how Kelsey did not take her eyes from my mother, not once, how she seemed sometimes to not even blink. Later, I would tag along while my dad drove Kelsey home. She sat in the middle seat in the back, right in between us, reaching over the center console to fiddle with the radio dial, her long fingertips the only ugly thing about her, nails kept short for guitar, the pads callused and chewed.

At Kelsey's, the kids were in charge. Diana worked evenings a lot, four to eleven, and even though I had to be home for dinner—my dad picked me up on his way from the hospital—Fiona needed to eat early, around five, and sometimes Kelsey and I would help Matt in the kitchen: sautéing ground beef from yellow Styrofoam packages (hunter-orange labels announcing sale prices, $1.99 per pound!) for Hamburger Helper, improvising chicken Parm with plain boneless skinless breasts, Prego sauce, shredded Kraft mozzarella. Dancing around Fiona in the

Copestenkes' tiny kitchen with the pendant Tiffany light I thought how adult it seemed, Matt and Kelsey teaming up to make dinner for Fiona, to make sure that she was in the bath by six, that this little person was cared for, tended to, made to feel loved.

I tried not to ask too many direct questions about Matt. Whenever I asked Kelsey about a boy, even in the most casual way—about Raff's friends Dan and Vinny; about Tyler Burns, a kid in my year who also worked at Camp Tahawus; about Alex Malcolm, Kelsey's ex from freshman year—Kelsey would jump right to romance. *Ohmygod*, she'd breathe, *do you* liiiike *him?!* It didn't matter how vehemently I protested; that I noticed a man at all meant I'd thought about fucking him.

Instead I pieced together Matt's story from a combination of clues—fragments Kelsey dropped or details I noticed in the hours spent at their house. Before Fiona, Matt was a drifter, a little aimless: he loved ice hockey but was never good enough to make the Thompson High team, in part because their family couldn't afford all the gear and ice time and club memberships that separated the really good athletes from the guys who casually played pickup on the lake in the winter. He liked animals and thought half-heartedly about vet school, but he got a C in biology. He considered the military, maybe trying to become one of the K9 handlers, but wasn't great about following instructions if he felt the orders were arbitrary.

After graduating from Thompson he took classes part-time at community college and worked at the marina, which is where he met Billie. She waited tables in the café, serving baskets of chicken tenders and fries while he repaired props and flushed engines and did touch-up paint jobs on scratched hulls. Sometimes, at night, they'd nick a boat from the dock and steal out onto the lake in the black midnight. He thought she was an adrenaline junkie. He didn't know about the amphetamines until later.

She stayed clean through the pregnancy, and for a little while after. Ultimately Fiona was no match for Billie's addiction, but for Matt she was a necessary sense of purpose. He dropped out of juco—waste of time, waste of money—and got the job as the pharm tech. He worked as many hours as he could get. He made sure Fiona had the safest car seat, books to read at night, that all the paperwork was done for Child Health Plus and that there was a little money in an account for orthodontia, sports equipment, cupcakes for classroom birthday parties. He seemed very serious to me, and eventually I understood that it was less about being a very young parent and more about the constant threat of a paperless custody agreement.

It happened once that fall, on a Tuesday in mid-November. We were at Kelsey's house painting Fiona's wall. (She'd asked for a pony for Christmas; Matt gave Kelsey a fistful of cash and sent us to the hardware store instead, where we bought six half gallons of paint in Mustang Brown and Palomino Beige and Pinto Red and planned a mural of wild horses.) The doorbell rang and Kelsey stepped around the splatters of paint to angle her cheek close to the window. "Fuck," she said.

"What?" I said, streaking a horse's tail with black.

"Why is she dressed like she hit the J.Crew jackpot at the Salvation Army?"

"Who?"

"Billie," Kelsey said, and I stopped and tried to position my face close to Kelsey's at the window. I could barely make out a petite woman with honeyed hair, wearing loose cropped jeans and a worn gray sweater.

"Why would she be here?"

"She does this sometimes," Kelsey said. A drop of Goldenrod Yellow landed silently on her calf, and I took the paintbrush from her hand and propped it on top of the bucket lid.

"Does what?"

"Gets sober for one-point-five seconds and says she wants to see Fiona."

I could hear the TV from the living room—the swelling contours of a Bryan Adams power ballad—and knew Fiona was planted in front of *Spirit*.

Matt stepped out onto the front porch. We heard the storm door rattle, then the slam behind him. Next to me, Kelsey went hard and still.

What was happening between Billie and Matt was unreadable. Neither raised their voice, gesticulated, allowed their face to crumple or widen or flex. It was as if they were in a battle to see who could be the calmest. After a while Billie walked back to her car—an old Volvo, the kind that's all square edges—and we heard the door shut behind Matt.

Kelsey immediately bolted into the hall. "What'd she want?"

Matt rubbed his fingers against one temple, pushing the corner of his eyebrow up, then down. "She wants to take Fiona to her parents' for Christmas."

"In Florida?"

Matt nodded.

"Well," Kelsey said, and she made a kind of scoffing noise, "that's not gonna happen. They don't allow toddlers in airport bars."

"She says she's been sober a month. Showed me the coin and everything."

"Wait a minute," Kelsey said, her voice high and sharp. "You're not actually considering this?"

"No, but—" Matt sighed. "We don't want any trouble in the big picture, you know? It might be easier . . ." He trailed off.

I watched how Matt's shoulders slumped, how his head rocked back slightly, how he played with his hands, forming fists at his side. I understood, all of a sudden, that Matt would not have wanted me to see him like this, if the choice had been his; that there was something private about his struggle. I thought of our name inked at the bottom of Fiona's new mural—*Cameron Cope* in looped black, Kelsey egging me on as I swirled the letters one after another. *Do you know how much this'll increase the value of the place when I'm famous?*

I had fundamentally misread the situation, I realized. I liked Kelsey's house because it was loud and playful and you could paint on the walls. It was a light chaos I attributed to whimsy, a certain joyful nonseriousness. In reality it was the constant tumult of an extremely precarious existence.

THE WILDFLOWERS DEBUTED AT THE GRAMMYS, WHERE WE sang "It Wasn't God Who Made Honky Tonk Angels" during the In Memoriam. Kitty Wells died that year, and although maybe another group would have chosen a more joyful moment to premiere, it felt right for us to begin by honoring the original Queen of Country Music, with a song that was one of the genre's first truly feminist anthems. We wore custom Nudie suits, mine with fringe detailing along the shoulders in the back, Rachel's snipped into a miniskirt, Annie's cut like a power blazer. The outfit felt like armor; Rachel and Annie like my protectors. I felt *validated* when I won Album of the Year the previous year, but there was a strength in numbers too. Standing side by side with the Wildflowers on music's biggest stage, I felt inoculated against the industry's whims, the delicate nature of my very new and very young success shored up by their sistering.

Later, I wiped off my makeup in Miles's bathroom while he stretched out on his bed, shirtless and tracing a finger over his own tattoos.

"People loved it," I told him.

"Of course they did," he said, a little absently.

"Adam called on the way home. He didn't apologize for doubting us, exactly, but he did say they were so proud of me."

Miles laughed in a shallow way. "Obviously. They got their token lady group without having to take on any kind of risk."

"'*Token lady group*'?" I repeated.

"It's a good thing," Miles said, although he didn't sound like he felt that way. "You're gonna be everywhere. You'll probably move a quarter-million units in the first week."

All night, I'd felt triumphant. Not just because we'd put on a good show, or because we'd proved the label wrong, but because I felt like I had finally arrived. I'd played the Grammys with two of the most influential women in the industry. I wasn't in the mood to recalibrate for Miles's cynicism. "We deserve to be everywhere," I said, pulling bobby pins from the nape of my neck. "The music is good."

"I didn't say it wasn't," Miles said. "I just said for these executives, it's not really about that. It's about feel-good dollars."

Someone else—a woman, maybe—could have made a similar point about our group as a version of capitalist-friendly girl-boss feminism, the kind that was on the precipice of taking over the marketplace then. But there's something suspicious about a white, straight man like Miles making the point, sneaking his own sexism through the back door of far-left politics. "Is it fun to be this much of a purist, Miles?" I asked.

"It's not a bad thing to care about your artistic integrity," he said.

"Fuck you, Miles," I snapped. "Just because your career isn't exactly going to plan doesn't mean you have to shit on mine."

I left Miles's house and walked to Rachel's. She also lived in East, a maze of streets on the verge of pricing out the locals sprawled between them. Paint chipped from a worn-down bungalow in the shadows of a forty-thousand-square-foot mixed-use development.

Natalie answered the door. "Dylan," she said, in a half whisper. "Let me get Rache." She padded quietly upstairs while I stood in the foyer of their craftsman, peering into their living room. It was warmly lit with small table lamps, cramped in a cozy kind of way with a little too much furniture. There was a small, vintage upright against the wall, and as I listened for Rachel's footsteps upstairs I tiptoed over, peering at the framed photos arranged on top of the instrument. Rachel and Natalie's wedding in Vermont. Rachel and Natalie on their honeymoon, somewhere with white sand and calm, clear water. Natalie cradling their daughter, Birdie, in the hospital, Rachel perched on the bed next to them. Rachel proudly holding Birdie in a strip mall parking lot, the awning of her namesake venue in blue behind them.

"Hey," Rachel said, her voice a little rasped. She still had her stage makeup on, but she wore sweatpants and a thin T-shirt, her brown hair piled high on top of her head.

"Sorry," I said reflexively. "I should have texted. I just—" I trailed off. I realized I was confused about the rhythm of my cowriters' lives. I couldn't articulate even for myself whether I needed them to mother me or mentor me or to be my friend; I only knew that I had overstepped, showing up after midnight to the place where Rachel's toddler slept upstairs.

"It's fine," Rachel said. "Come on, let me get you some tea."

While Rachel boiled water and set two mugs of tea on the counter, I told her about Miles. "He's jealous," I said, my voice rising, carrying the story to its natural conclusion. "He likes to pretend he's this super-secure musician who's just in it to make art, but I *know* he fucking hates that he's not as famous now as he was when he was in a boy band."

Rachel sighed deeply and fiddled with her tea bag in her mug, tugging the tag around the rim. "The worst thing about boys like Miles," she said finally, "is that they're always just a little bit right. That's why they get under your skin so badly."

This was extremely not what I wanted to hear. "How can you say that?" I said, my voice pitching upward. "He called us a *token lady act*."

Rachel flicked her eyes upstairs to where Birdie slept and put a finger to her lips, hushing me gently. I felt my shoulders tuck inward, making my body turtle-like with embarrassment. I was the child throwing a temper tantrum; Rachel was the reasonable adult. "What Annie always understood about this project was that we couldn't bully our way into it. If we rolled up to Music Row and started berating every sexist executive, we never would have gotten anything done. We *had* to make it easy on them. We had to make them feel *good* about playing us—not like they were apologizing."

It was Kelsey who'd first taught me this, how women in country had to camouflage their feminism with sparrowlike voices and familiar arrangements. Dolly Parton's *Just Because I'm a Woman* was a win for everyone, the label included; as much as I didn't want to admit it, I knew there was some truth to what Miles said about Melody: they agreed to let me play in the Wildflowers because the group was good for their brand.

"Guys like Miles turn their noses up at this kind of approach because they like to think of themselves as the true rebels. That way they don't have to blame their lack of success on their own artistic failings."

"It felt like he was saying we cheated, somehow."

"Well, it *is* a game," Rachel said. "But we didn't cheat. We used the rules to our advantage."

We heard Natalie padding across the floor above us, and then a garbled, distant cooing.

"Why did Annie ask me to be a part of the Wildflowers?" I asked Rachel. I'd always understood that there were commercial reasons for Annie's invitation; there wasn't a radio DJ in town who would pass on new music from Dylan Read, regardless of the subtext. But what if she'd seen something else in me—some uglier but no less valuable instinct?

Rachel sighed and scrunched her eyebrows together. "She asked you because she knew you'd get it. You show up on time and you get the job done, Dylan."

Natalie appeared then in the doorway. "Rache?"

Rachel turned as Birdie peered out from behind Natalie's body, her curly hair matted on one side, tugging at the hem of her pajama shirt. "Oh, little Bird," Rachel cooed. "You're supposed to be asleep!" She stood and walked over to her daughter, scooping her up and propping her at her hip.

"She wanted a song," Natalie explained. I thought of the track on our album about Rachel's own feelings of motherly inadequacy. She could sing to her daughter but she wasn't able to grow her in her body. What was our work worth, compared to this? In the scheme of things?

I stood from my chair. "I'm sorry," I said again.

Natalie smiled thinly. Birdie's head lolled on Rachel's shoulder. "Those kinds of instincts are gonna get you really far in this business, Dylan," Rachel said.

I nodded. I wanted to press her on it—I needed Rachel to tell me that I wasn't just a good girl; I was a gifted one too—but it was clear that it was time for me to go. They had a family and a life. I was a kid looking for a bed to shove my insecurities underneath.

KELSEY THREW ROCKS AT MY WINDOW, LIKE WE WERE IN A 1980s movie. I tiptoed across my room and pressed my nose against the fogged glass to see her fishing through fallen leaves for more pebbles. When she looked up again, taking aim, I waved my arms, frantically shushing her before my parents woke.

"Jesus *Christ*," she groaned when I opened the sliding door off the back porch. "You sleep like the goddamn dead, huh? I'm freezing my ass off out here."

"*Shh*," I said, hissing. She rolled her eyes and stepped past me into the dining room, trailing stale smoke and sour sweat. In the kitchen I watched her down three glasses of water in comical gulps, until she paused and put a hand over her mouth and lurched forward, briefly—

"Easy, killer," I said, grabbing her at the upper arm.

"The less fun part is starting," she said.

I tried not to laugh, rubbing her shoulder gently, three light circles. Upstairs I gave her a pale green oversized T-shirt from rec soccer a decade ago ("How did this fit you when you were in kindergarten?" Kelsey asked, holding the hem out wide from her body) and a pair of boxers

("You didn't steal these from your dad, did you?"). She sat very still and upright in bed, like she was performing sobriety, while I used a wet washcloth to wipe some of the makeup from the shallows of her undereye.

"You know," she said, her voice softer now, "I always thought it was the kids with the finished basements who were the luckiest." She looked over my shoulder to where the bathroom light cut across the floor in a triangle toward my bed, then leaned forward like a child sharing a secret. "But I think it's the en suite that's the real get."

"Oh yeah?" I said, laughing. "Because we can sober up in private?"

Kelsey collapsed back on her pillow, nestling into the sheets. "That, and you can have all the shower sex you want."

"Uh-huh. I think I should probably start with, like, regular lying-down bed-sex first," I said.

Kelsey giggled. "*Lying-down bed-sex,*" she echoed. "You're funny, Dylan Read. People don't know how funny you are." She sighed. Like my mom used to do for me, I pressed the blankets in around Kelsey's body, making a burrito of the comforter. "I had sex in a bathroom tonight, actually," she said.

"Oh?" I tried to keep my tone casual, worried I would seem freakish for wanting to know more. *What was it like? How does it work?*

"Raff was at Dan's, obviously," she said. "It was pretty lame actually. Steph was hanging around him like an abused dog."

I winced. Kelsey rolled her eyes. "She's pathetic. But it was annoying, because he and I have this, like, don't-ask-don't-tell policy, or whatever—"

"I don't think that's—"

Kelsey waved me off: "You know what I mean. We aren't exclusive. So it's fine, he can fuck Steph, but *as I was saying,* it was annoying because she was acting like he was hers. But then when she tried to get him to leave with her, he was all, 'nah, I gotta get my money back from this asshole,' because the guys had turned pong into a betting game, and she was like—" Kelsey made an exaggerated pouting face, mimicking Steph's disapproval. "So she left and Raff finished his game and made a big show of going to get fresh beers from the fridge in the garage but he gave me these eyes across the room, right? And so I know I'm supposed to follow him.

"And next thing I know we're in the bathroom off the kitchen and I'm leaning over the sink with my dress hiked up around my waist and I just think, you know, there's no way Steph and him are this good together."

I climbed under the sheets next to her. Kelsey turned on her side, slipping prayer-clasped hands beneath the pillow under her head. "I'm sorry, Kels," I whispered.

"It's okay," she said sleepily. "It's all material, you know?"

The following Monday the whole sophomore class crowded outside to watch a drunk-driving demonstration. I found myself tucked behind Raff and Dan while the police and fire departments towed in a mangled SUV, smashed and fire-crisped, and talked to us about the bodies in each seat: this victim had their ribs crushed inward by the dash; this one's neck broke when the airbag deployed. It reminded me of the antidrug ads that were everywhere at the time, meth addicts with chewed faces crawling on the roach-covered floors of gas station bathrooms. Didn't just *one* person in those meetings say, *Hey, do you think this is maybe a bit much?*

In front of me, Dan leaned toward Raff. "So Vinny says you and Kelsey fucked the other night."

Eyes straight ahead, Raff crossed his arms over his chest and made a scoffing noise.

I felt a static buzz at the corners of my eyes, like I was a radio dial tuned between stations.

"I'm done with her, I told you."

Dan looked at Raff skeptically. "I take my morning shit in that bathroom, man."

Raff lowered his voice. "Well," he said, "depends what you'd call 'fucking.'" Then he turned and looked at Dan, who raised his eyebrows. "All I can say is, if you don't wanna put your dick in it, there's a lot of things in a bathroom that you can get creative with."

I stopped breathing.

"Shit, man!" Dan said, his voice too loud.

"Gentlemen," Mr. Banks said from the back of the crowd.

Dan laughed under his breath. Raff leaned toward him, whispering now, and I tipped my right ear forward slightly. "I'm telling you, dude. The ones with daddy issues? Whole other ball game."

In the bathroom, after, I'd sweated clean through my cardigan, giant damp haloes beneath my armpits despite the November chill.

THE THING ABOUT GREAT COUNTRY MUSIC IS THAT THERE'S A choose-your-own-adventure quality to the writing. The listener's meant to fit themselves into the narrative. When *The Wildflowers* came out, Miles was in a high-profile relationship with a model named Serena Lane. All anyone saw in "Like Her" was that Serena was tall and I was short. A gossip blog posted photos of Serena and Miles—headed to brunch in LA, leaving a show in Brooklyn—and drew white drips out of Serena's mouth, on her dress. Online, my fans—who identified themselves as "Readers"—flooded her social media with book emojis, transforming the comment section into sagging shelves. One reviewer wrote that the only thing more brutal than a scorned woman is a scorned poet.

I felt badly that my song that was supposed to subvert the slut-shamey concept behind the "other woman" track had only, ultimately, resulted in more slut-shaming, but the truth is songs are misunderstood all the time. Just ask "Born in the U.S.A." What bothered me most was how nobody confused Annie's and Rachel's songs for the tropes they were undermining. It was only mine they read straightforwardly.

I had gotten so good at playing by the rules that I couldn't even break them when I tried.

My childhood bedroom seems stuck in a kind of arrested development. Surveying it from my bed in the clean morning light I notice the Beanie Babies slumped over with dusty noses on my bookshelves and middle school yearbooks stacked in a leaning pile on my desk but also a Peloton in the corner, my dad's dry cleaning hanging from the closet door. Everything caught between *mine* and *theirs*.

I peel myself out from under the covers and begin to walk a slow perimeter around the room, listening to the creaks and clatters of the house around me, the burnt smell of strong coffee wafting up through the vents, the indistinct murmur of my parents' and Nick's voices from somewhere below.

At the closet I pause and riffle through the clothes—my dad's suits, some dresses of my mom's. Nothing in here is mine anymore—except for the stack of notebooks on the shelf above the hanging rod.

I can't quite reach them, pushed back against the wall and in a haphazard stack, but the rule of being five four—the short side of average—is that you will try anyway, always. On my tiptoes I can rake my fingers across the wire spines of the notebooks, slowly creeping them toward the front of the shelf, until one comes loose and—

The notebooks landslide off the shelf, over my outstretched arm and head, into a shining rainbow on the floor of my bedroom. I bend and gather them back into a stack, then carry the pile over to my bed.

I still prefer standard grocery-store pads like these—Mead or Five

Star—in the three- or five-subject iteration, wire-bound (so they can lay flat), with their slick plastic covers in primary colors. The pages here are stiff with age and ink, a texture pressed into them with my ballpoint pen, and they crackle with each turn. Two of the notebooks are filled with poetry, lines about homeroom and playdates, AIM and middle school fashion trends. *The girls have matching leggings- in shades of fresh ripe fruit- cherries, lemons, sliced watermelons.* For a while I punctuate only and erratically with dashes. *I left your Name- in Bold print letters-.* This eleven- and twelve-year-old version of myself makes me smile with her devastating earnestness. There is a whole, terrible poem written for my sixth-grade crush, Jon Kleeman, where each letter of his name is capitalized:

> *Joy is too Obvious a word-*
> *Not enough Knowing- in its Life-*
> *Each and Every time- he asks-*
> *Must borrow A sheet of paper?*
> *No- this is delight.*

I'm still laughing about that one, still thinking about the hilarious use of *Must*, still thinking that maybe *Joy is too Obvious a word* is kind of a good line, actually, for a twelve-year-old, when I see the next notebook in the pile. Also wire-bound, this one is smaller than the others, with a flip-top—the sort that would fit inside your back pocket—and a mottled blue cover and thick, wrinkled pages that crinkle to the touch, as if the entire thing was dropped in water, fished out, and left to dry.

Its existence makes me sweat. I pick it up like an archeological artifact, as if it might turn to dust in my hands.

Inside, the pages are tie-dyed blue-black. I can see how the water spread from the bottom-right corner, a wave that picked up the ink and carried it toward the top left of the paper. The writing that remains is a tight, spiky cross between print and cursive that weeps at the threshold of wet and dry. I would know that handwriting anywhere.

Well, well, well, Kelsey says, clicking and unclicking each of the pens in the mug on my desk.

Stop talking like a Disney villain.

How'd that end up here?

I didn't forget about it, not exactly. If anything, I'd forgotten that Kelsey's old notebook was *here*, in my childhood bedroom. For months after she disappeared I found things like this: Kelsey's hairclips in my bathroom drawer, a bottle of Kelsey's nail polish mixed in with mine, a pair of her socks caught in our laundry. Each discovery made my stomach fill with slippery fish, my legs go to seaweed.

What are you gonna do with it? she asks me. *You can't even read most of it.*

No, but I can read some. I flip back to the start of the notebook. Even in the fragments I can see Kelsey's stylistic flourishes—the lines running like mirror images (*I've been waiting for my life to start / but I'm starting to think it already has* and *these drinks were on the house / but this house is made of cards*), something I'd thought of as uniquely Kelsey's but that I know now to be a classic country maneuver; the symbols grounded in boy behavior.

Doin' battle with iron giants / wonderin' if you'll betray this new alliance

Raff playing Halo, right?

Kelsey's doodling on her pant leg, inking a daisy into her denim.

I try to think of myself / like some sort of free-floating thing / turns out all along / that you've had your hooks deep in me

Also Raff, obviously.

Kelsey wriggles her eyebrows. *Haven't you learned* anything *from the way people talk about your lyrics online?*

Again I think about my fans, certain that a flower in my lyrics is not just a flower but a reference to a photo shoot I did in an old farmhouse, that a color is not just a color but a reference to an ex with blue eyes. I think of me and Kelsey in this bedroom, tossing these pages between the window seat and the bed, rewriting each other's lyrics, scribbling suggestions in the margins. Making a cipher of the art flattens it. They aren't always wrong in how they attribute a lyric to a certain person or party, but it's never the whole story.

"I'm gonna need to read those."

I snap the notebook shut. Nick stands in my doorframe, a mug of hot coffee in his hand.

"I need to know the name of your year-seven crush so I can beat him up."

"Jon Kleeman," I tell him. Nick laughs and I try to breathe through my hammering heart. He places the mug next to me on the nightstand and leans over to kiss me, smelling of skin and breath and humanness, then settles in at the opposite end of the bed, leaning his back against the footboard and bringing his socked feet up on the covers. I slip Kelsey's waterlogged notebook under the rest and shove the whole pile farther beneath the duvet.

"Sloane is downstairs," Nick says.

I pull the coffee into my lap, rotating the warm ceramic slowly against my belly. "She thinks we might have a quote, unquote 'tragedy problem,'" I tell him.

Nick raises his eyebrows. He isn't surprised by how the world talks about me, but he definitely thinks it's ridiculous. "What does that mean?"

What Sloane means is that my fans are over-pathologizing my relationship to Kelsey. Something terrible has happened to me, they've decided; I've been carrying this loss all this time, and nobody knew. It's the kind of thing they get really worked up about: not just *new* information but *deeply personal* information. I wouldn't be too concerned about it, Sloane texted this morning, but we have the new record to consider. "It's the kind of story that could become the *whole* story," I tell Nick.

A handful of pieces popped up overnight, clickbait masquerading as serious journalism. One quoted a "mental health practitioner" who asserted that the "autobiographical nature of Dylan Read's songwriting—and the extent to which it dwells in the years corresponding to the friendship in question—suggests that she is still actively engaged in healing." Another article claimed to be a "textual analysis" and brought in a Virginia Woolf scholar who said that writers "do not merely write what they *know*, they write what they are *processing*." The gossip influencer Raconteur screenshotted a series of DMs—usernames blacked out—about my eulogy and posted them alongside a photo of me speaking at center court. To some of the audience, apparently, I seemed *heartfelt*. Really *torn up*. To others I looked *uncomfortable*. The replies were memes about robots, Elsa from *Frozen*, Christina Ricci from *The Addams Family*. Conceal don't feel!

Nick tilts his head to the side. In the weightless sunlight I can see how the skin under his eyes is thin to the point of translucent. "You know not to look at that stuff," he says, gentle.

I sink lower under the covers, lifting my duvet over my head. "I *knowww*," I groan.

From the gossip blogs I clicked over to my subreddit, where someone had reposted the long-distance cell phone shot of me at the service. As a rule they are kinder on my sub. *She looks so sad*, they wrote. *I can't imagine what she's going through*. Someone shared a story about her freshman-year roommate who got ovarian cancer and died at twenty-one. *It's fucking brutal to lose someone when you're so young*. I thought of actresses revealing their eating disorders or sexual traumas years after the fact, the way their fans flocked to the old movies and red carpet photos and awards ceremonies, reframing the moment through the lens of tragedy or victimhood. On the message board it didn't take my fans long to do the same: *does anyone think shes been writing about kelsey from the very beginning? maybe its just me but I think lyrics like "floating like twin moons, Saturn rooting me to you"* seemed romantic initially but could also be about kelsey, who we know was a gemini (twins)?

In a single post the forum determined that I'd developed a linguistic pattern as a result of my relationship with Kelsey: moon metaphors (*Moonless!*) and solar eclipses and a tendency to describe the bigness and unknowability of certain things—of love especially!—in galactic terms. *You came and went / like Halley's Comet / trailing ice and dust / in your absence.*

At night I dream of galactic collisions / goddesses sick of their presumed disposition / all the beautiful destructive things named after women.

"So let me get this straight," Nick says. "Because Kelsey disappeared—" He pauses and corrects himself: "Because Kelsey died right before you moved to Nashville," he says, and I nod, because that part is true. They know, now, that Kelsey never left Thompson Landing. Her body was there the whole time.

"You're worried that everyone is going to assume that grief motivated your entire career," Nick concludes. *A whole new layer to her music,* they wrote online.

I grip my coffee tight in my lap. "Can't you see it?" I say softly. "Every article written about me will begin with something like 'Dylan Read, who moved to Nashville in the wake of the loss of her best friend,' or 'Dylan Read, whose debut album was made in the wake of tragedy,' or 'Grieving the loss of her best friend, Dylan Read moved to Nashville at sixteen—'"

"Okay, okay," Nick says, cutting me off. "I get it." He pauses and looks at me, concern etched in the lines of his face. I hate that he's looking at me this way.

"What?" I ask.

"You didn't tell me she was your best friend."

"I didn't?" He shakes his head. I've hidden so much from him for so long; over the past few days I've felt like a cracked dam, unable to keep track of the parts of the story leaking out of me.

I shrug at Nick apologetically. "I don't know how to talk about it," I tell him, which is a version of the truth, at least: Is it fair to call her my best friend, after everything that happened?

"It's okay," Nick says. "So what are you gonna do?"

"That's probably why Sloane is here. To strategize."

"Can I help?"

I shake my head.

"Okay. I'm gonna get a workout in, but if you change your mind, I'll just be downstairs. Your dad says you guys have some equipment in the garage?"

I nod. "And the Peloton," I say, gesturing toward the bike in the corner of my bedroom.

"No thanks," he says. "The only outdoor sport that's okay to play indoors is football." I've heard him say this before, but still it makes me smile.

"I love you," I say, and he kisses me again on the forehead. Only when the door is shut behind him do I notice that I've ripped a callus from the tip of my middle finger so deeply that I'll have to cut it off, or else risk tearing into the healthy tissue below.

DOWNSTAIRS, SLOANE IS PERCHED AT THE KITCHEN ISLAND, three devices spread in front of her like a makeshift war table. My mother flits around her, a pile of dishes in the sink and two pots going on the stove. The oven clicks intermittently; the air smells like onions.

"What's going on down here?"

"Oh, good morning, sweetheart!" My mother pauses to slide a bowl of fresh berries across the counter in my direction. "Picked them up at the farmer's market this morning."

I look at the clock. It's 8 a.m.

"Your mother has already made a lasagna *and* a baked ziti," Sloane says. "I think I'm learning where you get your productivity from."

"Lasagna and baked ziti are basically the same thing," my mom says. "It's not like I made two entirely separate dishes!"

I take a seat at one of the stools next to Sloane and pluck a blueberry from the bowl, trying to casually glance at her screens in my periphery. They are a blur of social media tabs, constantly refreshing themselves. "Is this for dinner tonight?" I ask, watching as my mother squeezes soap into the sink with all the restraint of a toddler making a bubble bath. In seconds it's a frothy mess.

"A few of us have been bringing food over," she says. "To Diana and the kids."

I think about how terrible it must be to have to do the grieving twice. Two rounds of soft voices over the phone and frozen casseroles and police officers with bad news. Two rounds of people staring in the grocery store or hearing your name called at the pharmacy or running into you at the diner and thinking, *That's the sad person.* Be careful around her. You don't want to catch it.

Thinking about Diana makes me panicky. I turn to Sloane, to the safety of action. Doing has always felt better to me than waiting. "So what's going on?"

Sloane also prefers strategy to emotional labor. "We're losing control of the narrative a bit," she says. "On the one hand I can imagine a scenario where we just let it play out. We're in this moment where it's getting a little . . . déclassé to get all worked up about a missing white girl, so maybe it runs its course quickly . . ."

"But on the other hand?"

"On the other hand, this is exactly the kind of ammo the label needs to push back on the record."

My vision goes white at the edges. "You think they'll scrap it entirely?"

"I think they'll say it's not the right time to release something, because it'll be impossible to separate this from the album. And so they'll tell us to take a beat, sit on it for six months or so . . ."

"And then hope the delay makes me reconsider the music." There are a million ways this industry will try to grind you down. "So what do we do?"

"I think our options are limited," Sloane says. "We can't do anything major—we're not sending you on *GMA* to talk about your loss."

"It's not *my* loss," I clarify.

"Dylan," my mother says from her perch at the sink, sloshing soapy water on the floor.

"Mom."

"Don't invalidate it for yourself."

"I can't go on national television and make this *about me*."

"It's a tricky line," Sloane says. "If we want them to stop making everything about you *about* Kelsey, then we need to communicate that you're okay. On the other hand, we can't let them think this hasn't impacted you at all, because that gets at the core of the issue."

Someone on Raconteur had mistaken the way my mascara blurred in the low-quality fuzz of the cell phone camera for proof that I was wearing false eyelashes. *Does this girl look like she's grieving to you?* they commented. *Fake eyelashes? To a funeral?*

Dylan Read was never the Disney princess, another person replied. *She was always the Disney villain.* Picture of Cruella, gif of Maleficent, meme of Snow White's Evil Queen.

The trouble was that I hadn't given them enough of my grief. Either I'd buried my trauma, or else . . . maybe I wasn't grieving at all. A familiar refrain in my career: maybe she's only *pretending* to care.

"So what do we do?" I ask.

"I'm thinking philanthropic," Sloane explains. I make a face: it feels dirty to use charity as damage control. "You know I don't love it either,"

Sloane adds, "but this way, we backdoor into the conversation. We get some local media to cover the initiative, allow them to ask a handful of questions; you keep the focus on the cause but work in how Kelsey inspired you to make the donation, et cetera, et cetera."

I nod. I can see the point of Sloane's game plan: a lightly publicized donation will quickly get picked up on social media, recycled up into the gossip sites and blogs, and eventually make its way into the ether without all the pomp and obvious performance of a major televised appearance.

"We just have to hold their hands a little more," Sloane insists. "Tell them how to feel."

Kelsey's waterlogged notebook comes to me, hidden upstairs beneath my own old journals. Ever since they found her, the story of us has shifted and warped beneath me just the same as that ink bleeding with wetness, the narrative slipping out from under my hands. For years I've worked hard to keep the girl I once was from the professional I've become. But the truth is that no matter how hard we try to obscure our past histories, they always have a way of seeping into the present.

The Divorce Album

There's been a lot of speculation about why I never played with the Wildflowers after 2013. Annie has performed under the name a few times since, with a rotating cast of other female country artists at significant venues—the Grammy Museum, Hall of Fame ceremonies, a revival of Lilith Fair. Sometimes Rachel is there too; sometimes not.

Never Dylan Read.

Anytime women collaborate, people mine for a narrative about cat-fighting or diva behavior, and I think my reputation in particular made the gossip blogs zero in. Stories about good girls are uninteresting; stories about girls only *pretending* to be good—girls who wear their sweet, polite smiles like masks—now *those* sell magazines.

But the boring truth is that Annie's group was a side project. It existed to make a point about women as more than merely the accent vegetables in country radio's salad (as one executive would describe us, later), and in that way it continues to live as a concept more than a singular band. Annie invokes the Wildflowers when she wants to send a message about the plight and potential of women in country, and after *Detour*, I just wasn't a country singer anymore.

In the end, though, it wasn't logic that prevailed over the Wildflowers gossip. The idea that I might be difficult to work with wasn't half as interesting as my divorce.

———

I FLEW TO LA ON A THURSDAY EVENING, LANDING IN A NEON peach sky, whisked from tarmac to freeway to hotel in the ombré of a forever sunset. From my suite balcony I could see the mountains that walled off Sherman Oaks and Studio City from Beverly Hills and West Hollywood, the jagged ridge where Mulholland switchbacked from the 405 all the way to the 101. I was there to spend a few days writing with Niall Hedlund, a long-haired Swede responsible for half the hits of the nineties and aughts, and whose approach to production was mathematical, with an emphasis on melodic tightness and syncopated rhythms. After the year with Annie and Rachel—and Miles too—I felt like Nashville was a closed box that had suddenly run out of oxygen. I was looking for new sounds, fresh ways to approach my work, and I thought Niall might have something to teach me.

The team at Melody humored me. They were used to artists bolting for Bali or Greece to write for a few weeks, seeking a change of scenery like a degreaser for the brain. They understood that musicians acted out on occasion. They were confident that I would come back to them, and in the meantime they could use my stint in LA to have me meet with people they thought I ought to know: film and TV executives; the CEO of a popular skin-care start-up; other young A-listers they wanted me photographed alongside.

I met Lilah Grant at an osteria with a brick-walled courtyard and market lights. Since we'd been seated next to each other at Paris Fashion Week—side by side at Chanel under the vaulted glass roof, oxidized green beams slicing through blue sky—we'd spoken only digitally, a handful of cautious messages in the sterile sans serif of social media. That day at the Grand Palais I'd spent the entire show aware of her body next to mine: how her kneecap squared when she crossed her right leg over her left, angled toward me; how she propped her elbow on her thigh and her chin on her fist, *The Thinker*; just once, I watched her wrap her right arm around her left side, quickly, fingertips against her rib cage, and I knew she was comparing her skeleton to the girls whose pelvic bones poked the floating gauze of their dresses on the runway. Something about our sameness made me territorial, uneasy, as if hanging out with her were its own form of mirror anxiety: I wanted to know; I couldn't bear to look.

When I arrived at the restaurant the seat across from Lilah was already occupied by a man wearing a white T-shirt under a midweight flannel, an intentional scruff groomed around a squared-off jaw. His name, I knew, was Hudson Nash; he'd won an Oscar that winter for a movie about rural Appalachia. In interviews, the director claimed a certain squirrel-eating scene was "one-hundred-percent authentic," and that Hudson had insisted on "really going for it." When Lilah introduced us, I shook his hand and thought about the rodent meat in between his white canines, gamey tendons caught in his beard. He'd been having a drink with a friend when he spotted Lilah, who he knew from a movie several years back, and he'd come over to say hello before he left.

"Why don't you stay for dinner?" Lilah asked, raising her eyebrows in my direction as if to say, *c'mon, be nice.*

"Oh, I don't want to crash your girls' night—"

"Please," I said. "Lilah says this city isn't half as lonely as people make it out to be, and I'd love to hear your take."

"Oh no," Hudson said, sliding into the booth next to Lilah, offering me the chair opposite. "It's the absolute loneliest city. I just happen to like that about it."

I wondered, throughout the night—over lamb ragù, beef carpaccio sliced to translucency, butter lettuce layered like leaves, drizzled with olive oil and lemon juice; Lilah and I only pretended to eat the meats and pastas—whether he and Lilah had already slept together. When she laughed, did she allow her shoulder to bump against his? And when he said something surprising, or charming, or funny, did Lilah touch his forearm like she was laying claim to him? And when we picked over the last of our tiramisu, did she snake her fork through the places his had been on purpose? Meanwhile Hudson told us stories about his work: how he was learning to fly for his new role, and how every time he went up he thought about when he went hiking in Tahoe with his dad and stumbled across the remains of a little prop plane, mossed over and hollowed out like a carcass. His sister climbed inside the plane's belly, searching, while he stood ten feet off shaking with the vague fear of having discovered a crime scene. "It felt sacred, you know?" he said. "Like a gravesite. But there was Jax, feeling around in the stuffing of the cockpit for bones." He laughed. "I should've known she'd end up a venture capitalist."

Watching him across the white-clothed table, I noticed that he slipped in and out of character, chameleoning himself into his stories. It was disorienting, to have a man tell me so much about his family and his childhood and yet to feel like I didn't really understand him at all, that he was as slippery as the fish he tried to pin down in Fallen Leaf, Echo Lake, raking a hand through the creek that crossed the trail up Tallac.

"He's single, you know," Lilah said, her voice low in my ear as we hugged good night. I wondered why she wasn't interested, but then I thought, maybe I don't know her well enough to ask. All the constant strategizing in my life had warped the way I understood my relationships, made me second-guess the difference between a friend and a tactic.

THAT WINTER, I ASKED FOR A GUITAR FOR CHRISTMAS. I BEGGED so intensely that my parents didn't even wait until the holiday—they gave it to me early, just to get me to shut up. Kelsey's guitar was a part of her process; sometimes a lyric grew out of an underlying harmony rather than vice versa. It seemed to me that was what separated a songwriter from a poet: a lyricist worked in tandem with the music, while I only thought about it later. If I was going to be any good, I needed to learn to consider the arrangement too.

But for however badly I wanted my guitar, I was nervous the first time I brought it to school; I felt like I was only pretending to be a music kid, like Amanda Finlay and Emilie Madden, who went to the orchestra room during study hall and told jokes about violas ("Why put your violin in a viola case? Theft protection."). During study hall last period I asked Mrs. Hopkins if I could leave ten minutes early to "get a form signed" by my guidance counselor, and waited outside for Kelsey. It was our standing plan to meet on the corner by the art wing and walk to her house, me mostly listening while Kelsey complained about her day: about how Vice Principal Friedman dress-coded her ("I have long legs and this is how clothing is cut. It's not my fault."); about how Señora de Rosier wouldn't let them do the Spanish version of "Cell Block Tango" from the musical *Chicago* for their Spanish Night performance ("I even said we could cut the sort of breathy *uh-uh* in the underlying rhythm, if it was too obviously a sex noise"); about how Raff didn't even look at her in the cafeteria line ("He can find *someone else* to buy his Doritos"). If the weather was bad and Matt didn't have to work, he'd pick us up and drive us home, arguing with Kelsey about the radio the entire five-minute ride. (Matt: "This is my car, no Mom Music in Matt's Car!" Kelsey: "Tanya Tucker is not *Mom Music*, she's *American Music*, dipshit!") Wedged in the back of Matt's Saab next to Fiona's car seat and the random miscellanea of adolescent manhood—an aerosol can of body spray, a crumpled fast food bag, an empty bottle of Surge; once, a condom wrapper—I felt like their child, an outside observer to their adult chaos. It both did and didn't bother me; most of all, it made me hungrier to prove myself when Kelsey and I would sit down to write.

"Of-fucking-*course* your parents got you a brand-new Gibson," she said that day, grabbing it and lifting it from its case, holding it out at arm's length. She looped it over her shoulder, adjusting it at her hips. "Tell me, what's it like to be loved this much?"

"Your mom loves you," I said weakly.

"Mhmm," Kelsey said, playing with the tuning pegs.

"Can you teach me how to do that?"

Kelsey looked at me, her eyes narrowed slightly. "Okay, but I don't want any of your overachiever bullshit here," she said. "We're gonna learn four chords and six strumming patterns and you're gonna have to trust me when I tell you that's all you need to know."

It wasn't that I didn't trust Kelsey; it was that I felt like a fraud, like even if I could hold my fingers in four positions on the fretboard and manage to shift between them while strumming, it felt like I was faking it. It was as if I'd learned a foreign language by memorizing a series of phrases rather than individual sentences and grammar; I could *borrow* what was given to me, but I could not speak in my own inflection.

Kelsey was impatient with my questions. When I asked for her to explain the difference between a chord and a note, she told me that *notes don't really matter* in guitar. (A chord is a combination of notes.) When I asked how you read music for guitar, then, she said, "Most people use tablature, not typical sheet music."

"And what's a capo do?"

"Changes the key," she explained.

"But shouldn't I be able to do that with my first finger?"

"What is this," Kelsey huffed, "the New York Philharmonic?"

I told her I didn't think there were guitars in professional orchestras.

"Okay, that's it," she said. "I get the Gibson for the afternoon."

So I bought a book and tried to teach myself music theory, but I was easily frustrated—it had too much in common with physics and precalc, a system made of rules that I had to accept without really understanding. I know many musicians say they just *picked up a guitar and taught themselves how to play*—Kelsey was one of them—and that music is supposed to be closer to art than to math, something you feel intuitively rather than something you *solve*, but the ghosts of inadequacy hovered over my shoulder and whispered in my ear. *They'll find you out.* I played until my fingers bled, jagged slices at the tips where the finger pad curves toward the nail.

Sitting in my window seat one afternoon Kelsey watched me apply wound glue in a thick layer across my skin. "It's better to try for fifteen minutes a day than two hours," she said, eyeing me skeptically. "You can't keep shredding them open. You've gotta let the calluses form."

Kelsey's own fingertips were mangled, scars etched into them in hash marks. She had a habit of fiddling with them, running her thumbnail along the grooves absently. It was gritty and gross and also something I desperately wanted for myself, a tangible marker of experience. "I can't stop picking at them anyway," I admitted. "Even if I'm not playing." I peeled off sheaths of my skin in math class, at the dinner table, in bed at night.

"Weirdo," Kelsey said, smiling. "Gimme that."

I held out the wound glue and she grabbed my left hand, flipping it in her palm so my gnarled fingers were exposed. It smelled like nail polish remover, bright and acidic, and after she painted each cut she lifted my fingers close to her lips and blew, lightly, her breath cool on my wet skin.

"No offense, but the pool feels redundant," she said, gazing out the window. "We have a lake."

"It just came with the house," I said, shrugging. She was right, but it wasn't the excess of the pool that made me feel embarrassed: it was that we were the kind of family that preferred a container of crystal-clear water to the murk of Tahawus.

"You ever go skinny-dipping?" Kelsey asked.

I smiled. "What do you think?"

Kelsey grinned. "We go skinny-dipping every summer at camp," she said, staring at the pool. "Once the kids leave on the last day. It's so . . . freeing, I dunno. Being naked in that much water. And at night every-thing seems . . . endless. Suspended."

I lived for these moments, when Kelsey could flip from ironic-detached-jaded to devastatingly earnest, open. "Were you nervous the first time?" I asked.

"Skinny-dipping?" She considered it. "I hadn't shaved."

"Your legs?"

"No, idiot. My vag. Like I just did my bikini line. And I remember seeing when all the older girls stripped down that most of them were fully bare and . . ." She trailed off, smiling a little at her own innocence.

"I was fourteen, I think. Summer before freshman year. I wasn't worried about anyone having to weedwack down there, you know?"

I thought of my own pubic hair. I trimmed the edges in the summertime when I wore a bathing suit, but that was it. I shifted in the window seat, pressing my thighs closer together.

Kelsey's gaze drifted back to the pool, brown leaves settled on the cover for the winter. They would be a soggy pulp by spring. "Raff and I had sex in the water once."

I felt my back tense. I hadn't told her about what I'd heard Raff say to Dan at the drunk-driving assembly. We hadn't really talked about Raff in a couple of weeks; I'd had the impression Kelsey didn't want to, that she was trying to move on. "Oh?"

"In the lake, last summer. On my birthday." She breathed deeply, once, twice, and fiddled with her Gemini necklace, running the charm back and forth along the chain. "I'm sure Steph is too vanilla for that."

I felt a hammering in my chest, as if she'd walked me to the edge of a very high cliff. "You deserve better than him, Kels," I said softly.

She murmured a vague *mm.*

"You deserve someone who doesn't lie about you."

Kelsey's face was flat, perfectly still. When she spoke her voice was absent its usual velvet, her enunciation crystal as the air. "What are you talking about?"

So I told her what I heard Raff say to Dan that afternoon at the drunk-driving demo. *There's a lot of things in a bathroom that you can get creative with.* "I'm sorry I didn't say anything, I just thought it was better to let you—" I stammered. "I thought it would just hurt you."

Kelsey blinked, her face golden in the early evening light. "We fucked," she said.

"I know."

"No, I mean—we didn't—we didn't do anything weird. Not that we haven't, or that I wouldn't, but like—I mean, what would you even use in a bathroom? The opposite end of a toothbrush? Raff thinks his dick is easily mistaken for a toothbrush?"

I didn't know what to say. I didn't know anything. I thought, horribly, of a plunger handle.

"I was drunk," she said. "But not that drunk . . ." She trailed off.

"Kels, I'm sure you remember it right. I'm sure he was lying."

"Why would he lie like that? What's the difference? Is this some Monica Lewinsky cigar bullshit?"

My mother liked to say that the Clinton affair shaped a generation's understanding of sex and power. "We can't pretend," she said, "that learning about a blow job at eight or nine because of reporters talking about a stain on a blue dress didn't impact the way you thought about consent and agency."

"He sucks, Kels," I said finally, an inadequate truth.

I watched her fury blaze in the setting sun.

IN LA I BROUGHT NIALL SCRAPS OF MATERIAL I WROTE ON TOUR, plus ideas the Wildflowers rejected. The songs had the rough shape of a travelogue, collected snapshots stored up in my brain: driving through Arkansas on a tornado-flecked night, lightning dropping from an oyster-colored sky; watching the sunrise over the Smokies, how the mist stretched between the trees and clouds like cobwebs. I wanted to call the record *Crossroads* because I felt as if I was at a crossroads then: five years into a career I still wore like borrowed clothes. The Wildflowers—instead of affirming my sense of belonging—had only further trapped me in amber as the young, unformed artist. I was desperate to find and present a new, more assured version of myself. I was going to make my *Nebraska*, the record that set Springsteen apart as a serious, thoughtful songwriter—not just a raucous, boyish rocker.

The problem was that I was trying to make a new sound using old material. Working with Niall was the opposite of the way we worked in Nashville—in country the writing process is lyrics-first—and he and his producing partner, Lars, would glance at my stowed-away rough drafts only fleetingly before choosing a drum machine, or a blend of hazy synths, and then send me off to redraft the concept to their harmonies. I'd return to my hotel room and write until two or three in the morning, recording voice memos from my bathroom while takeout slowly congealed on the dining table, desperate to make the experiment work.

Ironically, what happened with Hudson Nash defined me more than any of this scheming around the album or my brand identity ever could. I wanted to grow up, and there's nothing more adult than a failed marriage.

IT WAS HUDSON'S IDEA TO DRIVE TO HIS SISTER'S WEDDING.

"If anything," I said, the phone pressed to my ear in my Nashville kitchen, "I thought you would want to fly me in one of your planes."

He'd started collecting them, quickly assembling a tiny fleet of Cessnas and Skippers and Diamond Stars. He kept most of them in an airfield out in San Bernardino, but there were a couple puddle jumpers in the places he visited often: his ranch in Wyoming, his dad's hangar in the Bay Area. (Planes and horses: toys for very rich men.)

"Well, I thought of it," Hudson said on the phone, "but then I realized that would require you to pack light."

So I flew to LA, where Hudson picked me up in a vintage Mercedes, the palest yellow color of maple candy, with cognac leather seats and an interior stereo system updated with the latest Japanese tech. A car made for driving up the 1, he said, and as a joke-but-not-really he played "Bitter Sweet Symphony" as we stretched onto the highway, the water so close I seemed to touch it, dangling my hand outside the window.

He planned the whole route. We stopped in Santa Barbara and climbed up the laddered steps of an aqua-blue lifeguard tower ("From Hudson to Eternity!" the headline read in *Page Six*, alongside a picture of me leaning over the railing to kiss Hudson, barefoot in the sand). In San Luis Obispo live oaks stretched over a cramped main street and I grabbed Hudson's hand and said, "This feels like California saw a New England college town and was like, hey, we want one of those too," and he laughed and shook his head and told me, "You East Coasters are such snobs." ("Hudson Nash and Dylan Read: Taking it not-so-SLO?" asked *The Canyons*.) In San Simeon we pretended to be Daisy and Gatsby on the curved edges of the Hearst Castle pool. (This was the only place the paparazzi didn't follow us, because Hudson knew a Hearst and had the place closed down just for us. "Who's the snob now," I teased.) The highway in Big Sur rode a cliff peeling away from the water, and I said to Hudson, "Do you ever think about how this whole state is just splintering into the ocean?"

"Now you're talking like a Californian," he said, reaching for my hand across the shift and squeezing it tight. I thought of Princess Diana trailed by paparazzi to her death and guided his fingers back to the wheel. "Two hands," I said.

In Carmel, Hudson maneuvered the car through a twisted knot of tiny canopied roads, teetering houses tucked just out of sight beyond ranch gates and gnarled split-rail fencing. In a white plaster estate with moss-green doors we ate oysters and caviar and abalone and I felt, by the time the valet pulled the car around, that I could literally feel the fish swimming in my stomach, a tiny marine world gestating inside me. ("Lovers-by-the-Sea," *XOXO* wrote, with a photo of my head draped on Hudson's shoulder.)

From there the cheap Vegas feel of downtown Monterey, the surfers' pool off the rocks in Santa Cruz, water churning, Hudson telling me stories of coming down here as a kid to watch the competitions, how the swimmers would run off the lower rock ledge, diving straight into the whirlpool. "There's no way to wade in." He shrugged. "And nowhere for the wave to carry you. Every ride ends with bailing." I thought of vacations on Cape Cod and Nantucket, nine years old, knocked over by a four-foot swell, water stinging the back of my throat. Certain, if just for a fleeting second, that I was drowning.

Finally we hooked inland, slicing over the hills between the coast and the valley just like in LA, a narrow two-lane highway bridging water and desert via towering redwoods. Everything all at once in the golden land.

RIGHT BEFORE CHRISTMAS, I WENT WITH KELSEY TO A GIG. EVery December, Camp Tahawus opened its gates for a kind of holiday carnival, transforming the grounds for a weeklong festival of lights. They plowed the snow from the ice by the dock, making space for hockey and skating; they converted a lean-to near the beach into Santa's Workshop; they set up a small tent city along the paths that webbed through the cabins, market lights looped between booths where vendors sold blownglass ornaments and hand-carved nutcrackers and poinsettias wrapped in bright red foil. Children fed carrots to the reindeer through the mesh fence of their pen and amateur home cooks entered the gingerbread house contest; moms came in packs to craft homemade wreaths and beleaguered dads tied six- or eight-foot blue spruces to the tops of their Volvo wagons. The place that smelled like sunblock and bug spray found its air suddenly perfumed with mulled wine and roasted chestnuts, cloves and pine. They pinned a sign over the camp entrance, *TAHAWUS* covered with a red canvas banner: *THE NORTH POLE.*

Most of the camp's buildings remained locked to guests, but you could seek refuge from the cold in the cafeteria, where local businesses sold cookies and glass bottles of eggnog and craft beer and whiskey while bands played live music. Kelsey had an in because of her work at camp; the organizers would pay her a hundred dollars to perform, as long as she promised to "dress festively" and play "holiday music."

"Do you think it's a risk to do 'Hard Candy Christmas'?" Kelsey asked that Saturday evening, standing in front of her full-length mirror and wriggling into an emerald-green brocade jumpsuit, an empire-waisted seam wreathed with feathers. She was more nervous than I expected; she loved Tahawus, spent all summer playing guitar around its fires, leading packs of fifth graders two by two through the woods, filling the hours of a long hike with songs. "Can you come zip for me?"

I tried not to look at the black lace bra she wore as I slid the zipper up her back. "I mean, there are only, like, seven or eight Christmas songs everybody knows, right?" I said. "And you're the middle act tonight?"

Kelsey nodded, twisting slowly to the left and right, studying her angles in the mirror: the crux of her hip, the slope of her abdomen.

"Nobody wants George Michael on loop for three hours."

"Actually," Kelsey said, "they might."

"Okay, maybe. But sometimes people need to be told what they want, right? You always say that."

Kelsey smiled at me. With her index finger she tapped gently on the tip of my nose. "You're such a good little student," she said. "So I'm gonna do it third, then give 'em a couple more go-tos, but in the sad-Christmas vein—"

I nodded. "And then do 'Evergreen.'" It was the one original song we'd written for the show; I'd spent the previous week tweaking the lyrics obsessively, finessing the story of a tree-cutting into crystalline detail.

Kelsey hummed a little. *I had the best time playin' at timelessness with you.* "It's really good, Dylan," she said.

When she played it later that night, I had that feeling I always had when I wrote for Kelsey, that I was writing for her voice, leaning into vowel sounds meant for her brassy delivery, searching for the images that deepened in the luster of her slightly nasal vibrato—*sippin' brandy under dusted pines, giving thanks for some other kinda divine*—those long *eyes*, the drawled *ands*. Sitting alone at a table off to the side, nursing a hot chocolate gone cold and syrupy sweet, I felt like I'd slipped into her veins, put on the costume of her.

"She's good, isn't she?" The voice over my shoulder sounded like a 1930s movie star: in just four words, you could sense the practiced elocution, the lessons in enunciation. The woman behind me was in her seventies or eighties, small-boned and birdlike, with silver-white hair in a shoulder-length bob. She wore a black turtleneck underneath a Black Watch plaid suit, like some sort of punk-rock WASP. "These songs she's doing have a slightly different feel," she said next, "than what she usually does."

"Do you know each other?" I asked.

The woman smiled at me and extended a hand in my direction. "Adeline Coyne," she said. "I'm the president of the board here at Tahawus."

I shook her hand. "Dylan. Kelsey's friend. I—we've been writing together."

"Ah." Adeline nodded slowly. "Well, Art Garfunkel needed Paul Simon, didn't he?"

Before I had a chance to respond, she'd moved on, into the crowd, a host working her guests.

Later, Kelsey and I walked among the stalls, fingering taffeta ribbons and cinnamon-dusted pine cones, thirty-seven dollars in tips split among our pockets. Kelsey sipped coffee spiked with bourbon from the distillery and told me about Tahawus, pointing to the most popular bunkhouse (Macomb, because it was farthest away from the staff cabins and closest to the water); the hardest part of the ropes course; her favorite hiding spot for the scavenger hunt, in the hollow of a long-dead pine. She was a good tour guide, blending history with personal anecdote, navigating easily between the camp's origins as a tuberculosis sanitorium and its present-day iteration. Tahawus was built in the late nineteenth century, she told me, when the preeminent prescription for TB was simply "fresh air." Patients were instructed to spend as long as possible sitting outside, purifying their ravaged and bleeding lungs.

"Did you know TB is still one of the deadliest infectious diseases?" she said.

I didn't.

"Yeah, it's wild. The scientists who built this facility also founded a research center, and it's still one of the best TB labs in the world. That's what this is for." She gestured widely. "The North Pole. It's a fundraiser for the institute."

"I was wondering why the camp needed the money," I said. I knew how much Tahawus cost, and how well Kelsey was paid for her summers there. "It all makes much more sense now that I know it's for the *lab*."

Kelsey laughed. "Seriously. Have you *seen* the parents who send their kids here?"

"I *did* meet your board president," I told her. "Mrs. Coyne?"

"Oh—she's the shit, right?"

"She thinks you have real talent."

I watched the compliment land on Kelsey, how she blinked an extra time and hid her smile behind a hurried pull on her drink. It occurred to me that this didn't happen very much for her: Diana was overworked, and her parenting was mainly preoccupied with making sure everyone's basic needs were met; at school, most of the teachers saw Kelsey as an underachiever and carried a low-key resentment for the determined way her interests lay elsewhere.

Kelsey swallowed. "Duh," she said then, and nudged her hip into mine. "C'mon, let's go get a refill before Matt's done."

Matt was playing in a three-on-three hockey tournament out on the lake. I wanted to go watch, but Kelsey had no interest in "a bunch of sad-sack dads pretending they're good enough to play in the NHL." I suspected that what she really meant was that she didn't want to run into Raff and his friends.

The cafeteria was hot and full by then, a sea of Fair Isle sweaters and flannel button-downs, couples linked at the hips, cheeks red and eyes shining. "Nice set," a man said to Kelsey as he passed behind us, three drinks in two hands, a Santa hat cockeyed on his head. She smiled at him in a strained but polite way, and he leaned closer to her and winked. "I don't just mean the music." Kelsey's face flickered for only a millisecond, the tiniest twitch at the edges. He tipped his chin at me, and Kelsey finished the last of her coffee, tilting her head back to catch the remaining drops.

At a high-top near the front-left of the stage, a trio of men—jeans half tucked into Bean boots, one in a fur-edged bomber hat, the ear covers flapping lazily—huddled together over their table, working furtively, intermittently puncturing the room with a loud burst of deep laughter. The cafeteria pulsed with a kind of snapping energy, an uneven heartbeat. I turned to Kelsey, nudging her gently in the side. "Should we go?"

The men turned from their tabletop to the stage, where a group of women in Rockettes-style outfits kicklined to Brenda Lee. As the dancers moved into a triangle formation, the man with the bomber hat held a paper plate aloft, scrawled with a single number in jagged ballpoint pen. "Six! This one's a six!"

His friends laughed, their eyes squinting. Kelsey's jaw flexed. The dancer kept her chin out, straightened her back. They shifted formation, a laddered shuffle. A thin woman with blond hair twisted into a chignon took the lead.

Bomber Hat's friend held two plates up, seven and five. "Seven-point-five!"

"Is someone gonna say something?" I whispered to Kelsey. I searched the room for the woman in the plaid suit—surely she wouldn't let this happen—but she was nowhere to be found.

"This one's a nine, folks!" Bomber Hat yelled, twisting the six upside down, food grease gleaming in the light. I looked to the dancer: tall, with a long torso and a tiny waist, flat-stomached but with boobs and a butt.

Kelsey had the same closed-off look she did in my bedroom when I told her about Raff and Dan. She swallowed, then knocked her chin up in the direction of the dancer, gesturing. "The nine can," she said.

I watched her for a moment, the way her whole body had gone hard and armored. This was her entire worldview, I understood. Men had to give you power before you could use it against them.

THE HOUSE OUT ON ATHERTON AVE WAS NOT THE ONE HUD-son grew up in, he told me. His family moved from downtown Palo Alto to the wide boulevard that stretches from El Camino to Alameda when he was in his twenties. "My sister was more upset about it than I was," he told me, guiding the Mercedes past Italianate villas and turreted Victorians and sprawling craftsmans.

"Eclectic," I said, a forearm resting on the downed window.

"I think the word you're looking for," he said, turning the car into a gated driveway, the home shielded from view by tall boxwood hedges, "is 'rich.'"

Jax—despite not approving of the move initially—was married in the backyard of the new family home, wooden folding chairs leafed with eucalyptus in the shadows of the stately white French-country-style estate with its smoke-blue shutters and its fog-brindle shingles. She emerged from the pool house wearing a gown of lightly crinkled taffeta, dusted with arrowheads of beading, her dark hair in a sleek bun, and—sitting in the second row, behind the grandparents and next to an aunt and uncle from Connecticut who had the WASPy capacity to make conversation with absolutely anyone—I thought about how exactly *right* she looked, as if she was fulfilling a prophecy handed down at birth. Hudson and I made eye contact as Jax and her husband said their vows, and when he fumbled handing the rings to his sister his aunt leaned into me and whispered in my ear, "He'd lose his head if it weren't attached to his body." My chest ballooned with tenderness.

At dinner I was seated between Hudson and his father, Henry, who spoke very softly and had deeply tanned, weather-worn skin. I tried to sneak glances at him when he wasn't looking, searching for Hudson in the slope of his ear, the hunch of the shoulders. Hudson touched me through most of the meal: an arm draped over my shoulder; a hand on my upper thigh. I worried that his father would see the hand on my thigh and think I was a slut, easy, good in bed. I cycled through emotions: at first embarrassed; then, conversely, proud that a man wanted to lay claim to me in public—and then deeply ashamed again, appalled by the smallness of my own self-worth. I grabbed Hudson's hand on top of my leg and squeezed it tighter, reminding myself of the fact of it. Nobody asked me about my music, and I felt lighter for their indifference.

After we danced—after Hudson lost his speech and had to deliver an improvised version on the spot; after Hudson and I fucked in the guest room, his hand over my mouth to silence my orgasm; after I found Jax in the bathroom, trying to salvage her updo, and gently pressed her bobby pins back into place at the nape of her neck; after Henry asked for a dance, and let his hand slip below the small of my back just barely onto the curve of the top of my ass—Hudson and I made our way to the edge of the pool, where we sat with our feet dangling in the water as the party wound to a close.

"I wish Jax had gotten married at the Tahoe house," Hudson said, gazing up at the mansion in front of us, glowing amber.

"Why?" I asked.

"You can't see the stars here," he said, and I followed his gaze upward, where the Bay Area light pollution glowed at the edges of the sky like a vignette. "In Tahoe you can see the Milky Way."

I didn't tell Hudson that I knew stars like that, clinging together in whorls in a rural sky over a midnight-black lake, an afterimage of starlings in flight, collapsing and expanding as one glittering net. Instead I said: "Well, now you can get married there."

Hudson tilted his head toward me, a question knit in the furrow of his brow. He was ten years older than me but wore certain expressions with a boyishness that felt almost playful. I realized what I'd said—how I'd tossed the word "married" between us like a ticking bomb—but when I figured out my mistake I didn't feel embarrassed. Maybe it was the Scotch Henry'd been pouring with a heavy hand all night, but it didn't feel like a naive stumble. It felt, a little bit, like a provocation.

"Is that something you want?" Hudson asked. "To get married?"

"Do you mean generally?"

Hudson grinned. "What if I meant specifically?"

"STATELINE" IS THE STORY OF OUR MARRIAGE: THE MIDNIGHT flight from the private airfield in Palo Alto over Stateline, up through the purple-orange clouds and over the long black stretch of the Sierras and down into Nevada; the all-night chapel in the white A-frame and, after, the grocery-store champagne on the lake; the casino hotel where we fell asleep on top of the polyester bedspread, finally, properly wasted; the morning calls from our publicists, because of course someone at the chapel or the grocery store saw their chance for a six-figure paycheck; how differently shaped our shame was—the meticulously tended garden of my perfection obliterated in a single storm while Hudson's reputation as an irascible playboy was only further underlined, married (and soon to be divorced) twice now before he turned thirty-four. The sober, serious way our handlers reminded us that—even if this *was* something we wanted to do—we were not the kind of people who could get married without first lawyering up. *Your golden state, my bright young mind / A wedding day, not yours or mine / We raised the stakes, stopped pushin' time / Made a real big mess when we crossed that line.*

A lot of the music I wrote in the wake of that trip—*bein' with you's four-corner smoke at a western crossroads, July fires burnin' 'til my eyes run; cashier sells me a crystal and a dream catcher, says to bury one and hang the other / prayer sounds a lot like death out here, in a too-dry desert summer*—I could hear in a country vein. There's a long tradition of country divorce albums, dating back to Tammy Wynette's *D-I-V-O-R-C-E*, and I felt myself dancing along the edges of the trope. But it wasn't until I gave Sam the "Stateline" demo that I understood it wasn't right for the record, not one hundred percent. The mix Sam sent back had a kind of forlorn, neon honky-tonk vibe, heavy on the pedal steel, with plenty of *space*—like a glittering, feminine Willie Nelson. It was a portrait of a woman worn down by regret, enchanting in the waste of her mistakes.

But I had no intention of playing the part of the beautiful, damaged girl. I was embarrassed by my marriage, and my impulsivity, and sorry that I'd caused my label so much trouble—but I was also tired of feeling guilty. I wanted to make music that was good because it was *honest*, not because it was duly apologetic.

So I brought it to Niall. Together we made "Stateline" the cornerstone of a record that reframed my marriage as a town I was just passing through, with a crossover feel that suited the metaphorical travel—from one experience to another, from one sound to the next. Niall's initial "Stateline" production was less melancholy than what Sam drafted and more tense—like a Leonard Cohen record from the eighties, or "In the Air Tonight," or *Tunnel of Love*. There was less resolution to the writing, and Niall created in the mix the same push-pull I wrote into the lyrics. I was sorry to have left Sam behind, but I knew when I heard the first "Stateline" demo that I'd made the right choice. I was somebody new now, someone whose regrets didn't burden her so much as they made her wiser.

I played it live for the first time on *Ted Tonight!*, the week *Detour* was released. I worried that something so serious was wrong, tonally, for a comedic late-night show, but I also knew that I didn't have to play it straight, not one hundred percent. I practiced a pause after the bridge, a sly smirk, braiding the performance through with some knowing. I knew I was reopening the tabloid discourse, the tail of which had been far longer than our forty-eight-hour marriage, but I also knew that it was my chance to reclaim a narrative that had felt out of my control.

In the greenroom I twisted a Q-tip in my ear, used another one to dab gently at the corners of my eyes. In the seat next to my station a young man with medium-length brown hair and deep-set eyes fiddled with a book in his lap, running his hands across the matte cover. He caught my eye once, then twice in the mirror, a small slip of a smile flickering quickly.

"Congratulations," I said to his reflection, turning with the Q-tip in my hand, nodding my chin in the direction of his novel, *NICK DEVLIN* in large font across the bottom. The book was everywhere, glowing reviews followed by lengthy profiles, development deals splashed across

Deadline. A blistering indictment of the constraints of masculinity. The book about male friendship we've been waiting for: compassionate, tender, earnest. BOYS DO CRY: A NEW KIND OF MALE CHARACTER.

"Thanks," he said, and I couldn't help grinning: the hard cluck of the *k-s* noise at the end of his word, the clipped vowels.

"So you really are Irish, huh?" I said.

When he smiled he looked away, toward his lap, as if there were nothing more embarrassing than pleasure. "Guilty," he said.

"Is this your first time in LA?"

Nick nodded.

"How do you like it so far?"

"It's, ah—friendly?"

I laughed.

"You don't live here, do you?" He said *do you* in a blended way, *d'ya?* "Sorry," he added. "It's—"

I waved him off. "You get used to people knowing where you live," I said. "It's only creepy when they break in and shower in your bathroom."

He winced. "Fuck," he said.

"Sorry, too much?" I laughed, suddenly nervous. I found myself wondering what Nick thought about my divorced status. Did he care? Would he ask me about it?

"No, I just—it must be hard," he said.

"Well," I said, gently coaxing a lock of hair at the top of my head into place. "Nothing more annoying than complaining about fame."

Nick frowned. "I had to stop tweeting because I had a panic attack every time I hit post," he said. "And I only had, like, eleven thousand followers." He paused. "It just gets so noisy, you know?"

I knew exactly. It was normal to complain about the trappings of celebrity among my famous friends: the security breaches, the stalkers, the constancy of it, the always-on-camera-ness; the lost pleasures of the grocery store, wandering the aisles of Target, going for a walk. But this was different. Here was someone who understood how a writer's brain is her most important asset, how the work requires the material to spin on a low murmur in the background constantly, and what a loss it is—a death knell, really—when you find yourself straining to hear.

A PA appeared over our shoulders in the mirror, visibly anxious. "Mr. Devlin," she said, "it's time?"

He smiled at me. "It was nice to meet you, Dylan," he said. "Hope you find a way to keep it quiet."

"You too," I said, and I watched as he looked back over his shoulder once more on his way out, the quickest glance, his book hooked in his fist like a passport.

MATT WAS SUPPOSED TO DRIVE US HOME FROM THE NORTH Pole. As the night dwindled, Kelsey and I made our way to one of the firepits near the water and huddled around the flames with a few of our classmates—Bridget Neary, Alyssa Alonge, Kelly Corona—who passed a flask between them and heckled the boys on the ice intermittently. I watched through the smoke as Kelsey stole glances at Raff, his helmet tossed aside, cheeks flushed with effort. A little after midnight, as the volunteers came through and made half-hearted attempts to clear out the stragglers and the hockey players started packing up their gear, Kelsey stood to go to the bathroom. While she was gone I watched Matt skate in a loping, casual way, dragging the nets together and tying them up. He'd abandoned his gloves for the job and I watched as he brought his hands to his mouth, blowing to warm his fingers.

He changed out of his skates on the ice, slung his bag over his shoulder, and walked up to me at the fire, stick in one hand. "You guys ready?"

"Um." I paused. "Kelsey just went to the bathroom." In reality, she'd been gone more than fifteen minutes. It occurred to me I hadn't seen Raff in at least ten.

"Okay," Matt said. "I'll be in the car."

I nodded and texted Kelsey—hey, u ready to go?—and then waited five more minutes for a response I knew wouldn't come. Kelsey was notoriously terrible with her phone. She probably hadn't even brought it with her. I would need to find her myself.

I checked the bathrooms first—just a few girls with eyeliner trailing down their cheeks—and then the cafeteria (empty by then, only a handful of volunteers picking trash from the tables and pulling down long vines of twinkle lights). By the time I started for the cabins I knew where she'd gone. At Macomb I made my way around the side and stood on tiptoe to peer up through the window, a crack of frost spidering up the glass. When I saw Raff's head between Kelsey's legs on the lower bunk I didn't immediately look away. Kelsey's back was slightly arched, her skin milky in the moonlight, one long arm extended so that her hand gripped the back of his head, fingers clawing at his scalp. It looked as if she were devouring him.

Matt's Saab was one of the last cars in the Tahawus parking lot, idling a cloud of exhaust into the cold, empty air. "Where's Kelsey?" he asked as I climbed in the passenger side.

"She's getting a ride with someone else," I said.

Matt rolled his eyes. "Did that someone else get so drunk he slammed his chin into the goalpost tonight?"

Raff had lost control on a breakaway, curved away from the goal too late, slipped, and caught his chin on the corner. He lay on the ice for minutes, laughing to cover what was surely going to hurt like hell tomorrow.

I smiled at Matt but didn't answer his question. He shifted the car into reverse and pulled out onto the lake road, the twisting two-lane stretch that hugs the water's edge all the way around.

"Did you have fun?" Matt asked.

"I guess."

I felt Matt look at me across the center armrest. "Don't take it person-ally," he said.

"What?"

"Kelsey. Running off with a guy."

"I know it has nothing to do with me," I snapped. Matt raised his eye-brows, a universal recoil for *yikes*. We drove in silence for a while, and in my head I tried on different explanations: *I wish I was enough for her. I wish she found validation in other places. I wish I knew what that felt like, a mouth on me like that. I wish I could even picture myself trying it.* I closed my eyes and saw her again, her thighs wrapped around Raff's head like a vise.

"Look, nothing against my sister," Matt said, "but high school guys are idiots. I know from personal experience. You should be proud that you're not back there with one right now."

I didn't want Matt's pity. I only felt smaller, more childish. "I just feel . . . behind," I said.

Matt laughed a little, softly. "Well, better behind than with a kid at nineteen," he said. "Not that I would trade Fiona."

At Fiona's name I paused, curious but uncertain of the boundaries. "Is she going to Florida for Christmas?" I asked.

Matt shook his head. "We agreed that it would be too disruptive for her. She's never even spent a night with Billie."

I nodded. Matt wore his flannel cuffed and scrunched up to the el-bows, and I noticed how his forearms flexed as he gripped the wheel. "Did you love her?" I asked softly. "Billie, I mean."

Matt thought for a moment. "No," he said, and then: "Well, I don't know. I think it felt like love to me then."

"What do you mean?"

Matt considered this as he turned into my driveway, porch light glowing. "I think what I wanted most of all was a way to define myself. I was really, intensely mediocre. Not smart, but not ballsy enough to be a total stoner deadbeat. Dating Billie gave me something to be." He paused and leaned across the console, resting his palm just above my knee. It was heavy and warm on my bare skin. "You're lucky. You know who you are. I didn't. Neither does Kelsey."

"That is exactly the opposite of the way I would describe it," I said, staring at my parents' house. "Kelsey is specific. I'm like . . ." I thought of the little sand tray my mom had in her office, electrically charged grains that molded like something between dirt and clay. "I feel like kinetic sand," I said.

Matt tried to catch his laugh, choking on it slightly. "*That* is a metaphor only a writer would come up with," he said. He gave my leg a quick pat and put his palm back in his lap. His eyes were black in the darkness, catching the spark of our front light like a tiny ember.

I reached for his hand and led it, quickly, back to my leg, this time placing it at my mid-thigh, more to the inside, where the muscle curves gently. "You can keep your hand there," I said. He watched me, unblinking. I saw him swallow, the rolling wave of his Adam's apple. My hand still on top of his, I guided his palm up higher, pushing beneath my skirt to the top of my inner thigh. I didn't breathe.

"Dylan," he whispered, our hands still linked.

"I want you to," I said. "I want to know what it feels like."

He moved his hand underneath mine. His thumb grazed the edge of my underwear, the slightest dancing along the softest part of me. Something in me flexed, tightened. "Please," I whispered.

And then he pulled his hand from me, moving it to the top of the Saab's shifter. "I can't, Dylan."

"Guess I am just a kid to you," I said then, and as I unbuckled and opened the door I added, "but you know what? I'd rather be a virgin than a total fuckdoll like your sister." The metallic slamming echoed in the still night, a random ripple in a glass suburbia.

I READ MY REVIEWS. MOST ARTISTS WOULD ADVISE AGAINST this—to read the criticism is to let it in, and you'll find that you start creating in response to it. I think this is good advice if you only want to make art. I think that if you want to build a career, you have to know what they're saying about you.

Plus: I wanted to know what they thought of my version of the story.

On her previous solo records, Read demonstrated a knack for coloring inside country music's well-defined lines, Pitchfork wrote alongside a near-perfect 9.5. *What* Detour *makes clear is that this is an artist whose creative ambition has outgrown Music Row.*

The writing on Dylan Read's third solo album is as incisive as ever, Rolling Stone said, *but there is an inquisitive, curious stance to the songs on* Detour *that separates them from the resolution of a country record, and an overall intensity that belies her genre of origin.*

Dylan Read's made a name for herself as a writer capable of wrangling messy emotions with inimitable clarity and precision, the *Times* opined. *It seems now she has finally had the life experiences worthy of her sharp pen—and discovered the production sensibilities to match.*

They described the album as *a departure.* A pivot. A shift.

Maybe they just felt like it was tacky or lowbrow to zero in on the inspiration behind the record. Maybe they, too, were speaking in metaphor. Either way, all the reviews homed in on one thing: I wasn't just divorced from Hudson; I was divorcing myself from Nashville too.

On the day they announced the Grammy nominations, I woke up at 4 a.m. and spent three hours making a cake and another hour cleaning up the mess I made in my Nashville kitchen. It wasn't for celebrating; it was a distraction tactic, an elaborate coping mechanism. I didn't realize I had spilled batter on my phone until the publicist from Melody called and I smeared it in a streak across the unlock button.

"So we'll see what happens with Country," Mara began, "but in the major categories . . . it looks like *Detour* is not nominated."

All of my senses tunneled on Mara's voice on the other end of the line. I gripped the phone as if my hands could change the information on its way between her and me. "But the reviews," I said stupidly.

"I know. We can't believe it either."

"I won't be nominated in Country," I added, not that it mattered. Everyone knows the genre categories are consolation prizes.

Mara was quiet on her end of the line. "Probably not," she conceded, after a beat.

My insides went slick with shame. "It's not because it sounds too pop," I clarified. Pop-adjacent country records won Country Grammys all the time.

"Right," Mara said.

I thought it was only Nashville—a conservative town with Christian values and a deep pride in its power couples—that would care about my fuckup, but I was wrong. *Detour* was a terrific, critically acclaimed record. There was only one reason I didn't get a Grammy nod, and it was because I was a twenty-four-year-old girl who made a divorce album about her two-day marriage.

I thought I already knew that I couldn't afford to make mistakes, but I guess you need to learn some lessons more than once. Regardless, the day *Detour* didn't get a Grammy nomination was the day I decided I would never be foolish, or reckless, or impulsive ever again.

My appearances are negotiated. Not just when and where and for how long, but what sort of questions are permissible and whether I'll sign autographs and what kind of snacks and drinks should be on hand and how much small talk I'll make and whether photographs are allowed and if so by whom (e.g., press only) and in what context (e.g., posed versus candid) and, also, most importantly, what kind of security is available.

Accounting for the details is Sloane's responsibility. Knowing that they may not all materialize—that there might be surprises, that someone will sneak a video on their phone even if we explicitly said no filming, that a reporter will ask a question not on the approved list (or, more likely, they will manipulate a question on the approved list to insinuate or imply something else), that I will get stuck taking selfies with fans because they will ask and I feel bad saying no—this is my job. I handle the curveballs in real time.

We arrive at Thompson High in our small convoy: two SUVs, me and Sloane in one; my makeup artist, Lucie, and my stylist, Joe, in another. My security detail divides itself between the two vehicles. When we pull up to the building, a small corps of local news outlets is already assembled in the high school's looped driveway. We wave to them as we walk in, me at the center of my team's square formation, arm extended high into the air, gesturing over the fence of their bodies.

Principal Gleason is waiting for us inside, along with her own small entourage: the superintendent Mr. McFadden and a handful of school board members.

Look at these fucking suits, Kelsey says. *I guarantee McFadden hasn't listened to a new song since 1953.*

That's probably the year he was born.

Exactly.

"We're really so grateful for your contribution, Dylan," Gleason says.

My contribution: three-quarters of a million dollars, divided across two separate funds, one to endow a scholarship in Kelsey's name for a graduating senior who plans to continue their music studies in college; another to finance a program called, tentatively, New Voices—an advanced-study opportunity for seniors in music and the performing arts. When I was at Thompson, a small cohort of students with premed aspirations was selected each year for a program that allowed them to miss their morning classes to shadow researchers and physicians at the local hospitals. Now there will be something similar for students in the arts.

"I'm just sorry Kelsey didn't have an opportunity like this one," I say, "and glad that we can help to create it for future Thompson students."

Gleason smiles in a confused sort of way, and I realize that she didn't think we were already talking in sound bites. I grin, reach out a hand, and touch her elbow gently. "I was wondering if we could walk the long way to the auditorium, past my old locker?"

Gleason's shoulders melt. "Of course," she breathes, and together we lead the group down the English wing, chatting softly: about Mrs. Hopkins's old classroom (she's retired now); the staircase where Gina Smith broke her arm skateboarding my freshman year; the whiteboard outside Mr. Eisenhardt's room, victim to so many cartoon penises that, eventually, the image was burned into the surface, like a tube TV left on too long. I talk about learning to write poetry in Ms. Twyman's class, about a

Renaissance newspaper project we did in honors humanities, about the time I made a quilt for American history.

Ahead of us, Kelsey echoes a familiar guitar riff. *Ba-da-da-dum, ba-da-da-dum.*

I roll my eyes at her.

I had a friend was a big baseball player back in hi-igh school . . .

Shut up. I know what I'm doing.

The longer we walk, the more at ease Gleason seems. The power dynamic between us shifts, just slightly. She feels she has something to offer here: this is where we put the new computer classroom, these are the new smartboards we've added; as you can see, we redid the cubbies in the studio wing, no more portfolios all over—well, in theory at least. I'm glad to see her relax; the more comfortable she feels, the more seamlessly this will go. While most of the interview questions will be directed at me, she will stand in frame the entire time, so that the optics send a clear message: this is about the school, this is about educational programming; this is not—to the extent that such a thing is possible—a feature on Dylan Read.

I follow Gleason into the auditorium through the backstage entrance, the sounds of a small crowd muffled by layers of curtain. My fingers trail along the velvet, heavy, dust-cloaked, before I emerge on the platform and give a wave to the crew. "Hey, everybody!"

"Dylan!" In just two syllables I can detect the honeyed quality of a news anchor's voice, like an aural Xanax. Julia McCord is in her midfifties, with light brown skin and a smattering of freckles across her nose and cheekbones. Sloane chose her, in part, because she does a segment called Women of the Week, profiling various women in the community for their professional or charitable pursuits. I remember watching Julia on the morning news when I was in sixth and seventh grade, school closings scrolling below the chyron. It makes me sad in an abstract kind of way that she never made it out of local news. I imagine that no one dreams of spending their entire career at a midsize metro. I imagine that she wanted to be on *Today*.

Julia's hand is smooth and soft, her grip firm. "Thank you for sharing this initiative with us."

"Of course," I say. "I'm glad to see our community coming together in this moment." I know that the interview begins long before the cameras roll or the recorder gets turned on—that a good journalist starts framing her story the moment she lays eyes on you. That's why so many articles about me begin with what I'm wearing.

(Today: a black pantsuit in a textured bouclé with pointed-toe patent Louboutins. An outfit that will be shot sitting, standing, and walking is among the hardest sartorial assignments; weirdly, red carpet dressing is easiest—there's never a question about tone, and no one ever notices if a gown looks like a deflated tent when seated.)

Sloane swoops in, begins directing. "So we'll do a few minutes seated, then shoot some walk-and-talks, then do any additional questions standing onstage. Let's take a few minutes to set hair and makeup and we'll get going in ten?"

Julia agrees; Gleason nods; Joe and Lucie swoop in, a new pair of earrings in Joe's hands, Lucie aiming a powder brush at my T-zone. I'm aware of Gleason watching, consider offering my team to her, but it's a hard thing to do tactfully. I whisper in Lucie's ear—"Maybe you can delicately see if she'd like any touch-ups?"—and a minute later Gleason is nervously demurring in the way you do when you feel like you're *supposed to* decline: *oh, I couldn't, I'm all right, really, if you're sure?* And then Lucie has her knuckles under Gleason's chin, painting charcoal on her waterline while my old principal gazes skyward. When Lucie's done I watch how Gleason holds herself a little differently, shoulders back, chin pointed slightly up.

That was weirdly nice of you, Kelsey says, seated sideways in one of the auditorium chairs, her legs dangling over the armrest.

It's not easy to be televised next to me.

Bah! Do we think you're actually pretty, though, or just rich-pretty?

Fuck off.

Someone sets up a table and a trio of chairs, angled around one corner so that all three of us can face one another and the camera. We sit, adjust the lighting, Lucie rushes in for one last touch-up, untucking a piece of hair by my ear, and then Julia is asking me to explain New Voices to her with the cameras on, and I'm delivering a quick spiel Sloane worked up this morning: "Because a career in music shouldn't feel like a moon shot."

"Well, a career like *yours* might be one in a million," Julia says.

I drop my chin and smile in an *aw shucks* kind of way before slowly lifting my face to the camera again. "Yes, and while the truth is that I work very hard, I've also been lucky, and had resources and opportunities that are not available to everyone. I hope that New Voices can be one of those support systems for young artists here in Thompson Landing, not just in terms of opening doors for student musicians, but also in terms of broadening their understanding of the industry and the kinds of roles available. You can have a long, successful career as a sound engineer, as a producer, as a writer; you can work in film and TV; you can teach! There are so many ways to design a life around your creativity, but for some reason we internalize this idea that the only way is"—here I gesture up and down at myself, at my body—"this."

Once you have the thing everybody wants, it's very easy to say that something less might still have been enough. I know that I don't really mean it, that I only *wish* I meant it. Wouldn't it be nice, I think, to believe that I could be satisfied with anything less?

"That's a lovely sentiment. And so true," Julia's saying. "Now, you've endowed this program and a scholarship in the name of your friend Kelsey Copestenke. Do you think that's something Kelsey felt?"

"That a career in music wasn't really an option for her?"

Julia nods. I glance across the auditorium, to a row of empty seats to the left of the cadre of crew and print journalists, the school board, my team. Kelsey is dangling upside down in her chair now, hair spilling toward the ground, feet kicked over the back. *Don't look at me. You're the one who made me into a charity case.*

"Actually," I say, "Kelsey was ferociously ambitious. Principal Gleason might not remember that about her because her ambition didn't always manifest in, say, completing her history papers on time"—I nudge Gleason in the side, playing at chummy; she grins, laughs a little—"but she played her guitar every day. She carried a tape recorder with her—this was before everyone had an iPhone—at all times, so she could catch little snippets of song as they came. I think Kelsey believed in her own talent, and *that's* why I wanted to establish this program: to help every student find that faith in themselves."

Thanks for not calling me "poor" on TV, Kelsey says from the seats.

Not my first question-dodging rodeo.

Julia redirects to Gleason. She asks how they plan to select students for New Voices ("students will apply, and entry will be determined by committee, based on a combination of factors: GPA, community engagement, teacher recommendation, an audition or portfolio"); which partnerships they have lined up for the on-sites ("these are still coming together, but to begin with we're partnering with the state university and Alderidge, the small liberal-arts college thirty minutes south of Thompson, and Dylan has offered to put us in touch with some producers in Nashville who can volunteer their time remotely"); how they'll determine the recipient of the Kelsey Copestenke Memorial Scholarship from among the students in the New Voices program. Gleason talks about how they hope my initial investment will spur additional contributions, and that with the school board's support they can expand the resources available to Thompson students on campus. New lockers for the instruments, new acoustic paneling—a recording studio, even!

"That would be an extraordinary resource," Julia says. Gleason nods. "And you mentioned Alderidge before—did you know they have a recording studio?"

Gleason tilts her head slightly skyward, contemplative. "I'm not sure . . ."

"They do," Julia says. "In fact, we found an old demo Kelsey and Dylan made when they were in high school with the help of a professor there."

All the tenderness I feel toward Julia evaporates. I've spent more than a decade shifting the focus from the relationships that defined my past, battling a media that only ever wants to distract from my work.

"Wow," I say finally. "I didn't think we saved anything that day." And that's true: Kelsey was just testing the booth. I didn't know anyone kept the recording.

"Can we play it for you?" Julia asks.

Across from me, Sloane's face is frozen, a mix of fury and panic. The entire point of this was to give the internet *less* chum to frenzy around.

"Of course," I say. "Please."

Julia motions one of her producers over. He hands her his phone; I can see an audio file queued up. Julia holds the screen out between us, face up, and presses play.

The sound is better than I expected, crisper. You hear my voice around thirty seconds, coming in high and light under Kelsey, just enough to give her sound body, a choral effect. I am not actually trying to "harmonize," in the technical sense of the word—when this was made, I didn't even know what that word really meant, nor did I have enough vocal control to do it. I'm just singing along.

Most of the time I'm embarrassed by my voice on my early albums—the yell-y vocals, the vowels forced up through the nose, the cracking. I've internalized all the things they wrote about me, all the criticism that seemed both fair and not. Right now, though, I'm not embarrassed. My heart bursts: I feel it swell, balloon in my chest, choking out the bottom of my throat, and then just as suddenly I feel hollowed out, cracked into a million pieces. Some part of me always wondered whether I had Kelsey right. Maybe it was everything that happened, maybe it was all the time that had passed, maybe it was just the warped lens of my sixteen-year-old brain—but I couldn't be sure whether I'd applied a filter to the whole thing, worked the facts up into a mythology.

Now I know. Kelsey's talent was real. And she never got to see where it might have taken her.

When the audio stops, Julia looks up at me, expectant. I notice that Sloane has inched closer to us, hovering right over the mic operator's shoulder, weighing whether she should interfere. We can say we need to confirm that it's me on the file. We can fight to edit this portion out of the segment.

"We were so young," I say. I hope it explains everything.

AT HOME, WE WAIT. THE STORY IS SLATED FOR THE ELEVEN o'clock news. Sloane hides in my dad's office, operating two phones and firing off emails. She's no stranger to an audio leak—removing old demos and discarded tracks of mine from the internet is a constant game of whack-a-mole—but she's concerned that the tape is "an escalation in the narrative." Until this moment, I've avoided directly characterizing my relationship with Kelsey as a creative one. As far as the world knows, we were just two kids from the same town who both liked music.

Now they'll know we played together. It's the moment in the scandal when you learn it wasn't just a flirtation—it was a full-blown affair. Only this is a story about ambition and talent too, and they will hear that Kelsey was more gifted than me. They will separate out my unpolished alto from her shimmering soprano and suggest—without much subtlety—that maybe, if things had gone differently, it would have been her with all the Grammys. Because if there's anything the media loves as much as sex, it's pitting two women against each other.

My parents and Nick try to go on with their evening, tiptoeing around me, preparing dinner while I move from the pool to my window seat and back again, my nose in my phone, then in Kelsey's first-edition *Ariel*, then in her water-stained notebook, a wash-rinse-repeat cycle of self-harm and amateur sleuthing. *Who is L?* I want to know. *Is he in these lyrics?* The search distracts me from the media storm gathering on the horizon but also from my own guilt and shame and sadness; it's a puzzle to solve rather than an emotion to manage. I pause my obsessing only for dinner: burgers (made by my dad and Nick while I kicked my feet in the deep end of the pool); grilled vegetables from the farm stand; purple sweet potato fries, roasted to maximum sweetness. I rotate my corn in a pool of melted butter and stare at Kelsey across the table.

You're being kind of difficult.

I know.

And also a therapy cliché.

You would know.

See? Kind of a bitch.

After dinner—Nick helps my mother wash dishes; my dad scrapes the grill clean outside—I head back out to the pool, turn on the hot tub, and wait as it transforms to an angry sea. I sit on the edge and lower my legs in up to my knees, watching how they turn boneless in the roiling.

I start flipping through Kelsey's notebook again, pages slowly softening in the damp heat. It helps—searching for sense in the weeping ink—that I know Kelsey's imagery by heart. She writes about campfires burning, flames flickering in black irises; a lake at midnight, obsidian glass in the black; docks creeping with daddy longlegs and fishing spiders. What I'm hoping for is that moment of transcendent revelation, when an image reframes itself for you, lifts from the page and becomes something new, not what you thought. *Which one of these is a reference to L?*

Wake up in the morning, smoke caught in my hair like a memory . . .

Fiona picks crayfish from under rocks / stealing food from circling hawks . . .

I try to think of myself like / some sort of free-floating thing / turns out all along / that you've had your hooks deep in me . . .

I look at her floating in the hot tub in front of me, skin marbled in the golden-blue. This one is about Raff, right?

How can you be sure? It's sort of generic.

Generic isn't always bad. It allows the listener to insert themselves in the story. Anybody can picture themselves in a dive bar, driving through a hometown, snow falling in a hush. The key is to paint your secrets with the slightest camouflage of commonplace.

"Never go back to the old drafts."

When I hear Nick's voice I press the notebook to my chest, quickly, embarrassed.

"Hey, easy—I'm just teasing." The way he smiles makes me feel like an asshole. He takes a seat on the concrete next to me, not touching. "But if you're feeling stuck, I really don't know if the answer is in your middle school journal."

Kelsey blows a raspberry in the water the way she used to for Fiona in the tub, a sloppy gurgle. *He loves you.*

"This isn't mine," I admit. "It was Kelsey's. I found it upstairs with all my old notebooks."

I watch as Nick takes this in. A part of me desperately wants him to ask me more. *How did you get it? Why do you have it? Shouldn't you have given it to the police, way back when?* I am a coward when it comes to quitting; all I've ever wanted is for someone else to do it for me. Instead Nick says, "I'm really glad you have that."

"She was mad at me," I tell him. "Our last conversation was a fight."

He looks at me with infinite tenderness. "Don't be too hard on yourself. You were just kids." He glances toward the notebook. "Do you think it would help to take a break for a little? Come in and have some tea?"

It's one kindness too far. I snap. "I said you didn't have to come this weekend."

"I know," Nick says, wounded. "I wanted to be here for you."

"Well, it feels like you're fucking suffocating me."

Woo-wee. Kelsey whistles. *That escalated quickly.*

Nick rakes his fingers through his hair and takes a deep, loud breath. "I love you, Dylan," he says, with extreme patience. "I'm sorry that's so difficult for you."

After he leaves, I soak my left hand in the hot water until the blister on my middle fingertip turns jellyfish white, almost translucent. It peels easily, like the skin of a roasted peach, slippery but solid, there and then, with a single pinch, gone. Certain lines from Kelsey's copy of *Ariel* swim in my brain like mantras. *The comets / Have such a space to cross . . . Through the black amnesias of heaven.*

I could not run without having to run forever.

Will you marry it, marry it, marry it.

I pull my hand from the water and walk inside, where I wrap my arms around my boyfriend and whisper an apology into his sternum.

"What do you need?" he breathes into my hair.

So I ask if he'll come get a drink with me at Junior's.

THERE ARE REALLY ONLY TWO PLACES WHERE I CAN EXPERI-ence the world like a normal person: places where no one cares who I am (and I mean *true* indifference, not the feigned kind you get in LA) and places where no one expects to see someone famous. I've taken the tube in London and gone hiking on the AT and bought a pregnancy test at a drugstore on the coast of Ireland without anybody noticing me, or maybe just saying, *you look a lot like Dylan Read*, because there was no way that Dylan Read could be here, at a gas station in Idaho. Implausibility is the best defense against recognition.

Junior's offers both perspectives. Because despite Louie's best efforts to make his dive a Dylan Read destination, the truth is that his bar isn't worth the stamp on the passport. No one would expect me here because it's disgusting; anyone who sees me here doesn't give a shit. They're here for the same reason as me: to escape the world for a little while. I enter behind Nick with baseball cap slung low and feel my feet stick on the floor and breathe in the sour smell of cigarettes and urine. Everything is washed in a vermilion glow, neon signs and twinkle lights and the lit red beam of the jukebox, right now half blotted out by a large man braced against it, tabbing through the mechanical pages.

"I can see why you like it," Nick says.

"Charming, right?"

"It's the scene in the movie where the hero hits rock bottom and goes to the lonely honky-tonk to drown their sorrows."

"Just need a little Willie on the speakers," I joke, choosing not to argue about whether I'm the hero at rock bottom.

"Exactly. Come on," Nick says, "let's get a beer that tastes like water."

I spot Louie as we sidle up to the bar. He stands with an elbow on the flap, wearing a soft blue button-down and jeans and a clean shave, like an off-brand Tony Soprano. He fiddles with a cocktail straw wrapper in his hands, twisting it into a tiny crumpled ball, and eyes the bartender. She has her medium-brown hair pulled into a casual low pony and an impossible waist-to-hip ratio, and wears clear gloss on the kind of full lips that keep plastic surgeons in business.

Annoying that she's good at her job, Kelsey says, plucking a cherry from the garnish tray. I watch as she chews the syrup-choked fruit, then pops the stem in her mouth, twisting it around her tongue.

She's right. The hot bartender works quickly, focused. She flirts in a noncommittal way, never giving any one customer too much attention, never allowing a mess to accumulate, taking orders as she rinses her steel canisters and restocks the napkin holder. I wonder why she's here when she could be at the Hotel Tahawus or one of the mid-priced Italian restaurants in town, leisurely mixing vodka martinis and pouring table Chianti, shift over by eleven thirty.

Kelsey snorts. *You think those places hire eighteen-year-olds to bartend?*

I mean, it's legal in New York.

Lots of things are technically legal.

Nick turns and hands me a plastic cup, ice to the brim like a glacial lagoon. The frozen chunks move as one, a kind of adult slushy. The foam of his beer spills in a lazy rivulet. He gestures at a sign over the register. "This place is called the Jolly Roger? As in Captain Hook's ship?" he says. "Why do you keep calling it Junior's?"

I laugh. I forget that this is one of those local legends that needs explaining to outsiders. "I guess somebody at some point decided it was too much of a mouthful," I tell him. "So people started calling it 'The J.R.,' and then from there, 'Junior's,' because J.R. is short for—"

"Junior, I get it," Nick says, grinning.

"Exactly. And also it allowed teens to talk about 'hanging out at Junior's' without inviting parental scrutiny. Maybe somebody had a friend named Junior, you know?"

Nick laughs. "Brilliant."

A woman behind Nick turns from the bar with a pitcher and two glasses cradled against her chest, leaving me with a clear view of the patrons down the stools. Raff sits with his hands wrapped around the base of a pint glass, fingers tracing quarter arcs around the curves.

Nick follows my gaze, then looks back to me.

"That's Kelsey's ex," I explain. "Brendan Raffensburger." Just like in the movie scenes Nick mentioned, Raff looks sadder here, stripped of the menace I felt at Kelsey's memorial, the warm, low light of this place working on him like a desert sunset—casting everything in a nostalgic haze. I feel myself softening toward him: he lost something too, all those years ago; maybe, because of his age and gender, he felt as stifled and unable to express his grief as I did.

"Do you wanna . . . ?" Nick knocks his chin in Raff's direction.

I nod, then step forward and tap Raff on the shoulder. Kelsey's boyfriend turns slowly, peering up at me with his body hunched over his glass. His temple glistens with a light sweat, tossing off the neon.

"Hey," I say.

"Huh," he grunts, surprised. "Isn't this place a little . . . beneath you?"

"You should see some of the dives I played when I was coming up," I tell him.

"That was a long time ago," he says. "You're better than this now."

"Doesn't mean I have to be a snob about it."

Raff leans back on his stool, sizing me up. "Kelsey was a snob."

I raise my eyebrows. "Kelsey, whose favorite musician was *Dolly Parton*?"

"That was snobby! She was self-righteous about it, like she was the only one in the entire world who understood how brilliant Dolly was. It was fucking annoying," he adds, but I can see how the memory softens him. I feel the same way.

"I'm sorry, Raff. This must be hard for you too."

He takes a drink, buying himself time. "For a long time I blamed you," he says, and I feel something lodge in my throat. "For her breaking up with me."

There it is again. He keeps saying that they weren't together. The Kelsey I knew would have taken Brendan back in a heartbeat; the Kelsey I know *did* take Brendan back in a heartbeat.

But what if I have it wrong, somehow? I think of *L*'s initial in Kelsey's

Ariel. I'm missing *something*; I just don't know what, exactly—or how much it matters. "What happened between you two?" I ask.

Raff shrugs. "For a while things weren't black and white," he says, and I know this part is true. "But it was over for good in the spring. I told her I was sorry about Steph, and that I wanted to be different, but—Kels didn't want to hear it. She didn't want anything to do with me."

This doesn't make sense. "I don't remember it that way," I tell him. "I—I thought she loved you."

"Me too." Raff sighs. "But she just kept saying she didn't want to be like her mom."

"What?" Kelsey could be hard on Diana in the routine way any teenage girl can be her mother's harshest critic—but I also remembered Kelsey as *proud* of Diana: the way her mother took in Fiona; how Diana worked and scrimped and saved to provide for all three kids as a single mom on a nurse's salary. Kelsey pitched in around the house, used her savings to help with groceries. *I'm too young to be a fucking aunt-mom,* she would say sometimes, but then she would come home with a toddler flute, or a toddler guitar, or a toddler keyboard, and sit with Fiona on the couch for hours while she clumsily mashed her toddler fists against the buttons, wailing garbled nonsense. I always thought it was the four of them against the world.

"She said that Diana had no self-respect," Raff tells me now. "How did she put it?" He looks upward, like he's searching his brain for the memory. "'A spineless Gumby of a human,' I think." He pauses. "I hate to think she was comparing me and her to Diana and Luke, but—I dunno. Maybe she was afraid of making the same mistakes."

"But Kelsey didn't know anything about her father," I say.

Raff shrugs again. "Maybe. Or maybe she was too embarrassed to talk about it. You know how she could be. Wanted everybody to think she was so goddamn tough."

I'm trying to process this—I feel as if I'm looking at the last weeks of Kelsey's life through a thick fog now, something that was once so clear suddenly muddied by new information—when Louie appears at the bar in front of us. "How we doin', folks? Dylan, it's so great to have you back."

I don't like how he says it—like I owe him something. Like he wants to remind me he knew me when. Next to me, Raff immediately goes hard and sullen, the door he'd opened to me slammed shut.

"Starfucker," he mumbles.

"What's that, Raff?"

"Leave her alone," he says.

"Brendan," I say, "I don't need you—"

"I saw you on the news," Raff says to Louie, talking over me. "Tryin' to use her to make this shithole some kind of destination."

"You sure spend a lot of time in this *shithole*," Louie says, measured.

"Call it a public service," Raff says. "Someone's gotta keep an eye out for the flavor of the month." He sends a pointed glance in the direction of the hot bartender.

Louie inhales deeply. He seems to double in size. "I think we've had enough tonight, huh, Raff?"

Raff finishes his beer in a single, long drag and stands from his stool. "You're right. It doesn't matter which hot teenager you're trying to fuck," he says, tossing a fistful of cash down on the counter. "It's not my business anymore."

His shoulder narrowly misses Nick's on the way out. I try to meet the bartender's eye—to tell her I'm sorry about the dick-swinging contest, that she's more than a prop in their cage match—but she avoids my gaze, directs her attention to wiping down the shelves above the register instead. I wonder if it hadn't occurred to her yet that she isn't special.

Around us, the bar has gone relatively still and silent. Yaz's "Only You" loops its shimmering synths from the jukebox. Louie watches the door swing shut behind Raff before turning his attention to the room. "How about a round on the house, huh?" he says.

There's a couple of half-hearted whoops as the Jolly Roger's modest crowd moves for the taps. While Louie begins to pour, Nick places a hand on my back, a tentative question. He knows the game is over; I can't pretend I'm nobody anymore. We follow Raff outside into the night, where my SUV waits like a portal between worlds, ready to whisk me through the vacuous nothing.

WHILE WE'RE OUT, JULIA'S STORY AIRS, COMPLETE WITH ITS EX-clusive recording of Kelsey and me singing together. By the time we get back to my parents', it will have made its way through the fiber optics of the internet, Google Alerts to tweets to blog posts to "articles" on *Tinseltown Tonight!* and *Celebreality*, recycled and upcycled all the way to a trending topic, to my DMs, my mentions. The initial stories will have neutral headlines like "Clip of young Dylan Read singing surfaces: LISTEN." "College Professor Finds Recording of 16-year-old Dylan Read." "Dylan Read harmonizes with childhood best friend in new clip (AUDIO)." They'll mention that I'm singing with Kelsey, who "died tragically" or whose "death and disappearance rocked the town of Thompson Landing." Here is the clip you're here for, but first we have to acknowledge this weird, sad wrinkle!

One or two people will joke, darkly, that maybe Kelsey's death was not an accident after all. (A stranger will reply with a gif of SpongeBob wiping his forehead in relief. *Annie Carey and Rachel Pratt this morning.*)

Someone will tweet, *if there's one rule in the Dylan Read Cinematic Universe, it's that there are no coincidences.*

me trying to explain how Dylan Read, America's Sweetheart, is maybe a murderer [red string meme]

Meanwhile my fans will return to my lyrics. *What if all the references to water are also Kelsey references*, they'll wonder. *What if she did all of this for her.* A feminist blog will post a think piece under its Your Joke Is Lame and Sexist column arguing that pitting two young women against one another is derivative and reflective of broad sociocultural anxieties about female power. A columnist at a major news outlet will opine that we are a case study in the power of privilege: the girl with access beats out the girl with talent. The internet will work itself into a frenzy, wondering whether Kelsey and I were star-crossed best friends or—equally fatally—dueling frenemies.

But I will be too busy thinking about my conversation with Raff to care. As far as I know, Kelsey never met her father. But what if I'd somehow gotten it wrong? Brendan Raffensburger has done nothing to earn my trust, but Kelsey calling her mother a "spineless Gumby of a human" is one of those details that seems too specific to be made up.

The handwriting inside Kelsey's *Ariel* was a doctor's scrawl, a tight, hurried slant that was neither distinctly masculine or feminine, and the close—a simple dash, then a sole initial—told me nothing at all about Kelsey's relationship to *L.*

Now I wonder: Could it be an expensive gift from an absent father? *Turns out all along / that you've had your hooks deep in me*, Kelsey wrote in her notebook. *Made the same mistake the fish make*, Luke said, holding his hand up at Kelsey's service, a long scar notched in the soft skin between his thumb and index finger.

Could the *L* who gave Kelsey a first-edition Plath be *Luke*?

The Full-Pop

People would write, later, that I moved to LA because of Lilah Grant. They were wrong. The whole thing with Lilah Grant came after.

Despite *Detour*'s success, Melody wanted something safer for my fifth record—something that would restore my reputation in Music City and rehabilitate my image as a preternatural good girl. Only: Ambition had begun to buzz loudly at the periphery of my existence like a horsefly on a hot summer day. I tried to ignore it, but still I woke in the night clawing at bites on my neck.

I didn't want to do something *safe*. I wanted to do something *big*. And there is no place better at masking internal desperation with exterior flawlessness than Los Angeles.

So I told my team to look for a house in Laurel Canyon, where the streets accordion in switchbacks so tight that their curves pile on one another like ribbon candy. I wanted California to give my music the same juxtaposition: a looseness and a crowding, a warbling and a precision, a lightness that cut. I wanted to move to the place where American pop music was reborn a half century ago so that I could be remade too, and more perfectly this time.

You've never wanted to live in LA, my mother said. *All that traffic. The paparazzi!* She sent me videos of photographers launching their bodies on car hoods, surfing the back of moving SUVs, clogging the private entrances to restaurants like swarming ants. *Wouldn't New York make more sense?* my parents argued. *You've always loved New York.*

—

NEW YORK WAS A FAMILY TRADITION. WE WENT EVERY YEAR for my birthday, shopping and dinner and live entertainment—often a musical, once the circus, sometimes a Rangers game. When I asked my mom if I could bring Kelsey for my sixteenth, I expected her to say no, that it was a very expensive day already and it wasn't a small thing, really, to have to buy additional train and show tickets, and that anyway this was *our* thing, wasn't it? Instead she smiled in a sad kind of way and said, "I was wondering when this would happen." I looked at her sideways and she added, "It's okay for you to want to spend your birthday with your friends, Dylan. It's developmentally normal." I rolled my eyes and told her that, for a therapist, she had a truly remarkable capacity to make a person feel awkward.

"There's nothing *awkward* about psychological development!" she called down the hallway after me.

Upstairs I IM'd Kelsey. For weeks we'd spent every single afternoon together. I'd worried after the North Pole that we were over—that Matt would tell her about my hand on his; that Raff would take her back and she'd drop me for him—but instead she stopped talking about Brendan entirely, even when I tried to coax the conversation in his direction. At school he walked down the halls hand in hand with Steph Sweeney; at lunch, Steph spread cream cheese on his bagel, bought him a bag of Doritos, sat quietly next to him while raking her fingernails up and down the nape of his neck. Previously Kelsey would have unpacked these moments endlessly, but now when she ranted about her day it had nothing to do with him or her. They were collecting applications for next summer's CITs at camp. She pierced her tragus and it hurt like a motherfucker. Fiona was going through a *Tarzan* phase. *Fucking Phil Collins all the fucking time.*

As for Matt: eventually I understood the moment in the car as mutually assured destruction. At night in bed I thought about how he hadn't pulled his hand from mine right away, how he'd allowed his thumb to trace me just for a moment—I closed my eyes and slipped my hand into my pajamas and tried to mimic it, that faintest, tentative touching that only left me starving for more—and I knew that he'd crossed a line. We were polite to one another in the kitchen, leaned our bodies away from each other in the Copestenkes' narrow hallway.

Which show are we seeing though, Kelsey typed that night on AIM. Because I can't watch lion king in any form even one more time, not after last year. Last year Fiona was into *The Lion King*; Kelsey often accidentally lapsed into melodies that were clear interpolations of "Hakuna Matata," dissolving into a fit of giggles on her bed. What if my true calling is scoring animated movies?

The "circle of life" scene is really good tho, I wrote.

AAAAHHHHZZIN VETYANANA

I laughed behind my computer screen, scratch lyrics our secret language, music we wore like armor against the boys that threatened our private universe.

ULTIMATELY LAUREL CANYON HAD ITS LIMITS. THE PLACE WHERE Graham Nash and Brian Wilson wrote was hostile to today's celebrity. It was impossible—my security team informed me—to have the kind of privacy and protection I needed. *Look how close the houses are*, they said. *Look how tiny the streets.* They wouldn't be able to park a unit outside. They wouldn't be able to construct adequate fencing. Instead they showed me a portfolio of homes in places where other extremely famous people lived, where my privacy wall would be shared by someone else who also required a privacy wall. These houses had guest homes and security cottages and trees that blocked the view of my pool from the sky. "But isn't the point of the pool to swim in the sun?" I asked.

"In the late afternoon when the sun is low," they explained, "you'll have all the light you want."

So I would make my California Sound album from a sprawling Tudor in Beverly Hills. If I squinted, it wasn't difficult to imagine the exposed beams and built-in bookcases in a cramped and tilted craftsman, easy enough to see the cracked stone fireplace in a draftier house, simple to water my plants in the overcrowded conservatory off the kitchen and picture my bare feet on the same Spanish tile I'd seen in pictures of Cass Elliot in 1970. I listened to Joni while I cooked. Floated in the pool to Bowie. Played *Darkness on the Edge of Town* anytime I drove anywhere, but especially on a weekend trip to the desert, to a rented house in the nowhere between Palm Springs and Joshua Tree. I woke up at two in the morning with the cacophony of Lindsey Buckingham's guitars in my head, that smashed sound of neat and sloppy in harmony. I knew what I didn't want: the buried vocals, the live-music sound, the mistakes. I wanted a cleaner, shimmering aesthetic.

Soon after I moved, Lilah invited me over for lunch. She lived in Malibu, in a white house with an overwatered lawn and an infinity pool perched on the cliff so that you felt as if you were floating out over the sea. That afternoon she wore a high-cut swimsuit with a scoop neck, the kind that looks good only on women with bodies like hers: tiny waist, skinny limbs, still with ass and boobs. I felt embarrassed by my bikini, much too little coverage on a much less interesting shape, and on the chair next to her I wrestled with my towel, fidgeting into an angle that might make my body look like hers. My insecurity didn't surprise me so much as send me hurtling back through the years: I didn't know how to behave around Lilah because I hadn't spent time with girls my age since Kelsey. While I fretted and fumbled, Lilah told me about growing up in San Diego, in the house where her parents still lived ("they're really committed to *maintaining a sense of normalcy*"); about persuading them, via PowerPoint presentation, to let her audition for *Thirty Feet Down*, the show she starred in about elite diving; about having to finish high school in Encinitas despite her filming schedule, because her parents were convinced that she needed a backup plan.

"I even applied to colleges," she told me, her aviators tipped slightly down her nose, peering over the lenses at me. "I wonder if Georgetown would still have me, if/when this all falls through."

I told her I thought about the question of a backup plan all the time. I knew she understood that the point wasn't the money. The point was definitional. How would I talk about myself if I wasn't making music? Who would I be?

"I just want to make sure I pivot before it looks like I've been forced out, you know?" Lilah said.

It seemed everyone I met in Hollywood was busy pretending they were never nervous, that the work came easily, that they deserved everything they had and then some. In fact it was part of the whole reason I'd moved here—to learn how to hide the ugliness of my striving. But here was someone who knew how hard it was to get a seat at the table. Here was someone admitting to both her ambition and her anxiety.

I wanted to tell her everything.

Our lunches became a weekly thing. On Sundays and Mondays I worried over my phone, leaving it abandoned for long stretches in the hope that when I returned there would be a text from her, inviting me over on Wednesday or Thursday. I scrolled through her Instagram, stopping myself at a year or so back, panicked I would accidentally like something from long ago. How mortifying, to be caught that obsessed. I texted her only every third or fourth time I thought of her. I hinted, obliquely and in a joking way, at girls' weekends, meeting her parents, some sort of future. When she visited my dreams I woke vaguely ashamed. I tested the limits of my feelings with psychological experiments: Could I picture kissing her? More than that? Maybe; no.

I told her about Nick Devlin. We were DMing every now and then, but after Hudson I'd decided to take a break from men. I'd left my cowriters; I'd left country; now I'd left Nashville entirely. At every turn I'd shed a layer of my origin story like a molted skin. I wanted my fifth album to be defined entirely on its own: free, for the first time since the beginning, of any relationship baggage at all.

"Would you rather," Lilah asked, plucking a piece of watermelon from her plate and surveying it in the sunlight, "be the biggest, most decorated American musician of all time but never have sex ever again—or have the best sex of your life every time you fucked forever, but have to quit music tomorrow?"

It wasn't even a question.

THE FORTUNE TELLER WAS, OBVIOUSLY, KELSEY'S IDEA. WHEN we got into the city that day my mother suggested that we separate for a few hours—"you girls go have fun!"—and Kelsey grinned and grabbed my hand and led me through Penn Station to the subway, heading downtown. In SoHo we bought two hot chocolates at Le Pain and split a cookie the size of our faces at a bakery with a faded turquoise awning and a windowful of long, flour-dusted baguettes in paper sleeves. The late-morning sun angled across the cobbled streets and Kelsey's cheeks pinked in the February cold. I was thinking about how precisely she looked as if she belonged here when she paused in front of a brick townhome with a neon sign.

"No thanks," I said, when I saw the way Kelsey's eyebrows wriggled at *PALM READINGS* and *TAROT*.

"Come on," she said. "It must be good luck or something to go on your birthday!"

"Feels like going to mass when you don't believe in God."

Kelsey made a clucking noise, like a chicken.

"What are we, seven?"

But Kelsey already had her hand on the door.

Inside was all orange-pink light—the warm glow of candles and salt lamps—and the soft hush of layered textiles: overlapping Persian rugs; lush, velvet drapes; brocade-wrapped wingback chairs. In the back corner a black spiral staircase twirled to a second floor, a pothos trailing along its railing. After a moment we heard the pad of footsteps above us, then saw a pair of slip-on sneakers and knobby ankles on the top stair. I looked at Kelsey, whose face was absent its usual shrewdness—just briefly, no tight lips, no crinkling at the corners of her eyes. She was neutral, open, the same way she looked singing just us in her bedroom.

The woman was tall and blond and chic, dressed in skinny jeans and a thin, V-necked sweater, and as she extended a hand in Kelsey's direction she revealed fingers armored in silver rings and a wrist cuffed in a dozen thin bangles and beaded strands. "Welcome," she said. Her voice had the slight roughness of an eastern European accent. "I'm Vera."

Kelsey introduced herself and then pointed at me. "This is my friend Dylan."

Vera's handshake was firm, tight. "Hi," I said.

"How can I guide you today?"

"Well, this one is a little skeptical," Kelsey said, pointing to me, "but I'd love a tarot reading."

Vera looked at me, not unkindly. "Sometimes it's helpful to watch first," she said. She pointed in the direction of a Windsor chair pressed against the wall. "You can pull that over."

Once the three of us were nestled around the table, Vera picked up a deck of cards from among an orderly arrangement of tokens—candles, crystals, a knot of sage—and knocked them twice into a neat stack. She held the set flat in her extended palm toward Kelsey. "Rest your hand on top for a moment, please," she said.

Kelsey placed her right hand on the deck, gingerly. Vera closed her eyes and inhaled deeply. When she opened them again, Kelsey lifted her hand and Vera divided the deck into three sections, placed each pile on top of the other, shuffled, then instructed Kelsey to pull a card.

"Well," Kelsey said, placing the card face up on the table, "this lady looks like a bad bitch."

Vera smiled mildly. "Tell me what else you see."

Three times that afternoon, Kelsey pulled a card from Vera's deck and described what she saw: a crowned woman positioned between two pillars; a man and a woman drinking from large chalices beneath a snake-coiled staff; a busy scene splashed with ten gold coins, blotting the picture from view. The High Priestess, the Two of Cups, the Ten of Pentacles. Vera explained that the tarot is not meant as a forecast; it's meant to illuminate a way of thinking, to encourage mindfulness around certain habits, decisions, or tendencies. They talked about dualities, conflicts between ways of being, the creation of a third out of a union between two things.

Peering over the gold coins, Vera asked Kelsey if she thought about her legacy.

"I'm seventeen," Kelsey said. "Not a middle-aged man."

Vera stifled a laugh. "This card is generally a sign of good fortune. An inheritance, perhaps."

Kelsey let out a big, cartoonish guffaw. "There's no inheritance coming my way, I promise."

"So then tell me about what you intend to leave behind. Do you think about that much? Whether you're making the world a better place?"

Kelsey was quiet for a beat. "Well, there's my music," she said, before adding: "But I also have a niece. I help take care of her. I'm like her big sister and her mom and her aunt all in one."

"That sounds like a lot of responsibility," Vera said kindly.

Kelsey nodded slowly. "I'm going to be a senior next year," she said. "I guess I do wonder sometimes what it would be like for her if I wasn't around as much."

I felt the slick of panic, a cortisol rush. I was used to Kelsey talking about leaving—for Nashville, for New York, for some place she could play her music—in abstract terms. Hearing her factor her family into the equation made it feel suddenly more real.

"Well," Vera said, "I think there's no better way to move through the world than by thinking about what we're doing for those who will come after us."

Kelsey eyed the cards in front of her: the crowned woman, the drinking partners, the splattered coins. She touched them, one after the other, adjusting their positioning in a neat line, edges perfectly parallel. From the way she fingered her selection it occurred to me that she had hoped for something more out of this—a revelation of some kind, a guarantee—and I realized I, too, had thought something earth-shattering would come of Vera's cards: an omen of death, maybe.

In a way, it had. I understood that day that my friend was going to leave me.

COUNTRY MUSIC IS ABOUT RELATABILITY. JUST THREE CHORDS and the truth, as the saying goes. Pop, on the other hand, traffics in fantasy.

Weekend Read came about because I was worried about alienating my fans. I'd prepared them with *Detour* and its poppier stylings, but the difference between my third solo record and *Dylan Read* was between gazing over the side of a bridge and jumping into the water below. I needed to make sure they'd dive in with me.

So we rented out a hotel in Malibu, one of those places built in the midcentury, dusty white with baby-blue doors and the permanent scuff of sand underfoot, and created a weekend retreat around the album's aesthetic, designed to contextualize and preview the record for a select group of superfans while providing exclusive access to *me*. While my team worked up a menu of California casual cuisine and branded swag bags, I combed the internet, sifting through the rape and death threats and super-zoomed-in shots of my stomach after a big lunch (*is she pregnant?*) for the right assortment of disciples: They needed to be normal, not obsessive; devoted, but not zealots. They could not have threatened to murder any of my exes. They needed to have a sense of themselves outside of their fandom. I needed to know they would keep the secret of my album without the guardrail of an NDA (sure to ruin the mood, and the fact of which would almost certainly leak); I needed to know that I could spend two nights in a hotel with a hundred of my most devoted fans without worrying that one of them might create a hostage situation. I wanted to create the cozy atmosphere of a sleepover with your best friends without risking my life.

The night before they arrived, I practiced and practiced the interstitial monologues I'd deliver while I played the record. I wanted to sound natural, relaxed, like I was only playing an album for my friends—but I wanted to sow the seeds of a cohesive narrative too, because I knew these fans would annotate the lyrics and tweet about each track the night the album debuted. They would steer the discourse because they would be the ones with the insider knowledge.

"Listen," I said to them from the pool deck as the sun melted into the ocean beyond. A hush fell over the crowd, so just the waves on the beach murmured in the distance. "Listen to the coast. Hear the waves, how they swell and fade? And beneath that, the murmur of traffic on the 1 behind us—how it has a rhythm too?" I watched them crane their necks, tilt their heads, better position the ear to the sky. "The whole sound of LA is layered like a song, with harmonies that emerge depending on where exactly you are in this vast sprawl. Here on the beach we can listen to the seagrass rustle in the ocean breeze. In canyons at night you can hear the coyotes yip and howl. Down in the city the eucalyptus trees scratch as they shed thick peels of bark. And everywhere—from Malibu to Melrose to Orange County—you'll hear the intermittent sounds of human life: gates opening and closing, the smack of a mailbox, a dog barking." The catering crew moved among us as if on cue, their trays of fish tacos and avocado ceviche rattling lightly like a human percussive line.

I told them to think about a musical they'd seen—surely everyone had seen at least one, at least the movie version: *Les Mis*, probably, or maybe *Rent* or *Phantom*, or literally any old-school Disney movie—*Lion King, Beauty and the Beast*. "You know how there's always that big number at the beginning, the one that situates you in your new world? '*There goes the baker with his tray like always.*' It comes in thundering and kind of drowns you in the contours of the place? This is my version of that," I said. "This is 'East of Eternity.'"

For two hours that first night in Malibu I told stories about my life and stories about my art, braiding them together as one. There is no title track on *Dylan Read*, I explained, because the entire record is meant to be seen as a self-portrait. "Los Angeles Notebook" is a riff on a Didion essay of the same name, and presents the narrator studying her way through a new city, each verse a new neighborhood: Topanga, Encino, Silver Lake. "Elizabeth" takes its title from my middle name, and I could have written it like a country song, one that told the story of the grandmother who gave it to me and flipped the perspective in the last verse to my point of view, the narrator reflecting on her heritage; instead I wrote it as a pop song, verses structured in the lessons of a name—a queen, a matriarch, a romance-novel heroine. It was songwriting by synonym: splintering a concept again and again for the sake of showing how it all came back around, how it all met the same end.

As the sand turned silver in the moonlight and the ocean went to black beyond, as the events team lit bonfires on the beach and handed out sweatshirts and blankets stamped with the album art, as my fans made new friends from far-flung places, I stole away into the kitchen and texted Lilah. I think they're having fun.

Fun like this guy? she wrote, then a gif of Anthony Hopkins as Hannibal Lecter.

I laughed. Fun like summer camp!

You mean *stalker* camp.

Leaning with my elbows against the kitchen counter while the catering crew swirled around me, prepping individual s'mores kits in cellophane bags to deliver beachside, I stifled a giggle. A waiter looked at me and grinned as if we were friends sharing a secret. I imagined that if she hadn't signed an NDA she would tell a tabloid about this moment, how I seemed to be texting someone special.

AFTER KELSEY AND I LEFT THE PSYCHIC'S THAT AFTERNOON IN New York, we walked east through the Village toward Washington Square. A trio of boys rode skateboards around the fountain, catching their wheels on the concrete slope of the water's edge, a smack-hiss rhythm to their motion. The park was filled with NYU students, an army of purple and white, distracted and harried between classes.

"I could see you here," I said, flicking my head in the general direction of the university, its purple banners visible through the trees around us. New York wasn't far, I thought to myself. I could visit on weekends.

"In college?" Kelsey asked.

I laughed. "Yeah," I said, like it was the most obvious thing.

"I can't go to college," Kelsey said, and I felt immediately embarrassed. Kelsey nudged me in the side and added, "Twenty-two or twenty-three is too old to get famous." She grinned in that enigmatic way she did: both serious and not.

I exhaled and followed her gaze to where a man sat on a bench with a boom box perched on a shopping cart, the Cranberries on loud, *anything helps* on a piece of torn cardboard.

"I know it's not real," she said softly. "But I still wanted to hear Vera say that."

"Say what?" I asked.

"That I'd be famous one day."

"It's random, Kelsey," I said. "It doesn't mean anything at all."

Watching a busker set up an amp for his guitar, she smiled wanly and said, "Fame is random too."

Later during the musical I sat between Kelsey and my parents and wondered if even this stage was too small for my friend. I thought about how obviously talented the actors were, how they had to work incredibly hard to have ended up here, cast in what would become one of the longest-running Broadway shows of all time. I thought about voice lessons and fine-arts boarding schools and so, so many auditions and rejections and lines memorized and choreography learned but I couldn't help wondering, watching the lead, whether what she really wanted was to be a movie star. Maybe when she was little she watched the Oscars every spring and imagined that she would be on *that* stage one day, gold statue clutched in hand, her face beamed into millions of homes.

After the show we ate dinner at a fusion restaurant where the food was served on a lazy Susan in the center of a circular table. Edamame and basil pancakes and cold sesame noodles and sea bass were delivered to our table in waves, and my mother ordered a lychee cocktail with a slippery white orb in the center. When the waiter brought a small molten chocolate cake with a single lit candle in the middle, Kelsey sang "Happy Birthday" as if we were in a TGI Fridays, loudly and unashamed, and for a moment I thought maybe she was having a good time after all.

LILAH'S COMPETITIVENESS MADE MINE OKAY. WE CONFESSED our worst, most jealous thoughts in breathless texts, shielded by the separateness of our professional spheres: we understood each other, but we were not in direct contest. When an actress and writer was profiled in the *Times* for her slice-of-life dramedy, Lilah sent me the link to the story and a message that said simply *screams internally*.

The actress was exactly the kind of manic pixie dream girl the media loves: smart but young; pretty but not threateningly so; a little but not entirely aloof in terms of her social media presence. Her show was described—over and over again—as "a fever dream."

Aren't you home? I wrote. Can't you scream out loud?

She's a lock for the Emmy, Lilah replied.

In the space of my relationship with Lilah it felt safe to want. We wanted so, so badly. In a tenuous, shimmering way, this career had begun to feel like mine now—my kingdom to conquer, my crown to lose. A fifteen-year-old with dusty purple hair scored a nine in *Pitchfork* and I texted Lilah: the extent to which they award bonus points for newness is just 😵 💀 ⚰️.

"You know what I'm sick of hearing?" Lilah said to me while hiking one afternoon in Santa Monica. "That 'success is not a zero-sum game.' Like, guess what? It kind of is. Auditioning is *literally* zero-sum. If you get it, I don't."

"I understand exactly," I said.

"I know you do," she sighed. "I'm just sick of feeling bad about myself for thinking this way. Like I'm just fulfilling all the worst stereotypes about catty, jealous, backstabbing women." She kicked at a rock, launching a tiny golden dust storm. "Like, if you get nominated for a Grammy, and I don't get a nod for this season, I'm gonna feel . . . kind of jealous!"

I laughed, charmed by her truth-telling. "But that's apples and oranges. We're not competing for the same awards."

Lilah made a kind of frustrated grunt. "I know! But I can't stop comparing myself to other successful women! My brain just runs this endless reel of who got really big when and how long did it last for them and is it already too late for me to be talked about in the news in that breathless way that makes a sensation and . . ." She sighed. "I feel insane."

"You're not insane," I said. "You just work in entertainment."

As we made our way down the canyon a couple of paps caught us snaking through the ridge. Betrayed by another hiker, I thought, as if there's some sort of social contract in the hills.

Lilah pulled out her phone and snapped a series of selfies of us. Standing there with our fingers covered in dust and our faces sticky with sweat we selected and edited. As soon as we uploaded the pictures to Instagram the paparazzo photos would be worthless.

"We look so cute together," Lilah said, watching the likes accumulate. "We should go as dates to the shows."

So we walked the red carpets that award season as a pair, taking all of our pictures side by side, absolutely zero stand-alones; two for one or none at all, we told our publicists. We pressed our temples to one another, embraced with our hips and bellies touching, held hands. In between takes we dabbed at each other's mascara, pushed stray pieces of hair back in place. When the announcers took the stage to present Album of the Year, Lilah squeezed my hand in my lap. She found a callus on the tip of my index finger and made tiny circles over the top of it, the sensation dulled by the deadened nerves of scar tissue. "Would you rather," she whispered, "never win another award ever—or win but pee yourself every time you give your acceptance speech?"

My eyes didn't leave the presenters. "Too easy," I said.

Onstage, the Grammy heavier than I remembered, I searched for her face and worried that this was hard for her, watching me win. I wanted to tell her it didn't mean anything, but we both knew better than that.

IN MARCH THAT YEAR, MY PARENTS AND I WENT TO THE CARIB-
bean for spring break. The Friday before we left, Kelsey came to my house

to help me pack. She sat on my floor painting her toenails a dusty lilac while I rolled swimsuits into tiny bundles. I worried, frantically, about what might happen to our friendship in a week apart. There wouldn't be reliable internet at the resort, not the kind I could use to spend an hour on AIM; my phone wouldn't work abroad. Kelsey ran a thumbnail along the curve of her big toe, wiping excess polish from her skin.

"So I was thinking," she said, "that when you come back, maybe we could start to work on putting together a demo." She didn't look up from her nail.

I was wedging a pair of sandals into the front pocket of my suitcase. "Like to send to colleges?" I said absently.

"What?"

I looked up at Kelsey. "I heard Amanda Finlay talking about the same thing today," I said. "Recording a mix to submit with her applications."

Kelsey tipped her head sideways, peering up at me from under her dark hair, her eyes narrowed slightly. "Could be a good thing to have," she said.

Kelsey wasn't going to stay in Thompson Landing forever. The only thing keeping her here was Fiona, and I'd learned at Vera's that even she wasn't enough of an anchor. But if I helped Kelsey with the transition—if I could show her that there was a path available besides the dice roll of sudden fame; if I could support her on that journey—then maybe there would be a place for me in her future. Maybe it would even bring us closer together.

"Absolutely," I said.

In Grand Cayman my parents and I stayed at a sleek new resort with sand-colored floors and white pool chairs, at the end of a long strip of beach on the side of the island where the water lapped indifferently at the shore. In the mornings my dad and I rode borrowed beach cruisers to a smoothie bar, past five-foot-long iguanas sunning themselves in the morning warmth. *Island rats*, my dad said, laughing at his own joke. *Caribbean pigeons*. During the day I sat with my legs extended on a long lounge chair and scribbled in my notebook, melodic cadences matched to the tides. *The woman wore a crown but she wasn't a queen / and that made me think 'bout all that's not what it seems*. In the evenings we ate dinner at a restaurant right on the beach, plates of charred corn tossed with cotija and shrimp tacos dripping with lime, and at night in my pull-out couch in our suite I pressed my nose to my notebook until I fell asleep with new lines swimming in the front of my brain: *isn't seventeen the time for dreamin' / tell me why do I feel like I'm underachieving?*

When we got back on Sunday night, sunburn peeling on my shoulders, I IM'd Kelsey immediately. Wanna write tomorrow?

Duh, she wrote. Don't expect me to be happy about your new tan though.

At her house I hoped she'd have new melodies we could play with, that we could meld some of my new lines to her music, but she claimed to have been busy during the week, picking up extra babysitting shifts and doing CIT interviews for camp. I told her I'd done some research and that a good portfolio was probably about five songs, the length of an EP, and that we would probably want to find a recording studio to make a proper mix. I'd been prepared for Kelsey to say that she couldn't afford that, and to tell her that it could be an early graduation present from my family, no worries, but instead she just smiled affably without lifting her eyes from my notebook and said, "Good idea."

We had a little over one month left together.

LIKE THE OCEAN OR THE UNIVERSE OR THE EYE OF A HURRI-cane, fame is a thing you can't see clearly from the center. *Dylan Read* moved 1.2 million units in its first week. The tour sold out in minutes, eighty-five shows, stadiums only. "Star Chart," the second single off the album, would eventually be my first certified diamond single. You could not drive from your home to the closest gas station without hearing my voice on the radio. (Literally. This is knowable data: approximately how frequently, on average, my songs were played on the radio in a given metro area.) To everyone else, Dylan Read—and *Dylan Read*—was inescapable, ever present, *relentless*.

I said yes to everything. I did covers for *Debs* and *Rolling Stone* and *Chic*. I performed at the Victoria's Secret Fashion Show, dressed in a floor-length silk robe. When the call came from the NFL I dissociated so thoroughly that I didn't even think of Aaron, that I'd beaten him to his sport's greatest stage. We designed three set pieces for the Super Bowl—a drum-line version of "Star Chart," complete with a marching band and cheerleaders; a medley made of three other *Dylan* tracks; and then an arena-rock version of "Night Games," off *Sophomore*. Under a black tuxedo jacket I wore the kind of short satin dress I might have worn if I'd ever gotten to go to my own homecoming. That was Lilah's idea.

I headlined Coachella. A studio exec gave Lilah his Palm Springs house for the weekend and she threw an afterparty. The pictures were everywhere: some blurred with movement, hair fanned with a head toss; others close-cropped, frames crowded with long limbs and symmetrical faces and glossy hair.

Who the fuck is Delilah, I asked Lilah, referring to the name that was peppered in our comments, tagged with rainbow emojis and purple hearts.

Lmao, she said. That's us.

We cohosted the Met Gala. The theme was "Debutantes: Social Ritual from the Gilded Age to the Present." I wore a vintage Halston jumpsuit in white silk crepe, a nod to *Dylan Read*'s seventies aesthetic, with a massive faux-fur cape in a lush ivory. Lilah wore nude mesh embroidered with thousands of tiny crystals and a crown. "Couture prom!" she said. On the red carpet that year people wore thick brocade gowns with thirty-foot trains and capes that opened to reveal bright rainbows and dresses that were basically just corsets.

In a way the Delilah theories explain how easy it is to be too much and not enough. I'd reached a totally new level of visibility—a block-buster record, constant exposure on social media, an equally famous, equally public best friend—and yet there was this idea that I was still holding back some essential part of myself. Alongside the frothy gossip, more sinister ideas began to grow like weeds: Weekend Read was only a ploy meant to make me *seem* approachable; the emotions in my lyrics and delivery were fabricated for impact; my genre-hopping wasn't about artistry, but instead the much dirtier motivation that is ambition. The divorce had complicated my persona, and they used it to trace a throughline, writing about me the way they did certain female politicians: I just didn't seem very *authentic*. Who was I really, amid all this shape-shifting and reinvention?

When I came home on break from tour I hosted parties at my house in LA. Lilah brought her friends from *Thirty Feet Down* and I invited the models I met backstage at fashion shows and I hoped that the photos we posted online made us seem normal if also aspirational: "good" as in *real*; "good" as in *the ideal*. I installed an outdoor projector and we watched movies from the pool and in the mornings I woke to find my filter clogged with popcorn kernels and Sour Patch Kids swarmed with ants on the deck and bikinis that were not mine drip-drying in the bathroom. In the fall we had a week off around Halloween, a break between a Europe stint and an Asia-Pacific swing. I threw a costume party.

I hadn't seen Lilah since August. She came dressed as a member of a cult from a niche prestige drama, wearing head-to-toe white. Like the fictional cult members, she occasionally refused to speak, writing her thoughts on a yellow legal pad in Sharpie. Halfway through the night an actor I recognized but had not met arrived in a sheriff's costume, with a three-day scruff and aviator sunglasses.

I understood before Lilah linked her arm through his, before she lifted her chin to his face and he turned to kiss her, that this was her date—the show's hero is a tortured and grieving cop; their costume was a couple's ensemble. She hadn't mentioned Brooks to me, hadn't mentioned dating anyone at all except to say that the only way to kill the Delilah rumors was for one of us to get a boyfriend.

Fine, I thought. *If that's how you want to play it.* Late in the night, I allowed a model to take and post to her Instagram a selfie of us, knowing that Lilah and the actor would appear in the frame just over my shoulder in the background, their faces close, an unmistakable intimacy between them. By morning it was all over the blogs, in particular the fact that Brooks was maybe not one hundred percent broken up with his girlfriend.

It didn't work, obviously, in terms of the gossip. In the end all it did was hurt Lilah, who—in addition to the home-wrecker narrative—faced the knowledge of my betrayal. Lilah knew better than anyone about my meticulousness. She knew I would have noticed the entire composition of the photo. She knew I would have okayed its posting.

I could have just asked whether Brooks was a stunt or if she really liked him. But the truth is I wouldn't have liked the answer either way. It was much easier, in the end, to simply hit self-destruct.

IT WAS SOMEONE FROM CAMP WHO PUT KELSEY IN TOUCH with the Alderidge professor. ("You wouldn't *believe* the connections these people have," she said. "Anything you want is, like, one phone call away.") Kelsey borrowed Matt's car and on a Wednesday after school we drove down the highway to the college, Kelsey singing "You Ain't Woman Enough" at full volume. On campus we met a tall, soft-spoken man named Gene who carried himself like a recovering hippie. He had chin-length gray hair that he tucked behind his ears and he moved constantly, just like Kelsey: a tapping foot, a jiggling knee, arms crossed and uncrossed. We followed Gene deep into the bowels of an arts building, through a set of double doors beneath a gilded sign welcoming us to the *COYNE CENTER FOR THE RECORDING ARTS*. Inside, a black-walled room with soft flooring like a child's tumbling mat and a ceiling three times the hallway height held us like a secret underwater cave. Gene asked if it was our first time in a studio and when we said yes he seemed to light up. He moved from corner to corner in the space and clapped his hands and asked us to listen for the tail, to see where the sound went dead. In the vocal booth with glass walls on two sides he picked up a pop filter that had fallen to the ground and explained how it muffled the air so that it was your vocals that caught, not your exhalation. He hooked it to the mic and gestured for Kelsey to come forward, bring her face close. "Come on," he said, smiling. "Give it a try."

Kelsey was never shy. But she hesitated before Gene that afternoon, waved her hands in front of her chest like, *oh, no thank you*. She tried to make it about him: "You don't need to show us—"

"No, really! It's not a problem. This is fun for me." He grinned, and I remembered a science teacher in seventh grade who kept a menagerie in her classroom: lizards and snakes and tanks full of fish. Some people just love what they do.

I nudged Kelsey in the back with my elbow. "Go ahead," I said.

Gene navigated around us—the vocal booth was small, and he was careful not to accidentally touch either one of us. I thought of him as kind, respectful. "I'll just be right in there," he said, pointing to the control room.

When he closed the door the room went still. Kelsey took a tiny half step toward the mic, then looked back at me. "This is weird."

I thought of the day Kelsey showed me the training room under the old rink. "Just pretend you're in the shower," I said.

"A naked body is much easier than a naked voice."

"Poetic."

She rolled her eyes at me. "What should I sing?"

Through the glass, I watched Gene position himself on a swivel stool at the control panel. He looked our way and gave us a double thumbs-up. "First thing that pops into your head," I said. I wriggled my eyebrows, a playful urging.

She made a kind of huffing noise, *ughfine.* As she stepped to the mic a clicking noise came through the booth, then Gene's voice. "I'm ready whenever you are. Just step up and start."

Kelsey's voice filled the air around us, crisp and clean, a kind of precision to her vocals I'd never heard before. Her twang cut. *Everybody is wonderin' what and where they all came from . . .*

I understood why Kelsey chose the song. The original track was minimally produced, very vocal-forward, Iris DeMent's voice bright and loud, almost abrasively so in the opening verse. In Kelsey's arsenal, it was a song that made sense to sing a cappella, on demand. "Let the Mystery Be" was also a safe pick tonally: its *sound* doesn't necessarily reflect its lyrical melancholy.

Kelsey smiled as she reached the first chorus, then waved her right hand at her hip, motioning for me to step to the mic. I shook my head. She grabbed my wrist and yanked, pulling me next to her. I didn't know all the words—just the chorus—so I dropped out on the second verse, then rejoined on the hook, fattening Kelsey's lead vocal with my backing. By the time we reached the final chorus Kelsey was looser, easier, and she pressed her hip into mine and tilted her temple in my direction and I followed her lead over the closing lines, adding an extra straining, up-note syllable to the final *let the mystery be-ee.*

After, in the mixing booth, Gene spread his arms wide over the console and said, "Now, this is really just for show," and then tapped into a computer screen that mirrored the mixing board, all the controls digitized. When he adjusted a fader on the computer it moved on the display, sliding up and down as if maneuvered by a ghost hand. "In reality all of this"—he waved at the panel—"can be done on here." He motioned at Pro Tools. "But some people prefer the feel of an actual board." He played the recording back for us, tinkering with the software for the purpose of demonstrating: *see, we can pitch it up here, down over here; Kelsey, you came in a little flat here, which we can always re-record but we can also just tweak.* I asked if this meant we were "autotuning" the recording and he shrugged and explained that when people use the phrase "autotune" colloquially they're referring to the sound you get when you run an entire vocal production, start to finish, through Pro Tools. This—making minor tweaks here and there—wasn't really the same thing. He put his palms on his knees. "So I hear you ladies are looking to record a few demos?"

I glanced at Kelsey, who was running a finger along the curved edge of the mixing board. "We write songs together," I explained, and when Gene said "cool" in an unfussy way I felt like he'd given me a gift: *yes, you belong here.* "Kelsey is a year older than me and will be applying to colleges in the fall, and we wanted to make an EP for her supplemental materials."

Gene turned his attention to Kelsey. "Excellent. Where are you looking?"

Kelsey tucked her hands into her jacket pockets and smiled the way she did when she was flirting, one of a million shifting turns I'd seen her deploy in Raff's presence. I knew it meant she had her armor on. "Oh," she said, "I'm not sure yet."

Gene cocked his head slightly. "Well, you should think about Alderidge if you're into music." He spun on his stool, tiny quarter-moon rotations in each direction. "We've got everything you need!"

Kelsey grinned, sphinxlike. "Sure seems like it."

Gene stared at her mildly for a beat, then switched his attention to me. "Well, you let me know when you want to get in here, and I'll make sure everything's set up for you. It'll be simple—it's just vocals and guitar, right?"

I nodded.

"And—what, three songs? Four?"

"Maybe five," I said, worried I was testing the limits of his generosity.

"No problem. I'm happy to help," he said.

In the car on the way home I buzzed with the energy of having learned something new. Gene had used an entirely different language with us—"visual duets" and "live open sounds" and "overdubs"—and I wanted to know how to speak it fluently. But Kelsey was quiet, barely humming along to *Jolene*. When I said, "He was super nice," she only nodded, made an assenting murmur.

I counted the mile markers on the side of the highway, numbers flicking past. Ten seconds from one to the next. "I think we should do 'Rust Season,' 'General Store,' and then probably something slightly more ballady, right?"

Kelsey kept her eyes straight on the road.

"Is something wrong?" I asked. What I meant was *Did I do something wrong*?

"No," she said. But I knew she was lying.

LILAH'S NEW LIMITED SERIES PREMIERED WHILE I WAS IN AUS-tralia. I had a cameo in the second episode. We shot on a ranch inland from LA, on a sprawl of acreage once reserved for old Westerns, in nineteenth-century dresses with our hair in windswept braids. I'd asked the set photographer that day to send me any stills she had of me and Lilah together, and when I got home after tour, the photo I'd selected was waiting for me in my entryway, still wrapped in the framer's brown paper.

In the shot, Lilah and I are looking at something off camera. My head is tilted toward hers, and I appear to be whispering something in her ear. She's laughing, lips parted, eyes crinkled at the corners. Between the costumes and the secret-sharing, we look like two little girls playing make-believe, disappeared into a world that existed only in our shared imagination.

At the time I thought there was something charming about it, the playful, almost childlike intimacy of the moment. But in the end I never sent the photo to Lilah. The illusion, by then, was broken.

Kelsey used to calculate driving time in songs. The distance from Thompson High to her house was two songs, for example. A detour to Fiona's day care added another two. A person could listen to five radio hits on the way to the mall, at least, and during the holiday season you might get stuck in traffic out Route 50 and be gifted with two more. The Stewart's was just three minutes from her house, and Kelsey liked to play radio roulette: *You get one shot here. If we're lucky, it's S.H.E. If God hates us, it's the Grave Brigade.* (Kelsey hated sad dad bands.)

My parents' house to Kelsey's is three to four songs ("three-point-five," Kelsey would say), although more solidly four in our current era of 2:40 singles. On the drive over I think about how I left things with Nick. We woke up in the morning in a lightly hungover daze, our headaches just as likely due to the stink still clinging to our hair and bodies, Junior's lingering like some kind of toxic residue.

Nick wanted me to come back to New York with him. "Mike can trail in the SUV," he said. "We can stop at that place in Woodstock. Maybe go for a walk around the reservoir." He propped his head up on his elbow, looking down on me as I burrowed under the duvet. His St. Christopher pendant dangled at the hollow of his chest, less a talisman of his faith (Nick was Irish Catholic in upbringing but not in practice) than a super-stition.

I reached up, my head still on the pillow, and rubbed it between my thumb and index finger. "I need to stay here for a bit," I told him. "You go ahead without me."

Nick pulled away slightly and the necklace fell from my hand. "What for?"

I'd decided on our way home from Junior's. For fifteen years, I'd had only one version of how things went down between me and Kelsey. But ever since they found her—ever since I set foot back in Thompson Landing—I'd started to feel the narrative shifting beneath me. And between last night's conversation with Raff and my discovery of Kelsey's first-edition *Ariel*, I just can't escape the feeling I might have gotten something wrong. What if the story didn't end with me and her? What if there was some way to lessen the burden I'd been carrying?

"I want to go talk to Kelsey's mom," I told Nick.

Nick cocked his head slightly, the tiniest flicker of confusion. "Didn't you see her at the service?"

I pulled my head from the pillow and sat up, shoving the duvet down to my waist. My hair fell in front of my face and I could barely breathe for the smell. "I didn't really get to talk to her, though."

I avoided Nick's eyes. I could tell he knew there was more here, that I was holding something back. He's always known. The difference between him and my fans is patience, and trust. "The past few days can't have been easy on her," he said about Diana. "Do you think maybe she'd like some time to herself? Maybe you wait a week, give her a call?"

Nick's empathy toward Kelsey's mom cut too close to the bone. I was already drowning in guilt where Diana was concerned. I already knew that my presence was a hurricane. "Are you saying you think it was a mistake for me to come here?" I snapped.

"What? No. Not at all—"

"Because I'm perfectly aware of how much oxygen I suck up, Nick.

And if you aren't up for that, then maybe you should rethink this marriage proposal you keep shoving down my throat."

A sudden stillness opened between us. *I'm sorry I'm sorry I'm sorry*, I thought. Please. I lash out when I'm scared.

Nick picked at a loose thread on his pillowcase. After a moment, he looked at me, his eyes so green they looked golden. "Remember the other night at dinner when I told your mom I don't ever feel lonely?" he said.

I didn't nod. I didn't say anything at all. I felt paralyzed by my own cruelty and stubbornness.

"It wasn't true," Nick said. "I do feel lonely sometimes, but not because I don't feel understood, like your mom was saying. I know you understand me better than anyone. And that's why it feels really lonely—because you still won't let me in."

I didn't argue. He was right. But I couldn't share any more of myself with him until I knew which story I wanted to tell.

DIANA ANSWERS THE DOOR WEARING LEGGINGS AND AN OVER-sized sweatshirt, pilling in spots, frayed at the cuffs. Her hair is pulled back in a haphazard bun at the nape of her neck. Without makeup, Kelsey's mother looks even more tired than she did at the service, or more middle-aged. "I was wondering if you'd stop by," she says, scanning over my shoulder as she opens the storm door to clock my security. "Do the thugs want to come inside too?"

"Only if you might try to kill me." I smile.

She laughs in an empty kind of way. "I don't think I have the energy."

I follow Diana into the kitchen, where she invites me to sit at the table while she fills the kettle for tea. My mom teaches her clients to respond to anxiety with an activity called *I see, I hear, I feel*: you identify five things you see, five things you hear, and then five things you feel. (You can repeat the activity, identifying four things for each sense, then three, and so on, until you feel grounded and present.) I try it now, in Kelsey's kitchen, but everything is a loaded gun—I see Fiona standing on her step stool in front of the sink; I hear Kelsey humming while she fiddles with the oven knob, the gas clicking until it catches; I feel the chill off the drafty back door, the sudden breeze where the cats came and went through the flap.

Diana puts two mugs of tea on the table and sits across from me. For a moment we stay like that, the drinks steaming between us, me watching as Diana rotates her cup gently in half circles, clockwise, then counter-clockwise.

"This house meant a lot to me," I say.

Kelsey's mother looks up, meeting my gaze with her eyes slightly narrowed. I have no idea what Diana thinks of me, not really, this girl who zipped into her daughter's life and left with everything she ever wanted. An impulse to beg forms in the bottom of my throat, a strangled knot of discomfort and guilt. "I liked hearing the two of you like that," she says after a beat. "On the news last night. Don't get me wrong," she adds, "I'm not thrilled about them trying to turn my daughter into a celebrity footnote."

I wince. "We didn't know they had the clip."

Diane waves me off. "But I haven't heard Kelsey sing in a very long time. And I'd be lying if I said I didn't want to listen to that track every day for the rest of my life."

I think about how my mother is careful to say things like "I hear you" instead of "I understand." Do not presume empathy. "I always thought of Kelsey as so much older and wiser than me," I admit. "But hearing her voice on that clip was like—" I fumble after the right phrasing, the song-writer in me resistant to clichés. They're allowed only if you turn them a little. "It was like when your eyes have to adjust to different light. I don't think I had it wrong before, I just think I had a different perspective."

"You were both just kids," Diana says.

"Exactly," I agree. "You know, the day we made that recording—Kelsey was . . . different."

Diana tilts her head, curious. "How so?"

I think about how in live shows the music is always slightly faster, especially if we're not all wearing ears and using a click track. The energy and adrenaline boost the tempo. I have to remember to breathe, to be patient, to steady my heart. I thought I would be the one with questions today—the miner sent alone down the shaft. But it occurs to me that Diana and I might be co-explorers, each of us searching for absolution in the dark.

"I thought she was mad at me," I tell Diana. "I've wondered about it for fifteen years. Do you know if there was something else going on around then? Did something happen?"

Kelsey's mother sighs. I see how a piece of her hair has slipped from the bun at the base of her neck and curled like a small tail. I hear the grind of the fridge, a mechanical churn. I feel the hard spindle of the chairback against my shoulder blade. And then Diana tells me, for the first time and in her own words, about Kelsey's father.

HE TOLD HER HIS NAME WAS DEAN.

It wasn't really a lie because she had his full name right there in his file, Lucas Dean Sullivan, but when she performed his intake in the ER he told her that people called him Dean, after his middle name. She said, "Well, I usually call people by their last names anyway, Mr. Sullivan."

From the beginning, a deception, but he would insist—still not getting it—that it wasn't, not exactly. She made him sound like such a monster.

He'd run his hand through a table saw. It could have been worse. Just two slices across the tops of his index and middle fingers. Given the state of his hands—gnarled, swollen knuckles, scars everywhere—she was amazed he'd come in at all. She knew plenty of people who would have tried—foolishly or not—to make do with some gauze and tape.

"Yeah," he said when she told him it didn't look too bad, "I was mostly worried about tetanus?"

He needed two stitches in each slice and a new Tdap. As she prepped each cut for the doctor he sucked air in between his front two teeth, a hiss in reverse. "Don't these things usually have automatic stops of some kind?" she asked while she flushed the wound.

"Mm," he grunted. "The nice ones do." He had a strong jaw and dark, thick hair pulled into a small ponytail.

"Isn't that a bit like saying, 'well, the *nice cars* have seat belts'?"

"Yeah, and?"

He made her laugh.

She had a thing about bringing men around Matt, which was a little difficult to navigate because she had a thing about men too. Couldn't live with 'em, couldn't live without 'em. But Matt was in pre-K and she worked evenings at the hospital so Lucas Dean could come over in the middle of the day without having to meet her son.

He was one of those men who cobbled together work. He painted houses, led fly-fishing expeditions, grabbed one-offs as a handyman for his buddies—plumbers, contractors. Sometimes he couldn't come over because he got called to a job. *Baby,* he'd say, *you know I gotta take 'em when they come.*

Of course, she'd say.

Her schedule made things difficult too. He didn't stay over because she didn't get off until after midnight. She had a sitter who watched Matt until she got home, and then she had to get up to get Matt to school and then it was back to bed for another couple of hours. So they didn't do things that a normal couple did: no dinner dates; no movies; no Saturday walks with going-cold coffees. It was okay, she thought. She was a twenty-five-year-old single mom. She didn't have time for that sort of pageantry.

He was the kind of aloof that was magnetic. He would offer nothing of himself and then, suddenly, out of the blue, decide to tell you about learning to fish with his father when he was seven, eight. He was a restless kid, he said, always getting in trouble in school because he did his worksheets standing up or he used the lunchroom garbage can as a basketball hoop. But in the quiet summer mornings on the river he found something in the cast-and-reel rhythm, the soft satisfying noise of the lure in the water. She saw him as a little boy, black-haired in the clean light, finding peace for the first time.

His mother had bipolar disorder. She slammed doors, resolved fights by storming out, forcing the children—Luke had a brother two years older—to pursue her, to tentatively knock with their small soft fists and peek inside her dark room and apologize for something they only vaguely understood. Later, she wore her housecoat around the living room all day and berated their father.

But these moments of vulnerability and longing were tiny blips in an otherwise armored existence. Diana would want to know about his day and he would say, *Don't be like that.*

Like what? she'd ask.

Don't make us into a boring sitcom couple, like we have nothing to talk about besides our routine.

Instead they had sex. It was very, very good, although he didn't like to use condoms and preferred to come on Diana's stomach or back. She would lie there with him dripping into her belly button while he went to the bathroom for a warm, wet washcloth. He wiped her off in a small circle, fishing into her navel, grinning.

It was a coworker, Tracey, who told Diana he was married. This was before anything you needed to know about a person was online. More or less you had to take somebody at their word. Tracey caught Diana in the parking lot one night and asked, "The guy you're seeing—he's a handyman, right?"

Diana nodded. She hadn't talked about him much at work; she'd always had a preference for keeping the various parts of her life compartmentalized.

"What's his name?"

"Dean. Well, Luke, but his friends call him by his middle name. Do you need something done around the house?"

Tracey and her husband were having their first-floor half bath remodeled. The contractor brought in another guy to do the paint, Tracey said. She thought it was him.

"Oh, that's funny," Diana said.

Tracey waffled from foot to foot, took a deep breath, then said, "I want you to know that—whatever's going on—I'm absolutely not judging you. And I wouldn't say anything if I thought there wasn't a chance you didn't already know this."

Diana felt her heart at the back of her jaw. Maybe, she thinks now, somewhere, she knew. The fact that he never stayed the night. That he was noncommittal about his plans, that he was always rushing to a job.

He was married, Tracey said. He kept talking about his wife.

From there Diana made a lot of mistakes. It seemed—in hindsight—that every time she got to a fork in the road, an option to confront reality or to burrow further, deeper into her fantasy, she chose the latter. And he had an explanation for everything. Yes, he was technically married but they were living separately. Divorce was expensive. He told her that he married his wife because he felt bad for her, because her mother had died suddenly and she'd gotten pregnant and had a miscarriage and it was too much trauma for a person; she needed Luke to be a life raft. So he'd married her. It was the good, upstanding thing to do. But he didn't love her.

"She calls you Luke?" Diana asked.

"Because she doesn't know me like you," he said. "You know what I like."

After that he slept over for the first time, as if to prove the point. She introduced him to Matt. They went on a weekend ski trip, spent a Saturday night in a cabin in Vermont. Luke paid for the sitter.

She stopped talking about him at work. She made her life smaller.

Another parking lot night. "I didn't know if I should tell you this," Tracey said, "but your ex was in here."

Same heart thudding, stomach plummeting, intestines slimed to her toes.

"A little girl," Tracey said. "Seven pounds, five ounces."

When you want something to be true badly enough, you find your way. He slipped, he said. Got her pregnant one night when he was over at her house fixing the dishwasher. It was in those couple of months when things were rocky between him and Diana. It didn't mean they were getting back together. Diana was the one he wanted to have a family with.

Still when they fucked he pulled out. Like teenagers she ended up pregnant anyway. When Kelsey was born he came to the hospital. Tracey saw him leaving and that was the last of their friendship.

The fog of new motherhood. Kelsey had trouble latching. Twice they saw a lactation coach, who explained that Kelsey had a slight tongue-tie. Diana's nipples bled. Luke divided his time between his children. When Diana asked if Kelsey could meet her half sister Luke said that her mother wasn't crazy about the idea. "She's insane," he told her. "I'm working on it."

When Kelsey was six months old, Matt tipped over the cheap Vick's humidifier in his room and spilled boiling water all over his pajamas. The hot wet fabric clung to the skin on his left thigh. She paged Luke over and over again from the ER but he didn't answer. She spent the night with an infant strapped to her chest while her son's leg oozed through layers of gauze, new bandages every two hours. Luke told her that he left his beeper at a job earlier that day. He was so, so sorry.

Two weeks later she brought Luke lunch while he was painting a house and then parked her car around the corner until he finished. She followed him, imagining herself like the Soviet spies that had loomed large in her adolescent brain.

He'd told Diana he was living with his brother, but as soon as Diana saw the A-frame at the end of the winding road that peeled away from the lake, she knew that wasn't true. Two dogs roamed the lawn, a lab whose belly swung beneath him and a shepherd mix with arrows for ears. A tire swing pendulumed from a maple in the side yard. One of those red-and-yellow plastic pedal cars in the driveway.

After work she drove back. The sitter would wait an extra half hour; sometimes Diana got stuck at the hospital. She parked down the road slightly and walked up the street to the driveway. Something—not her—set off a motion detector light over the garage. One of the dogs barked, then the other. She tucked behind the maple tree.

The A-frame had a large porch with sliding glass all along the front. Those houses were built to catch the rising sun. A light flicked on somewhere deep inside, illuminating the depths. Diana knew right away that the figure moving toward the windows wasn't Luke. She was too small, too controlled in her motion. Luke was rangy, arms swinging, shoulders held up tight. The woman peered out into the yard, face pressed against the glass. She put her hands on her hips and rotated slightly, stretching her lower back. Sending her melon-shaped belly into profile.

For a long time that was the end of it. Luke wasn't going to risk blowing up his real life for his fake one—as a custody battle would have—so he let Diana go. Matt asked, once or twice, why Mommy's friend Dean didn't come over anymore, because Matt was going through a dinosaur phase and Luke kept a dollar-store tube of plastic dinos in his car for when he stopped by. When Matt emptied his bucket of toys on the carpet in the living room he might occasionally stare at the faded stegosaurus and be reminded of the guy who used chase him around the couch, elbows tucked into his sides to make his arms small like a T. rex. But kids are resilient. They move on.

Kelsey, of course, had no memories of her father. When she was in third grade and playing Barbies at her friend Jessica's house, Jess's mom overheard Kelsey narrating an elaborate story wherein her Kelly doll chose to "leave" one Barbie family for another because the other family had a daddy. This surprised Diana because Kelsey had never said a thing about wanting a dad before. There are all kinds of families, Diana told her. This was upstate New York in the mid-to-late nineties, so in reality almost all of Kelsey's classmates had traditional heteronormative family structures, but Diana found books about queer families and adopted children and single parents and read them to Kelsey at night.

But teenagers will be teenagers. They shoot to kill. Every now and then it would come up in confrontation: when Matt was fourteen or fifteen and he missed curfew he might say to Diana, *What's the worst that could happen? I'd get somebody pregnant?* Or *It's no wonder our dads left. You're such a fucking nag.* By the time Kelsey was the same age, Matt was going through a rough patch, dating Billie and getting stoned a lot, and the fights were worse. Suddenly both kids were impossible.

Diana ran into Luke, of all places, picking out a Christmas tree with Fiona. He was alone, the beleaguered dad sent to pick up the tree on a too-cold December night. When she saw him across the picked-over rows of pines, face half in shadow, her first thought was: *run.*

Her next thought was that he was one of those men who only got better-looking with age. The gray suited him, as did the slight weathering around the eyes, across the forehead. He looked more powerful than ever. Meanwhile she only looked more tired.

Fiona shrieked from down the row. "This one! This one!" That's when Luke looked up and over.

She slept with him the first time because she wanted to know what it would feel like, to fuck him with a full understanding of who he was. She slept with him a second time because he called and said that he couldn't stop thinking about her and it felt good—so good—to be the one calling the shots, to be *answering* the phone rather than waiting by it. When he told her he was unhappy in his marriage, that he always had been, that the only reason he stayed was the kids, she pressed one finger to his lips and slipped another beneath the sheets. She was done wasting energy on whether he was telling her the truth. Every time they fucked she felt as if she was making some sort of payment into a debt of selfhood: he took so much of her so many years ago, made her feel so small and uncertain and unloved, and now here she was, making a choice for herself, telling him how she liked to be touched rather than worrying if he liked how she felt.

She knows now that it wasn't as simple as that, that still on some level she was deriving validation from her abuser. But these things are not easily untangled.

It happened on a Wednesday in March. Fiona was down for her nap and Luke was working a job nearby. They had just finished when they heard the clatter of the front door—the storm glass needed replacing; it vibrated in its slot—and then Kelsey's voice. "Mom? You got company?" They heard her singing next, a soft warbling, and then the opening and shutting of the cupboards. They hurried to dress, hissing at one another. *Why is she home?* Diana shrugged. It was spring break. Kelsey was supposed to be helping out with spring cleaning at Tahawus, opening up and airing out the buildings after a long winter.

Fiona called down the hallway. Diana heard Kelsey's singing switch to *Beauty and the Beast*: "Bonjour! Good day!" Diana stopped at Matt's door on her way down the hall. Kelsey sat on the edge of Fiona's little toddler bed, stroking her dark curls. "I thought you were spending the day at camp?"

"Pipe burst in the kitchen," Kelsey said. "Above my pay grade. Who's here?"

Luke appeared over Diana's shoulder. Kelsey looked from him to her mother, obviously suspicious.

"This is Dean. He came over to fix the showerhead." The lie came easily. "Maybe he can fix that pipe too," she said, laughing weakly.

Kelsey blinked, swallowed. Diana wondered if she saw herself in her father. She hung her hopes on the narcissism of adolescence. "Uh-huh," Kelsey said, and Diana knew her daughter didn't believe her for a second.

"Sure thing," Luke said, and then he looked at Diana. "Let me know if there are any issues. Nice to meet you girls," he added, and he was gone.

Kelsey brought Fiona into the kitchen and began assembling a plate of carrot sticks and cheese squares. When she spoke she used her kid voice, kept her tone light and pleasant so Fiona—busy cantering her plastic ponies across her plastic mat—wouldn't take notice of any emotional disturbance.

"So is this what you do?" Kelsey asked.

Diana was packing her dinner for her hospital shift. "What do you mean?"

"Squeeze in quickies with random men while your granddaughter naps?"

"Kelsey," Diana said, her voice low and stern—a warning.

"Matt trusts you to take care of her."

"I do take care of—"

"Are you fucking the mailman too?"

Diana steadied herself against the counter, tried counting down from ten.

"It's too bad there's no such thing as a milkman anymore. I think that would be the housewife trifecta—"

The thing is that Diana had spent so long feeling so much shame about Luke. She couldn't understand why, all those years ago, he had such a pull over her. Why she couldn't leave. Why she chose to believe his lies—because it was a choice, wasn't it? She knew a different reality existed. She was weak and pathetic and insecure and—

She smacked her hand down on the counter, a flat-palmed thud. Kelsey looked as if she'd been slapped. Fiona froze. And Diana spoke without thinking, a defensive, angry reaction to her daughter's slut-shaming. "I'm not fucking the handyman, Kelsey," she said. "I'm fucking your father."

She would regret it—not that she told the truth, but that she told it the way she did, deployed like a grenade, intended to wound rather than inform—for the rest of her life.

DIANA STANDS FROM THE TABLE AND MOVES TO GATHER THE mugs, but I stop her, wave her off. "I've got it," I say, and I take both handles through my right thumb and walk to the sink. A string of pearls drips from a macramé nest anchored at the ceiling. On the window, someone taped an octagon of tissue-paper stained glass. I think, briefly, of all the crafts Kelsey never saw Fiona make, how good she was at treating her niece's toddler drawings like Basquiats. I drizzle too much soap on the mugs, turn the water on to the hottest setting. Now I understand why Kelsey behaved the way she did at Alderidge: the week I'd been in Grand Cayman, she'd walked in on her mother fucking the father who abandoned her. Raff's story also makes perfect sense: Kelsey wouldn't have gone back to him after this. She would have done what every teenage girl does at least once and run, as far and as fast as she could, in the opposite direction of her mother's behavior. But that still leaves a hole in the plot.

"Do you think it's possible that Kelsey and Luke were in touch at all after that day?" I ask Diana, thinking of the first-edition Plath, signed with an *L*.

"Why?"

I towel off the mugs and rest them in the drying rack. "I wonder if she might have asked for his help," I say.

"With the college thing?" Diana asks, referring to the news story.

"Maybe." Kelsey wanted a ticket out. I can see how she might have tried to exploit her lemons for lemonade.

"Luke didn't have any more money than we did," Diana says.

"So he wouldn't have given her an expensive gift? An early birthday present, maybe?"

Diana doesn't try to hide her confusion: her eyebrows furrow, her lips roll inward; *what are you talking about?*

"I found a first-edition Sylvia Plath on Fiona's bookshelf," I explain. "It was Kelsey's, I think. It would have cost . . . a lot. I thought Luke might have bought it for her to prove he cared, or something. To try to get back into your lives."

Diana considers this. "That's not just an expensive gift, Dylan—it's a thoughtful one too. Even if he was trying to make up for seventeen years of absence, Luke just doesn't have the . . . ah, *interpersonal skills* to come up with something like that. The nicest thing he ever got me was a Banana Republic sweater." She sighs. "Plus, you know how stubborn Kelsey was. I can't imagine her asking him for anything."

"How can you be so sure, though?" The Kelsey I knew was headstrong—but she was also scrappy, resourceful, ruthless. She wasn't principled so much as she was unrelenting.

"Because of everything with Billie," Diana says, like it's the most obvious thing. "If she didn't believe Fiona's mom deserved a second chance, she couldn't very well have given one to Luke."

Of course, I think. So much of this story is tangled around our response to Billie and her perceived threat to the Copestenkes' delicate unit. So much of this knot comes down to who we forgive and what for and why.

The Misstep

We had another scandal, when the men were falling like dominoes. Every day, a new industry titan: first, a chorus of voices online—me too, me too, me too; then, in print, bold headlines, above the fold. For weeks the pieces ran. The facts were always roughly the same. Movies were canceled, then uncanceled. Corporations were renamed. Some men were arrested but many—most—merely had their lives dismantled, lost jobs and marriages and legacies. I thought about the men who surrounded me, who made up more than seventy percent of my collaborators, my company leadership, my band, my security and transport teams. Stacks of articles rose and swelled in my brain, multiplying daily, and I understood: it was unlikely that none of them had ever done something that merited a hashtag. Chances were.

It was my publicist at Melody who told me. The *Times* called for comment (the publicist knew how to play the game so that the story would read that they had "made repeated attempts to contact Ms. Read, without success" rather than that I had *denied* a request for comment, a small but critical distinction). They had four women, two of them on the record. The stories were credible. There were patterns.

The first question I asked was whether any of them were rape. The publicist barely hid her disgust. Now you know, I thought: That's the kind of person I am. Someone who ranks trauma.

The second question I asked was whether any of the women were—I waved my hand vaguely, as if my living room in Beverly Hills was representative of... what? My company? "You know," I said. "One of us."

"No," she said, "at least not among this set." She didn't have to explain what she meant by "among this set." There would be more women; there always were.

Still I felt a flash of fury, then the lock-jawed grit of defensiveness. "So I'm supposed to answer for his behavior even though it had nothing to do with me? I'm not his employer! I haven't worked with him in years!"

When the publicist said nothing, I asked my third question. "Do you think people will stop listening to my music because of him?" I thought about how all these men have blast radii—a field of destruction beyond their worst crimes, all the actors and directors whose careers began on their sets, their tainted résumés and origin stories and awards; I thought of children in elementary school art class, learning to paint by styling replica Van Goghs, or writers in high school fiction workshops, trying on voice in the vein of David Foster Wallace. Would they write in rambling, footnoted sentences forever? Would that ruin them?

The publicist spoke carefully. "You're the biggest name on his slate. That's just a fact. Every story about him will mention you." She paused. "But the good thing is, nobody really understands how music is made. A producer's influence—it's abstract to most listeners, especially in a case like yours."

In my mind I tallied all the things I'd made with Sam Jordan. I thought about *the only night games I'm playin' are the games that I'm playing with you* and *we got our shooting stars crossed* and *tellin' me white lies to avoid what lies ahead*. I thought about describing sounds with colors and moods and how he'd listen and then say, "Okay, so I think that means you want to bring the vocal forward," or if I said I wanted a song to feel "thin" and "strained" and "pleading" he'd say, "Okay, so let's play that guitar slightly out of tune." One time I told him I wanted a song to feel anxious and he gave me my first lesson in bars, which I'd previously understood only mathematically: In a 4/4 time signature, one *bar* is composed of four beats. But you can manipulate where a verse ends within the bar count to give the song a weird or rushed or, yes, *anxious* feel.

At the time, I hadn't taken any music theory. I didn't know that when I was using words like "warm" or "tinny" that I was describing timbre. Other producers like Niall and Lars would give me more advanced lessons in syncopation and musical math but Sam Jordan was the introductory course. It's like how your first real lover—not necessarily the person you lose your virginity to, but the person with whom you have that first prolonged, experimental, startlingly intimate relationship—informs how you fuck everybody else. We hadn't worked together in years—not since we'd disagreed over the production of "Stateline" and I'd made my final, permanent pivot to pop—but the truth was that I learned to speak the language of music from Sam.

His influence was not, in other words, at all abstract to me.

I decided against releasing a statement. I remembered how Aaron had tried to warn me about Sam, how I'd fought with him over barbecued ribs on his patio in Lakewood. How had I gotten it so wrong? I wondered. Why was it so hard for me to see the difference between condescension and care?

Maybe I deserved a public skewering. Maybe I even wanted one.

In the storm that ensued I lost sight of the villain. There were think pieces about the albums on which Sam had producing credits and think pieces about the think pieces. In the comments I found a handful of bright impassioned defenses—*for the one millionth time women are not responsible for the bad behavior of men; for fuck's sake she was 17*—swallowed up by righteous anger, the certainty that I must have known, that I was an enabler, that men like him only get away with their crimes because some women are willing to be shields. My Instagram filled with novel-length treatises on my complacency, my complicity. I let them fight among themselves for a while before wiping my feed, unfollowing everyone, deleting the app from my phone.

My contract with Melody was up. Despite my embattled status, they weren't about to walk away from their best-selling artist. But I wanted a clean slate—how had I not seen that before? I thought Nashville was the last link between me and Kelsey, but it was Melody: they'd signed me only because Adam McIver had found Cameron Cope's MySpace. Sam was just one more stain in an already-tarnished origin story. So we signed with Prismatic and I hired my own publicist rather than take one from in-house. About my social media secession, Sloane said simply, "I wish you'd talked to me about this beforehand."

But "beforehand" implied having thought it through. There was no thinking. There was only holding my skirt down as I climbed out of large SUVs and Google predictive search adding *nudes* to my name and a long history of women I'd abandoned, or who'd mutually abandoned me, and the question of whether or how much of it was, after all, my fault.

FOR A COUPLE OF WEEKS AFTER WE VISITED THE ALDERIDGE recording studio, Kelsey made excuses about not being able to get together. Fiona was taking toddler ballet lessons after school and Matt and Diana both had to work, so it was on Kelsey to handle drop-off and pickup. She had an English paper due on *Beloved*. She picked up a few hours of babysitting for the Randalls across the street, because the grandmother took a fall and was still in the hospital. These were normal reasons Kelsey might not have been able to hang out, and it occurred to me that I was just being paranoid—that she wasn't *avoiding* me; that this was just life—but I couldn't stop thinking about how quiet she'd been in the studio, how still and small her body had become, even if only briefly. I thought helping Kelsey plan for her future would guarantee my place in it, but what if all this talk about next steps only emphasized how soon she would have to leave me behind? Had she begun to harden off, to protect herself from further loss? I did my math homework, checked AIM constantly, read poetry before bed. I tried to write new songs but nothing came: only a hurricane of worries.

Finally Kelsey asked me to hang out on a Friday, when Matt and Diana would both be at work and when I could stay as late as I wanted, because my parents didn't force me to be home for family dinner on the weekends. We could write and play music and make tacos from the grocery store kit and I would teach Fiona how to dot the lettuce mound at the top of her shell with rings of black olives so they looked like eyes.

After dinner I did the dishes while Kelsey steered Fiona into the bathroom. I saw the business card as I was tightening the lid on the salsa in front of the fridge. *Amedore & Clark LLP*, it read, and in a neat line beneath the practice name, a list, the items separated by diamond bullet points: *Divorce ◆ Child Custody ◆ Child Support ◆ Adoption ◆ Domestic Violence.*

From the kitchen I could hear Kelsey's singing, Fiona's toddler gibberish like an underlying harmony: *I keep a close watch on this heart of mine . . .*

I leaned closer to the business card, as if the embossing would tell me anything more than what I could already guess: this was about Matt and Billie.

I quickly finished cleaning and tiptoed into the living room, to the family computer in the corner. After confirming that Kelsey was still busy with Fiona—I could hear them haggling over the specific number of bedtime stories, cribbed from Kelsey's campfire tales—I shuffled the mouse impatiently, urging the desktop to life, and then clicked online. Amedore & Clark's website featured a number of stock photos of women holding children, arms draped around their toddlers on a sunny afternoon, swinging them in the air in the golden hour, blowing dandelion pods into the wind. *The dissolution of an intimate partnership can result in more than emotional fallout. Our team can help you with the complex legal challenges that often arise from such a life transition.* Under "Areas of Practice" I selected "Child Custody," where another drop-down menu appeared.

I was scanning through the entries—*enforcement, modification, visitation*—when a new IM window popped up in front of Firefox.

GTBrigadier82: hey beautiful

My heart throttled forward, careening against my rib cage then traveling up my chest into my throat. It pulsed in my ears, at the back of my jaw. I watched Kelsey's away slip in automatically (brb), then waited, frozen.

GTBrigadier82: I have a present 4 u

Was *this* why Kelsey had been avoiding me? Had she started to see someone new? Or was this Raff—had she gone back to him, knowing their days were numbered anyway?

I had to know. My birthday's not til next month, I typed.

GTBrigadier82: who says its 4 ur bday
GTBrigadier82: maybe i just like to spoil u

My vision tunneled, the living room around me blotted to nothing. I drilled over the keyboard, thinking of what to say, how to step into Kelsey's voice.

copeofmanycolors7: well I hope you're not expecting any random gifts from me
GTBrigadier82: i know better than that
GTBrigadier82: neway theres only one thing i really want;)

A door opened then shut, slowly and quietly. I heard Kelsey twisting the knob carefully, easing the latch into place.

copeofmanycolors7: shit, I g2g

I x-ed out of the chat, quickly punched in our MySpace where Amedore & Clark had been, and pretended to be rearranging our friend list as Kelsey walked into the room. She launched herself over the back of the couch, landing on the cushions sideways. "Fucking kid needed to do the moose song four times through." She put her open hands to her temples, miming moose antlers. Kelsey sang Fiona camp songs sometimes at night, and only when Matt wasn't around—*they get her all riled up*, he'd say; he wasn't wrong. "Anyway," she said, looking at me, "what are you doing? Cybersex?"

"Gross," I said. My heart hammered in my ears.

"Don't knock it till you try it," Kelsey said. "But if you're gonna use my AIM to do it, you better put on a good show. I don't need anybody diluting my brand."

I wondered if I could coax her into telling me about GTBrigadier82. I kept my tone dry, dismissive. "You do not use this computer for cybersex," I said.

"You think Matt isn't watching porn on that?"

I lifted my hand from the mouse as if scalded. Kelsey cackled.

"That seems sort of . . . unboundaried," I said.

Kelsey was still laughing. "Boundaries?" she repeated. "There's no boundaries when you're poor!"

She reached for her phone on the coffee table and texted with her head dangling off the seat, the soft milk of her throat exposed to me. "Do you wanna go to Bridget's tonight?"

"What about Fiona?"

"When Matt gets back," she said, still typing. "Then we can take the car."

I chewed the inside of my lower lip. "Is everything okay with Matt?" I asked.

Kelsey didn't look up from her phone. "What? Why?" she asked.

I teetered at the edge of our cliff. On the one hand, it's not like they were hiding the business card—it was right there on the fridge. On the other, Kelsey was mercurial about what she kept private—she never told me she hooked up with Raff at the North Pole, nor had she told me about GTBrigadier82. (It had to be Raff, right?) "I saw a business card on the fridge," I admitted. "For a family lawyer?"

Kelsey swung around, sitting upright, and tossed her phone to the other end of the couch. "Oh," she said. "That."

I waited. From our MySpace, "Play It Backwards" murmured on low, Kelsey's timbre somehow more velvet with the vocals made indiscernible.

"Billie wants custody." She began picking at a chip in the lacquer on the coffee table. I tried to force my face into her sight line, but she wouldn't take her eyes from the peeling wood.

"Is this because Matt wouldn't let Fiona go visit over Christmas?" I asked.

Kelsey shrugged. "She's moving to Florida, to be near her mom. Says it's good for her sobriety. And she wants to take Fiona with her."

"Wait a minute—" I pushed out of my chair and kneeled on the carpet in front of Kelsey, hands on the table between us. "This isn't, like, she wants to take her on weekends and every other holiday? She wants *full* custody?"

"I'm not worried. She's done this before."

"Matt's had to go to court before?"

"Well," Kelsey said, "no. But Billie's threatened to do this."

Kelsey could pretend not to worry—but I couldn't help worrying *for* her. "I'm sorry," I said feebly. "I didn't know."

"Because there's nothing to know. *If* Billie stays sober long enough to go to court, it'll take the judge two-point-five seconds to see her for what she is, which is a white-trash piece of shit who just wants a WIC card."

I think she wanted me to laugh. I let out a quick puff of air, forced through my nostrils.

"Come on," Kelsey said, standing up. "You can't go out like that."

"Like what?" I asked.

"Like Joan Baez went shopping at American Eagle."

NICK DEVLIN CAME TO LA. HIS NOVEL'S ADAPTATION WAS OR-dered to series. His office overlooked the wash and a golf course, kept a startling green despite the drought. At 11 p.m. on a Thursday night he texted to invite me to a cast member's birthday party in Venice. I guessed he was a little drunk.

I live in Beverly Hills, I wrote, a classic LA response: nope, too far.

It's 11PM. The roads will be empty.

I couldn't tell Nick that I was trying to be invisible. I didn't know how to explain to him that venues that describe themselves as "private" are actually breeding grounds for paparazzi, for waitstaff looking to make a quick buck off a *Page Six* tip.

I wanted to shield him from my reality, which is exactly how I knew I had feelings for him.

I have to write, I told him.

He replied immediately: Coffee first?

We met at a twenty-four-hour diner in Culver City, on a block snared in gentrification: an hourly motel across the street from a tech company's sleek new office space; a mom-and-pop taqueria next to a shop that built custom bikes for five figures each. I saw Nick from the parking lot, seated in a booth against the window and framed in white fluorescent light like a Hopper painting. As I entered, a couple men at the counter turned to look at me, then turned just as indifferently away.

Nick pushed a bowl of creamers and a plate of sugar packets in my direction. "I didn't know how you like it." His accent clipped his words, smashing them into each other. I worried—frantically—that I would accidentally mimic him, that I might find myself thinking so hard about my vowels that I'd imitate his truncated ones.

"Just black," I said, pulling the coffee closer. "So how was the party?"

Nick smiled into his drink sheepishly. When he lifted his gaze to meet mine it looked as if he was about to confess something. "I don't love this part of the job," he said.

It made me want to crack him open. "The parties?"

He nodded. I laughed for what felt like the first time in months. "I knew that coming here would mean a lot of . . . socializing," he said. "But . . ." He exhaled in an awestruck way: *Whew. Sheesh.*

"You're an introvert, huh?"

Nick smirked. "I'm a novelist."

"Who wants to be a TV writer."

He tilted his head. "I guess . . . I just don't know how long they'll let me stay, you know?" He laughed to himself then. "So if I get this show made, that might help me make another one, which could help me sell more books—"

"—so that maybe—one day!—you'll be able to stop worrying about whether it's too late to go to law school instead."

When Nick laughed it was in a quiet kind of way—not stifled, exactly, but gentle. Tender. Knowing. "I don't know if it's reassuring or depressing that you understand what I'm talking about."

It was true that I was a long way from needing a backup plan. Even with the massive expense of private security, I had enough money to last more than a lifetime. But I knew as well as any artist about a process that makes you feel like you can never stop running. That was the thing about Nick: he made me feel normal. I was a writer in a shitty diner commiserating about the hamster wheel. There were a million people just like me in cities all over the world.

I lowered my voice and leaned across the table, close enough that I could smell the party's silage stuck to his clothes: stale smoke and liquor. "The treadmill *never* stops," I told him.

Nick laughed. "Now tell me something I *don't* already know."

His understanding washed over me like an absolution. I feared I could tell him everything.

WE HIRED A NEW PRODUCER, WYATT GALLOWAY—WYATT HAD an emo band in the nineties and worked on a bunch of pop-punk and pop-rock stuff in the aughts—and I sent files to him at odd hours: five a.m., midnight, three thirty in the morning. Sometimes he listened to my demos right away, shot back words of encouragement: *keep going*. Other times I waited two, three hours, and checked my email to find a folder of stems. *Let me know what you think*, he'd say.

I picked Wyatt because I knew I was making a pop-rock album, and rock is supposed to feel messy: rock vocals are yell-y or grating; rock instrumentals are raw and noisy; rock records have a kind of cacophonous live-music feel, the whole band at once in the studio. My own creative instincts all run in the direction of polish. I'm not a very technical singer and I'm a perfectly average instrumentalist, but when I put all the parts together I want them to *fit*, every element locked neatly in place. The songs I was writing in the wake of the allegations against Sam were angry and brittle and I knew that my own production tendencies would sand the edges, give everything a slick gloss. Wyatt would help show me how to keep the texture.

He understood that there were three of us in the studio. On a Tuesday morning, three weeks into tinkering with "Shadow Play," we argued over the line placement in the chorus: I wanted it on the beat, while Wyatt insisted it was too *neat* for such an emotionally messy song.

"That's the fucking *point*," I said, "that we're doing a tethering and an untethering in this track, that the beats should match the speaker's struggle."

"Just *listen to it*!" He played the track as we had it again. "The problem is that it sounds flat. Boring, like a doldrum."

"So let's speed it up."

He looked at me sadly, a pitying frown just barely tipping the corners of his mouth.

"Sam gave you the syncopated chorus line, didn't he?" The name felt like a slap.

"Sam didn't invent running the lyrics offbeat," I said.

"Obviously! So why are you making *every single rhythm decision* in reaction to the work you made before?" He paused. "Do you know what no one else does like you? Those melodic tumbles, the cascading note at the end of a verse. And the way you unspool entire stories in lines? How sometimes the breath is impossible in your lyrics?"

"I don't need you to tell me what I do well!" I felt small and pitied, uncertain and snared.

"You're forgetting what you know! Sam didn't give you your instincts. He just gave you a tool kit that you could have gotten anywhere."

We laid down "Lessons" with crunchy guitars and blown-out electronics; I talk-sang over the verse, plotting and ruminating: *late at night I think of all the things I can't make right / stuck in an endless fight / just me against myself.* In "Madam" I wrote about a woman who stole millions of dollars from the robber barons, a Gilded Age huckster who died by suicide rather than be locked away for life. She slit her own throat, I read; they found her body in a tub of her own bloody water, the wound pale and clean. We gave her song the radical unpredictability of a dancehall drum line. In another life I would have gone to Lilah's house and shared the music with her as it was in process, would have told her how I wondered whether anyone would want to hear my work ever again. But that was over now. In a Google spiral that began with paparazzi photos of her getting coffee at Alfred on Melrose, I read that the name Lilah comes from the Hebrew word for "night" or "darkness."

Like most things on the internet, my findings had a choose-your-own-facts quality to them. One site said Lilah's name meant "night creature" or "night monster." But another said that it was used to describe how the night is darkest before the dawn.

I GOT DRUNK AT BRIDGET NEARY'S. PLAYING FLIP CUP ON A sticky card table in the basement, I thought about GTBrigadier82 and took shots between rounds. I wondered what the "82" was for—was it his birthday? August second? I stole cranberry juice from the Nearys' fridge and mixed it with vodka from their freezer and imagined the gifts he might have bought for Kelsey: lingerie, flavored condoms, candy thongs. I thought about how easy things were for me, how neat and tidy my life was, and how maybe Kelsey kept secrets from me because she thought I wouldn't understand. What did I know about sex, what did I know about addiction, what did I know about money, what did I know about problems.

At some point I found myself on the grass, with Megan O'Neill and Bridget yelling at me from the boathouse roof. My top got tangled on my ponytail as I lifted it over my head and I worried about the underwear I was wearing, pink-and-white striped, and how the white would dampen to translucency once we dove in.

I don't remember the feel of the water. It's one of those memories that has become a photograph rather than an experience, something I've read about but not actually lived. I know that when I came up from underneath, Bridget and Megan were inches from me, arms spread, goose-flesh blue, screaming a warrior's cry. I screamed back, mouth open wide to swallow the moonlight. We sat in flannel blankets next to the fire, close enough that a stray flame might catch the fibers. A boy I didn't know sat between me and Bridget and after five minutes or fifteen he put a hand on my bare knee, casually, and that was when I realized I hadn't seen Kelsey in I didn't know how long.

I turned to the boy—dark hair shorn short, the kind that seemed like it would have a satisfying roughness if you were to run your hand across it—and asked if he knew where my friend went. He looked at me like a person might look at a toddler. *You silly girl.*

Across the flames Dan said, "She left."

"What?"

Dan leaned his body into Bridget, who curled under his arm. "She left."

I looked around the deck, at the small smattering of people still jumping into the lake, through the oily windowpanes of the sliding glass doors. I was looking for Kelsey but also for Raff.

"I can give you a ride," the boy next to me said, and I remembered his name: *Tyler.* "Yeah," he said. "That's me."

I laughed. I didn't realize I'd said it out loud. "I think I should go home now," I said.

"Okay," he said. "You should probably put some clothes on?"

I looked down at my legs, the skin of my sternum beneath the blanket, orange in the firelight. "I guess so."

Tyler smiled at me. Shadows raccooned under his eyes. "I'll get your stuff," he said. "You left it down on the dock." He moved his hand up from my knee and squeezed my thigh, slightly, fingertips dug into the curve of my adductor.

When he came back he pressed his stomach into my shoulders, leaning over me to place my clothes in my lap. "Ready?"

Tyler held the door for me. I maneuvered through the party's thinning crowd with the blanket notched at my neck like a cape, Tyler trailing me, to the bathroom off the family room. With my feet pressed against the tiling I turned over my shoulder and asked Tyler if he wanted to help me get dressed.

"I'd prefer to help you get undressed," he said, and stepped inside the bathroom, shut the door, turned out the lights.

When Tyler asked me if I was on birth control I lied. Maybe it was just because I was and always will be the kind of girl who has the resources to deal with an unwanted pregnancy. Maybe the conversation I'd had with GTBrigadier82 had left me feeling reckless, unboundaried. Maybe I heard Kelsey's voice in my mind—*they hate having to use a condom, it's so much worse*—and most of all, more than anything else, I wanted to be thought of as good at this.

NICK'S SHOW WAS SET TO WRAP IN A MONTH—IN HOLLYWOOD, that meant six to eight weeks—after which he'd return to Ireland, managing most of postproduction from abroad. Until then he was renting a place in Studio City, a white clapboard house with a New England shabby-chic feel and a firepit in a secluded backyard. He shared the home with his director, Colin, who was from England, and I called it the frat, even though I couldn't imagine either of them having joined a frat had they gone to American universities and not, as had been the actual case, Trinity and Oxford, respectively.

Mostly he came to my house. We weren't spending the night yet, but he stayed late and together we watched the long sunsets of a California summer. He left when the night settled into its starless dusty black, and I worried about him whipping around the boulevard's S-turns, imagined a coyote in the beam of his headlights, his rented Volvo SUV careening off a cliffside. I felt too needy to ask him to text when he got home, but maybe he knew I was afraid: I had fun tonight, he'd write, or send a selfie of his head leering over Colin, asleep on the couch with a video game controller in his lap.

I have a thing about air-conditioning—I don't like the way the chill settles into your bones and joints, the way you forget, after just a few hours inside, how air is supposed to smell: layered, thick, present. I use the AC on only the hottest days in LA, preferring to bake in my house like a brick oven. When we had sex Nick's sweat dripped from his nose and forehead and hair onto my face, my chest, my lips. We laughed when it landed in my eye, salty and stinging, and switched to me on top, our bodies slipping as we tried to find a new rhythm. I ordered new lingerie in bulk, bouquets of lace thongs in aquamarine and lapis and cerulean with matching bras. I bought casual wrap dresses and wore them without a bra, untying myself for Nick like a gift. I forgot, for a while, that the internet even existed, that somewhere, many someones were writing that I was a liar, an enemy to women, an ice queen.

He packed his things on a Saturday in late July and drove to my house in the afternoon. No one knew about us, except for Colin and whoever saw us in that diner booth on a Thursday night in Culver City. We were uncharacteristically quiet; he was a little hungover, one too many whiskeys at the wrap party the night before. I felt strangled by all the things I wanted to say, like if I opened my mouth I would force us to confront what we had tacitly, wordlessly agreed to try: something long-distance. We were wealthy and had flexible careers and it was easy, really, to hop on a ten-hour plane ride, especially when you can charter them yourself.

I grilled steaks so lightly they were still violet inside and we ate them with shoestring fries delivered from a restaurant he liked in West Hollywood. We would have had sex right there on the striped cushions of my pool deck chairs except I was worried, of course, about cameras with long-angle lenses and invisible recording devices wedged into the vines that cloaked my privacy fence, and so we went inside and fucked wordlessly, faces pressed close together, and I didn't come because I was too sad, too mad at him for being hungover, too confused about what it meant that he was choosing to go home when wasn't this the best thing we had ever had?

For two weeks after he left I wrote nothing, not a word. The time difference was hard; we texted while I ate the last of the season's berries in the dry whip of the Santa Anas and he picked over mussels in a pub down the street from his office. At night I studied my angles in my bathroom mirror, click-clicking away at shots with my hands over my nipples, pressing cleavage into existence. I deleted them all, paranoid about hackers. Instead I sent words. I miss touching you.

There was a fire. The winds carried the smoke out to sea and the sunsets turned sandy, a wash of dusty taupe. He texted and asked if I planned to stay and I said, we can't leave every time there's a fire, and he typed, deleted, typed, deleted, and then finally said: is it terrible that I'm trying to use a natural disaster as an excuse to get you to come visit

The tabloids, I wrote. They're even worse in Europe.

I know. His ellipses blinked. We can rent a place in the country.

Work? I asked.

Let me worry about that. And then: Just come.

We rented a place an hour outside Dublin, an eighteenth-century estate with a long, crushed-gravel driveway surrounded by a hundred acres of parkland and forest. A working horse farm, the stables housed two dozen warmbloods in gleaming chestnut and dusty dun and pearled honey. I liked the foggy chill, the way the air tempered the animal tang of the barns. At night Nick and I drank whiskey in two-finger increments and wandered to the stables, slipping through a small gap in the three-hundred-year-old door, creaking it open just wide enough to fit, so the horses shuddered and exhaled but did not fuss. I wrapped my leg around his waist as he pressed me against the stone and felt the smell on me for days, warm and peaty.

I read that in California the horses had to be evacuated by the truck-load. They carried them inland to farms in the Central Valley, where cattle are slaughtered by the hundreds daily. I understood that we had made an oasis for ourselves, a paradise of purple heather and rose-colored roans and bitter tea and morning buns. I never learned to like the thick coffee taste of Guinness but I loved how the hops hung on Nick's breath after. When he went down on me and came up again I brought his lips to mine and tasted myself but also the earth and wheat of booze. I thought about all the private things between us that I could never write about, and understood that this was intimacy: the knowledge that something is unique only because you choose to frame it that way. As an artist I had never felt more inspired, but as a lover I only wondered how bulletproof I could make our bunker, how long I could keep the world out.

FROM EUROPE I SENT WYATT SONGS ABOUT HILLSIDES OF VAR-iegated green and stormy beaches and moss-covered bridges made of crumbling stone. *White house on the corner with the back door / come here, let me give you the full tour / stranger in a strange land, here's your safe port.* I imagined them against wailing strings or finger-plucked guitars or dampened piano chords, a tender and delicate production totally counter to what we'd been writing in the wake of the allegations. I didn't want to throw away the old tracks, I told him; I wanted all the dissonance on the album, the heartbeat bassline of glam-rock next to the distorted electric guitar of classic rock alongside these soft, sweet pop ballads.

"Shipwrecked" was the last song we wrote. I worried about tacking a guiding theory on at the end—shouldn't you know your thesis at the beginning? "It feels like we're shoehorning a song into existence," I argued. "We're only writing this because I liked it as an album title."

"How many times has the last song you've written been your best one?" Wyatt asked. I thought about it. "Did that make you go back and re-engineer the whole album?" No. "It's actually really creatively honest, right? You found your way through the material. It's a capstone." He paused, sensing that I was unconvinced. "We arrived at the concept because it was there in the existing lyrics, as a kind of subtext."

Wyatt was right. But I had long ago forgotten how to trust my gut, how to search for treasure in the minefield of my subconscious.

I CALLED KELSEY IN THE MORNING, PHONE PRESSED AGAINST my cheek with my head still on the pillow. I tried three times, then hung up and texted her *can you not be terrible about your phone for just one second, and then, call me.* In those days you had to be eighteen to get the morning-after pill; I knew girls at school sometimes went to Planned Parenthood for contraception, but it seemed so much easier—and so much less embarrassing—to just ask Kelsey to use her fake. I rolled over in my bed and slept until ten, until my mom knocked on my door and said, *okay, sweetie, enough of this.*

In the kitchen I shuffled from the fridge to the toaster, assembling a pile of Kashi waffles (*even your frozen waffles are expensive,* I heard Kelsey say, *and I bet—yep! No fake syrup here, just Vermont's finest*), nesting a handful of too-early blueberries on top. My knife crunched through the toasted ridges, and I ate three bites before I allowed myself to check my phone, then three more, then three more. It was one of those spring mornings where summer seems possible, and out our back door I watched my parents putz around the yard, wiping down the pool furniture, sweeping the deck, arguing half-heartedly about whether the fence needed painting. I rinsed my plate in the sink, watching the last of the syrup streak in ripples, before loading it in the dishwasher.

In my bedroom I showered until the water ran cold, one shoulder slumped against the wall, the pounding in my head dulled by the steady pressure of the faucet. I stared at my face too long in the mirror, wondering whether my skin always looked like this, sunken and pallid. My hair felt brittle in the bristles of my brush, tiny tangled knots everywhere. I didn't yet understand how a hangover can function as a kind of slow-motion panic attack, a radio dial set to self-loathing on a low murmur in the back of my brain. I hadn't learned how it makes you numb and spiky at the same time. I thought I was sedated; instead, I was a third rail.

I spent the afternoon working on my chemistry lab report, the kind of tedious assignment that didn't require much of my brain. My mom yelled upstairs to say that she and my dad were running to the garden shop, and I tried Kelsey's cell again. jfc, I texted, and then tried her home number.

"Hey, Matt," I said when Kelsey's brother answered. "It's Dylan."

"You sound like shit." He laughed.

"Thanks. Can I talk to Kelsey?"

"She's not home," he said.

Sitting with my knees pulled to my chest, feet on the seat of my desk chair, I frowned. "Oh. Do you know when she'll be back?"

"No idea. I haven't seen her this morning. I guess I thought she was at your house."

I shut my eyes tight. "I need a favor," I said.

I DIDN'T WANT TO DO ANY PRESS FOR *SHIPWRECKED*—NO INterviews, no appearances, no private preview concerts at tech companies. By the time the project was ready, I said, I'll have made myself invisible for a year. I don't want to reemerge on *Good Morning America*. They'll ask too many questions about where I've been, about what made me leave. "I don't want to talk about that," I said. *I don't want to talk about Sam.*

"We can negotiate the questions," Sloane said.

"All that I want to say is in the music," I explained. "And if *I* don't believe the music can stand on its own, then why would I expect listeners to think that?"

Sloane frowned like there were cracks in the logic. "You might be giving your listeners too much credit," she said. "No disrespect to our fans, of course, but consuming your art is as much a craft as making the art. And not everybody is up to the challenge."

I didn't disagree. "But that's not on me. It's my job to make the music." For just a moment, I wanted it to be like it was in the beginning. It had been such a long time since that was the entirety of my job.

And that's when it came to me.

I think they thought the dive bar tour was ridiculous. My team told me that—even given, you know, *everything*—if we did eighty to ninety stadiums we had a shot at the highest-grossing North American tour of all time. There was no money to be made in dive bars. Actually, we would *lose* money on the enterprise, when you factored in travel and the cost of the crew.

"It's an idea," Sloane said, and I could see her wheels spinning. "Would you announce it in advance?"

"No," I said, not having thought it through. People would show up to a bar expecting a live band and they would get Dylan Read. My music like guerrilla warfare.

"And how many of these do you want to do?"

"A couple places in LA, a couple in New York . . . maybe one in Nashville?"

She nodded. "And we'd do it ahead of the album?"

"Right," I said. "It'll replace the usual press circuit, and any singles."

"It's kind of cool," she said after a moment. "A real word-of-mouth, grassroots experience. People *love* being able to say they saw U2 at their college Fountain Day in 1980 or, like, Springsteen at the Stone Pony in '76."

Wyatt pointed out that it would help position the music correctly: give my first rock-leaning album a rock star's origin story.

"And it'll help with the whole"—Sloane made a circular motion in the air, vaguely directed at me—"pop star pigeonholing."

Someone asked why we didn't just do another Weekend Read.

"It's sort of an extension of that," Sloane said thoughtfully. "Just as intimate, but less elite."

"It's not a safe space," I said, and only then did I truly understand the impulse. I didn't merely want to begin again. I wanted a baptism by fire.

MATT'S CAR SMELLED WARM AND ANTISEPTIC, LIKE PINE-SOL. Tom Petty came through tinny and slightly uneven on the old speakers. "Thanks," I said, sliding into the front seat.

"It's not like I haven't had to do this before," he said, not unkindly, and I wondered if he meant for Billie or for Kelsey or someone else entirely, maybe several someone elses. I watched his back as he walked into the CVS from behind the window, and picked at my calluses while I waited. Little flecks of peeled skin fell from between my fingertips like snowflakes.

Back in the car he handed me the bag and a Gatorade. Change rattled in the plastic. "You should take the first one now," he said, nodding at the drink, and so I opened the box there in Matt's front seat as he reversed the car. Something about the whole thing felt like an anticlimax, confusingly easy; from both the sex and the pill I'd expected meaning, weight, a sense of difference. I imagined playing Never Have I Ever and being able to put down two more fingers.

At home in my bedroom I cut the box into two dozen tiny pieces, wrapped it in its own garbage bag, and buried it at the bottom of my bathroom trash. I had the second pill—it was a two-step process then—in my hand, searching for an overnight hiding spot for it, when my phone rang on my desk.

"Did Matt just take you to get the morning-after pill?" Kelsey's voice was loud and low, glimmering at the edges with delight.

"Did he tell you that?"

"He was very gentlemanly about it, don't worry. I bullied it out of him."

I walked from my bed to my window seat, where I let the back of my head press against the wall. I rolled my neck from side to side like a metronome, allowing the wood to massage my aching skull. "Where've you been?"

"I have told you *so* many of my sex diaries and you *finally* have an entry to share and you *still* wanna talk about me?"

I was quiet on my end of the line.

"It was lame, okay?" Kelsey conceded. "I'm over shit like that. I left."

"Without me?"

"I'm not your babysitter, Dylan."

It was a knife into my deepest insecurities about our relationship: that Kelsey saw me as a child, a little sister toddling after her, a shadow rather than an equal. I fought to keep my voice steady, to speak like I was brave rather than wounded. "I know you're not my babysitter, Kelsey. But I thought you were my friend. And I needed you."

I could hear Fiona's indistinct wailing-along with a movie on the other end of the line, the distant, faint curves of a melody. "I'm sorry, okay?" Kelsey said.

I didn't believe her. "I just don't understand why you keep going back to him."

"Who?"

"I know you're seeing Raff again. He IM'd you." I said it like a winning shot: *There. See?* If Kelsey wouldn't open up to me, I would force my way in. I would prove to her that I was paying attention; that I was smart; that I noticed things.

"Were you fucking *snooping* on me?"

I felt a rush of panic. "It just popped up while I was on the computer," I explained, defensiveness mounting. "I wasn't even sure GTBrigadier82 was him, I don't know Raff's screen name, but now since you're not denying it—"

"Oh my God. You know, I thought it was cute that you're a little obsessed with me, but now I see how truly fucking delusional it is."

"I'm not obsessed with you—"

"Did you even *want* to fuck Tyler? Or did you do it just to get my attention?"

"You're just jealous."

Kelsey laughed, a raspy, angry *bah*. "Of Tyler's stubby little dick?"

"How many times have you gone crawling back to Raff after he's dropped you?" I spit. "At least I have some fucking self-respect."

I meant for it to hurt; I just didn't know how badly. I didn't even know that it was our last real conversation.

WE DROPPED *SHIPWRECKED* BY SURPRISE ON A FRIDAY IN APRIL. Later I would learn that many critics thought the whole event—the dive tour, the surprise drop, the album content itself—lacked self-awareness. I was playing the victim when there were *real* victims here. They said a surprise drop smacked of ego, that I wanted to have my cake and eat it too: that I could not both be in celebrity exile *and* think I had the influence to pull off *a stunt like this. Dylan Read*, they wrote, *has learned that cardinal rule of contemporary celebrity: nothing is an opportunity like scandal.*

Once they got down to the music, though, they were more thoughtful. *Once again Dylan Read is testing the limits of her genre, this time molding the sounds of rock and punk to fit her lyrics-forward pop. While it seems that this album was crafted in response to the allegations against an early producer and collaborator, the truth is that Read has a habit of reinventing herself with every new release, and* Shipwrecked *is no different.*

But I didn't know any of that yet. I was in Dublin with Nick, eating linguini with clams in his kitchen and purposefully tuning out the feedback until my team digested it on my behalf. Nick brought my foot into his lap under the table and rubbed my arch with his thumb while I picked at my clamshells, searching for yellow hearts of meat to swallow whole.

"Tell me something I don't know," he said, a phrase borrowed from our first date. In a world that saw my art as public property and my life as entertainment, "tell me" was our way of reminding each other that some things could be just ours.

I looked at him across the table, smiling at me, and tossed a clamshell back into its pasta nest. "I wish I'd brought you to one of the shows," I said. "I'm sorry I didn't." We'd decided we weren't ready, that it was safer to keep us private.

By "we," I obviously mean "me." *I* decided, and Nick agreed.

Nick placed my foot gently on the floor and leaned forward, taking my hand across the table. "So why don't you take me now? We'll go down around the corner."

I looked at him. He wasn't kidding. "I can't—" I began. "I can't just drop into a pub and demand the mic."

"Can't you, though?" His eyes met mine, searching, daring. "Hey," he said, softer, "you don't have to. I'm in this for the long haul, whether you let me see you play or not."

I grinned. "You're in this for the long haul?"

"Was that not clear?"

I thought about the first time I landed back in LA after visiting him in Ireland. My face hurt from crying and I had to hide inside a half-open umbrella to walk the ten yards from my plane to my SUV so the three paparazzi waiting with their long-angle lenses wouldn't catch a shot of my swollen eyes. In the car I took four ibuprofen and swiped in and out of my phone again and again, waiting for a text from him that wouldn't come because it was barely 5 a.m. in Dublin. When I got home I let my driver carry my suitcase in through the front door and said thank you and good night over my shoulder and walked upstairs to my room, where the summer before Nick and I sprinted, naked and dripping, from the shower to the bed, the smack of cold threatening to ruin the moment, necessitating we redo the foreplay.

I was brushing my teeth when he texted, thinking about how my dentist kept threatening me with gum surgery. I needed to be gentler, he told me, and gave me a special toothbrush that shut off when I pressed too hard.

Make it in ok? Nick asked.

I took a selfie with my toothbrush crooked in my mouth, a little bit of white froth at the corner of my lips, my head cocked just slightly to the left.

This feels more intimate than a nude, he wrote. And then: heart-eyes emoji.

He typed, deleted, typed. I pressed my toothbrush into my back molars.

I like this better, he wrote.

Looking at Nick over the remnants of our clam sauce that evening, I understood we'd been making something solid from the start. I squeezed his hand harder across the table. "Come on," I said.

We walked down the street to a pub with exposed beams and white plaster walls. A band was already setting up in the corner, on a small raised platform with a couple of standing mics and a couple amps. The guitar player had a buzz cut and wore a midweight gray Henley, unbuttoned to its bottom notch. He looked at me in the way people do sometimes: *Are you—? You can't be.*

"Hi," I said. "I was wondering, and I know this is kind of rude, but that's my boyfriend over there"—I looked over my shoulder to where

Nick sat at the bar and waved—"and it's his birthday today, and I would love to just play him one quick song."

It wasn't Nick's birthday. The guitarist looked at me with his mouth slightly open. "Uh, yeah," he said slowly. "I think that'd be all right. Guys?" He turned to the rest of his band—a bassist and a drummer—who both nodded dumbly.

"Cool. And one other thing—" I clasped my hands in front of my chest. "I didn't bring my guitar. Could I borrow yours?"

He searched behind me for cell phones aimed to record, the paranoid way we all wonder if we're being made the butt of a public joke. "All right, then," he said, and he held it out to me.

The guitar was out of tune, and the acoustics were terrible, but the latter had been the case in all the dives we'd played. I sang "White Flag" the way I did the first time I ever demoed it, with a slight warble and a little distance, the finger-plucked guitar lighter and lovelier than the way we produced it for the album track. *You want me to let all our dreams in*, I sang, *but I built this armor 'round me for a reason.*

I dropped the guitar for the final verse, singing alone over the intermittent hiss of the tap, a glass set down on damp wood, bodies rustling against one another in their rain jackets and spring sweaters. *What if this is all we have / what if we just can't make it last?*

The pub had filled quickly, swelling to overflowing in a single three-minute song. Snippets would end up online. As it was happening I was aware that this was the irrevocable moment, that with every sung note captured on film I was launching our relationship into the infinite discourse—but I understood, too, that we couldn't stay holed up forever.

Secrets and boundaries are not the same thing, my mother always said. But I'd long ago lost sight of the difference.

Diana walks me to the door. We stand together on the small flat of linoleum where Kelsey used to leave salt-crusted Uggs and high-top Chuck Taylors and worn cowboy boots in a jumbled heap. *Of all the things my mom could care about*, I hear Kelsey saying, wedging her left toes against her right heel, kicking off her sneakers and rolling her eyes, *"no shoes in the house" is the* one *rule she chooses to enforce.*

Well, I think, you'd be happy to know she finally let that one go.

"She would be proud of you, you know," Diana says to me. "All that you've done."

"It could have been her," I say. "It should have been her."

Diana's eyes narrow slightly. Her head tilts. "You didn't take it from her, Dylan," she says then, and there's something suddenly precise about her tone: a crystalline quality, all the tiredness sloughed away.

The air between us hums. Am I only hearing what I want to? Or is Diana trying to absolve me of my guilt? "I'm sorry, Diana. About all of it—"

She pulls me into a warm hug and I let my chin fall onto her shoulder, into the crook of her neck. She smells like I remember: Herbal Essences and Dove bar soap. I close my eyes and breathe in. "This is not your fault," she whispers.

As we pull apart, I notice the basket of mail on the table next to the door, where Kelsey and Matt used to toss their keys and sunglasses and other random minutiae: Fiona's My Little Pony; a tube of hand lotion; a found mitten. "Wait a minute—" I say, reaching for the mail. "Is this your class?"

Diana eyes the card in my hand. It's a flatlay, with a photo on one side and an invitation on the other. In the picture, a couple hundred kids pose outside Thompson High in stacked rows. The girls have teased hair; all the clothing is too big—straight-legged jeans and oversized flannels and bomber jackets with roomy shoulders.

"It's our fortieth reunion," Diana says, gesturing at the year on the bottom: *Class of 1982.*

"Will you go?" I ask.

"I've never left Thompson Landing. My entire life is a class reunion," she says. But then she tilts her head and smiles at the photo, softening. "Can't seem to toss it out, though. I mean, look at us!"

I examine the picture again. "Is that—" I bring my nose closer to the photo, trying to distinguish the faces from one another. "Is that Louie?" I ask, pointing to a boy in a letterman jacket in the top row who looks a lot like the owner of the Jolly Roger.

Diana nods. "Another lifer," she says. "Found a way to turn throwing house parties into a career, I guess."

I laugh, a single *hah*, because I know I'm supposed to. "I had no idea," I say.

"Why would he leave, right? Things were never going to be better for him than they were right here."

But that's not what I meant. I had known, probably, somewhere, in the vague way we all store our hometown gossip, that Louie went to Thompson. Maybe I'd even known he was roughly Diana's age. What I hadn't known, or what I hadn't puzzled into place until this moment, is that they graduated in 1982.

SO WHAT'S YOUR PLAN, EXACTLY? KELSEY'S SAYING TO ME IN the back of my SUV, streaking through Thompson Landing while my phone lights up in my lap: text from Nick, text from Sloane, call from

Sloane. *You think you're gonna walk in there with a rough memory of a fifteen-year-old AIM conversation and this guy is gonna be like*—she raises her hands up, palms by her ears—*you got me! I was* totally *fucking a teenager.*

I pick at my left pinkie with my left thumbnail, checking for the weak spot in the toughened skin at my fingertip. The IM conversation isn't all I have. Tucked against my right hip is my purse, with Kelsey's notebook and her copy of *Ariel* inside. The same old fragment of a memory—Kelsey's hip pressed into Louie's—flickers before my eyes.

I was wrong about GTBrigadier82, I see now. It wasn't Raff, like I thought fifteen years ago. I hadn't misremembered the sexual undertones, as I'd started to think when I considered it might have been Luke. (Was it possible to read "I like to spoil you" more neutrally?)

No. GTBrigadier82 was the owner of the Jolly Roger.

I explain to Mike how to pull around to the edge of the alley, where the back door to Junior's is propped open with a sagging liquor box. "Wait here," I say, and jump out of the car before he can protest.

Ahead of me, down the narrow lane, Louie emerges from the back of the bar with two trash bags in his hands.

"Hey!" I call out. My voice pings off the brick around us, funneled up through the closeness of the buildings.

Louie turns at the dumpster, cranes to see. He's wearing jeans and a Junior's T-shirt. "Dylan," he says. "Thanks for stopping by last night. Would've loved for you to post about it on your Instagram, but—"

"Were you fucking Kelsey?"

Whoa, Kelsey says over my shoulder.

His face makes a fist. "Excuse me?"

I hold up *Ariel*. "You gave her this, right?"

Louie's face contracts further, unreadable. He's not going to make it easy—but after fifteen years in the music industry, I know how to call a man's bluff.

"She wrote about you," I say, pulling Kelsey's notebook from my bag now. "I have one of her journals from that year."

Kelsey cocks her head and raises her eyebrows. *Huh. Not bad.*

Louie looks from me to the book to the notebook and back. "Why don't you come inside for a drink," he says. "Let's not do this out here."

Junior's is different in the off-hours, overhead lights on—unflattering, fluorescent—and stinking of bleach. The bar mats are pulled up and dragged off to the corner. Cash lies in piles on the counter, stacks of fives and tens and ones. The ice vat is empty, and the garnish trays are upside down on towels, drying. A daytime talk show plays on mute on the TV in the corner.

Louie tucks behind the bar and begins filling two glasses with ice. One hand grabs the soda gun while the other pulls a bottle from the well. The liquids are poured simultaneously, two streams into the glass until full, and then he slides a cocktail napkin in front of me and places the drink on top.

Finally, he speaks. "I don't know anything about that book." He juts his chin in the direction of *Ariel.*

I slip the notecard from inside. *The best songwriters know their poets!–L.* I tap the single initial. "I know you bought her things," I say, thinking of GTBrigadier82: *I like to spoil you.* "And I can't think of anyone else who would have given her something so expensive."

He almost laughs. "Look around you, Dylan. Look at me. You think I give women *poetry*?"

"She was *seventeen*," I snap. Not a woman, I think. A girl.

I slap Kelsey's waterlogged notebook on the bar top and begin flipping through it furiously. When I find what I'm looking for, I rotate the page in front of Louie, displaying the text for him. *I try to think of myself like some sort of free-floating thing / turns out all along that you've had your hooks deep in me.*

"I told you, I'm not much for poems."

"Your bar is named after the *Jolly Roger*. Captain *Hook*'s ship."

Louie laughs for real this time. "So I'm supposed to think that's about me?"

Kelsey has her ass up on the bar, feet kicking in the air. She shrugs good-naturedly. *It was a good try.*

I pull the notebook from under Louie's hand. "Maybe if that were the only reference to the bar in here," I lie, pressing it shut against my chest. "But it's not. And if there's one person the police would trust to decode Kelsey's lyrics, it's me."

Louie's eyes narrow slightly. For a moment we stare at one another, each of us waiting for the other to flinch. "The investigation's over, Dylan. Cops said it was an accident."

"I know," I say. "But that doesn't mean things wouldn't look pretty bad for you if I were to hand these things over."

This isn't gonna work, Kelsey says.

"The journal is yours if you tell me what happened," I say to Louie. I see him eyeing its warped front cover, how obvious it is that it was once soaked and allowed to dry out. The drowned girl's sunken notebook is a powerful piece of evidence, however you want to spin it. Enough for the cops to take a second look, especially if there's a new suspect to consider.

And Louie knows it. "And what about that?" he asks, eyes flicking to *Ariel*.

"It's not from you, right?" I say, a little daring. "If I believe your story, you don't have anything to worry about."

Louie sighs. Eyes the notebook, then looks up at me. And he begins to tell me about Kelsey.

FIRST OF ALL, SHE LOOKED SO MUCH OLDER THAN SIXTEEN, seventeen—and she acted like it too. He knew the bartenders slipped her shots every now and then, that the free soda she had every Monday often had a little rum swirled in the bottom, like we're drinking now. He liked how she could handle it, how she never tipped into the glassy-eyed territory, how she drank just enough to make her pale cheeks a little rosy. She was playing to a mostly empty room, he thought. Let her have a drink. God knows he was doing worse than that at seventeen.

And she was funny. Mostly he ignored her while she played, but every now and then he'd stop and listen to her little jokes between songs. *My English teacher says I have to stop writing about my ex-boyfriends, especially when they're in class with us, but I just say, Mr. Bridges, it's an* honor *to be my muse.*

Anyway, she was fun to be around. Sometimes she would hang out after her Monday set. She liked to sit at the corner stool and pick at cocktail olives, spearing them from the garnish tray with a straw, and ramble about her life: school, music, Fiona, Matt, her mother, me. Sometimes she didn't talk at all and just scribbled lyrics. She stole a million pens from the register that way.

He taught her to play darts. One time they were shooting pool and he saw how she pushed her ass out as she was angling the cue and he thought, *that wasn't a mistake. She knows how that looks.* Another time she told him she liked when he wore button-downs. She touched him then, for the first time, her fingers grazing his collar, then patting, once, twice, at the top of his chest, below his clavicle. When she wasn't at the bar they texted a little, and then she made him an AIM account and they chatted that way. Sometimes it felt like flirting but he wasn't absolutely certain, and of course that only made him want her more.

He looked it up. She was seventeen; it wouldn't have been illegal, not in New York, not technically. Sleazy, maybe, but you can't go to jail for being a sleaze.

He started surprising her with small gifts. Marbled guitar picks, in pearlized ivory and pink and turquoise. That sour candy she liked. A fancy leather notebook for her writing. Once, a silver bracelet with a music note charm.

Never a book of poetry.

One night that spring she was leaving out the back alley when he was taking out the trash. They paused and talked. She wasn't wearing a jacket and her teeth chattered and he reached out and rubbed both of her arms. And that's when he kissed her, or she kissed him, or anyway they kissed, and she tasted like sweet mint gum and booze and he got hard almost immediately, but that was it.

A couple weeks later his phone rang while he was working. It was late on a Saturday night and things were getting messy, like they did at a dive. She was calling from a number he didn't recognize, and she was drunk. "I need a ride," she said. "Can you come get me?"

One of the bartenders was screaming at a couple she found fucking in the bathroom.

"I'll be right there," he said.

He picked her up at one of those houses that looks like everybody else's house. She was at a party with some kids from camp. When he began navigating the car back to Diana's she stopped him and said she needed to go to Tahawus.

"Why do you need to go to the lake?" he asked.

To camp, she clarified, and then added, "I just do." And he was stupid enough to think that maybe what she wanted was to bring *him* there.

In the car on the way she asked him whether he made any money as a restaurant owner. "First of all," he told her, "a bar isn't a restaurant." And second of all, he owned a bar because he didn't need money. His grandfather had owned a regional chain of furniture stores, sold them for eight figures, and left plenty to the grandkids. He was surprised she didn't know this about him. Everybody knew Louie's granddad.

"Right," Kelsey said. "So why'd you stay here? I wouldn't have."

A potentially insulting thing to say, he thought, but he'd heard worse. "Where would you go?" he asked.

She sighed. "Doesn't matter," she said. "I lost my ticket out."

He pulled through the gate into Tahawus. Putting the car in park in front of the main house, he said, trying to follow the thread, "Somebody wrote you out of their will?"

Kelsey laughed in a hollow way. "No." She paused, then added, "I thought I had somebody who cared about my future. But not anymore."

Then he did the sleazy thing. He reached across the console and put his hand on her thigh. "I care about you," he said. She looked at his hand like someone might appraise an ugly stray dog. *Huh.* But she didn't tell him to stop. He leaned over and slipped the other hand into the deep V of her sweater—into the cup of her bra—at the same time he brought his lips to hers. Her tits were perfect. He felt her nipple in between his first and second fingers. But then he realized she wasn't opening her mouth and he pulled back, returned his hand into his lap, ran the other through his hair.

"Sorry," he said. "I thought maybe that's why we came here."

"I came here to be alone," she said. She got out of the car. The door slam echoed in the quiet.

That was the last time he saw her: walking down toward the lake from the main drive, a black shadow in the thin moonlight.

"IT WAS JUST BETWEEN ME AND HER," LOUIE SAYS. "SO I KEPT MY mouth shut. And can you blame me, really? Like you said—it wouldn't have looked great if her forty-two-year-old boss was the last one with her."

"I get it," I say, and I do. I understand exactly.

Guarantee I am not the only girl he's tried to pick up at the bar, Kelsey said, twisting open the jar of olives and using the spoon end of a stirrer to pluck one from the depths.

"But you're fucking the other bartender, right?" I ask. "The hot one, with the tiny waist?"

"Seriously?" Louie says.

"I'm just curious. It wasn't just Kelsey, it's that you've got a thing for younger girls. And you didn't want anyone digging around in that."

He lifts one hand into the air and makes a kind of exasperated exhale, like, *what do you want from me.* "I might not be a great guy," he says, "but I'm not a monster. Kelsey was wasted, went for a swim, and drowned. I shouldn't have left her, and I'll be sorry I did for the rest of my life. But I'm not the reason she's dead."

No, I think. You're not any more responsible for that than I am.

The Visual Album

Light travels faster than sound.

First came the new way of posting. All of a sudden the fashion bloggers and mommy bloggers and lifestyle bloggers with their photographer husbands and their editorial spreads and their overwater bungalow vacations weren't it anymore; their feeds were too perfect, the entire reason social media was ruining everyone's lives. A new generation took to the apps with understated edits and photo dumps and mirror selfies in ugly places: highway rest stops, fast food joints, mall dressing rooms. They flipped their hair, stuck out their tongues, held the camera too close to their faces. No more palm trees and sunsets and three-hundred-dollar swimsuits; no more charcuterie spreads and coordinated holiday shoots. You had to tell people about your *real life*, and in our real lives we are all a little unfinished and a little cheap.

That was the most important thing. You could not appear as though you were trying.

The sound followed. It came in high and breathy, an airy falsetto. It whined, it whisper-sang; it never belted. Sometimes they sounded gravelly, the vocal fry of Los Angeles translated into song, or the rasp of a lifetime smoker delivered in the body of a seventeen- or twenty-one- or twenty-five-year-old.

They put their music online in forty-five-second clips. Under the vocals you could hear the way their fingers made contact with the piano keys or the guitar strings, the soft muffle of skin against something hard and metallic. The mic caught all the breath, the missed inhales, the strained exhalations. Someone somewhere called it "bedroom pop," and the name stuck. It was a way of embracing the synth- and electro-pop leanings of the moment while stripping some of the artifice; it was a way of talking back to the idea that pop was too clean, too produced. You heard the dog bark in the track, a dumpster clatter, the inconsistent acoustics of a futon positioned under a lofted bed. It was the new grunge; the return of an insistence—one we come back to in cycles—that authenticity is found only in the mess.

This new/old emphasis on disorder was, to me, just a rebranding of the same old trap: *effortlessness*. I am not effortless. I never have been. Not as a person, not as a writer, not as a musician. For once I sought refuge in my age. I was not so young anymore. It would have been ridiculous for me to try to pull off the bedroom pop aesthetic, sonically or visually. I didn't want to be thought of as a messy kid. I wanted to be thought of as a professional.

Because I wasn't the same artist I was when I moved to Nashville at sixteen, afraid to own the most significant relationship of her life, hiding her deepest secrets in plain sight. I wasn't even the artist I was when I put out *Detour*, desperate to disentangle herself from her roots. I was a multi–Grammy Award–winning, Platinum-selling, global superstar.

And I was in love.

NICK'S LEASE EXPIRED AND I TRANSFORMED THE OPPORTUNITY for conversation into a fight.

"It's like you need to keep some kind of safety net," I said, standing in my kitchen in LA with a Bolognese simmering on the stove. "A backup plan."

Nick sat at the island. "You knew I rented," he said, and his helplessness—the way he refused to fight back, to stoop to my level—only increased my fury.

"I don't keep track of your lease terms," I snapped.

"Do you want me to give up my place?"

"I don't want to *tell you* to do anything!" This was true, despite my tone, despite the way my voice pitched upward, desperation evident in its warble. I didn't want to tell him what to do; I wanted him to live with me, always and forever; for him to say, *let me be with you.* For the first time in my adult life, I'd found something that made me want to stand still. But I needed Nick to give me the permission I had never been able to give myself.

"I didn't ask you to tell me what to do. I asked you to tell me what you *want*."

I felt a prick of heat on my back and yelped involuntarily: the sauce had boiled, flicking a splash of tomato on my shirt.

Nick motioned with his hands, beckoning me over to him. "Come here."

"It's fine," I said, twisting my body to try to eye the damage in the center of my back.

He stood and walked around the island. I cooked; Nick did the laundry—we didn't divide our labor so much as choose the tasks we liked most. I found cooking meditative in the same way he felt accomplished after folding a load of laundry. "Take it off," he said. "It'll stain."

I waved him away. "It's tie-dye. You won't even notice."

"I'm not trying to use my stain-fighting powers as a way out of this argument," he said, smiling.

I thought: *But what if I wanted you to remove my stains for the rest of my life? What if I don't want anyone else to know this about you, that you are proud of your fastidiousness sorting delicates, that you never accidentally put a sports bra through the dryer?* I thought: *Why do you want a washing machine in Dublin when I'm right here?*

Instead I slipped out of my sweatshirt and gave it to Nick, our hands brushing in the exchange. He disappeared into the laundry room while I scraped the stuck bits from the bottom of the pot. When he walked back into the kitchen I heard the hum of the washing machine behind him, the mechanical rush of water. He looked like he loved me.

"I don't want a backup plan," he said, quietly. "But sometimes I feel like you do."

I felt suddenly blown open, like a town after a tornado's spun through. Despite soft-launching our relationship at a pub in Dublin, I'd insisted we keep a low profile. I told the world about Nick, but I didn't need to let them document our every move. I hadn't seen how the secrecy was hurting Nick; I thought he understood that I was trying to protect us—that years of tabloid coverage had made me nervous about opening a relationship to the discourse. There was Aaron, furious after Lana's piece (*they're calling me a cradle robber*); there was Hudson, winning an Oscar the same year I didn't even get nominated for *Detour*; there was Lilah, showing up to a party with Brooks (*the only way to stop the Delilah rumors is for one of us to get a boyfriend*). No matter how hard you tried, it was impossible to truly tune it all out; fame hung in the ether like an invisible gas, poisoning my personal life or my professional one or both.

"I know you feel you're protecting us by keeping us private," Nick continued. "And I don't even really want to argue with you about it, because first of all, there's no way for me to do it without sounding like I'm asking for a share of your spotlight, and that's not the case." He said it in the rambling way he could, the syllables smashed into each other, his accent tripping over itself. "And second of all, I know I'm out of my depth. There are so few people in the world who can truly understand your kind of—" He flailed after the right word. *Celebrity* was a thing we pretended I didn't have; to refer to it that way felt almost anthropological—an abstract concept instead of the reality of my microscope. "I've never had to navigate this kind of attention," he continued. "I have to trust that you know your way, because my eyes haven't adjusted to the glare. But sometimes it feels less like you're trying to shield me than that you're ashamed of me."

I realized then that I'd been following an old playbook, one that no longer applied but that I used out of habit. It was Kelsey who taught me how to hide a relationship; I was operating with the same furtive, surreptitious demeanor that helped me conceal what happened back then, and I hadn't seen how Nick might misunderstand my behavior for what it was: fear. I had been afraid to tell the world about Kelsey because I thought I would lose my career; I was afraid to tell the world about Nick because I thought I would lose him. "I'm not ashamed," I told him. "I'm scared."

Nick pulled me close, holding me tight. "When you feel like you have something to lose, that can make you feel really vulnerable," he said. "But I think another way to look at it is, can't it make you really brave?"

That was the difference between me and Nick. He saw our soft spots as our strongest. I believed the tender bellies needed protecting.

LATER THAT NIGHT, AFTER KELSEY AND I FOUGHT ON THE phone, I went on AIM in my bedroom and watched for her to log on. I thought I might say sorry, or maybe—more likely—I'd message her and see if she was still mad. Instead daddy4504 appeared in my *online* list.

Hey, I wrote to Matt. Thanks for helping out today.

> **daddy4504:** np
> **dylanthelibrarian:** no work tonight?
> **daddy4504:** just got in
> **daddy4504:** winding down
> **dylanthelibrarian:** good shift?
> **daddy4504:** eh

I felt stupid for IMing him. I didn't have anything to say. I wanted to know if Kelsey had told him about our fight. I wanted to know if he thought I was a slut, trash, a mess. Instead he sent so u gonna tell me who the lucky guy is

>**dylanthelibrarian:** I think it's "was," past tense
>
>**dylanthelibrarian:** a one-time thing, i'm pretty sure
>
>**daddy4504:** that bad, huh

I laughed. Drums beat in my chest.

>**daddy4504:** it's always bad with teenage boys
>
>**dylanthelibrarian:** weren't you one of those once
>
>**daddy4504:** unfortunately
>
>**daddy4504:** not anymore, tho

An entire percussion section pulsed in my lungs, in my arms, up my neck.

>**dylanthelibrarian:** maybe you can introduce me to some of your friends
>
>**daddy4504:** that would break my heart
>
>**dylanthelibrarian:** don't you want me to have what I deserve
>
>**daddy4504:** I do

My fingers fluttered over the keyboard.

>**dylanthelibrarian:** tell me
>
>**daddy4504:** ??
>
>**dylanthelibrarian:** tell me what I deserve

I waited, typed, deleted, breathed.

>**daddy4504:** im better with my hands than my words
>
>**dylanthelibrarian:** so come over

He was there ten minutes later, parked down the street. I slipped out the back door wordlessly, feeling like I might vomit. In the passenger seat I buckled, then unbuckled, unsure if we were going anywhere, the car engine turned off. He laughed, and then I kissed him, maybe to make him stop laughing, maybe because the laughter felt like a dare. He pulled me on top of him, one hand up my shirt, the other slipped down my waistband. He put a finger inside me and moaned: "You're so wet."

I felt embarrassed and turned on at the same time, a swelling inside the core of me.

His phone rang while I was unzipping his pants. "Do you want to get that?" I asked.

"Absolutely not," he said, his breath hot on my neck.

I wriggled out of my shorts, kicking them to the floorboards. His thighs were white, hairy. I didn't know how to guide him into me, worried about squeezing him too hard.

"Should we use a—"

"I just took the morning-after pill. Pretty sure it'll cover this too," I said.

My phone rang when he was inside me. Matt reached for it, smacked it from the cupholder across to the passenger side, under the dash. While I moved against him he put one hand on me, rubbing me in small circles. It was too much.

"Is that good?" he whispered. "Is that better than what he did?"

I made a hiccuped affirmation.

"Are you coming? I want you to come," he said. "I want to show you what it feels like."

But I am afraid of edges I cannot see. Instead I yelped in a pattern I hoped mimicked something like the cries of an orgasm. He pulled on my hair, lightly.

"That's right," he said, and he came then—I only figured it out as he was finishing, how he rocked into me more slowly, once, twice more, and then stopped. He breathed into my chest and I wondered what was supposed to happen next.

"That was great," he said, and he moved his hips under me and I took that as a cue to slip off of him, over into the adjacent seat. The car was stale-smelling and hot.

"Someone really wants to talk to us," I said, reaching for my phone under the glove compartment.

Matt shrugged, shoving himself back into his pants. "I think they'd understand," he said.

"Weird," I said, looking at my phone. "I don't know the number."

"Did they leave a message?"

They had. As soon as I heard her voice on the other end of the line I knew something was wrong. Kelsey's speech was garbled and distant, her normal velvet warmth gone brittle. "So, you were right," she said. "Turns out I'm just a fuckup who's gonna be stuck here forever." She exhaled loudly into the line. "Worse places, I guess, at the end of the day. Hey, I think I have something," she said. "*Body of stars*. How's that for a metaphor, Roberta Frost? It's a body of *water* but tonight it looks like it's made of stars. I should write this down—eh, fuck. I think I left my notebook by the dock. Anyway, Matt's not answering his phone and I need someone to come pick me up."

The line went dead. I turned and looked at Matt, also listening to a voicemail. I could make out the tune of one of Kelsey's camp songs through his tinny speakers: *THE MOOSE, THE MOO-OOSE! HE'S SWIMMING IN THE WATER!*

When he hung up he turned to me in the car, his face shadowed in my garage light. I felt a dampness in my shorts, both of us dripping out of me still. "We have to go find her," I said, and he put the car in reverse and drove.

"TEXT PAINTING" IS THE TERM MUSICOLOGISTS USE TO DESCRIBE when the instrumentation of a track echoes the lyrics. For example: a line mentions "walking," and we hear the clip-clop sound of heels on pavement; a verse notes the passing of time, and we hear the ticktock of a clock's hand moving around its circular face. When Leonard Cohen sings *it goes like this, the fourth, the fifth / The minor falls, the major lifts*, the chords shift exactly according to his lyrical direction. *That's* text painting, and it's one of my favorite things about production.

As a writer and poet, music had given me ways—like text painting—to add meaning to my language. But six albums in, even sonic metaphor was feeling like *not enough*. It wasn't the same restlessness that defined my earlier albums; this was a purer kind of ambition, a confidence in my talent I hadn't felt before. If *Shipwrecked* and the thing with Sam Jordan had helped me to feel artistically reborn, dating Nick made me feel newly powerful. I didn't want to merely reinvent; I wanted to innovate.

Nick understood. He told me once that he liked writing scripts more than novels because he had more tools at his disposal. We can add meaning with sound and image in a way you can't with prose, he once said. "Well," he added with a laugh, "maybe a better novelist could." And that's when the idea came to me.

When I pitched the visual album to my team I didn't tell them that I was hungry, or that I needed a challenge, or that I was trying to make a magnum opus. We had no way of knowing that by the time the record was finished, a once-in-a-century pandemic would have rendered us all housebound, and we would be looking for ways to fill the void created by the absence of live music. My case for the project rested simply on the fact that I was writing about love, and love demands an artistic arsenal. While bedroom pop tried to be ironic about its emotions—styling them in lowercase letters as if a refusal to capitalize could make the heartache smaller—the truth is that it was extremely deep in its feelings. *The Book of Us* had the courage—the *wisdom*—to own the complexity of a universal faith.

I am not the first artist to explore love as a form of spirituality. Poets have been using the language of religion as a metaphor for love for centuries. But *The Book of Us* is a soup-to-nuts commitment to the analogy, every single song and the accompanying film intentionally trafficking in the language of faith as a way of explaining the experience of love. I would use the sonic stylings of different subgenres of rock as a way of highlighting the emotional meter, crafting breakup songs like "Myth of Me" with the rawness of classic rock to mirror the anger that comes with dissolution, or songs of grief (like "Wilderness") with the dazzling bigness of arena rock. "The Gifts of You" and "Skin and Bones" are both ballads in the vein of Peter Gabriel or Leonard Cohen, styled with a tonal ambiguity created by straddling major and minor chords. They're neither sad songs nor happy ones; to me, they most closely echo the experience of love—that annihilating, affirming vulnerability.

If I can do all that with sound, I said to my label, just imagine what I could do if you gave me the power of visuals too.

I BOUGHT A PLACE IN NEW YORK, IN THE VILLAGE, CLOSE TO the West Side Highway with views clear across the water to New Jersey. I woke in the very early mornings and bought a coffee at the bodega on the corner and walked out across the piers and down the island, someone from my detail ten paces back. On the way home we might walk up Broadway into SoHo all the way to Washington Square and then west again. The first time I took the right grid of streets and passed the neon signs announcing *TAROT, CLAIRVOYANT, READINGS* I thought simply, *Oh. Here it is.* I thought memories like this were supposed to hit like cheap shots, a sucker punch—but that happens only if you have a soft spot, and I'd made sure to build a bunker there. Nothing but thick, hard, calcified rock. I began tracing my route past Vera's every time I walked, a little test of the sense memory: *Still nothing? Good.*

The house is mine but we started to make it feel like ours. Nick's books cluttered the shelves in the office. Our toothbrushes stood next to each other like soldiers in the bathroom. He kicked his shoes off next to the door and I tripped over them when I walked in, his ridiculous too-big duck feet. In New York we felt looser than we had in California or Ireland, maybe because it hadn't already belonged to either one of us. We could mold it together. And there were ways to slide through the city with some anonymity, if we were careful. An NFL player lived on the corner; in the building next to mine an actress who earned something like two million per episode in her latest prestige drama. All three of us slipped in and out of our underground garages, shuttled to the back entrances of concert halls and private rooms in restaurants.

Nick and I picked and chose our joint appearances: we went to the *Vanity Fair* Oscar Party together; we skipped the Met Gala; I went alone to a celebrity wedding where we knew there would be reporters. At best our decisions felt arbitrary; at worst, hypocritical. What did it matter if we were photographed at a premiere together if I was writing lyrics like *he's a missionary in my foreign land / preaching pleasure with his holy hands*?

On a weekend in February, as news of a virus in China hovered in our periphery and *The Book of Us* went to postproduction, Nick and I watched a movie about a crumbling marriage that was—rumor had it—a thinly veiled roman à clef about the writer's now-failed union. To his credit, both partners came off badly. It was the kind of intimate two-hander that fries the nerves. Sitting with my legs crossed beneath me on the opposite end of the couch I worried about whether the project had contributed to the dissolution. The writer and his ex-wife were broken up by the time the film premiered, so it wasn't the press that did them in—if anything, it was the process. Could it have gone either way? I wondered. If he'd written about something else, would they have found their way back to each other?

"Do you think you'll ever write a book about me?" I asked Nick.

Nick was calm and thoughtful as he loaded the dishwasher. "I think I'm always writing about you," he said. Meaning: the sausage is a mix of real life and imagined.

I flicked my chin toward the TV. "I mean, like that."

"Well, I hope we never end up *like that*," he said, smiling.

"You know what I mean," I said, a little frustrated. The movie had sharpened my spikes; I also knew Nick *knew* this, and was working to talk me off the edge.

"Do you think you'll ever write about me?" he asked.

I hadn't told him about the premise of the record. He knew it was a visual album, and he'd heard snippets of the songs as I noodled them around the house—but I hadn't admitted that I was making a concept record about our relationship. Without knowing it, Nick had homed in on my hypocrisy, the way I was projecting my anxiety onto him.

"I am writing about you," I said.

He didn't look at me like he was angry, or hurt, or afraid. He didn't look like someone who spent a lot of time worrying the thread out of which we'd woven our tightrope, wondering whether it would hold as we crossed the abyss of my fame. He looked at me like I'd given him a gift. "It better be the best thing you've ever made," he said then, grinning.

"I think it might be," I told him, which was the truth. *The Book of Us* was starting to feel like it could be my *Purple Rain*, my *Rumours*. A career-defining apex, something worth shirking the bedroom pop trends of the moment. "But what if it's too much?" I asked, soft.

"I trust you," Nick said simply.

And that's when I understood: I wasn't only worried about whether the world would see Nick. As long as I kept my past from him, I would worry about what would happen if he ever really saw *me*.

—

MATT PULLED THE CAR BENEATH THE OLD RANCH GATE, *TAHAWUS* in sharp spikes of wood, pieces puzzled together to make a chicken scratch font, and parked in the driveway in front of the main house.

"Wait here," I said, and in his wordless nod I knew Matt understood. This was never about him. Part of the reason he shone so brightly for me was because of her.

I walked quickly down the path from Tahawus's main house toward the water, the thin trees with their small leaves tossing human shadows in the starlight. I thought I saw a coyote, a bear, a hunter. To quell my fear I tried to remember the grounds transformed for the North Pole, or to imagine camp as Kelsey described it every summer—filled with children, group songs, shrill plastic whistles—but it was hard, in the darkness, to think of anything but Tahawus as it was a hundred years ago, filled with the dying; hard not to conjure Kelsey's ghost stories, women in bloodstained white tipping the deck chairs over at midnight.

Finally I made my way to the beach, a thin sandy stretch not more than five feet from grass to water's edge, where the lake shushed against the shore. I looked to my right, where fifty yards on the woods ran right up to the water, then to my left, where the beach stretched farther to a small dock and boathouse. Nothing. Staring out at the lake I realized Kelsey was right: you *could* imagine yourself floating in the galaxy here, surrounded by stars.

Maybe it was because of the way the moonless night flipped the cosmos, suspending me in between universes. Maybe it was just the thrum of panic. But it took a moment for my eyes to decipher the shape out on the water, the boat pitching waves harder against the shore with its interruption.

I called Kelsey's name once, twice, three times. I knew she wouldn't answer. I carried all the stories in my back pocket the way you do in a place like Thompson Landing: the teenagers who got high and slipped out onto the water on their prom night, the drunk Jet Skier, the late-season ice fisherman who had too much whiskey in his coffee, miscalculated the melt. Accidents happen here.

But the mind goes slippery with terror and denial. I kicked off my shoes and thrashed into the water. The adrenaline carried me at first, then made my breathing go ragged, everything on overdrive. I flipped onto my back, floated to steady myself, swam five or ten more paces, tread water, swam, lost myself in the darkness, needed to reorient my path toward the boat. All the while a string of apologies unraveled in my head like a chant. *I'm sorry, I love you, I'm sorry, I need you, I'm sorry, I believe in you.* My breathing was already uneven with cold and effort and exhaustion but it began to mix with the watery choke of sobs—

They say it's a kind of temporary madness. Confusion. Panic. You forget yourself, your surroundings, your body. It can happen—even to strong swimmers—in very deep, very cold water. Your heart hammers. Your lungs work overtime. Instinct tells you to keep swimming when the right move would be to rest, let the water carry you.

A hand grabbed at the back of my sweater. I screamed, my voice trailing endlessly across the lake. A voice—a low register, authoritative—shouted my name. Matt.

I stopped resisting, stopped fighting. Let him lay me on his chest and swim backward, a lifeguard's retrieval, toward the boat. He rolled me off him, gave me a push as I lifted myself up and over. The metal knocked into my ribs, my spine.

Matt landed next to me with a thud. "You were taking too long," he said. "I came looking for you—" Matt stopped short. "I saw—" Again he couldn't finish.

And then I saw her notebook. Small, flip-top, wire-bound, tucked half-under the seat at the bow. I scrambled after it, fished it from the inch of water that Matt and I had tossed into the boat when we climbed in.

I crawled to the edge of the dinghy and began screaming Kelsey's name. Matt shushed me, grabbed at me, wrestled me away from the side, covered my mouth until I bit his hand.

"We need to go get help!" I yelled, grabbing at the oars. "Come on! Help me!" I said it over and over again. *Help me, come on. Come on, help me.* Matt's body began shaking, hypothermia setting in, a stunned look on his face.

When he spoke it was barely a whisper. "It's too late," he said, and I knew he was right. As soon as I'd seen the notebook I knew for sure. She was here and now she was gone.

My teeth chattered. I began to recognize the psychological onset of shock, could hear my mother talking about the brain's ability to act like a shield, how there isn't—really—any defense against it.

Matt's face was contorted, stretched. "I can't," he said. "Fiona—Billie—I can't be here, Dylan," he said.

"It was an accident!" I screamed, but the fog was descending fast, a body that had been in overdrive suddenly crashing, synapses fried, cortisol depleted, blood oxygen gone.

Matt motioned between us. "This wasn't," he said.

I clutched Kelsey's notebook to my chest as he rowed us to shore under a blanket of stars.

FROM ABOVE: TEN TOES SINKING INTO WET SAND. A WAVE LAPS forward, burying the feet, then washing them clean again. The water ebbs and flows, forward and back, the only sound the rhythmic shushing of the shoreline. From behind we pan out and up to reveal a WOMAN, bedraggled in a damp WHITE DRESS, standing with her arms at her sides, watching the horizon on an empty beach. The sky is gray with receding storm, and the grasses up the dunes rustle in the breeze. This isn't paradise, but there is some sort of peace here.

The woman turns. On a hill up the dunes she sees a small white building, like a missionary chapel. There's a shift in her: she seems to make some sort of decision.

A QUICK POP: A still, empty bedroom in an OLD HOUSE—wide-plank wood flooring, crown molding, a dusty fireplace. Morning light slants through a wide, eastern-facing window, across a desk positioned underneath. Another quiet place.

Back to the beach. The woman makes her way up the dunes, holding her dress above her calves, dropping the fabric to her bare feet when she reaches the chapel door. She presses both hands to the dark wood.

INSIDE: A modest, one-room meeting house, also empty. A half dozen wooden pews along each side of a center aisle, leading to a raised platform stage. A series of small wooden engravings rings the walls at eye level. With the door shut, the ocean is a distant bassline, far away. This, too, feels like a sanctuary.

Another QUICK POP of the bedroom, this time with our angle closer on the desk, writing scrawled on a notebook. *At night I make confessions / as if all my weaknesses / can't be turned into weapons.*

Back in the church, the woman walks barefoot around the edge of the room. She pauses at one of the wooden carvings, leans closer to the image. Her face contracts slightly: *What's this?* She holds her hand up as if to trace the panel—but thinks better of it. She continues on to the next square. This time we see what she does: a rudimentary carving of a man and a woman, their backs turned to each other, slumped over with their chins on their fists. Beneath the portrait, a single word: *DISAPPOINTMENT.* These are not the Stations of the Cross—this is some other devotional.

The thrum of a fat bassline interrupts our quiet, far away, more of a vibration than a distinct harmony. The woman hears it too. She turns away from the carving, over her shoulder to a door she didn't notice before, at the front of the church to the left of the stage. She crosses over to it, her hair and dress dripping on the wood floor, and turns the knob.

A shadowy set of stairs appears. The music is clearer now. She considers: the damp, dark unknown; the clean, bright stillness of the empty chapel. We get one more QUICK POP of the bedroom desk, a breeze flipping the pen-wrinkled pages of the notebook. Back in the church, the woman makes her choice.

The Book of Us is a song cycle: each track has its own distinct universe, but when listened to together the songs make a cohesive whole. As the woman descends deeper into the labyrinth beneath the church, she navigates these worlds, each temporary landing (each song) earmarked with a title card: *EUPHORIA, CURIOSITY, DOUBT*, et cetera.

We begin with INFATUATION. The woman sits with a MAN—dark hair, green eyes—in a lonely diner, haloed in white light, her body next to his in a corner booth. The jukebox plays a tinkling, distant version of "Golden Age." Our heroine looks from her date to her coffee and back again, as if the brightness of him is too much. *This golden age / is making me feel so afraid / I know that it can't stay this way / when trouble's at the door.*

EUPHORIA is all skin, twined feet in rumpled sheets, gleaming bodies, warm light dappling ecstatic faces. *Tell me how to say I love you / 'cause I do / but I can't seem to find my words.* The woman and the man from the bar tumble into each other, alternatingly frantic and tentative—sweating foreheads pressed close together, her body arced over his, a fingertip tracing the curves of her, trailing down the midline of her stomach, her lips on his neck.

In INQUIRY our heroine tiptoes around the bare bones of a construction site at night: her flashlight flickers across drywall, rafters, ceiling joists, load-bearing beams; the tangled plastic and frayed copper of exposed wires, electrical work in progress. A QUICK POP to a flare of memory: the same girl, younger, tiptoeing up a slatted staircase after a gaggle of friends; a beat later, the girl sits with her feet dangling from a second story, in the middle of a group of preteens. Back to the woman, creeping through the house bones.

We disappear further into childhood in ENLIGHTENMENT. Through "Skin and Bones," the woman and her lover navigate each other's memories like ghosts. A boy—like the woman's lover, rounder-faced and rosier-cheeked—reads an essay to his fifth-grade class. The girl makes a butterfly of sequins for an art project, using a pair of tweezers to lay the glitter down piece by piece. The boy slices his heel on a sharp shell at the beach. The girl catches a snake in her grandfather's garden. The woman turns her hand over to show her lover the scar, a tiny white dimple on her ring finger. *If you could see me to my bones / you would see they're carved with poems.*

As we move through these beats—station to station, title cards rolling one after another—we continue to pop to the writing desk in the quiet room, occasionally with our heroine sitting at the chair, with her fingers tracing the lines on her page, chewing at the tip of a pen while gazing out the window. There's the sense that she has two worlds available to her: the labyrinth of her thoughts, and the maze of this man.

DISAPPOINTMENT flashes over a pageant stage: rodeo queens dressed in cowboy hats and fishtailed gowns, detailed with rhinestones and grommets. The camera lingers: on the stitched whorls on the soles of her cowboy boots; the shining metal on her belt buckle; the worn leather of her horse's browband and reins. Our heroine wears a sash: *Miss Upstate.* She rides a bucking palomino in a dusty ring, plays an out-of-tune guitar to accompany a reedy performance: *they told me I could be anything / turned out the bargain came with strings.* In the dressing room she wedges hair extensions against her scalp, smears Vaseline on her lips. From the stage she watches a mirror image of herself—in the audience, dressed casually, relaxed—share a giant pretzel with her lover. She follows her alter ego through the rodeo grounds, navigating the carnival lights of a state fair—ring tosses, fried Oreos, a duck-shooting game. Her lover wins her alter ego a giant teddy bear. He looks happy. This is what he wants, our hero thinks: an easier woman to woo; someone less challenging than a queen.

We enter the wilderness, and "Wilderness." A hostile, wet forest, somewhere where the lushness of summer looks like a menace: branches sagging with moss, land sunken with swamp. This is DOUBT: wandering, map-less, searching for the trail. Night falls and our heroine builds a camp, makes a fire. The flames lick and spit in her eyes. Suddenly she stands before a barrel fire on a lonely steel bridge, a notebook clutched to her chest. SABOTAGE. As the woman tears pages from the journal we INTERCUT with images of conflict: her face, tear-streaked, as she shouts at her lover in a sparse kitchen; a slammed door; a shattered glass; a car peeling from a driveway; the man standing, hands hung helplessly at his sides, in the woman's rearview mirror. She tosses the last of her words into the fire, turns, climbs easily up to the bridge railing. Steadies herself. Then JUMPS.

A glittering net of starlings, swooping low over a lake and then up again. RESTORATION flashes on the screen. Our pacing begins to slow; the cinematography warms. Cue: "Fruits." The woman wraps ties around her tomatoes. She carries a basket of them, bright and disfigured, into the house and sets them on the counter. Her lover rinses them in a colander at the sink. They are in a cottage somewhere, the sea visible out the window over the basin. She slices one, lets it bleed on her cutting board while reaching for olive oil and salt. He opens his mouth to her. She feeds him from her garden.

The cottage becomes a farmhouse for "Shelter," and RELIANCE. Their oasis expands to include goats, chickens, potato plants; dogs yipping across great fields at her lover's heels. The woman leans against a porch railing and watches the world they've made. *I can build a home for us / just this once / and maybe that'll be enough.* She crosses her arms, a flicker of melancholy on her face: they can't stay here forever. The man whispers to her: *This is what we'll make inside ourselves.*

The woman goes inside, upstairs, through a shut door—into the bedroom with the desk. Cue "The Gifts of You"; DEVOTION flashes on the screen. Our heroine takes a seat at her notebook, and for a moment checks her own reflection in the window. Then she begins to write. *Kneeling on the rug of your unrolled wonders / prayin' to God and heaven that there aren't more hunters.*

We arrive at a sense of denouement with FAITH. The word flashes over our heroine's shut eyes. She opens them and it disappears. She is back inside the chapel, staring at the final wooden carving. She turns, but her head blocks the image from our view—faith is not something you see. There, in the middle of the pews, is her lover.

She makes her way to the chapel piano. Her fingers hover over the keys.

At the end of the song, she stares out at the man, watching her, proud. Just the two of them, in a church, her in a white dress. What now?

CUT TO BLACK.

IN THE CAR ON THE WAY HOME, HEAT BLASTING ON OUR FRO-zen bodies, Matt made his case. "I'm twenty-two," he said. "You're six-teen. I could go to jail." He paused, then added: "Not that I need to go to jail to lose my daughter in a custody battle. Statutory rapists don't get to keep their kids."

I didn't know if it worked that way. Wouldn't my parents have to press charges? It didn't make sense, otherwise; I'd done it willingly. But everything was garbled for me, like I was still underwater. "What if there's some other explanation?" I asked. I imagined Kelsey untying the boat, placing her notebook on the seat, then pushing it out onto the lake like a funeral barge. Maybe she went to the lake to make a sacrifice, to return her songs to the place that inspired so many of them. To wash herself clean of the burden of her dreams. Or else—"Maybe she left it there so no one would look for her!"

Matt looked at me pityingly.

"We can't just leave her!" I cried.

"I can't lose my daughter," Matt said. There was a kind of steely resolve to his voice.

"Can't we just tell them . . ." I pleaded, "I dunno, she called me, and . . . and I didn't have a car, so I called you, and we went to find her together?"

Matt drove with one hand on the wheel and held his other up close to the heater. I thought I remembered something about how a hypothermic body needed to be carefully brought up to normal temperature. Were we doing it wrong? Would he lose his fingers, his hand? "The best lies are the simplest ones," Matt said. "We won't risk messing up our story if its clear-cut. We were never here." He paused, then added: "Dylan, I can't be involved in any kind of trouble right now, not with everything with Billie. I can't risk losing Fiona."

"So we just—" I faltered, flailing at the vastness of it. "We just keep that secret? For the rest of our lives?"

Matt didn't say anything. He navigated the car off the lake road, up the hills that begin to snake away from the water.

"What about your mom?" I asked.

He shook his head. "I don't know," he said, but then he added: "But I think she'd understand that there's nothing I wouldn't do for my daughter. And I think Kelsey felt the same way."

I pictured Kelsey running the hose down Fiona's playset slide and tracing sketches on Fiona's back with her fingertips at naptime and feeding Fiona glass after glass after glass of water when she emerged from the tub wailing at the roughness of her pruned fingers. *You just have to, like, fill back up!* I ran my hands over Kelsey's waterlogged notebook in my lap and began to cry then, a weeping that lodged in my throat, the kind that comes from everything all at once.

The Triangle Diner is in a mint-green building with cracked shingle siding on a wedge-shaped corner of a three-way intersection. When Mike opens the back door of my SUV, the car floods with the smell of bacon, hot and smoky and a little sweet. I've told him that he's welcome to come in and have a bite but that he doesn't need to worry about anyone bothering me here. The crowd at the Triangle does not care about Dylan Read, Pop Star, unless it is to remind me that I had better not forget where I came from.

I choose a booth in the back corner and watch as Kelsey slides in opposite me, pulling her whole body up on the vinyl and stretching her legs long on the bench. *Why are you here, anyway? Just go home.*

I tap the face of my phone on the tabletop, waking it, a pile of missed calls and texts in their round-edged rectangles. I've gleaned that since the New Voices interview dropped last night—with its audio of me and Kelsey singing at Alderidge—the online chatter has reached a fever pitch. Sloane wants me to make another statement. She says the label has already emailed about the new album, about the elephant in the room. *We feel it might not be the time . . .* She wants me to do what I've been trying to avoid since she first asked me about the missing girl: own the story, fully.

She just doesn't know exactly what that means.

It's your fault for trying to be perfect, Kelsey says, twisting a piece of her dark hair in front of her face. *Take it from me. If you fuck up all the time, nobody pays any attention to what else you might be hiding.*

I wasn't trying to be perfect. I was only trying to be good.

The waitress comes. She does a fleeting double take, then pours my coffee from a carafe dappled with condensation. "Anyone joining you today?"

"Yes, he should be here soon. He'll have a coffee as well."

I called Nick after I left Louie. He was already on his way out of town, guiding his Range Rover away from the lake, southbound toward the city. "I have work to do, Dylan," he said, not angrily—just patiently reminding me, as he has so many times before, that he has a career to manage as well.

"It's a diner. Your food comes in three minutes," I said. "Plus," I added, "I need to tell you something you don't know."

Now I watch him through the dirtied window, my good, reliable Steady Eddie of a boyfriend, and feel a twitching in my abdomen. I stare at my hands in my lap, watching the tremor at my wrists.

He'll still love you, Kelsey says to me.

I don't know about that.

Sure he will. That's why you feel like you don't deserve him. She peels the top off a creamer and downs it in a gulp.

Gross.

She sticks her tongue out at me.

Nick smells like citrus and cedar and his hair is combed and still a tiny bit wet in the thick at the crown. He slides into the booth across from me and looks around.

"Do you remember our first date?" I ask him.

Nick flips the menu over, eyeing the laundry list of platters. "Of course I do," he says. "I wanted you to come to a party and we met at a diner instead." He looks up at me. "You wanted me to know the real you."

Some part of me always wanted Nick to know. I've loved him from the moment we met backstage at *Ted Tonight!*, when he saw right through my skull into my noisy, overcrowded mind. I didn't tell him about Kelsey because I was afraid of losing him—but I also understood there was no future for us as long as I kept this part of myself walled off. "I do want you to know the real me," I say. And I tell him everything.

I SPENT THE SUNDAY AFTER KELSEY DROWNED IN MY BEDROOM, waiting for Matt to text, for the police to knock on the door, for the balloon inside my chest to burst. I told my parents I had to write an essay, that I'd left it to the last minute. It wasn't like me but they were too hungover from a dinner party the night before to ask questions. Finally Diana called on Monday afternoon. I was at my desk, mindlessly copying definitions from my history textbook, when my mother came to tell me.

"Honey?" she called, knocking lightly.

I felt my abdomen go molten. "Mm?"

She opened the door tentatively, peeking her head through the crack. "Can I come in for a sec?"

No. "Yeah." I put my textbook down and pulled my knees to my chest, then unfolded them long again, aware of bodily contortions that yelled *self-protect.*

My mom took a seat at the foot of my bed. "Diana Copestenke just called," she began, and then I evaporated from the room.

"Dylan?" She looked at me with her eyes narrowed slightly, the wrinkle between her brow folded like a surgeon's midline. "Will you do that for Diana?"

"Do what?"

I saw her lips press together, the tendons along her neck flex. She took a breath and softened her voice even further. "Did you hear anything I said?"

I hadn't.

"Diana hasn't seen Kelsey since Saturday. She needs you to come over and help the police look through her things."

I didn't understand. My mother would have said *Kelsey died*, or *Kelsey drowned*. She wouldn't have been oblique about it. Which meant—

"They haven't found her?" I asked.

"They need your help looking."

Some part of me thinks things might have been different if they'd discovered her right away. A body is hard to ignore. But as soon as they decided she was *missing* rather than *dead*, my sixteen-year-old brain decided, *okay, the story's not over*. Intellectually, I knew what happened, but emotionally I wanted to believe otherwise; I wanted to live there, in the long, murky middle, for a little while longer.

"SO I LET HER STAY THERE," I SAY TO NICK NOW. HE'S LISTENED to my story with a writer's focus: interrupting intermittently to ask for clarification, tracking the beats like a plot diagram, repeating a detail to make sure he didn't miss something important. "For fifteen years, I let my best friend stay under the water. It was a terrible, unforgivable thing."

Nick is quiet for a moment, his green eyes fixed to my gray ones. "Is this why you won't marry me?" he asks.

The question feels like whiplash. I've just told him the worst thing I've ever done, and he's still curious about our future. Shouldn't he be sprinting for the door? At a minimum, shouldn't he be furious? "We understand each other because we're both writers," I say to him. "So much of our relationship is all tied up in how we talk about our craft and our creativity. But the truth is I never would have started writing music if Kelsey hadn't found me in the library that day."

"We might not have even met."

"I owe everything to her," I agree.

"And you think sabotaging our relationship is the best way to pay her back?"

"It's not that simple," I say, a little frustrated. "It's everything. It's that I'm afraid of what getting married would do to our relationship—because of the money and the scrutiny and the intensity of the spotlight. I'm afraid of what being married would mean for my career, because the conversation around my relationships and the fact that I write about them has undermined my success as much as it has contributed to it. And yeah, I guess I am afraid that being married to you will be just another thing I have to trace back to Kelsey. Multiple things can be true at once."

"*Exactly,*" Nick says. "What happened to Kelsey isn't your fault, Dylan. It was a whole hurricane of things. It was Luke and Diana and the custody battle and Louie and even then, at the end of the day, it was an accident. Kelsey got drunk and drowned." He pauses. "If you don't want to get married because you did it once before and you've decided you don't believe in the institution, that's fine. If you don't want to be with me, that will break my heart—but I can't force you to stay. But if the real reason we've been *stuck* is because of your guilt . . ." He pauses, then shakes his head. "No. That's not a good enough reason."

I think about this for a moment. "I came home this weekend because I felt guilty, but also because I was scared—I was so afraid the whole truth would come out, and I thought being here would help me control the narrative. And then the story started wrinkling for *me* too. All this time I thought she got wasted because of our fight, but the harder I looked, the more I started to feel like there were things about Kelsey I didn't know." Thinking of the note in Kelsey's *Ariel*, I add: "Probably some things I'll *never* know."

Nick smiles at me in his winking way. "I know you're used to everything being about you, but sometimes it's not."

"But I still missed her call. I still left her there. For fifteen years."

Nick reaches across the table between us, his hand extended like an offering. I place my palm in his. I know he has experience with forgiveness. I know that he knows people make mistakes. I know that he believes in second, third, fourth chances. Some part of him hopes his sister will make it back, one time, eventually, for good. It's not stubborn, stupid optimism. It's an understanding that some people take a while to figure out their stories, to put the pieces into place.

"You can't always make it right," he says then. "But you can take responsibility for it."

We sit like that for a moment, my callused hand in his, allowing him to trace the chewed and mangled parts of me. I do want to own my part in this. But first I need to give something back.

THE DAY MY MOM BROUGHT ME TO KELSEY'S, WE PULLED INTO her driveway behind a sheriff's vehicle and an unmarked investigator's car. The front door was open, as if the house was a crime scene. My mother called to Diana from the front steps, still waiting for permission to cross the threshold.

I noticed then—it hadn't registered on the way over—that she had brought a tray of enchiladas. "You're giving her our leftovers?" I asked, appalled.

My mom's voice dropped to a whisper-hiss. "I made extra last week and froze them for later! I figure Diana can use a night off from cooking more than me."

"Hey." Matt appeared in the doorframe, his dark hair greasy and finger-combed, his skin like clay.

"Hi, Matt," my mom said. She held up her dish. "Where can I put this?"

Matt stepped to the side. "They're in the kitchen."

My mom walked past Kelsey's brother, through the living room. I moved to follow but Matt stepped in front of me, blocking my way. He smelled warm and sour, and kept his voice low when he spoke. "How are you holding up?"

My breath lodged at my clavicle. "I'm managing," I said, throat-choked.

Matt reached out a hand and patted my shoulder. I fought the urge to shrink from his touch. "Just stick to the plan," he said.

I looked at Matt in the hallway then, his face stretched, eyes sunken, and for a moment I did understand that the stakes were different for him. My life was engineered around perfect grades and SAT prep and college prospects. His was about caring for a toddler.

I'd always felt young and insecure around Kelsey. If I wanted to grow up, I needed to understand grown-up choices.

"I won't say anything," I said. "I promise."

He looked at me for a moment, like he wasn't sure whether he could trust me. And then he stepped aside, allowing me to pass.

In the kitchen my mother sat across from Diana, their hands knit together on the tabletop. I wondered whether they were closer than I realized or if this was just my mom at work: delivering tenderness, touch, a sense of safety. A uniformed officer looked on, one hand on his holster. I tried not to look at him the same way I sometimes avoided a teacher's eye in class. "Dylan," Diana said, looking up at me. "Thank you so much for coming."

"This must be the friend?" A woman in a blazer stood in the kitchen doorway. I could see that she wore a plastic-sheathed badge at the end of a long chain, looped around her neck.

Diana nodded, then extended an arm toward the badge. "Dylan, this is Detective DiNuzzo. She wants to ask you a few questions about Kelsey's things, see if there's any information there that might be helpful."

I nodded and followed the woman down the hall to Kelsey's room. Her pants were too tight and the lining of her back pockets showed against her ass. I felt embarrassed for her, then ashamed that I had this reflexive meanness, then annoyed: I already knew this about myself, didn't I? I was only pretending to be a good person, wearing the outfit like a costume.

Standing in the doorway of Kelsey's room, the detective seemed to read my mind. "I know it feels like we're invading her privacy," she said. "And—honestly—we are. But sometimes you have to commit minor wrongdoings in the name of the greater good."

I frowned. Everyone was making the same argument, scaling their transgressions. "That sounds like something a comic book villain would say."

The detective laughed in the way of someone trying not to—she curved her body away from mine, hiding her face. "Kelsey will forgive you for reading her diary if it helps us save her life."

"You don't know Kelsey," I said, and then: "She doesn't keep a diary."

Detective DiNuzzo pointed to Kelsey's notebooks, spread out on her bed, opened to their bleeding hearts. "What are these?"

I stepped forward for a clearer look, but I already knew. A flash of the wire-bound notebook in the bow of the boat, now lying flat to dry at the top of my closet. "They're her songs," I explained.

"Ah." DiNuzzo nodded. "I thought they were poems. There are little snippets of . . . regular writing, though?" She peeled through the pages of one of the booklets, the paper crinkling in her hands.

"Sometimes we might do a little freewriting about the ideas behind a song," I explained. "Like journaling, sort of? If you have a story but you can't find the images yet."

She looked at me like she had no idea. I imagined her job worked the other way: she had the images but not the story. "Anyway," she said, "if you want to just take a look at these, let us know if there's anything you see that might be useful."

I tried to do as I'd been told. I stepped closer to Kelsey's bed and looked among her scribbles and crossed-out phrases for anything that might function as a kind of revelation. But Detective DiNuzzo was hovering too closely, only pretending to look at the pictures tacked to Kelsey's wall, flicking her eyes in my direction every minute or so. "What are you looking for, exactly?" I asked.

"Sometimes you don't know until you know," the detective said. "Just tell me if anything catches your eye. Anything unusual, anything you don't recognize . . ."

I let my fingertips trail over my friend's writing, the pages textured with the press of ink. I wasn't reading, not really; I knew what they said. Still I felt the need to be a good student, to give this woman something. "Most writers have motifs," I said, and the detective looked at me like this was not what she wanted, actually—to get into a discussion about poetry with a sixteen-year-old. "Images we come back to—"

"I know what a motif is," DiNuzzo said.

"Right. Well, Kelsey likes summertime. It's all over her work."

In Kelsey's songs, lovers jumped from docks hand in hand and bare feet pressed into thick grass and campfires licked the sky in someone else's eyes and bodies smelled like sweat and smoke and calamine, oily and warm. I thought about Kelsey showing me how to press my nails in a crescent-mooned x over the top of a bug bite to alleviate the itching, a targeted pain to remedy a hazier one. It was a trick with an expiration date; when the crosshatch faded, the desire to scratch returned.

The detective nodded. "Yeah," she said, "I was thinking more, like, is one of these about a person, or about a place . . ."

Outside, I heard Fiona squeal on her playset, the delight of Matt pushing her higher, higher on the swings. "A lot of these are about her niece," I said, finally, and pointed to a couplet about a *bathtub sea*. "But I imagine you already figured that out."

Detective DiNuzzo glanced down at the page, then up at me. "She really loves her," she said.

I nodded, too afraid to speak. *Loved,* I thought. Past tense.

"Well, why don't you take a few minutes with these," she said. "I'll just be in the kitchen talking to Mrs. Copestenke."

I nodded. When DiNuzzo left the room I stood still for a moment, then moved across the carpet to Kelsey's egg chair, collapsing into it. I twisted around and swung my legs over the back like we both had so many times before, scanning her space from the upside down, her dangling Mardi Gras beads and her cheap scarves and her necklaces pointing skyward.

There, on her dresser, exactly where I'd seen it hanging a million times, was the golden constellation. I righted myself and listened for the distant murmur of voices down the hall. I slipped the necklace from its hook and felt the diamonds in between the pads of my thumb and forefinger, tracing the celestial twins. I teased the clasp open and wrapped the chain around my neck, allowing the pendant to come to rest against my sternum.

"Dylan?" my mother called down the hall. "Are you ready to go?"

Only when we were in the car on the way home did I realize I was still wearing the Gemini necklace.

I FIDDLE WITH THE CHARM NOW, SLIDING IT BACK AND FORTH across its chain as I watch Tahawus come into view out my window. The trees make a tunnel over the dirt road into camp, branches thick and heavy with peak greenery, the forest floor to either side of us crowded with ferns so large they seem prehistoric.

In my lap, my phone rings. Sloane, again. I'm not this kind of person, I think. I do not make life difficult for my team by being unpredictable and unavailable. (If anything, I am difficult because I am overly communicative, because I worry too much, because I require going over a thing—a strategy, a plan, an idea—again and again and again.) Then a new thought occurs to me: What if I have been this person all along, and the other one—the good girl, the one who always says yes, the one who answers when called—was the mask? And anyway, at what point does the costume become the reality?

But if I talk to Sloane right now, as my bodyguard guides my SUV into a throng of families dropping their children off for a week or two of summer camp, teenagers and cell phones at the ready, she will tell me to turn the car around. We can take care of this some other time. I haven't even had Fiona sign an NDA.

The last thought makes me giggle inappropriately. What madness is my life.

We pull into the driveway in front of the main house, the gravel loop humming like a hive: trunks popped up, car doors thrown open, the grass piled with duffel bags and laundry baskets and storage bins filled with Cheez-Its and individual-sized packets of trail mix and the big jars of Skippy peanut butter. Camp counselors—white polo shirts, green shorts, clipboards and lanyards—shout instructions, point in the direction of cabins. The night I swam after Kelsey dims on and off in front of me, every blink transporting me between then and now—midnight to morning, budded trees in spring to summer lushness, the dry yip of distant wild dogs to a chorus of families.

Mike eyes me in the rearview, some concerned skepticism in his brow. *Is this a good idea?* "It's busy," he says, eyeing the stream of cars ahead of us.

"Sunday. Drop-off day," I tell him, remembering—somehow—that camp runs Sunday to Friday. High school memories stick to the ribs, even the most trivial. "It'll be okay," I add. "No one knows I'm here."

I wait for Mike to open the door, then step out into the light as he follows a few paces behind. Immediately the heads turn. The black SUV isn't particularly noteworthy at a place like this, where moneyed families deposit their children, but the same can't be said of a suited 230-pound man. Still, I *do* have the benefit of surprise: no one expects to see Dylan

Read here, and maybe for a moment or two or four they think that I'm just a very wealthy (very young?) parent. I remember Kelsey telling me that sometimes Tahawus hosted the children of heads of state, senators; the daughters of men who traveled with armed guards in Mexico, Haiti, the Middle East.

A counselor approaches us quickly, her eyes shaded by a green baseball camp, the serifed *T* of the camp logo situated in a crest at her forehead. She's in work mode—I recognize the way her eyes don't quite meet mine, how she speaks with the clip of a very happy robot—and for a second she has no idea what's about to happen.

"How can I help y—"

And there it is.

"Hi," I say, reaching my hand out. "I'm Dylan. I'm so sorry to bother you on such a busy day."

She scrambles to shift her clipboard and pen into one hand, tucking both under one arm. We shake. "I know who you are," she says. She's probably in her early twenties, listens to me all the time.

I smile. In my periphery I clock several arms holding cell phones aloft, some angled more surreptitiously than others. "I wonder if you could help me find Fiona Copestenke."

The counselor nods, eager to help. "She just brought a new camper down to her cabin, but she'll be back up this way soon. You can wait inside if you want?" She looks around, noting the cameras. I imagine some of the videos are already online. I know what they'll say. Lots of surprised faces, captions like *when Dylan read shows up at move-in*, or, if they're meme-curious, *she doesn't even go here*, or maybe snippets of my lyrics, *you make shadows in my summer escapes* or *they say one swallow does not a summer make but I think this dock looks a lot like a plank.*

"It'll be . . . quieter in there," the counselor adds.

"That sounds great," I say.

Inside, the main house resembles an old Adirondack Great Camp, the ones built by the robber barons and railroad tycoons: wood paneling, stone fireplaces, chandeliers made of antlers. I walk a slow loop around the main hall, pausing to examine the old photos and trophy cases that line the walls. A camper holds a massive largemouth bass aloft, proudly displaying her catch; a pack of girls huddles at a mountain summit, the wind whipping their hair; a trio of young women poses in front of a newly built cabin, one wearing a tool belt, their faces grimy with dirt.

Eventually I come to a series of portraits of each summer's camp counselors, posing together in rows on the steps of the main house. I know, as soon as I see the gallery, that Kelsey will be here, and something about this moment feels different from seeing her face in the news or even at the service. This is more sacred, as if I am finally visiting her grave.

It doesn't take long to find her dark hair gleaming from the porch in 2005 and 2006. She smiles with all her teeth visible, like the photographer caught her laughing. I search the girls around her, wondering if they're in on her joke: Is that a stifled smirk on the blonde next to her in 2005? A caught grin on the girl with the glasses in 2006?

I always thought of my friend as fiercely independent, the kind of girl who *wanted* to go it alone even more than she may have *needed* to. I always felt as if I was trying to prove my usefulness to her. But here now, seeing her in the context of this space, enshrined in its history, I see how it meant something to her to belong, to have a support system, to be counted on and asked to contribute.

Wasn't it Kelsey who volunteered to play with me at the talent show?

Wasn't it Kelsey who dragged me to the old training room?

Wasn't it Kelsey who *asked me* to write with her?

I continue my walk back through Kelsey's history, at the generations of Tahawus counselors who came before her, watching the uniform styles shift with the decades, the colors recede to sepia then black and white, until I'm staring at a cadre of white-shirted girls from 1943. There's a self-awareness to them, a primness to the uniform that charms rather than rankles—as if they know it's a little silly to be posing in brogues with silk scarves around their necks at a rugged outdoor camp. In the bottom corner, a woman with thin, long limbs perches on the balustrade, her wrists crossed almost lazily at her knees.

Something about her looks familiar. I wonder if it's just the way old photos tend to bleed into one another—the way all pictures of women from 1950 faintly resemble my own grandmother, because of the clothes and the posture and the framing and the hair. According to the caption, her name is Lena Coyne; it doesn't ring a bell, but I can't shake the feeling that I've seen those closely set eyes before, clocked the jut of that chin.

On the wall opposite me, the fireplace is flanked on both sides by trophy cases, filled with plaques and certificates. I walk across and scan the honors, the annual tennis tournament champions and Campers of the Year and Spirit Award winners collected in their glass boxes. I'm looking for Kelsey but I'm also looking for Lena, scanning the names on the trophies like a roster until I realize—

Each of the Camper of the Year plaques is stamped by Tahawus's board president, a handwritten signature etched in the metal. From 2000 to 2007, Tahawus was led by Adeline Coyne.

And then I remember: a woman with silver hair in a plaid suit, styled like a cross between Joan Jett and Queen Elizabeth. I *have* met "Lena"— Adeline introduced herself to me at the North Pole, the year I wrote "Evergreen" for Kelsey to perform.

I look at the name again, and it's that moment when the cluster of stars becomes the fish, or the hunter, or the scorpion's curved tail. I know that handwriting.

I pull the copy of *Ariel* from my bag just to be sure. *The best songwriters know their poets!–L.*

It matches the signature exactly. L wasn't Luke or Louie; it wasn't a random Leo or Logan, someone I'd never met or heard of.

It was Lena.

I quickly pull my phone from my pocket and google her name, suddenly ravenous for anything I can find about this other woman in Kelsey's life.

Adeline was born in 1925, I learn, the granddaughter of a man who made millions in railroads. There's more about him than her online: endowed buildings at Columbia, private clubs in Manhattan, named boxes at opera houses and named wings in art museums. Lena was one of seven, and every summer she and her siblings were sent to Tahawus while her parents vacationed in Europe. She spent eighteen months as a Wave radio operator during the war, then enrolled at Alderidge in the fall of 1946. After trying—and failing—to get a job as an A&R rep, she settled for work at an ad agency, where she slowly proved her ear and eye to her male colleagues, and eventually became VP of marketing at Pulse in LA. From there she helped to steward the careers of many of the notable musical acts of the 1960s and '70s, including the June Foxes, Betty's Garden, Ship Kingsley, and Frankie and the Four. A longtime trustee of Tahawus and Alderidge, Adeline died in May 2007.

Two days before Kelsey.

I'm gonna be stuck here forever, she said in her voicemail that night. *I thought I had my ticket out*, she told Louie. Maybe these weren't only broad drunken ramblings, a hyperbolic reaction to our fight, or even a delayed meltdown about Luke. Kelsey was at a party with camp friends before she called us; she could have learned about Lena's death there, and when she did, it was more than just losing a mentor. Maybe Kelsey felt Lena could have opened doors for her; clearly she was invested in her musicality—

And then I remember one more thing: a name in a stately font over a set of double doors down a long basement hallway. The Coyne Center for the Recording Arts.

Lena was the reason we recorded at Alderidge that day. But it didn't have anything to do with college—that was the assumption of a girl who saw the expected path as the only valid one. Maybe *that's* why Kelsey never told me about Lena: she thought I wouldn't understand that she was making other plans. Or maybe Lena and her vague promises were a secret long before I came around, the way we sometimes hold our wildest dreams like cards close to the chest, afraid of exposing our hopes to the harshness of the world . . .

I read Lena's obituary one more time. Her birthday was in June, I realize—she was a Gemini, like Kelsey. *This rich lady I know from camp got it for me*, Kelsey told me, sliding the diamond pendant back and forth across its chain.

Fingering the same golden sky at my throat now, I see how I did to Kelsey what the world has done to me. For most of my career people have only ever defined me in relationship to the men in my life. They look for them in my lyrics, search for their influence in my production credits, say that I wouldn't be here if it weren't for all the men in suits who saw something in me. I hated it, but I did the same thing to Kelsey. I never imagined any other kind of story.

I'm thinking about this when a voice calls out across the foyer. "What are you doing here?"

I whip around, feeling caught. Kelsey's brother stands in the doorway, holding a large box of fishing equipment—supplies for making flies, I think, from the feathered pieces I can see. "What are *you* doing here?" I ask.

He lifts the box higher, as if showing me. "Fiona asked for some of my old fishing stuff."

I decide then that I'm going to tell Matt everything I've learned. But first we have to own up to what we did, even if it's just to each other. "We should have told your mom," I say.

If I expected Matt to argue, he doesn't. Instead he sets the box down at the foot of the stairs and walks over to me, so both of us are standing in front of the trophy case. "I did," he says.

"When?"

He shrugs. "Not long after. A couple months?"

Diana knew. I feel a hollowing out in my abdomen, the bones of my ribs disappeared. It's something like relief—but there's exhaustion too. "Why didn't you tell me?" I ask.

"You were gone."

I could be angry with him, but a part of me thinks that maybe this was my penance: holding this particular weight. But Diana isn't the only one we hurt in all this.

"What about Billie?" I ask.

"Billie dropped the custody thing a little after Kelsey disappeared. At the time I thought it was just typical Billie, you know? She probably didn't have the money for a lawyer, wasn't actually ready for a kid . . . but I think maybe she knew we'd been through enough, as a family. Didn't want to hurt us any more than we already were. She went to Florida and got sober, then moved back here and rented a shitty place over the deli so she could be close enough to do birthdays and weekend movies and whatever. She and Fi are more like sisters than mother-daughter, but it works."

"Is that why you decided to tell Diana?"

Matt shifts from foot to foot. "Yes. But it was wrong not to tell her in the first place," he says, then looks at me, meeting my gaze squarely in a way he hasn't all weekend. "I'm sorry I asked you to do that."

I try to reconsider Matt at that moment, a twenty-two-year-old single dad, flailing after some sense of adulthood. His grief never had any space either.

And then one more thing occurs to me. "That's why Diana told me about Luke," I say, more to myself than Matt. "She shared her piece of the blame so I would have the courage to share mine."

Matt looks at me a little crooked. And then I finally tell him what I've learned over the past few days: how Kelsey walked in on Diana and Luke; how that pushed her to ditch Raff, finally; how she and Louie had a thing, sort of; how she called him the night she drowned, when she wanted a ride to the lake so that she could mourn a woman who also loved this place, whose gifts to Kelsey were tangible—she had wealth and connections—but spiritual, too, the rare adult who saw Kelsey's dreams as plausible realities; most of all, how none of this absolves me and Matt, but how I can see, finally, more clearly than ever, that the burden of what happened to Kelsey belongs to all of us at once, a constellation of wrongs.

AFTER, MATT FOLLOWS ME OUT ONTO THE PORCH AS THE LAST of the arriving campers unpack their cars in the drive. We do not hug, or touch, or even say a real goodbye. We've been saying goodbye for fifteen years, each of us tugging on an invisible rope between us, trying to pull free of the other's anchor. We're ready to go now.

"Do you want me to help you find Fi?" he asks.

"No," I say. I want to do this last part alone. "I know my way."

He nods, a single bounce of the chin. And then we go our separate ways.

I follow the same thin, curved path through the trees toward the beach that I ran on that dark, moonless night fifteen years ago. This time, the shadows do not make ghosts. The warm afternoon sun dapples onto the forest floor. The leaves are thick and lush now, and they shush against one another in the breeze. The whole of camp feels hushed, settling into the weight of its new guests.

I find Fiona down by the water, chatting with the lifeguard while some eager new campers get in their first swim. One after another they sprint down the dock and launch into the lake, fists clamped around their noses, the other arm held high in triumph. I watch her watching them, her long, dark hair gleaming in the summer light, her skin pinked in the August sun, her clipboard cocked against her hip like a standing desk. When she laughs it's just like her aunt, wide and unselfconscious.

After a beat, the lifeguard spots me. Fiona's gaze follows, and I raise a hand sheepishly. *Hey.* "Can we talk for a second?"

Fiona looks to the lifeguard, who nods, and then leads me along the beach away from the dock, out of earshot. The voices of the campers cannonballing into the water get a little thin with the distance; in the high sun the lake is more brown than blue, the color of the dirt and trees. It becomes what we see in it.

"It was a whole thing when they found her," Fiona says, staring out at the nearest island. "We thought we were going to have to cancel this week's session, because what's camp without the beach . . ." She trails off, then shrugs. "I'm sure we'll have to manage some especially sinister ghost stories. Make sure the older kids don't torment the Juniors by turning Kelsey into the Lady of the Lake."

"She might have liked that," I say. "A legacy that's just a little bit menacing."

Fiona nods. "That makes sense. From what my dad has told me."

Right, I think. Kelsey is a stranger to her, a specter. I wonder if Fiona feels burdened by this. I want to tell her that I know something about existing as a projection. Instead I reach into my pocket. "This was Kelsey's," I say, holding my palm flat in between us.

Her Gemini necklace glints in the light, the diamond-pricked sky tossing white spots on Fiona's face.

"I think you should have it," I say.

Fiona reaches for the necklace. She allows it to dangle between her thumb and forefinger for a moment, the pendant twisting in the wind, before dropping it into her palm, a golden nest.

"May I?" I ask.

Fiona hands the necklace back to me, then turns around, holding her dark hair up. I loop my arms over her head, dropping the charm against her chest and bringing the clasp to close at the nape of her neck.

"Why are you giving it to me?" Fiona asks.

"Because Kelsey loved you," I say. "Because she wanted the world for you even more than she wanted it for herself." And then I realize that I'm talking in sound bites, the kinds of things that sound lovely and elegant and offer a clear, simple logic. But they aren't necessarily the whole truth. "I don't need it anymore," I say, finally. "I have plenty of Kelsey without it."

The Tribute

L eonard Cohen once said that if he knew where the good songs came from, he'd go there more often.

I've always been jealous of that answer. It's the perfect evasion, charming and true *enough*. Because everybody always wants to know: Who's the song about? What's it based on? Does the artist have the same origin point as the art? Could you find them both on a map?

When we played *Split the Lark* for my label, it was clear they wanted a different answer to the question. I'd set out to make a record that embraced my writerliness in a way I hadn't before, because I was trying to say that the music came from a place of effort. But people are used to my songwriting feeling *diaristic*, and something about *Split the Lark* just didn't feel confessional enough.

In a way, they were right.

Lakeshore is the story of us, of me and Kelsey. Both elegiac and retrospective, the album is informed by her life, her musicality, and written in honor of the influence and inspiration she had on me and my career. Lyrically, you'll find her attention to storytelling; melodically, I tried to capture the cadences and rhythms I remembered not just from her writing but from our conversations—the swings from a rapid rat-a-tat to a patient, easy silence; the way we could be serious and playful at the same time. Sonically, I tried to engineer a production that took its cues from Kelsey's favorite things: the fat slap of the lake lapping at the sand; the constant pulse of the bugs in high summer; the coyotes yodeling in the distant nighttime. My voice—fully developed now, and with hours of lessons under my belt—can access the lower registers that came naturally to Kelsey.

There is so much about creativity that seems like magic, and so much about success that seems random. When your outside world gets noisy it's very hard to keep the inside one quiet, and over time I started to believe the lies I told myself: I didn't know how to write; I didn't know how to sing; I didn't know how to perform. I was just mimicking my dead best friend. I slipped on her skin suit under the cover of a black early summer night and forgot, long ago, where the boundaries were between her and me. Instead of embracing the seams I sought to hide them, to hope that no one but me would ever notice. It walled me off from my best art, and from the people who loved me most, including my husband.

But friendship, like music—and like love—is a collaborative and creative act. Kelsey has a writing and producing credit on every song on *Lakeshore*; the royalties are divided between her family and Tahawus. I believe Diana would rather have her daughter than the earnings, but I can't bring Kelsey back. This—honoring her artistry and its influence on my work—is the closest I can come. It's not enough; Matt and I made the wrong choice that night, and no amount of honesty now will bring me the absolution I crave. But revisiting our story *did* help me to look again at the life I built after her death, and to trace my path from that moonless night to this album on a route made of hard work. Kelsey had more natural talent than me, but I made up for what I lacked with a different kind of goodness. For a long time I thought it was a less worthy course, but now I see that multiple, seemingly conflicting ideas can be true at once. I do not believe that all of my success is due to Kelsey. I also believe that I would not be here without her.

And there's this: My fans have been begging me to do a return-to-roots country record for years. This album for Kelsey is the truest expression of that request.

I hope they're happy.

Acknowledgments

For facts, terminology, and general information on music production and music theory, I am grateful to the following resources:

Numerous podcasts, including *60 Songs That Explain the '90s, Bandsplain, Dolly Parton's America, Every Single Album, Popcast, Rolling Stone Music Now, Song Exploder, Switched on Pop,* and *Zane Lowe*;

Several music documentaries and concert films, including *Billie Eilish: The World's A Little Blurry, Dolly Parton: Here I Am, Echo in the Canyon, Gaga: Five Foot Two, Homecoming, It All Begins with a Song, Miss Americana, Song Exploder* on Netflix, *Springsteen on Broadway* on Netflix, and *Madonna: Truth or Dare*;

Broken Horses by Brandi Carlile, *Her Country* by Marissa Moss, *Born to Run* by Bruce Springsteen, *How to Write One Song* by Jeff Tweedy, *How to Write About Music* edited by Marc Woodworth and Ally-Jane Grossan, and numerous volumes in the 33 1/3 series;

Music journalism and criticism at the *New Yorker,* the *New York Times* (including the Diary of a Song series), NPR, *Pitchfork,* The Ringer, and *Rolling Stone*;

The city of Nashville, especially the producers who welcomed me into their studios, the friends and family who pointed me to the locals-only experiences, the artists I watched share their work in rounds and at open mics, and my copilot, Nina.

I also spoke with several music professors and musically talented friends early in this project, and their expertise, patience, and generosity helped provide the foundational knowledge needed to embark on this novel. To Ross, Kate, Leigh, and Steph: Thank you.

My thanks as well to:

Lisa Grubka, Hilary Zaitz Michael, Chelsea Dern, David Stone, Ellie Klein, Scott Goldman, and everyone who supports my work at UTA, WME, TFC, and FKKS;

Victoria Hobbs at A.M. Heath;

My editors, Kate Nintzel and Katie Bowden, and everyone at Mariner and 4th Estate who has championed this book or supported Kate and Katie in their efforts to do the same;

Mike Lombardo, Sharon Hughff, Jenna Bush Hager, and Ben Spector, my partners in adaptation;

Ellie, Zu, Daisy, and Lucy;

My therapists;

My friends and family;

And my husband, the love of my life and port in the storm—you and me on the rock, babe.

Finally: This book is dedicated to my cousin Kristen—my earliest creative partner and cowriter of numerous living room plays, whose wild imagination and magnificent mind gave my own more room to grow.

About the Author

EMILY LAYDEN is a screenwriter and the author of *All Girls*. A graduate of Stanford University, she lives in upstate New York.